Anthony Delano

Dateline: Rome

P

Palatino Publishing

Also by Anthony Delano

Too Much Good Time

Slip-Up: How the Daily Express found Ronnie Biggs and Scotland Yard lost him

Joyce McKinney and the Case of the Manacled Mormon

Maxwell: a Portrait of Power (with Peter Thompson)

Guy Gaunt. The Boy From Ballarat who talked America into the Great War

They Sang Like Kangaroos: Australia's Tinpot Navy in the Great War

Breathless Diversions

Too Much Good Time

A slick, sophisticated tribute to a tight-knit bunch of men and women thrown together by the caprice of the news cycle from London to Dallas to Saigon to Tel Aviv to New York, with detours to such inviting watering holes as the Savoy and P. J. Clarke's. Read, remember and enjoy! - Peter Thompson, editor, *Sunday Mirror*.

Foreign correspondent Anthony Delano led the kind of glamorous life that movie stars can only dream about. Read this and you can share the dream. A terrific piece of work by a natural storyteller. - Michael Molloy, editor in chief *Mirror Group Newspapers*.

A vivid saga of what it is like to be a foreign correspondent headed for the chaos of war while everybody else is fleeing in the opposite direction. 'Media studies' students should step outside their comfort zone for a while and take note. - William Ham Bevan.

Some of the best thriller writers were foreign correspondents before they turned their hands to fiction. They've seen it all – and know how to tell a good story. Now, Frederick Forsyth, Gerald Seymour et al are joined by one of the best, Tony Delano, who has crafted a first-rate thriller from a lifetime's experience of reporting wars, assassinations, hijackings, treachery - and sex intrigues. - Ivor Davis, Los Angeles correspondent, *Daily Express*.

Slip-Up

No journalist can afford to miss this cautionary tale… the story of the in-fighting and downfall of all concerned has one rolling in the aisles. Mr Delano's eye is astute, his ear a credit to his profession at any level; and his wit is accompanied by the ability to write clear English.-*The Times*

Marvellously funny and told with ease and wit... The best stories are sometimes the ones behind the news. There never was a more hilarious tale.-*Daily Mirror*

Anthony Delano, a reporter of much experience, has written the most useful, intellectually coherent and - yes - serious action-study of the British Press that anyone has given us for years... and hysterically funny… A beautifully articulated case-study of the Code of the Street in action. - *New Statesman*

The funniest book of the summer. With expertly witty hands, Delano uproariously describes how 'the biggest comeback of a condemned man since the Resurrection' was bungled... Lovely fun. - *Cosmopolitan*

Delano mercilessly exposes the savage Fleet Street competition that underlay the Biggs scoop, and the tale is pacey, absorbing, humorous. - *New Society*

Has an authentic ring. For anyone interested in the inner workings of a popular newspaper, it is enlightening and amusing. A readable and entertaining piece of work. – *The Listener*

I'd say it's the funniest book about Fleet Street since Evelyn Waugh's *Scoop*. I stayed up half the night to finish it. It's one of those you-can't-put-it-down books. SLIP-UP includes some devastating portraits of Fleet Street characters. Delano's wicked pen spares no one. - *Phillip Knightley, UK Press Gazette*

A Billy Wilder-style comedy of muddle, mistrust, and misplaced zeal. - *New York Times*

Gripping... Delano tells it superbly. It's hard to think of a book since *Scoop* in which double-dealing, grappling ambition, spectacular successes and the glaring ineptitudes of daily journalism are examined so sharply and with such wit. - *The Australian*

A story worth telling, not only for entertainment but also for the light it throws on journalistic practices. The characters are vividly and sympathetically presented. - *Times Literary Supplement*

Dead-eye Delano has done it... He has taken on two of those worthy - if somewhat frowsty - British institutions, Scotland Yard and the *Daily Express* and demolished them with wit, pace and a keen eye... A hilarious straight-through read. Very, very good value for those who like a laugh. For journalists, it is a must. - *The Scotsman*

Joyce McKinney and the Case of the Manacled Mormon
From a lifetime at the sharp end of journalism, Delano knew that even though the story of Joyce McKinney was a cracking read, the story behind the story was probably even better. The result of Delano's investigation is a thrilling roller-coaster ride. Delano is an ace story-teller, and if Jeffery Archer gets to read his books, I suspect he will feel a shadow cross his grave. - Brian Hitchen, editor, *Sunday Express*

The Manacled Mormon is a fantastic read... if you come across it, leap on it and lap it up. It's really top quality tabloid sensationalism. - *TrashFiction*

Told with much verve and a great eye for detail anyone who's worked in the media will find themselves smiling and nodding knowingly throughout this rocking good read. - Christopher Ward, editor, *Daily Express*

Anthony Delano

Dateline: Rome

P

Palatino Publishing

First published in Great Britain in 2020
by Palatino Books
This paperback edition published in 2020
by Palatino Books
2nd printing 2020

ISBN (Paperback) 978-1-907841-16-3

www.anthonydelano.info
palatinobooks@gmail.com

The Author

Anthony Delano moved to London after an early newspaper career in Australia to work for the *Daily Mirror*, which at that time sold nearly five million copies daily.

He earned the best jobs old Fleet Street could offer: Chief European Correspondent, working out of Rome and Paris. Chief American Correspondent, based in New York and Washington DC, and finally Managing Editor.

When the monstrous tycoon Robert Maxwell took over the *Mirror* it was time to go. He became Professor of Journalism at the London College of Communication.

He now lives in the South of France.

Then and now

Most fiction is a product of the writer's observation and experience reprocessed through imagination.

Apart from those specifically referred to, all the characters in this book are fictitious and any resemblance to persons living or dead is purely coincidental.

There *is* an *Associazione della Stampa Estera in Italia*, the foreign press club, in Rome (though it is now in a different part of the city, and in the halcyon *Dolce Vita* days I worked out of the old one as a fledgling foreign correspondent.

A few characters in this book *do* bear some resemblance to fellow members of the *Stampa* back then, particularly Reynolds and Eleanor (Pibi) Packard of United Press.

Their other colleagues from the era might think I let them off lightly

For
My wife Patricia,
daughter Francesca,
and
grand-daughters
Lily and Alice,
Venetia and Sybilla.

A wire service has a deadline every minute...
-Joe Morris, United Press International

-1-

No matter what Rome might be like the rest of the year, in February it seemed much the same as any other big town in Europe: grey, chilly, everyone in the streets just wanting to get home. The main thing on my mind when I arrived there one late afternoon in 1957 was finding somewhere to sleep that I could pay for. I had a job, but payday was the best part of a month away. A hotel, even for a night or two, was out of the question, but after twenty-eight hours sitting up on a train I needed hot water and a soft pillow.

I wasn't entirely confident about the only address I had that might be helpful, scribbled down a few nights earlier in the gloom of a London dive called the Mandrake Club. A map bought at the Stazione Termini, a vast clanging hangar, showed that I'd got the name of the street right at least, Via San Nicola da Tolentina. The number, however, was open to interpretation. Was that *160* I'd written? *180*? *760*?

The person I hoped to find behind the number was a girl I had not seen since well before I left New York months ago, Marsha Ford. She had been a year behind me at Columbia, and while I didn't really know her well I remembered her from dances and parties. She'd married a guy I worked alongside at Century NewsWire, the world's most dynamic global news agency, as we who belonged to it were frequently reminded. Seemed she was now in Rome and the only person I knew — knew of — who might be able to help me out. The last thing I needed was having to explain the embarrassing state I had

1

gotten myself into to my new colleagues at the CNW bureau, where I was not expected to present myself until the following morning.

Via Tolentina, to where, in the interests of orientation, leg-stretching, and economy I headed on foot, was a straight and narrow downhill stretch lined with nose-to-tail cars. In addition to my portable typewriter — an Olivetti Lettera, 22, standard foreign correspondent item — I was lugging a suitcase that held everything else I possessed.

The entrances to the buildings I passed were forbidding: huge, heavy wooden doors bound with iron fittings, set in stone arches. Most had an array of buttons and bell-pushes alongside. The sky was darkening. When I started my halting progress there had been only a few people on the sidewalks. More began to stream from doorways, their workday presumably ended. They shouldered past me, making it even harder to read the numbers.

But even if I did happen upon figures that matched my scrawl, then what?

Umbrellas sprouted, not just the black ones that had choked the streets of London like poison mushrooms, but a motley array of colours and shapes, dainty little numbers hoisted by men as well as women. Since I was somewhat taller than most of the people waving them around, my eyes came under threat.

Preoccupied with fending off spokes, it took me a while to appreciate that I was getting wet.

In the typewriter case was a nifty little fold-up hat that came in handy at such times. I stepped into one of the stone arches to pull it out and, straightening up, experienced one of the more improbable coincidences life has to offer short of simultaneous orgasm. On the other side of the rain-slick street, framed in a similar doorway, a young woman unsnapped one of those menacing umbrellas and shook it out. In the instant before it obscured her face I thought I got a glimpse of the very person I was hoping to find.

'Marsha!' I yelled.

As I started across the street a large vehicle came sloshing down the hill. I was swamped in a struggling mass. Brawl? Pickpocket caught in the act? Someone throwing coins around? My first experience of a bunch of Romans all trying to board a bus at the same time. Conditioned by the sullen and resigned Londoners among whom I had spent most of the previous year, I stood staring as the bus drew away, limbs flailing from a half-closed door, expostulations hanging in the exhaust fumes.

The target umbrella was half-way down the hill on the other side of the street. I took a grip on bag and typewriter and dodged out into the rain. Marsha — as I was now convinced it must be — had on a light-coloured raincoat, but I had to take my eyes off it to sashay through the merciless traffic.

Relatively safe on the opposite sidewalk I picked out the raincoat again. One such raincoat, anyway; there now seemed to be several. I galloped on, hauling up alongside one umbrella-toting woman after another to check them out until I caught up with the right one at the bottom of the hill. 'Holy shit,' said Marsha when she got me in focus. 'Shelby Stone. Aren't you supposed to be in Budapest?'

The café — bar, whatever — was as noisy as the street, crowded and steamy, crockery clattering, customers gabbling. Almost all were men, most of them standing at a long counter though not for long. As we looked around for somewhere to sit, one after the other gulped down his little cupful and headed out again. It put me in mind of jailbirds I had watched on an assignment to Sing-Sing stepping up to swallow the tranquilisers that quietened them down for the night. We

3

found a chest-high metal table the size of a dinner plate with a couple of teetering chairs to match. I made to go towards the bar. Marsha grabbed my arm. 'I'll do it. What do you want? *Espresso*?'

What else? When in Rome, I thought stupidly, watching her go to a cash desk we had passed coming in, then over to the bar counter.

'You pay upfront,' she explained, bringing back the tiny cups on wet saucers. 'Then give the receipt to the *barista*.' My first insight into the level of good faith Italians placed in each other.

She got back up on the stool and gave me a wary once-over. 'You haven't come looking for me, have you?'

'Only kind of.' I explained about the guy in London who had given me the vague steer to her. 'My new job's here. Rome bureau. Deputy chief.'

'That's fantastic!'

We talked about that while I wondered what she'd meant about looking for her. Far as I could recall she had worked at one of the big publishers, but marrying a Centurion had made her, as the joke went, an agency moll, as hip to postings and in-house politics as a staffer; and to the strange lure of working for the wire.

Wire-service work was not for everyone in news. A lot of people I knew with jobs on big-city papers and radio stations looked down on the news agencies, even the original one, the pompous, prestigious Associated Press, aka Old Apathy. Journalism school graduates, in particular, didn't care for the pared-down, bare-bones, just-the-facts-ma'am reporting that was agency style.

'You know what a guy came out with when I interned there?' one of them moaned at a bull session up at Columbia.

'Those readers out there don't want to know what you *think,* he told me, first day. 'They just want to know what you *know*.'

I didn't see anything wrong with that but the J-school guy felt not being able to introduce interpretation meant he was just some kind of postman. I, though, didn't go to his school; I was wafting through an Eng Lit major, with fanciful minors that included Western Philosophy. Nevertheless, I got newspaper jobs right away, first on the *Hartford Courant*, near home in Connecticut, then at the Baltimore *Sun*. The Centurions I came across in the reporters' bars talked about firing as much as hiring, but also about epic exclusives over the other wire services, United Press and International News Service as well as Apathy. Above all, they talked about foreign postings, which seemed to me the natural way for someone who could keep his eyes open and turn a phrase to fulfil a young man's dream of faraway places and far-fetched events.

Those postings seemed more easily come by at CNW than at the others and so it proved after I spent a grinding year in the home newsroom on East 42nd Street in Manhattan where Marsha's husband, far as I knew, still worked. I was hired by — I guessed — the guy who'd hurt the J-school grad's feelings, Richard Hammond the managing editor. He didn't offer any guidance on objectivity but when he handed back my clippings book he said, 'No adverbs.'

'Excuse me?'

'Don't go in for adverbs here. Not a high count on adjectives, either.'

'I thought Ted might have sent you. To bring me back.' Scribbling down that address in the beery dark of the Mandrake, I hadn't given much thought to why Marsha might be in Rome.

When she had sprung to mind as a possible solution to my problem, a marriage break-up seemed the obvious reason.

5

Interesting, but no real business of mine. Ted wasn't really a close friend. If we were working different desks I might not see him for weeks.

The Big Room on East 42nd was an archipelago of desks: Stateside, International, Sport, Business. At the back was Rewrite Row, old hands with headsets clamped over their green eyeshades wrestling with the disjointed accounts phoned in by legmen. Above them loomed a huge mural in the industrial style of Diego Rivera, centred on the figure of a guy in a hat, pencil poised over notebook. Everyone called him the Reporting Angel, after the dreadful prints you saw in pious households.

Beneath it was engraved the intro that the prototype war correspondent William Howard Russell wrote for his account of the Charge of the Light Brigade:

> I shall proceed to describe, to the best of my power, what occurred under my own eyes, and to state the facts which I have heard from men whose veracity is unimpeachable.

That was actually a fair summary of the kind of guy from CNW that beginners like me wanted to become: the straight-up reporter who asked the right questions and knew how to handle the answers.

Beginners like me, though, learnt the ropes sitting around the rim of one desk or another, rewriting local area newspaper stories that came in via Western Union to be distributed on our own circuits to Century clients around the country and across the world. I learnt the knack of running recapitulation, to call the pages of a story 'takes,' and to finish up with ENDIT because 'end' could be mistaken for a word in the copy. It was newswork at its most plain and simple: who, what, when, where. Only rarely did we get around to why. Why things happened wasn't thought to matter too much to the reader figure we were urged to keep in mind: a soda jerk in Wisconsin. What did matter was getting it to him fast. Evening papers and radio stations that took our rip'n'read service needed to be first with everything — news breaks, sports results, stock prices. Beats over our rivals were valued by the minutes they hit the wire ahead of the opposition.

Even so, the copy needed to be sound. In a dreary corner of the Big Room where there was a water cooler and a coffee machine hung a blow-up of a little guy in an old-fashioned army uniform. This was Roy Howard, the United Press correspondent who back in 1918 threw the world into considerable disorder by reporting that the Great War had ended two days before it actually did. People all over the world came out to dance in the streets but the armistice terms were far from settled and all concerned were still shooting each other. It took twenty years and a new world war for UP to live that down, and we still made gags about the Roy Howard Memorial Award.

With so many services to feed we had to type up copy in 'books', eight sheets interleaved with carbons that jammed the rollers of the old iron typewriters. Pounding away eight hours at a stretch was like five rounds in the ring with Joe Louis. Nothing was wasted at CNW except the hope of earning what we were worth. The most frequently used word in the service messages regularly fired off from the back office was DOWNHOLD. As in DOWNHOLD WASHINGTON PHONECALLS, DOWNHOLD STRINGER PAYOUTS, DOWNHOLD VACATION COVER.

Those were distilled from the tightwad spirit of Colonel John Coldfield, company president and legendary stalker of the soda jerk. He hadn't invented the wire service, but he'd done more to make it what it was than anyone since Baron von Reuter started up his pigeon post, keeping our output aligned to the hard news stream, but widening it with stories that appealed to ordinary folk. Even so, Centurions were expected to stick to the facts and report only what they had seen heard or been told by a source to which it could be attributed. IMPERATIVE UPBACK ASSERTION... would be a servicer even less welcome than DOWNHOLD.

Old John, as he was always spoken of, still owned Century, or as much of it as he needed to. He was indeed old now and never came down to East 42nd, but his was the unseen hand on every keyboard. In recent years he had set out to make sure he would be remembered. He had bestowed a John Coldfield fountain on the Columbia University campus. Down in Wall Street a bronze Alexander Graham Bell nursed his epochal telephone on a plinth with the CNW logo. Sardi's restaurant had a Century Critics' Corner off the main room and each year the National Baseball League handed out the Newswire Sportswriter Cup. Gossip was going around of a crowning project, some kind of neon light display to outshine the news ticker over Times Square.

Seemed nothing could stop CNW growing, two hundred bureaux across the world, 1500 staff. Still trailing Apathy, though even if they outnumbered us we usually out-filed them. Over there the deskmen dressed as though they worked for IBM, white shirts and glued-on jackets. We could sweat away in shirtsleeves, but the ambitious kept a knit tie in their jacket on the rare chance of being sent out somewhere they could flash their shield-shaped Working Press pass. One of those roll-up ties was my only parting present when I was tapped for a job in the London bureau, hub of the European operation. I went over on the SS *America* — modern-day steerage class, four-berth cabin shared with strangers. I was a tyro foreign correspondent.

I'd seen the movie. I went out and bought a Burberry trenchcoat.

One of my weaknesses as a reporter, I had been told by some shit of an editor in my early *Courant* days was that I wasn't an aggressive enough questioner. I preferred to see that as a strength. If there was time to wait a little, quietly, people generally told me more than I might have got out of them by going on the attack. And, sure enough, Marsha started to unload.

'This was just the first place I thought of. Well, the second, actually. The first was London, but there were too many people there we — Ted and I — knew. Rome sounded, well, kind and easy-going.'

'And is it?'

'Sort of. The natives are friendly. Too damn friendly sometimes.'

If she meant Italian men that was hardly news. 'But some of them are *really* nice.'

'Specially to blondes, I'm told.' No expert, me, but I thought her hair might be just a tad lighter than I remembered. It had been cut short and smart. She seemed a little thinner, but healthy-looking and clear-eyed with a nose that stood up for itself, not a silly snub blob. All in all, she was a pleasure to look at: just the sort of straight-up, great-looking American gal I had learnt to steer clear of. No matter how ingeniously sexy they might have been in high school and college, they seemed to graduate straight to panty girdles and *Bride* magazine. Once married, though, they were back with the guys, sporty and talking dirty but still unattainable.

'I guess.' She reached across and brushed hair back from my forehead. 'You're blond, too, Shelby.'

9

True. Tow-headed, I'd always thought, though it was a term I'd never uttered, not knowing whether it should be pronounced as *toe* or *wow*.

Nor had I ever considered it much of an asset, just part of a pretty average 26-year-old WASP male package, five-foot eleven inches tall, 150-some pounds, rest in proportion.

'I suppose you knew about Ted, didn't you? That he was...that way?'

That way. No, I hadn't known. If I had I would have been plenty worried for him, even if he wasn't a close friend. *That* was the way to plenty trouble in the United States.

A couple of years back Senator Joe McCarthy's clearout of people in government he labelled 'commies' and 'comsymps' also swept up plenty of guys who were suspect for *that* reason. 'Only people against me,' said Senator Joe, in an un-publishable confirmation that there was a Pinklist as well as the Blacklist, 'are commies and cocksuckers.'

'I hope it won't shock you, Shelby,' said Marsha, those clear down-home eyes glistening, 'But I've been making up for lost time.' I fished about a bit conversationally for some details about this disarming revelation while waiting for the right casual moment to bring up the reason I had been anxious to find her.

'His name's Lorenzo. I met him when I went to the Berlitz School to see about teaching English. Or learning Italian. I need to look for a job, though Ted's giving me a sort of pre-alimony allowance. I'm staying in his *nonna*'s apartment. His grandmother's. Where you spotted me.'

'You've moved in with him?'

'Are you crazy? I'm in the women's wing, right up under the roof. Lorenzo's in close custody, I don't even know where in the building. Has to report to *nonna* for lunch and dinner. His parents live somewhere out in the country and Lucia's got orders to keep him out of trouble until he hears if he's been accepted for the *Carabinieri*.'

'He wants to be a policeman?'

'Hush your mouth! The *Carabinieri* aren't policemen. Or not *just* policemen. It's a very elite institution. A lot of people think they actually run the country. The men are hand-picked and the officers are chosen from the highest of flyers in the army.'

'Like Lorenzo?'

'Yes. He's already an army officer, but he has to be pure as pure.'

'And not sully himself with sex?'

'Not so anyone knows.'

'So if *nonna*'s got him on a leash...?'

'He can't take me on dates. I have to eat lunch and dinner alone.'

'So how....?'

'There's this long stretch in the middle of the day when everything shuts down.'

'Siesta.'

'*Sonnino* it is here. Or *riposo*. Lorenzo's friends with a physiotherapist who's got an office on the ground floor. That's where we date. *Riposo*, and in the evening after *cena* when he's allowed out for a couple of hours exercise.'

'Twice a day?'

'Shelby, it was a long drought. Though I've gotta say that crank-up massage table is no treat.'

'Marsha,' I said, offhand as could be, the old college chum, 'is there any way you could lend me a couple of hundred bucks? Lire, whatever. Just for a while.'

I hauled a thin sheaf of dog-eared bills from my pocket. 'This seems to be all I've got.'

'But, the bureau...?'

Even the most rigorous reporter know how to shuffle facts for best effect. 'London practically shovelled me out the door. No time for the paperwork. I've got an American Express transfer on the way.'

Well, I would have next month.

Amex! Poor darling. You could starve waiting. Americans here say that if you ever need to get rid of a body just chop it up and send the packages off by Amex. Never be seen again!'

'It wouldn't make a very good impression to show up at the bureau and get them to break out the petty cash. I don't know any of them except Charlie Flynn the bureau chief and I particularly don't want to hassle him. I just need a loan for a few days. Get a hotel.'

'Hotels here cost the earth. If you're broke, you need to be careful.' She took one of the bills from my skinny roll, strode over to the cashier and came back with a clanking fistful of metal that she arranged in a little cylindrical pile. 'Now you know how to order an *espresso*, here's Roman life lesson two. *Gettoni*. Fifty lire apiece. Can't make a phone call without one.'

'For pay phones, right?'

'Right, but there aren't any pay phones. Not in the street like back home. You'll see signs outside bars.' She nodded to a grey metal box and handset on the wall and picked up the topmost *gettone*. 'At least we'll get you a bed for tonight.'

Back from the phone she handed me a fold of banknotes. I could buy us a drink. She asked for Campari. When I winced at the thought she said, 'You could have an *americano*. Gin in it. Specially created for hard drinkers like us. Or you could have a *babee*.'

I blinked. 'A *babee* whiskey. The barman will know. It's what they say. Scotch if you're lucky. Neapolitan if you're not.'

'But why...?'

'Who knows? Italians think whiskey is more dangerous than the home-grown booze, so they take it in small doses. *Babee* doses. You can have a *babee* or you can have a large *babee*.' I was turning towards the cashier — fast learner, me — so she did not see me wince.

'Anyway,' she said when I brought the drinks over. 'Tell me about Budapest.'

'I will. But where's this I'm going to?'

'Where I'm staying. Mamma Lucia's. That's Lorenzo's *nonna* I mentioned.'

*

A brisk downhill walk the following morning and Via della Mercede was as easy to find as Tolentina. This time I could read the street numbers. Twenty-two, on the corner of Piazza San Silvestro across from a grim, rust-streaked building with a sodden *tricolore* dangling over its entrance, Rome's main post office. There were a few nameplates outside, all newsy. Century NewsWire was the topmost. The one on the bottom the longest: *Associazione della Stampa Estera in Italia*. I started up to the fourth floor. No elevator.

Hadn't been one back at Tolentina either, my home for... not too long, I hoped. Waking up there had been even more bizarre than going to bed. Well, to sleep.

The night before I had followed Marsha's instructions and knocked on a first-floor door. After a lot of bolt-shooting and rattling of chains, I was let in by a caricature mamma, round as she was tall. A hand shot out of the black garment that concealed most everything else. Marsha had told me what to pay and I handed over the bills.

Mamma Lucia — *Luchee-a* — led me into a vast dark space that to judge by the sideboard and long table ought to have been a dining room. But the table had been shoved against the wall. In the cleared space several club chairs were arranged facing away from each other and there was a high-backed couch angled into one corner. Lucia patted one arm of it, then a folded blanket and a pillow.

'*Buon riposo.*'

For about five minutes before fatigue wiped them out, the shades of London danced around in the gloom.

-2-

For a breakthrough foreign posting, London hadn't felt all that foreign. Mostly, it looked the way it did in old black-and-white movies, The CNW set-up just off Fleet Street worked much the same way as the Big Room on East 42nd. One difference was everyone kept their jackets and ties on. Not so much because it was the English way, it was just damn cold. Another was that everyone used everyone else's first name instead of the American newsroom convention of surnames only, just as we slugged each take of copy. Here, it was all first names even for the European News Manager, Roger Traynor.

I mentioned this to a fellow rimrat, Herbert from Boston. 'Sure,' he said. 'But it doesn't make us buddies.'

True. We rats were too competitive for that. Too intent on scoring the break-through assignment that would take us out in the field, the dateline that would raise awe in Wisconsin, envy in East 42nd Street and turn us into real foreign correspondents.

So instead of a roll-up knit in the pocket, everyone packed a passport. 'Don't come in without it,' Roger told me first day. 'Never know where you might end up. Days off, pop around the main consulates, get visa-ed up. Mary's got a list of places Americans need visas for.' Mary, middle-aged and war-wearied, was the newsdesk secretary; only woman in the room.

Signs were good. It was a helluva time for news. Out in Egypt, President Abdel Nasser had nationalised the Suez Canal, effectively confiscating it from its British and French operators

15

who had assumed they had rights not only to the waterway but the strip of Egypt it ran through. Ships headed for Britain had to divert around Africa for fear they could be trapped in the middle of the desert. Nearly overnight, it seemed, Britain was swept back to World War Two black-and-white. There were warnings of food shortages. Fuel rationing was introduced. You had to get coupons from the post office to buy gas. Sorry: petrol. Seemed to me the British loved it. Reminded them of their finest hour.

*

The desert dust had usually settled on the story by evening. Fleet Street pubs were wild, even if they closed at ten o'clock just as things were livening up, but there was often a party someplace. One such raucous event over in South Kensington brought about my convergence with Verity Venn, VeeVee to her friends, who were many and varied and, in most cases, more wary of her than I. She sold me a used car. To be accurate, she introduced me to a friend who sold it to me, guy in a Royal Air Force blazer and matching moustache: Jeremy.

It did not take a lot of selling. The car was a Jaguar SS 100 open roadster built in 1936. It looked great as we walked towards it outside a gas station: a 'bonnet', as the English call a hood, stretching to infinity, wire wheels, cute little doors in the open body that I could swing a casual leg over and slide down into the driving seat — positioned exotically on the right. Even to my inexperienced eye and ear, it had a few problems but I wanted it.

Those were my initials on it. Forget the other connotations.

It was actually a pig of a car in everything but appearance: hard to start, harder to stop, leather upholstery that seemed to have been cleaned off with a steel scrubber, and a mad drunkard's thirst for petrol. Even so, I loved it. One hundred quid down was the deal with Jeremy. Fifty quid the following month and another fifty the month after. Two hundred in all, or $560, a month's CNW salary. I handed over the first payment in fivers, those wonderful white £5 notes twice the size of a dollar bill that would buy dinner for two at the Savoy Hotel. If you unfurled one to pay for drinks in a pub someone would say, 'Don't break into that, old chap. Let me get it.' They were only printed on one side. You could write notes on the other.

I bought a little soft cap with a bill — peak, to the English — and wore it when I drove around London, at least when it wasn't raining, sneering at people in post-war cars that looked like surgical boots. When I could get the SS to start, that was. And when I could afford the gas.

After I had been to bed with VeeVee a couple of times, a far less complicated matter than my experiences with American girls, we got to be a regular couple. Although we didn't spend that much time together she was really good fun.

She helped run a vintage dress shop in the King's Road, Chelsea, and shared a little apartment with the girl who owned it, Sally someone, in Adam and Eve Mews, off Kensington High Street. The address alone would have endeared her to me.

There was always something happening there, drop-ins, flake-outs, party time always ticking over. Sometimes VeeVee came to my place. I had a bed-sitter in Bloomsbury, a quick bus ride from the bureau, in which I had installed a couple of oil heaters. At A & E Mews there was a little stove thing in the living room, but VeeVee's bedroom was like an icebox. Until we were between the sheets, of course, and even they needed a while to warm up. She didn't.

'It's best to call first,' she said to me at the start. 'I never know if Sally has someone in and she can be a bit noisy when she's...

entertaining.' She picked up on my smirk. 'Like an air raid siren. Woo-woo-woo…' They must hear her out in Ken High.'

'I suppose you heard that? When you were a kid.'

'The sirens? Oh, yes. Sally's *woo-woo* was the Alert. The All-Clear was *wooooooooooo*.'

That was one of the sillier reminders of how close the war still seemed to London even though it had ended ten years earlier. The scars stood out all over, weed-covered bomb-sites around Fleet Street going back to the Blitz of 1940, gaps in the facades of Chelsea terraces where a German 'buzz-bomb' took out a house.

In the States, we'd practically forgotten that war, moved on to the Korean event for which I, in college at the time, had escaped the draft. She was always hard to get on the phone, though whenever I did get the go-ahead I'd bowl over with a bottle or two and park the Jag outside for the neighbours to admire. She'd come down to open the door and I'd follow her back up the narrow staircase, usually knocking over the stack of unopened brown envelopes sitting by the mailbox. 'Bills,' she said when I asked about them. 'Always bloody bills.'

I completely went along with her dismissive wave. We were all broke, everyone I knew. My CNW salary went further in pounds than dollars but London was expensive. So what? I was having a helluva time mainly thanks to VeeVee, who dealt with whatever came along with admirable directness. One of the places we liked to go was a Chinese restaurant that seemed indifferent to the weird English laws about liquor. You could get a drink with food into the early hours, if you didn't mind pouring it out of a fancy little teapot into a fancy little cup. Once we ordered Peking duck and the waiter was explaining how to put stuff on the pancakes. 'You spread thin,' he said. 'Real thin so enough to go round everyone.'

My non-buddy Herbert was one of the crowd that night. He actually wanted to be liked though he had a strange way of going about it, taking digs at people all evening. He was sitting across from VeeVee, a bit drunk. 'Spread thin, enough to go round everyone.,' he said with a sloppy leer, mimicking the waiter. 'Sounds just like VeeVee here.'

She had to half stand and lean across the table to deliver her punch, but it was a real roundhouse right that knocked him off his chair. He slunk off in the direction of the john and never came back, 'Just trying to get out of paying his whack,' someone said.

Whack? We all thought that was hilarious.

I was proud of her.

She had one of those Dutch cap things. It didn't make for an entirely smooth bedtime experience, but it was a huge improvement over the dispiriting roll-on precautions that might otherwise be required. We, or rather I, called it Hans Brinker. 'Name of the little Dutch boy who put his finger in the sea-wall and saved Holland from being washed away,' I explained. 'A story that exemplifies myth transformed into reality.'

'How interesting.'

'Don't sneer. It's true. The little boy in the story was totally invented by an American writer called Mary Maples Dodge.'

'Why do Americans always have three names?'

'They don't. I don't. Anyway, the story became so popular that American tourists in Holland always wanted to see where this momentous event had occurred. It never had occurred, but not wanting to disappoint their guests the Dutch chose a likely spot along the dyke and put up a statue there to young Hans. See, myth into reality. Sort of thing that could happen with news if we don't watch out.'

Hans Brinker sometimes added a little gaiety to our intimate moments. VeeVee might forget to insert him until proceedings were well advanced and I would be called on to help. Slathered in contraceptive gunk and rolled up for insertion he could slip from our grasp and take to the air like a miniature flying saucer. Once she made a lucky catch with her big toe. Once she didn't and the thing ended up on the floor. I retrieved it, covered with dust and who knows what else. House-cleaning was not a priority around A & E Mews. Nor on this occasion was contraception. 'Put it down over there,' said VeeVee as I shifted from foot to foot on the freezing linoleum, enthusiasm beginning to droop. 'We'll live dangerously this once.'

The whole damn world was living dangerously. Britain and France decided to liberate the Suez Canal by invading Egypt — in conspiracy with Israel, although that took a while to establish. Then the Hungarians revolted against their Communist government, a significant crack in the Soviet Bloc.

It was sparked off by Poland next door having second thoughts about the Warsaw Pact, the deal Moscow had bullied its Iron Curtain satellites into a year earlier to build a united front against our Nato alliance.

Things moved so fast or threatened to that the Europe desk used an off-line Teletype to punch out tapes ready to be slapped into the A-wire machine:

      FLASH-RUSSIA INVADES HUNGARY.

      FLASH-ANGLO-FRENCH ALLIES SEIZE SUEZ CANAL.

The rim cleared and rats hit the doorsteps of power all across London: Foreign Office, Houses of Parliament, US Embassy. Rewrite was overwhelmed. DOWNHOLDS went out the window as we dived into those chug-a-lug London cabs to get back and bang out copy straight on to the wire. Passing the machine that brought in servicers, I peeled off an incoming and took it over to Roger, snapping it up in a peripheral glance as I went.

BUDAPEST UPWARMING CANST UPBACK PRONTO STORIFY COLORFULLEST?

Roger handed the message to Mary. I stared down at my typewriter keyboard while he scanned the underpopulated room, looking past me to whoever had just come in.

'Herbert!'

There was a flurry of coats and scarves alongside as Herbert stripped off his outer layers, flopping the side of his jacket over the arm of my chair. A side pocket gaped and I caught a gleam of green and gold. Roger raised his head from a note Mary shoved in front of him and let his glance slide past me.

'Got your passport?'

Herbert slid a hand down his Harris tweed. Swivelled round, and tried the other pocket. Stood and patted himself all over, a flush deep as ketchup rising to his crew cut. I didn't dare look, stricken by what my own right hand had done, seemingly by reflex. Unhindered by reflection or fear of consequence, it had strayed across to Herbert's pocket and extracted his passport with a two-finger scissor lift that any Broadway dip would be proud of. Maybe I wouldn't have done it to a buddy. Maybe I would have. There was a beat while Roger took another look at Mary's note.

'You?'

Face straight, eyes front, I held up my own passport. 'Flight's to Vienna. You'll have to find your own way to Budapest.' He pronounced it *pesht*.

'Get him some dollars, Mary.'

In the lobby, I handed Herbert's passport to the commissionaire. 'Must have dropped it on the stairs.'

Then I grabbed a chug-a-lug home to collect my trenchcoat.

-3-

The first Russian tank I saw was between me and where I needed to go. It was a chilling sight, nudging its way out of the mist swirling around the road leading out of Hungary towards Austria, a dark rounded shape low to the ground, sinister and... the word that came to mind was 'saurian', but I wasn't going to serve that up to the soda jerk.

I had been in Budapest for a week or so, covering the events that by then were being headlined as the Hungarian Uprising with two experienced correspondents, the resident bureau chief Sean Walker, and Charlie Flynn, a heavy up from Rome. Although the government was dutifully communist, Hungary had even more doubts than Poland about doing as Russia wanted. Then pro-Soviet hardliners in government pushed Imré Nagy, a liberal national leader, out of office. There were outbreaks of popular defiance. The feeling built up that things might end badly.

I thought the Hungarians were great. Most of those demanding that the government thumb its nose at the Soviet Union were students and young workers around my own age. They wanted a better life, sure, but they also enjoyed making trouble.

There were plenty of pretty girls around. 'They don't wear brassieres, you know,' said Charlie Flynn. He was a few years older than me with a boozer's vein-laced face. He was English, although as a CNW lifer he had been around Americans so long he might easily have passed for one had it not been for an unhealthy fascination with what he called football and we called soccer. That's soccer with a sneer.

I envied Charlie his beat. Rome was the professional last resting place of my inspirational hero figures, the legendary reporting duo Elwyn and Cadence Rickard. They must have been on the far side of fifty by now, Elwyn anyway, but they still filed for CNW sometimes.

'You see much of the Rickards?' I asked him. 'Oh, yes,' Charlie said, not enthusiastically. 'Too much sometimes.'

I knew by now that was his style and I planned to ask about them again, but that bit about brassieres got in the way.

'Really?' I asked. 'Why not?'

'No idea. But it's a well-known fact among sexual foragers. Accept it. Hungarian women don't wear bras.' 'Is that true?' I asked Marco, the Hungarian driver we used, a sharp-witted guy in his thirties. He shrugged. 'They don't like. I don't like either.'

I asked Sean, citing in evidence the Merry Widow-style bodices flaunted by the hookers haunting the Hotel Radzinsky, where most of the correspondents had put up.

'Those are Avo issue. Microphones sewed in.' Avos meant AVH, the State Security Service and its agents. Ordinary police and the few soldiers around Budapest seemed unconcerned by the protesters who had become a regular sight on the streets, but at a glimpse of the dark grey Avo uniform or word that Avo gumshoes were around, the protesters would fade.

I never got to settle the matter first-hand. Some of the girls were friendly enough and spoke English of a sort, but none seemed interested in the tatty splendours of the Radzinsky. Marco said he knew hotels where the help was less likely to be Avo snitches but my efforts were pretty half-hearted.

Any case, I expected to be back with VeeVee in a few days.

As the government came to seem more confused and ineffectual ordinary Hungarians became bolder. A student group got into a state radio studio and broadcast a list of demands. One was an end to compulsory Russian classes at school, which seemed eminently reasonable to me. But the one that hit the spot was that a giant statue of Josef Stalin the Russians had planted in the Városliget, the city's main parkland, be removed. People came from everywhere, thousands of them trudging through the early snow, rolling up in trucks. Some had serious tools, cutting torches and hacksaws.

There were no Avos around and the police and soldiers just let the crowd get on with it. In a matter of hours the 25-metre high figure was down, nothing left standing but old Joe's bronze boots, a marvellous emblematic picture to light up the copy.

Another Century maxim around was *Your Story Ain't A Story Until It's On The Wire*. It was becoming difficult to file out of Budapest. Telephone lines went dead in mid-conversation. The bureau Teletype sometimes worked in one direction, sometimes the other, rarely both.

That was the first machine I had seen with a non-English keyboard, Z where you would expect Y, accents and diacritical marks sprinkled around. The *Here Is* key that let the other end know who was connecting was labelled *ITT VAN*. In the state telegraph office, you could hand in a cable, watch the operators click out the dots and dashes on an old-fashioned brass gadget Samuel Morse himself might have used but only rarely did a message land where it was aimed at.

Same with pictures. The wire-photo machines in the state news agency were off-limits to foreigners, but some photographers had their own. They'd mix up developing fluid in a hotel bidet, process their film, make a print and wind it around the little shiny cylinder. If a phone connection came up they'd unscrew the handset, clip the leads on the machine to the contacts and hit the button. If the picture went, cause for celebration. Except, maybe, for the next person to use the bidet. But nine tries out of ten the call dropped out.

This time the shots of old Joe's bronze boots did get on the wire along with the story. There were plenty less iconic pictures waiting to be sent and more copy, too. All of us had a file of mailers we'd written, low priority background and sidebar pieces that in days gone by would actually have gone by mail rather than on the wire, off-peak. They offered release from the stricture of hard news reporting, scope for an occasional adverb.

'You better get on up to Vienna,' Sean said to me. 'Send a pile of stuff on from there. Can't trust the trains. Marco can drive you. It's only 150 miles. Bring back all the newspapers. And some cash. I'll tell London you're on your way.'

'And don't forget to bring back the copy after it's been filed,' said Charlie. 'Keeps the by-lines honest.'

Reporters joked about by-line bandits. Unable to file a piece yourself, you'd hand your copy over to someone to send it. The story would end up under his by-line rather than yours. 'Sorry, buddy, guy on the other end must have misheard me.'

I just grinned and shrugged. Most people seemed to accept such quasi-jovial insults as part of Charlie's style but not all of them liked it; he was unsettling company, making you wonder whether he was going to pat you on the back or pick your pocket.

The road west was jammed with trucks and buses. 'People head for frontier,' said Marco. 'Maybe I not come back too.' He was grinning, but I could see that he was entertaining the possibility. Daylight began to fade at the halfway point, a place called Győr. That was when we saw the first of the tanks, tiny sidelights glinting, as they lurched out of a side road and started down the middle of the highway towards us. Marco spun off on to the verge and we counted them going by, so close we could read their markings.

At least Marco could.

'Not Hungarian. Soviet.'

'Jesus, Marco. We've got to find a phone.'

'Phones no good, I'll bet.' Marco was probably right. Vehicles behind that had also pulled over to let the armoured column pass started up again and were driving around us, getting ahead. Vienna was still a three-hour drive away. The tanks could be in Budapest before I was able to file.

Marco wound the window down and peered out into the gloom where a group of locals had come to watch the roadshow. He quizzed them a bit and chewed over what they told him.

'There's something.'

Minutes later we pulled up outside the railway station. 'Forget it, Marco. I get on a train either it won't go anyplace or it'll just stop in the middle of nowhere.' Marco hadn't been thinking of trains. He walked us around the buildings until we found an office occupied by three guys wearing uniforms that looked to be made of carpet underlay. They listened to Marco, indifference briefly turning to interest then back to shrugs. One picked up a telephone — the kind you see in period movies, handset in cradle, mouthpiece like a daffodil — and wiggled it at me.

But I had already spotted the likely reason Marco had headed off here. In one corner stood a fairly new-looking Teletype. There was another exchange of views among the compatriots.

'Connects to Vienna,' said Marco, smug. The keyboard was like the one in Budapest. Tentatively, I punched the *ITT VAN* key. The machine clattered into life and, after a few mashed attempts, the *Ostërreich Post und Telegraphenverwaltung* accepted my CNW charge code and opened a line to London.

Now, punching *ITT VAN* ought to ring the bell on whichever machine I had been connected to in the London newsroom. Ten bells for flash, a few cryptic words to presage a top priority story. Five for bulletin, the story distilled into a paragraph.

Deep breath. Correspondents went through their careers without getting to punch out a first magnitude bellringer. Or without getting themselves lined up for the Roy Howard Award.

Suppose the tanks had merely been going down the road to park up for the night?

But if I felt any presence apart from Marco spelling out letters in my ear it was not Roy Howard but a hero figure from my idealist days at Colombia. Charles Sanders Peirce, America's first great logician. Applied in this case, his theory of Logical Inference suggested that a fleet of tanks would be heading for where the action was.

Old Charlie Peirce had also said, Belief is that on which one is prepared to act.

I rang up the portentous ten bells. That would bring people in London to their feet, stepping over to the Teletype, peering over shoulders at the pulsing print-ball waiting to see what-the-hell?

What if they had just been looking for a short cut eastwards out of the country and home?

I counted off thirty seconds so someone could switch the circuit over to the A Wire that would feed it straight to Century clients across the world. I banged out five bells.

'What's the name of this place, Marco?'

Remembering to hit Z if I wanted Y, I picked out:

> SHELBY STONE-GYOR, HUNGARY. FLASH. RUSSIAN TANKS
> ADVANCING ON BUDAPEST

Another bit of Century dogma was that any story short of the end of the world could be told in a lead of no more than twenty-three words, not counting dateline and by-line. The end of the world wouldn't even need that many. Nor did this.

> BULLETIN---23:10:56.2015. SHELBY STONE-GYOR,
> HUNGARY. RUSSIAN TANKS WERE TONIGHT ROLLING
> TOWARD BUDAPEST TO PUT DOWN A POPULAR UPRISING
> AGAINST THE SOVIET-DOMINATED HUNGARIAN
> GOVERNMENT.

J-school guys had a concept called Reporter Sovereignty: academic slush that meant having control of a story. Applied to the present situation it would mean I couldn't blame anyone else if I got it wrong.

But what if they *had* merely been looking for somewhere to hole up for the night?

Too late now. The story would already be stuttering out in a thousand newsrooms, the State Department, embassies, ships at sea. All around the world radio stations would be ripping and reading, newspapers would be making over the front page. Governments calling each other.

And so the news is made.

*

I had expected to go back to Budapest, once I'd got to Vienna and checked in with London, but Roger Traynor had other ideas. 'Stay right there. On the frontier. We're hearing there are no trains and the roads are full. Russian stuff going one way and Hungarians the other, getting out. There's going to be a flood of refugees into Austria. Important people. Maybe even the Hungarian government.'

He was right. Thousands of people poured out of the country, a running story that paralleled the dramatic coverage of the events they were fleeing from. Tribes of international reporters fought over them, and over the copy that some of them brought up from incommunicado colleagues in Budapest. By-line banditry was rife but there was plenty of good filing anyway, though no more bellringers. It was after Christmas before I got

UPWRAP VIENNA REBASE LONDON.

*

'Hope you know everyone thinks you did really well out there,' said Roger. We were in an impressive eating club called the White Elephant. You needed to be a member to get in. It was in Curzon Street up near Hyde Park, the sidewalks lined with more hookers than I had ever seen in Times Square.

I did know. In the wire service mafia that crucial bulletin telling the world that Soviet suppression of the Hungarian Uprising was underway had made my bones. I also knew I had been lucky those Russian tanks had actually been going where I said they were.

Roger, too, had a share of the glory. Big stories leave a comet trail of bright shreds that light up all involved. He had given me the assignment, his bureau handled my copy. I was his boy. He ordered pints of champagne that came in silver tankards. VeeVee wouldn't even let me drink beer in pints, said it was vulgar and working class. 'Just like me.' She made like she was joking; Brits always did when they talked about class, even if they weren't.

The barman put a dish in front of us. Small greenish shells and a little pile of salt. 'Gulls' eggs,' said Roger. 'Eat up. They'll be illegal soon. Along with those whores out there.'

A debate was rumbling on in parliament and the pubs about whether streetwalkers should be outlawed or just made to work indoors. I told him about the wired-up hookers in Budapest, which got us halfway through a damn fine meal. I was up for this European way of things. No one in New York had ever been bought so much as a doughnut.

'How did it go with Charlie Flynn?'

The question was a shade too offhand. 'Fine. We didn't see a lot of each other, really.'

'No problem with this?' Roger hoisted his glass of the fruity Bordeaux that had come along after the champagne. Or, as Englishmen like him called it, claret.

'Not far as I could see.'

'While back, I thought he might be heading for trouble. Heard he was getting pissed twice a day rather than the usual once.' English pissed meaning drunk, rather than American meaning pissed off.

'Really? He seemed OK to me. We just had a couple of drinks in the evening usually.'

'Anyway, good to know you got on with him. Not everyone does. Even on his own home ground.'

There were a couple more hints about Charlie as the meal went on, crude invitations to badmouth him some way. I might have worried that Roger thought I was stupid enough to join in if I hadn't been grabbed by what he went on to say about Rome. In fact, I felt the visceral quiver usually brought on by the prospect of sex or a scoop.

'What a great beat that is. Most glamorous city on earth. Power of the movies. *Three Coins in the Fountain, Roman Holiday*. Everyone wants to go there, ride around on one of those Vespa things with Gregory Peck or... whatshername?'

'Audrey Hepburn?'

'Yeah, her. Though most of those Italian girls have more going on the top storey. Then there's the pope. What a showman! That Holy Year stuff a while back hauled in a bigger audience than the National fucking Football League.'

Undoubtedly true, that. No matter how miserable Old Pope Pius XII made Catholics feel about their sex lives they seemed to love him just the same. Was Roger actually trying to sell me a job any rimrat would have traded his sister for?

'We need to beef up the coverage down there. Newspapers all over are going fucking rainbow. Advertisers want colour, and that means colour for our pictures. Colour supplements. Magazine pieces. Rota-fucking-gravure spreads.'

This was the stuff Centurions were talking about non-stop. CNW had bought up a photographic agency and changed its name to Century Newspix. It also set up a syndication agency to sell stories and pictures beyond the hard news client base.

'So we want colourful words, too. Completely new kind of mailer service. Interviews. Stories about the big names. Grace Kelly's just around the corner. Prince-fucking-Rainier for God's sake!'

Tmesis, another vestigial echo from my Colombia era reminded me: the rhetorical term for levering an emphatic word or phrase into another, as in National-fucking-Football League and Prince-fucking-Rainier.

'What if I send you down there with that as a brief?'

Hot-fucking-dog was what came to mind. But what I said was, 'Gee, Roger. That'd be great.'

'Just remember you'll need to stay on the right side of Charlie.'

Outside, the doorman rattled like a kid's toy when he raised his arm to hail a cab for us, pockets full of big half-crowns. Mellow, I remembered I would be sharing a dateline with my heroes of reporting. 'I heard the Rickards are still in Rome.'

Roger's look reflected the exasperation Charlie had shown when I asked him if they were still around. 'Oh, yes. You'll be running into them.'

I thought it might be difficult to pick up where I had left off with VeeVee. In the two months I had been away we had only managed a couple of crackly phone conversations. Getting through to the mews was tedious and often no one answered. But when I called she said, 'Darling! It will be marvellous to see you.'

The Jaguar's battery was flat as British beer, but it responded to vigorous cranking and I drove around and pulled up outside her door. Stopping in the right place required careful judgment and pressure on the brake pedal just short of pushing it through the rotting floorboards. I reached out to turn off the ignition, but before my finger reached the switch — keys were yet to come when my treasure had been built — the engine stopped of its own accord. The fuel gauge had been suggesting — it never did more than offer a hint — that the gas tank was a quarter full. I tapped it, trying to remember when I had last put some in and how much, but the needle lay dead.

'You've got petrol coupons, haven't you?' asked VeeVee. Of course, I didn't. 'Never mind. Jeremy will have some.' Of course, Jeremy would.

We went out to eat. The pile of bills at the foot of the stairs seemed high as ever.

'I'm afraid you won't be able to come back tonight. Fiona's got someone.'

'Woo-woo-woo-woo?'

She didn't laugh.

More from politeness than prospect, I asked if she might like to come see me in Rome sometime.

'I'd better talk to Jeremy about the Jag? Looks like I'll have to sell it.'

'I'm going to have a baby.'

*

The next couple of days were all paperwork and personal administration. My landlord wanted the lease paid up. CNW said that was my problem. Sure was, since it cleared out my bank account. I would need a work visa for Italy. That was their problem. So were the train tickets London-Paris-Rome, a trip of more than twenty-four hours. First class? You kidding? This is CNW. But I wheedled a month of living expenses in advance: $950. It came in American Express travellers' cheques that I had to sign in front of the office manager. 'Pretty soon we'll get all you guys in the field one of these,' he said, showing me a slice of plastic with *Diners' Club* stamped on it. 'Credit cards. Amex are going to put out one of their own. That way we'll know exactly what you spend and where.'

'Can't wait.'

VeeVee called me at the bureau. 'Fiona knows a doctor.'

Once again, I admired the girl. She knew where we stood. There was not the slightest hint of blame. Let alone of marriage — and this was, after all, the way plenty of people got hitched. So, a man's gotta do what a man's gotta do. 'How much, do you reckon?'

'Five hundred pounds. In advance. Tomorrow.'

We met at the Chinese restaurant where she had slugged Herbert. I countersigned all the Amex cheques and handed them over, together with most of the cash I had.

'It's going to be next Thursday. When are you leaving?'

'Wednesday. Bad timing.'

'Fiona will look after me. She said when she had hers it was no worse than a bad monthly.'

'Will she be at the mews tonight?'

It wasn't the same. Or rather it was, in one regard. Matters were well advanced when it occurred to me that I was receiving an inappropriate signal. I backed out and checked with my fingers.

'What are you *doing*?'

My sensitive parts had not deceived me. Hans Brinker was as firmly in place as a finger in a dyke. You should pardon the expression.

We parted in silence. I gave the pile of bills an understanding pat in passing. And off I went to Rome, sadder, wiser and broker than I'd ever been. I didn't even think about the Jag.

-4-

The door to the bureau was open. At the end of a short passageway I could see Charlie Flynn with a couple of other guys at the usual cluttered desk. On the wall behind them was a map of Europe and another of Italy with all the provinces delineated. He waved me in. '*Benvenuto*!' he said. 'You look a bit rough.' I remembered from Budapest that he had a way of jarring people like that. Trying to put them off balance.

'Long trip. Not much sleep.'

The last part wasn't true. I'd slept like a corpse, settled into my couch in Mamma's dining room. Getting out of it, however, had taken some handling. Sitting up in the morning gloom I found that I was not alone. Other strays who could only afford a couple of thousand lire for a place to sleep had come in after me. Heads began to pop up from the big club chairs, spiky with yesterday's brilliantine. There was even a guy asleep on the table over by the wall, a topcoat over him.

The air was thick with yesterday's breath and the morning's farts. A line for the bathroom put a shower out of the question, but there was hot water for a rushed shave at a basin in the passageway. I had a clean shirt in my bag. Mama posed a question that, with the aid of a fellow guest, we reduced to the operative word: *stasera*? Tonight? Where else was I going to go?

I had no idea what part of the cavernous building Marsha might be in, but thought it best not to ask. She had left me outside Mama's door and scooted up the next flight of stairs. From the landing, she signalled me to push the doorbell and when I looked around she had gone.

I locked the suitcase and left it in Mama's kitchen. Had to take the risk. Toting my Olivetti, I went into the bar where we had been the night before, put a greasy five hundred lire bill in front of the cashier and said, *'Cappucino per favore'*.

It worked. I took the paper slip to the bar and said it again. Without a word the guy ripped it in half and turned to the hissing machine that had Gaggia inscribed across its tinny front. I saw that other customers were leaving a few coins from their change so I did the same, carefully picking out the least valuable-looking of the little discs that seemed to have been stamped out of an old aluminium saucepan. I can deal with this town, I told myself as I stepped out across the Piazza Barberini.

The rain had gone and the early sun seared through the top coat of paint on a corner building. A stencilled slogan showed through like a watermark. I got used to seeing these decades-old reminders of the Fascist days but this was my first.

Credere. Obbedire. Combattere. VINCERE.

Just like CNW, really.

*

'It's great to be here,' I said to Charlie.

He introduced me around. Aldo: short, fat, sweaty. Cristof: short, thin, sallow. Later impressions of them were better. Aldo knew the Italian peninsula from hip to toe. Cristof spoke most useful languages including romanesco, the city's earthy slurring dialect. In all of them, he talked around the stub of a foul black cigar with a twist in it like the tail of a pig, a *toscano*.

They all had chairs around the kidney-shaped desk but Charlie was obviously in the slot. The set-up was much the same in every CNW bureau, a scaled down version of the rims I had ratted on in New York and London.

Here though, I knew, I would get slot time myself. It would be like having the con on a ship. You were in charge, but at any time the captain — the bureau chief — might come along, tap you on the shoulder and take over. Meanwhile, however, you had first shot at every story that came in. To decide if there *was* a story. Whether a set of events, circumstances, purported facts was worth writing up — by yourself if it was good enough, someone else if you wanted to pass — and being sent to London to go on the A-wire. Gate-keeping, the J-schools had started to call it, and it was heady stuff.

Clatter from the other side of a partition suggested the A-wire Teletype was there along with, I would discover, an operator called Rinaldo. There was also a machine carrying the CBW feed distributed in Italy, together with our servicers and one for the ANSA wire, Italy's version of Old Apathy. If the slot was the bridge of this ship I was joining that was the engine room. I wouldn't go so far as to liken the sound to a mother's heartbeat, but it was a reminder of where I was and what.

Charlie took me into his office, a windowless closet with a slightly less cluttered desk, a couple of filing cabinets, some shelves and a large old-fashioned safe. One of the cabinets had a faded label: Rickard. He must have realised that his greeting had been a bit short on warmth so he said, 'Good to see you again, old chap. We're damn glad to have you here.'

We talked about Hungary a bit, where he'd stayed until the story settled down. We'd exchanged a few messages while I was filing from Vienna, but he'd never mentioned my mighty exclusive, even passed on the kind of sour compliment Centurions tended to come up with when someone pulled off a good one. Anyway, he seemed to want to be encouraging, picking up on what Traynor had told me in London.

'That's fine by me,' he said when we had compared what each of us thought was my brief. 'Long as writing that colour stuff doesn't get in the way of the news. You'll still have to do stories, take the slot whenever we need you.' Doubling up on news was fine by me. I was so keen to make a hit in Rome that I would have crawled across the Alps like one of those St Bernard dogs, copy in my mouth.

'If you go after the movie crowd you'll be coming up against Rita.'

'Rita?'

'Rita the Meeter. She covers Cinecittá for us on pay-as-you-go. Ciampino Airport too. It's just up the road.'

I looked around.

'Never comes up here,' Charlie said. 'Sends her stuff in by hand. Can't do the stairs. Can't do sentences, either.'

Back at the desk, they showed me the phones and intercoms. Most stories, or at any rate the intimation of them, would be phoned in by stringers on local newspapers and radio stations, legmen paid by results. Apart from a couple of handsets, there was a grey, industrial-looking instrument with a second earpiece. I had seen a counterpart on Charlie's desk, presumably an extension. 'The *tipolino* phone,' said Aldo, emphasising the *tip*.

They explained the joke. A Fiat 500, the tiny automobile that would eventually become my next set of wheels, was known as a to*polino* — little mouse. Ti*polini* were the bureau's informants: local newsmen, vice squad detectives, traffic cops, hairdressers, headwaiters, hotel concierges, bank clerks and *funzionari* — public servants. The most valued, Charlie explained, were in the Vatican: priests and *monsignori* of varied nationality, bureaucrats, below-stairs workers. They were also the most expensive. A couple of times a month, Cristof would go round town doling out cash to those who had earned it.

There was a rudimentary archive, a four-drawer file cabinet stuffed with newspaper clippings and tear-offs. One drawer was marked *Montesi*. 'Still running?' I said. That story had been rattling on for a couple of years, drifting further and further down the news schedule. A young girl had been found dead on a beach, her underwear re-arranged. Theories embraced unsavoury aristocrats, politicians, sex parties, drugs. Allegations had been made against several well-to-do degenerates.

'Might never end,' said Charlie. 'Italian policeman, Italian lawyer, Italian judge gets a hand on something, any hope of finding out what actually happened is gone forever. Also, you need to forget all that American openness. Here, no-one will want to talk to you about their business. Not even tell you if it's raining outside their window. It's not that *omertá* stuff everyone writes about the mafia. Just the national way of life.'

'And when it comes to the *Sala Stampa*,' said Cristof. 'The Vatican press office. Never believe anything they tell you about the pope.'

'Nothing?'

'Well, maybe his name and number.'

Pope Pius XII and everything to do with him called for delicate handling, careful interrogation of the holy *tipolini*, usually by Cristof. The old boy was eighty and his death would be a world-class event.

To say nothing of the election of his successor.

*

By seven in the evening, I had a pretty good grip on things. The phones stopped ringing. There was intermittent mechanical chatter from the Teletype room but Rinaldo had his jacket on. Cristof, who had been out all afternoon, came back, settled into the slot to read the Outgoing file, a thick wedge of tear-offs on a clipboard. 'Bar time,' said Charlie. 'Come on downstairs and meet the inmates.'

Like working the slot, the layout of the *Associazione della Stampa Estera* also reminded me of a ship, or any rate the cabin class lobby of the SS *America*, the only ship I had been on. We came into it on a vast circular mezzanine overlooking the floor below. Around it were telephone cabinets, mailboxes, a couple of desks manned by guys wearing black schoolmaster-style gowns. '*Buona sera, dottore*,' they said to Charlie.

'Dottore?'

'We're all *dottore* here. That's what Italians call anyone who's been to college. Some of us are *professore* or *commendatore*. These *uscieri* — ushers — here will decide whether to promote you.'

A few gawkers leaning on a rail around the mezzanine kept us in shot as we went downstairs to a space scattered with big chairs and sofas — a flash-up reminder of my night to come at Mamma Lucia's. When Charlie had asked where I was staying, I invented some friends. 'Fine,' he said. 'Save on your outgoings. Just leave us a phone number.' He had already forgotten about that, heading for the bar and the first of many *babees*.

The bar that ran along one side of the ground floor was fringed by pods of drinkers. Other groups sat out in the room, well apart it seemed at my first brief glance. Everyone turned to size me up. New blood.

It would be hard to operate as a foreign reporter in Italy without the *Stampa*. Not being a member would mean having to work without a press pass — the glossy little *tessera* — and much else that was helpful.

Benito Mussolini started out as a newspaperman. In the Fascist heyday of the 1930s he wanted a good press and he knew that one way to get it was to make life easy for those who might provide it. He made the *Stampa* a comfort zone for foreign reporters, offering phones that worked, cable facilities, an ANSA hook-up, cheap travel on the newly punctual trains; even tickets to the opera. Above all, it had this bar where they could interview each other.

Many of those old Fascist-time privileges and concessions were still to be had. Discount railroad vouchers meant that a first-class wagon-lit to Venice cost as little as 10,000 lire, less than twenty bucks. The main downside to the place was the weirder members, shadowy figures of uncertain accreditation and questionable connections who hung around on the fringe of conversations. In Italian. the official language of the place, they were *spazzatori* — scavengers. In English, the drinking language, they were shitpickers.

'This here's Digby,' Charlie said over his shoulder, peeling a guy away from the bar. It was all I could do not to laugh full in the face that turned round to me. It was a Halloween mask of that British military caricature Colonel Blimp: red, bloated and wreathed in a truly awesome moustache that curved up to merge with fluffy sideburns. In London I had heard them called Bugger's Grips. Under it, however, was a big welcoming smile and the eyes above it gleamed with goodwill.

'Digby Tucker,' said the mouth amid the hair. 'Welcome to Rome.'

'Fuckin' *Special*,' said Charlie, *babee* in hand and noticeably happier. '*Daily Express*.'

We'd been talking upstairs about 'Specials', staff correspondents for newspapers and radio outfits who were the bane of every CNW bureau. They felt entitled to stroll in and look over the Outgoing. 'Then the shitbags go send off their own stories with stuff added that they'd never share with us,' said Aldo. 'Real one-way street.'

Couldn't stop them, though, Charlie said, if they worked for CPW clients. Just make it hard for them to poach our exclusives. Stick the hot story on the bottom, of the file. 'Even in the drawer,' said Aldo.

Now Charlie threw an arm around the Englishman's shoulder. 'Digby's OK though, aren't you Digby? He's one of the good guys.'

He was playfully aggressive, too, with the next guy he turned to. 'Our doyen, Kurt Leder. Deutsche Presse-Agentur. DPA. The CNW of Germany.'

'More the AP⁴⁄₂ Herr Leder said.'

'Kurt's pretty straight, though. For a Kraut.'

This Kraut, steely-eyed, thick-set crinkly hair working back from his forehead, grinned politely; he looked to have Charlie's measure. Others might have been less gracious had they overheard the assessments delivered *sotto voce* in my ear as we continued around the bar.

London *Daily Mirror*. Crazy. Watch out.

The Times. Umbrella up his arse.

Vanguardia, Barcelona. Spick pederast.

Agence France Presse. Spy.

Newsweek. Creep.

Catholic News Service. Pious creep.

'Over there's TASS.' Charlie pointed to a couple of stolid men in unmistakably Russian suits parked side by side. 'One's the correspondent the other's the commissar. Can't remember which is what.'

The Russians turned towards him in tandem. One lifted his glass a centimetre. Up yours.

Only slightly embarrassed by Charlie's commentaries, less *sotto* as more *babees* were delivered, I was having a marvellous time. He told the bartender to open a tab for me.' He'll let you know when he wants you to settle up, won't you, Gino?'

Expansively, I ordered the next round. Beyond the stand-up drinkers, a couple of groups around tables deeper in the room were beginning to break up. I had been taking peeks across there and was now pretty sure what I was looking at.

'Is that...?'

Charlie scowled over the rim of his *babee*. 'Indeedy, my boy. Those are — that is — the world-famous team of him 'n' her newshounds, Elwyn and Cadence Rickard. Poisonous fuckers.'

He pushed me over there, front and centre. 'New addition to the bureau.'

There were more people at the table than I first thought. They had evidently just finished a game using cards with designs I had never seen before. As Elwyn Rickard began to stand up and stick out a hand towards me I felt I should throw a bow. Charlie started around the table.

'Jean-Claude Hollande, *L'Humanité*, Commie. Claude Cameleon, some Greek rag. Willy Schmeik, *Neues Deutschland* — that's *East* Germany. *Communist* East Germany. What is this, Rick? Huddle of the *Stampa Estera* commie cell?'

Elwyn Rickard was still pitched forward, unfolding himself upright. Not the best posture from which to loose off a punch. Nevertheless, he tried. Charlie hopped neatly backward and Elwyn went face down into one of the big club chairs.

'And this,' said Charlie, extending an arm over Elwyn's heaving back, 'is the celebrated Cadence.'

The woman began to rise. I had thought she was standing already. Although I had idolised the Rickards for years, I had never seen a picture of them. I had no idea they were so *big*.

43

'Hi, Caddie.'

She was still unfolding, rising higher and higher, easily passing the six-foot mark. 'Fuck off, Flynn.'

Elwyn was back on his feet. He seemed to have forgotten about slugging Charlie. He looked down at me, a little unfocused. 'New kid on the block, eh? We'll have to show you around a bit.'

'That'd be great... Mr Rickard.' And, thinking I'd better include her, 'Mrs Rickard.' The towering — literally — presence of this epic couple made me feel like a copy boy.

'Elwyn,' said Elwyn. 'Call me Elwyn.'

'Call him Rick,' said Caddie. Her voice sounded like a great door creaking. 'Everyone calls him Rick. As in prick.'

*

The evening exhausted itself in a restaurant called the *Re degli Amici* that we reached by straggling through a maze of streets behind the post office. The Rickards led, striding out. It was hard to tell at first whether we were a party or if some were just going the same way. Charlie had disappeared. I remembered he was married and presumably had a home to go to. I fingered the slender sheaf of bills in my pocket and tottered along between the English moustache and a small rounded woman on full alert who, I belatedly realised, was Rita the Meeter.

As the bureau guys emphasised in my induction session, the major story-flows in and out of Rome — apart from national politics that even Italians could rarely make sense of — did indeed rise in the foothills of Cinecittá and the Vatican; also from the Food and Agriculture Organisation of the United Nations, a vast temple to international bureaucracy on the edge of town. Quite a lot, though, trickled in from the airport, Ciampino. It was the last fuel stop for planes leaving Europe for Africa and the Mideast and the first for those coming in.

Desirable interviewees could be intercepted and shaken down for quotes that would be in print before they got to London or wherever. Equally, if airport reporters somewhere up there missed a departure story the target could be caught up with in Rome. By Rita, it would seem. It sounded like she had a good beat there. Cinecittá, on the other hand, might be too good for her.

We ended up seven for dinner, the other two a sharp-faced American in her thirties, Esther, who wrote a column in the *Rome Daily American*, the local English-language newspaper, and her rather younger Italian friend.

'Fernando takes simply marvellous photographs,' she wanted me to know. 'Ask me, he's gonna be wasted working for you-all.'

Whether anyone asked her or not, Fernando turned out to be chief of the Century Newspix operation in Rome, having been included, it seemed, in the buy-up. 'I just had to come along tonight to make him tell me all about his new *fidanzata*.'

Fernando was uncomfortable, partly, I guessed, because he was the only Italian among these boisterous *stranieri*, also because Esther evidently had a prior claim to his attention that she was unhappy to see expire.

The reception as we shambled into the restaurant had been theatrical. The maître d' led a troupe of waiters crooning like a barbershop quartet, 'Signor Rickard! Signora, *buona sera. Buona sera tutti. Che piacere! S'accomodi!*'

Nevertheless, I picked up the resignation on their faces as we were herded to a large round table in the middle of the room.

It was after 10.30 and the night had a way to run.

I ended up alongside Cadence. I worked up a cheerful, slightly drunken grin but I had to tilt my head way up to let her see it. It was like sitting next to that statue of Joe Stalin.

Wine came. Litre carafes of white or red that were emptied in a round of the table.

Rita helped me order something I would never have thought of, *spaghetti all chitarra*.

'Means guitar,' she said. 'Did I hear we might be working together?'

I let the sharp edge to the question scrape by. 'Square spaghetti?'

'That's the *alla chitarra* part.'

'But guitar strings are round.'

'They push the dough through a wire mesh thing. That's the guitar.'

'And it's yellow.'

'Eggs. I hope you're not going to expect me to share my contacts with you.' The territorial imperative. First day in my new job. First potential antagonist. Maybe the second, given my uncertainties about Charlie.

There was a sauce with the pasta, some kind of meat with little peas. I shovelled it up. 'Blotting paper!' said Digby across from me, moustache flecked with spinoffs from his own dinner.

Rick, as I now warmly thought of him, took delivery of the next wine consignment, splashed it into every glass he could reach and bawled for more. Esther for one didn't need any more. She had probably intended to make a show of dealing gracefully with Fernando's new interest but had left it half a litro too late. 'You want to tell us a bit about this new lady?' she asked him, a snarl beneath her slur. 'The beautiful Lucinda.'

'Yeah,' said Rick, tuning in. 'What's she like in the sack?'

Fernando seemed to be happier to deal man-to-man rather than come up with something to quieten down Esther. 'Too soon to be sure,' he said, only the flick of a leer. 'She's still *in rodaggio*.'

Rick guffawed. I looked to Digby. 'Being run in. Like a new car.'

He hadn't really got me in his sights before, but Rick decided to deliver some advice to the newcomer. 'Never stick it to a *signorina*.'

'Thanks for the tip,' I said waiting, but evidently that was it.

I turned back to Cadence lowering over me like a Mount Rushmore face. 'Guess you're regulars here,'

'Been coming for a while. Matter of fact we had dinner here the day Italy declared war on the United States.'

'Here? This restaurant? In 1941?'

'December 7. Day of Infamy over here, too.' Rick, sitting across the table had heard her. Everyone heard. That voice cut through the rumble of other people's conversations like a buzz saw. 'Luigi put us behind that pillar there so the Fascists at the other tables wouldn't come over and gloat about their Jap pals hitting Pearl Harbor.'

This was the kind of stuff I wanted to hear. I looked from one Rickard to the other. 'Must have been a hell of a day in the bureau.'

'He wasn't there when the flash came in,' said Cadence. 'He was home having lunch with Ezra Pound.'

Ezra Pound! This was too much. I didn't go in for literary heroes, poets especially, but I'd always liked this great American oddball. At college, I had sometimes found a few of his lines useful. 'A tree has entered my hands...' What my hand had usually encountered at such a time was a forked trunk of panty-girdle, elasticised armour impervious as ironbark. The next line was something about sap rising, as my female companion would have worked out for herself by then.

'I filed *all* the stories,' boomed Caddie. 'Not that there was much. Much that got past the censors, anyway.'

'I wasn't exactly sitting on my hands.' This was evidently well-established repartee. 'I was on the phone to the embassy trying to make sure we didn't get slung in the pokey.'

'But we *did*. You did, anyway.' I wanted to hear about that, of course. But having orderly habits of information assembly I asked Caddie, 'And what about Pound?'

'I never let him in the house after that. Soon as he heard the news he started stomping around the place giving the Fascist salute and yelling *Viva il Duce*! Frightened the shit out of our cook.'

'Well, we weren't *in* the house much longer after that. I was in Regina Ceoli. Then we were all herded off to Siena.'

'Regina… ?'

'Regina Ceoli.' Digby again. 'Prison over on the other side of the river. The Tiber. Nasty place.'

I took over the prompt. 'But you got back to the States eventually?'

They must have because of all the war reporting they did afterward.

Not so Pound, who had shown ludicrous obstinacy by staying in Italy all through the war, broadcasting nonsensical Fascist propaganda.

The US government hadn't wanted to put him on trial. It was easy to imagine the kind of exuberantly subversive stuff he would have spouted in a courtroom. So they called him crazy and put him in a looney bin in Washington DC where he was still, regularly holding court with disciples and scholars.

'Sure we got back,' said Caddie. 'But it took a bit of fixing. The Duck and Hitler swapped us for the Italian and German correspondents stranded in the States.'

'The Duck?'

'That's what everyone called Mussolini back then. Americans, anyway. *Il Duce*. The Duck.'

'They made us stay in Siena six weeks, half a dozen American correspondents, all frustrated because they couldn't file on the story. Most of us hadn't gotten on all that well even before we got slung together.'

'We went into a little hotel up there as mere surly rivals,' said Rick. 'Came out lifelong enemies.'

'At least you came out.'

'Early 1942. Train across France, Spain. Ship from Lisbon to New York.'

I wanted to hear more of this but the Rickards had lost interest. The evening was winding down in a cacophony of clattering plates, shouts for waiters, squabbles starting up. Rick grabbed the *conto* that had been scribbled out on an order pad and was counting heads. Esther had left earlier after slightly fuddled goodbyes. Fernando didn't go after her, but probably wished he had, now that he was up for her share as well as his own.

'*Cinque mille!*' bawled Rick. I slipped out my skinny wad under cover of the tablecloth and found a five. Caddie looked at me across the table her broad face expressionless, but something in her eyes made me feel she could count what was left in my wallet.

-5-

My salary, once it began to flow, went further in lire than it had in British pounds. No one could say I wasn't earning it though. As and when required, I took my turn in the slot, usually at night when things were quiet. Rinaldo was in the wire room if I needed language support. I had signed up at Berlitz and was making fair progress, but I found Italian telephone habits annoying. Answer a ring and the voice at the other end would ask: *Chi parla?* That's what *I* should be asking — who's calling me? Once, getting up to stretch, I idly tugged at the handle of the Rickard file cabinet. Locked. Mostly, though, I just got on with punching out my twenty-threes.

> 06: 04: 57: ROME. ITALY'S HIGHEST COURT TODAY RULED
> THAT A TRIAL TO RESOLVE THE MYSTERY OF WILMA
> MONTESI'S DEATH MUST BE HELD IN VENICE NOT ROME.

Fumetti, Aldo and Cristof called stories like the Montesi saga, after trash publications that down-market Romans loved, comic-strip magazine serials using Polaroid pictures with paste-up balloons of text — the *fumetti*, smoke clouds. Montesi-inspired variations were churned out every week, a new Wilma lookalike making a debut.

The main prosecution witness in a string of hearings and trials was a young woman called Anna Maria Caglio. She claimed that her former lover, the wayward son of a government minister, had left Wilma Montesi drugged and dying on a beach. After a particularly malevolent court performance, the trash faction writers labelled her the Black Swan. That was a good headline, but a back story as long as the gospels and a notable absence of facts made the going hard for a wire service.

Judges said the three accused, one the son of a former cabinet minister, would not receive a fair trial so close to where the girl's body was found in 1953.

I usually ate lunch at a *rosticceria* a few doors up Via della Mercede. You yelled out your order or just pointed at the dishes on offer and ate at a stand-up table alongside anyone else who could squeeze in. A *specialitá della casa* intrigued and repelled me: long skewers packed with barbecued birds the size of sparrows. The counterman jammed them into chunks of bread, little beaks and feet sticking out. Birdburgers.

If I didn't have to go back right away I might give my digestion the benefit of a seat in the cinema next door that only cost a couple of lire. The box office also sold sweets, stamps, lottery tickets and smoking essentials. Eric got his awful *toscani* there and I bought Lucky Strikes that were furtively slid out from under the counter. It was quite legal to sell American cigarettes but either the state monopoly, whose main brand was the foul *Nazionale*, wanted them kept out of sight or there was some kind of nostalgia for the black-market days not long past. In the present, quite a few customers bought their *Nazionales* one at a time, slapping down a couple of aluminium slugs and firing up from a lamp wick on the counter.

The movies were black-and-whites from the 1930s and 40s called *telefoni bianchi* because the May West-ish heroines usually fondled a white telephone. Dialogue was sparse and declarative, a helpful supplement to my language lessons.

More often, though, I went back and worked on my mailers, which were getting a good reception around the States and in

Latin America where the market for God and mammaries seemed insatiable.

> EX NY FEATUREDESK 250557 REPORTED GINA
> LOLLABRIGIDA ENGAGED WET NURSE TO FEED NEW BABY.
> PLEASE STORIFY HOW FEELS TO INFILL PROWORLD'S MOST
> FAMOUS BOSOM.

A less problematic variation on the tits theme was provided by a young woman artist called Novella Parigini. *Life* magazine had run a picture of her in her Rome studio, painting girls in microscopic bikinis while wearing one herself. Not painting pictures *of* the girls. Painting *on* the girls. The bikini was a new erotic artifact and CNW clients wanted everything about them that we could file. As it happened, I knew where to find Signorina Parigini.

*

I had come across the Via Margutta on my visits to Newspix. The picture operation was about twenty minutes' walk from San Silvestro on the top floor of a commercial building between Piazza del Popolo and the Tiber. I had two routes to get down there. The Via del Corso was a thundering, asphyxiating rat-run of Vespas and Fiats, but on the side closer to the Tiber rose the mighty column of Marcus Aurelius, an eighteen hundred-year-old *fumetti* in stone. I would stroll by the Palazzo Chigi, home to whoever was prime minister that week, and the Palazzo Montecitorio, the Chamber of Deputies. Neither elegant facade offered any suggestion of the chaos within.

My other itinerary lay more to the east, although compass points didn't matter much until the end of the day when, if I could get up to the Pincio Hill, I would watch the sun go down behind St Peter's across the river. I was delighted to find there was a Via del Propaganda, home to an extraterritorial outpost of the Vatican, the College for the Propagation of the Faith. Opposite it was a marvellous shoe store that always made me feel uncomfortable in the clumpy Florsheim wingtips that were all I had.

Just in back of the College was a tall building whose shutters were always closed. Appropriately enough it was a *casa chiuse*, the last legal whorehouse in this part of town, and about to be *chiuse* forever thanks to a campaigning woman senator, Lina Merlin. State licensed brothels were shutting down all over Italy and this one would go when the Legge Merlin went on the statute book in a couple of months.

Then I would be in the Piazza di Spagna, the dread American Express on one side of the Spanish Steps and on the other the house where John Keats died. Opposite were the glittering shopping streets, Via della Croce, Via dei Condotti, Via Frattina and, at the end, Via del Babuino — Baboon Street.

It took me a while to discover that parallel to Babuino, which was as clamorous as the Corso, ran a far more enchanting byway. Narrow, cobbled, shaded by tall facades on either side, Via Margutta seemed like a village backwater. It reminded me of Adam and Eve Mews. Except for the vivid flowerboxes, elegant lanterns, lush trees rising behind sun-drenched orange-yellow walls and a fine marble fountain. And the phantom brushwork under peeling paint: *Il duce ha sempre ragioni*. Mussolini is always right. Bum product slogan, they would have called that on Madison Avenue.

Novella Parigini's studio was at 53b, seventh floor. My Seventh Heaven, she called it and those were the only English words at her disposal unless you count 'bikini'. She was an enticing young woman with whom I might have taken up the pressing matter of how to get laid, except that my Italian was not up to a flirtation. We stumbled through a rudimentary

53

interview, me coming up with a lot of leading questions and her answering *Si*.

I looked in at Newspix every few days to see if there were any shots that might inspire a mailer. There was always a big hello from Fernando, understandable perhaps since I probably outranked him. He introduced me perfunctorily to a young woman, dark, small and distant: Lucinda, I remembered. In *rodaggio*.

I liked the atmosphere there, a sharp chemical smell. If the darkrooms were not in use I could duck under the clusters of film rolls hung up to dry like socks and look through piles of damp prints warm from the dryers. Colour was beginning to make an impact, but I liked the dramatic depth of the black and white images.

The demand for pictures of Rome's famous and infamous was catered to by a tribe of feral photographers called *scattini* — annoying insects. Flashgun shots of misbehaving or indiscreet celebrities snatched outside bars and nightspots in the early hours were an important currency. Packaged up with routine pictures of Vatican visitors and the occasional Italian personality recognisable elsewhere, they went out to CNW subscribers by airfreight.

*

I saw the *scattini* in action soon after it was warm enough to sit out in the early evening. Though the Via Vittorio Veneto was world famous, the part that mattered was only about a quarter-mile long. It curved gently uphill from the Gigi Fazzi restaurant by the American embassy to Porta Pinciana, a gate in the Aurelian Wall, a 2000-year-old chunk of brickwork.

On the right side going up the places that mattered were the Hotel Excelsior, Cafe Doney, Jerry's Bar and Grill and

Bricktop's nightclub. Across the road were the Caffé Strega and Rosati's. No need to step inside to see who was out on the town. Each joint had staked out a stretch of tables on the sidewalk where the clientele was on open display. Actors and actresses anyone might have heard of favoured the right, along with Hollywood carpetbaggers, and Italian fixers — *i sigaroni*, for their big cigars.

The left side was mainly starlets, whores, politicians, gangsters and the phone book aristocracy. The post-war Italian republic did away with noble titles, but lots of people found them hard to give up — or easy to invent. And waiters liked to sprinkle *contessa* or *marchese* around.

Sometimes I'd go on patrol up there with Digby. He'd get *buona sera, dottore* from every second waiter and plenty of friendly nods, even from some *sigaroni*. Even from some of the girls they were with. Even from people I had actually seen in the movies. 'It's the moustache, old chap. Kind of a trademark. People remember me.'

At Doney's a raddled couple remembered him at such length that I sat down at a table and ordered a beer to wait out the conversation. I was never sure exactly what happened next but if my eyes could have been pointing in opposite directions I think the right one would have lit on a tall, dark-haired woman about twenty-five and a much older man strolling up from the Excelsior. The left one would have picked out a couple of guys in blue jeans, cameras up and ready, breaking into a downhill trot. In reality, I didn't see the approaching *scattini* at all until one tripped over my left foot, which had been sticking out from the table, crashed down on the sidewalk like a felled tree and the other tripped over him.

I jumped up but the photographers stayed at knee level, scrabbling around for bits that had fallen off their cameras and thus in no position to get a shot of their target stopping to kiss me briefly on the cheek.

'Thank you,' she said and was gone in a puff of scented breath, a flash of perfect lips and wry, pale blue eyes. Enthralled, I watched her saunter off with the old guy. I barely registered him, but I wouldn't forget her.

'What the hell happened?' Digby helped me haul the lead *scattino* upright. He was heavy-set, short and sweaty. Affronted, too. I hadn't meant to trip him, I explained. He'd tripped himself. I gave my shin a rub to make the point.

Digby wasn't interested in cause and effect. 'Don't you know who that was? Bloody Arabella Frost. I've been trying to get her to talk to me for weeks.'

I actually did know who he meant, although I hadn't recognised her in the fleeting moment she paused to show her appreciation for something I hadn't done: a mid-market English actress with a few familiar films behind her. But I didn't really grasp *what* she was to Digby until I looked out some clippings. She was also La Principessa Arabella di Bergamonte et Murano, estranged wife of Principe Riccardo of the same ilk.

The *Daily Express* wanted her badly because she had applied to the Italian courts for sole custody of the young son of the marriage that had landed her that mouthful of a title. The marriage, she claimed, was no longer functional. The title however was. Riccardo came of the Black Nobility, the papal aristocracy created way back to humour the offspring of popes and cardinals and thus beyond the power of the Italian state to rescind. It brought him, in addition to much unseemly servility, the privilege of carrying some relic like the Holy Foreskin in papal processions.

There had been several dramas like this around: impressionable young actresses, usually British, sometimes

American, falling for silky Italian noblemen then finding they were not so noble in their ways. Finding also that there was no divorce in Italy and that an Italian court would rarely award custody of children to a foreign mother. This would not be a wire service story, except probably for the outcome, but the sensational London papers would jerk every possible tear out of it.

*

Rick and I ran into each other practically every day in the *Stampa*. He had breakfast there. Gino the barman would fry him three eggs in butter that he ate with some kind of pizza crusted with salt: *focaccio pugliese*. Gave me a bit of it once and I nearly cracked a tooth. It was a while before I found him there alone, mid-afternoon and the place deserted apart from a few dozing *spazzatori*. Big as he was, his broad facade sliding downhill, he found it hard to get comfortable. Sitting, he moved his ass around all the time making the chair creak. He would stretch a leg right out then haul it in again, scraping the heel of his shoe on the marble floor. Even standing at the bar he was never still, half-turning one way then the other like a wrestler shaping up for a throw. 'I reckon you want to know about us,' he said. 'Caddie and me. How it works?'

Indeed I did. I wanted to know everything they knew. Stuffed in that bulging pair was all the curiosity, craft and cunning of getting out there and bringing in the story, back in the days when it was a damn sight harder to do. Not just that. The arrangement by which they seemed still to be Centurions but never came up to the bureau or, far as I could tell, filed anything, was tantalising, to say the least.

So far I hadn't heard much from either of the Rickards about the noble art of reporting. I had, however, learnt more than I really wanted to — from Rick, anyway — about sex Italian-style. Well, sex Rickard-style. Every time I got him around to the romance of period newsgathering he would start in about who he had boffed on whatever assignment and, in lavish detail, how. It was no different when Caddie was with him. Apart from firing off the occasional genial insult, she would just sit quietly, looking around wherever it was in that distant, flat-eyed way.

The only opportunities he wasn't interested in were those that seemed to abound on the streets of Rome. Only the night before he'd picked up on that gnomic warning against Italian womanhood. After another late dinner at the *Re degli Amici*, a gaggle of us had lurched around to the last place still open in that part of town, a haunt of printers and typesetters from *Il Messagero*, familiar shades to us all from newspaper days. They were eating *spaghetti all' amatriciana*, we kept on with red wine or segued on to Vecchia Romagna, the local brandy.

'The only thing about sex that interests a young Italian woman,' said Rick, 'is that it leads to babies. Unless she's a mother she's no one, just another useless little *ragazza*. But for that, she's gotta have a husband. And the best way to get a husband is to get pregnant. She's got no time for fun. That virgin quim is her ticket for the guy who's going to give her the magic *bambino*. Pity the poor guy, too, because marrying that succulent young piece of ass means marrying everyone else in her life — mama, papa, *nonna* and all her jailbird brothers. So sure, young buddy, they're enticing, all that honey-coloured flesh and curves. But fun, pleasure, interesting variations, forget it. The only use that little *signorina*'s got for a prick is to plant a sprog in her. Steer clear!'

When I felt vibration underfoot I thought the *Messagero* presses across the road must have started up, but it was Rick stomping on the worn tiles. '*Olé!*' yelped Rita, clapping her hands. 'He's Spanish. The guitarist.'

I had not paid any particular attention to the guy with a guitar in a corner. There was one hanging out most places in Rome. 'He only comes in sometimes. Rick loves him. Says it reminds him of the Civil War days.'

Rick was out amid the shaky tables, wobbling his hips like a stripper. He kept time with the music, little steps in a square pattern, stopping to drum his heels. Someone started to clap, that double-tap thing flamenco dancers do. It didn't last long. The guitarist tried to pace him, but after a few shuffles, Rick ran out of moves. And breath.

Then Caddie stood up, glided over towards him like a circus tent caught by the wind. The guitar came up with a few more chords. Her clothes were, as usual, in the style of mission handouts, but she twitched the hem of her skirt with a hand and it swirled and lifted. The calves unveiled were bare, firm and shapely. Her shoes were chunky, low leather heels. No good for clicking on the floor, but she went into a little routine in front of Rick. He stuck out his chest or tried to, lifted up his arms like a magician hauling a rabbit out of a hat and twirled. She twirled, too, swooped, fell back on that confident rectangle of steps. They went on for a while, circling, inviting each other with swivelling gestures, pausing to drum out a burst on the floor. It was like watching an elephants' mating display, though they knew what they were doing. Quite a little show.

Now, shaking *focaccio* crumbs off his front, he said, 'Goldfish bowl.'

'Excuse me?'

'Me and Caddie,' said Rick. 'A goldfish bowl.' The nature of my interest seemed to have been misunderstood. But what could I do other than shut up and listen?

'Right from the start, we said our life together was gonna be transparent as a goldfish bowl. We wouldn't ever hide anything from each other. Or anyone else, come to that. Anyway, it would have taken a hell of a lot of hiding, 'cause let me tell you, man, we were both out to do a lot of fucking. Hell, only reason we bothered to get married was to save the trouble of *not* being married. You know, travelling, hotel rooms together, that sort of stuff.'

'You gotta remember when we started out it was back in the 1930s. For young 'uns like us, seriously horny, America was a straitjacket. Where we wanted to be was Paris. Scott Fitzgerald, Henry Miller, they were our heroes. Caddie and I were going over there and behaved even worse than those guys, but the only foreign job I could get was in China. China! Did anyone even know if the Chinese fucked? Turns out they did, but that's another story. Anyway, we stayed there awhile, then eventually we got to Paris. It was like our real life just began. There was fucking in the very air. Paradise.'

A pause implied a round of drinks. I ordered. 'We were gonna be the Scott and Zelda of newspapers. She was a fine-looking broad back then, my Caddie, apart from being a great bare-knuckle buddy in a bar-room brawl. Had these great long legs that wrapped around you like a giant squid and a quim like an intelligent vacuum cleaner. All the hot guys were fascinated by her — and vice versa. So the deal was that each of us could do whatever — whoever — we wanted, long as we told each other. Oh, hi there, Miss Frisk.'

I swung around to where Rick was looking past me, and confronted a vision from a play by one of those perky Scandinavians. Ibsen or Strindberg would have written this one as the elderly aunt giving the young heroine a hard time: a stern-faced woman, quite old, turned out in perfect start-of-the-century fashion: full-length dress in a spriggy fabric, short jacket, wide-brimmed hat. I couldn't very well peek down at her shoes, but they were sure to have rows of buttons.

'Miss Frisk is our *doyenne*,' said Rick. 'The wise woman of the *Stampa Estera* and the most distinguished correspondent of a distinguished Swedish newspaper. One of the *Dagbladets*.'

'*Svenska Dagbladet*, actually.' Her English was barely accented. She offered a hand gloved in some sort of netting. The other one twiddled a nifty little umbrella, no…a *parasole*.

'Miss Frisk is the great love of my life, but I never get to see enough of her. She hides away in the Vatican.'

'And other places, Mr Rickard.' We chatted a bit, then she offered her glove again and glided off as though on skates. I'd never seen anything like it outside of the theatre.

'She's looked like that for twenty years,' said Rick. 'And that's what people said about her twenty years ago. Father was Swedish Minister to the Holy See.' The See, I'd learnt on my first day, was the political concept of the Vatican, the barefaced pretence that it was a state, a genuine country with citizens, passports, duty-free booze. 'He was a stern old Calvinist and so is she. But she's known those pious phoneys over there all her life and they can't put much past her.'

Then we went back to sex. Intriguing as Rick's disclosures were in general, the detail became a bit wearing since his taste ran less to glamorous Mata Hari figures and international society hostesses than to whores, and pretty workaday ones at that. He seemed to have total recall of every encounter racked up in the civil and military brothels of a dozen nations.

I gave up trying to get him to tell me what sort of a deal they had with Century that let them file what they liked whenever they felt like it, without any bureau duties. Casually as I could, I asked Charlie.

'Wish I knew. Though if I did it would probably just make me mad. They're not on the bureau payroll — thank God. They've got their accreditation through us and they can put anything they want on the wire. But some boardroom-level deal means they get paid from New York, even though they're only rolled out for stories they want to do.'

If I wanted to know about the amazing life that lay behind those legendary joint by-lines I guessed I had better try Caddie.

-6-

Along with everything else, I was trying to get some kind of orderly sex life together. Having been so drastically warned off the local prospects I decided to open negotiations with Marsha, of whom I had not seen much for a while.

Although Rick seemed unaware of it, the Italian sexual attitudes he railed against were not all that different from those back home. Most of the young women — like Marsha — I grew up alongside also wanted marriage and babies and pretty quick, too. They usually hitched up with someone in the interlocking circles of college days and early jobs, switching from prey to pal, the friendship link as effective as an incest barrier. Or a panty-girdle.

However, one who had broken loose — like Marsha — was a different matter, a woman who had got into the habit of sex and spoke wryly of her long drought. A woman of experience recovering from a sexually unhelpful husband with a socially unobliging Italian lover. There could, at the least, be a case for consolidating our requirements.

With paydays regular I had been able to move out of Mamma's and into a small strange apartment up near the Stazione Termini that I found advertised in the *Daily American*. It was sublet by an elderly Dutch woman who stuffed her treasures into the main bedroom and locked it off.

What space that left me was adequate enough, but the place was on the top floor of an eight-story building under an immense PanAm Airways sign. At night the little terrace was bathed in neon blue, with intermittent flashes of red from a counter in the centre of the display that flicked out the number of PanAm flights that hadn't crashed that day. It fit my budget, even though there was a weird extra: the tiny elevator would only go up when one of those ten-lire aluminium stamp-outs was dropped in a slot. Going down was free.

I invited Marsha to look the place over then took her to dinner. I wanted to show I could manage the Italian meal experience on my own, bawling *'Senta!'* — Listen! — to call the waiter and if he didn't jump to it, tapping my wineglass with a knife like every other impatient diner. Try that in New York and you wouldn't want to eat what the waiter brought you.

Before I arrived in Italy I had always thought of a plate of pasta as a full meal. Spaghetti for dinner, that was it. Maybe a dessert or some ice cream. Not in Rome. The main event only came *after* the pasta. Veal, fish, a pork chop. Plus vegetables, salad. Then a dessert. The sheer amount Romans put away always surprised me.

Most of the menu items had become familiar and even in an upmarket *trattoria* there was little danger of embarrassment over the wine list; the choice was simply between *rosso* and *bianco*. Both came in those open *carafi*. The only decision was whether to have half a litre or go the whole hog.

'What I'd like to know', Martha said. 'Is why they always give you damp table napkins?' It was true. Even in an upscale *ristorante*, whether it was lunch or dinner, the napkins would be soggy and limp. I knew why because Esther had told me at one of those *Re degli Amici* events. 'They only run to one set. The waiters take them home for their wives to wash and iron between meals.'

We had a fine time together. Since my earlier assessments hadn't really been lustful I had not fully appreciated how appealing Marsha really was: clear blue eyes, neat ears with little gold pins through the lobes. And that nose: straight and narrow with tight oval nostrils. I wasn't sure if women wanted to be complimented for their nostrils, so I shut up.

As a former agency moll, she was keen to know how I was getting on in the bureau. The Lollobrigida baby request made her giggle. 'Did you do it? Get the wet-nurse?'

'Had to tell them sorry. Lady in New York obviously didn't know what the baby had been called.'

'Which was?'

'A traditional Yugoslav boy's name chosen by Gina's Yugoslav husband.'

'Such as?'

'Milko.'

'Oh, dear!'

She seemed so relaxed and cheerful I was sure I could get her back to the apartment to watch PanAm colour her bare skin like a Paragini. But at nine-thirty she began to emit departure signals.

'Lorenzo?' It wasn't jealousy or resentment I felt. Frustration, sure, though not just the old itch. I had forgotten the pleasure to be had in hanging out with someone who spoke the same language; not literally, but without needing to have stuff explained. Marsha was on my wavelength. Pity the signal got blocked

'Don't be disappointed, Shelby. I really like you and some other time... well, maybe we could have. But...'

'Don't tell me you're a one-man woman.' I tried to keep it worldly and light-hearted.

'One at a time, maybe.'

'Or that you've fallen in love?'

I was careful, as always, to pronounce the word in quotes.

Seemed to me that was where all the trouble began. As I once heard my own kid sister, the soul of kindness and affection, explain to a girl friend and fellow conspirator, 'I would never break up with a guy before I got him to say he loves me. That's what matters most of all.'

'*Magari!*' said Marsha.

'Excuse me?'

'That I've fallen in love. *Magari*. You haven't heard that? It's a wonderful word. It means...well, *maybe*, but more like *I hope so.*'

'Well, I guess I hope so too.' Hell I did.

*

I had a fallback position: the smallest bar in town. Smallest American bar, anyway, a basement just off the Via Veneto into which could fit, at a push, two dozen people: The Colony. It was underneath the California Cafe, a version of the wholesome down-home drugstore counter where homesick Americans could get milkshakes, sodas and a club sandwich. Even spaghetti and meatballs.

Lots of Rome restaurants proclaimed American Bar on their awnings, but the guys who put them up had never been in one. Bellying up to the bar, foot on the rail, was not the Italian way of drink.

Such life-enhancing moments were available in very few places. Beside the Colony there was Jerry's Bar, a reasonable facsimile of the New York experience in a basement on the Veneto heavily patronised by movie migrants. For later in the evening there was Bricktop's nightclub, right across the staircase from Jerry's. In all those places the barmen knew how to set up a proper drink. In the Colony it was Alfredo, who had served his time with the Italian Line.

Unlike the tourist refuge upstairs, the Colony appealed to strays who were in Rome for the long haul, an ill-assorted but mostly friendly crowd: off-duty marines and clerks from the embassy nearby, slummers from the FAO, con men of fluid nationality, simple seekers of booze and company. And sex. I occasionally got lucky there with adventurous tourists, usually schoolteachers from the sticks, and a couple of times with an embassy secretary named Betty, who had a relaxed attitude to the matter. She took the initiative after the usual exchange of credentials and a couple of highballs.

'Come on…'

'Shelby.'

'Shelby. Nice name. Come on, Shelby. Walk me home.'

I never did work out Betty's sexual value system and enquiries were not encouraged. She was not a permanent presence in the bar. Apart from anything else she worked strange hours at whatever she did, about which she was just as dismissively vague. Nor was she interested in dates. I called her a couple of times before coming to accept that she didn't go in for scheduling.

But when she did show up, usually with her room-mate Wendy tagging along, she was invariably ready and willing. If I got in early. When the moment came she was likely to choose the nearest guy who appealed to her. First come, first serviced and latecomers could only concede graciously.

Wendy, also at the embassy, seemed to have a different programme. She would swap wisecracks with the marines or anyone else around but not, so far as I could see, ever make out with them. On the occasions I scored, Betty would lead me into a sort of closed-in terrace with a mattress on the floor. She'd leave me there and ten minutes later come back in a bathrobe with a bottle of Jack Daniels and a pack of condoms. 'Courtesy of the PX. Where would we be without it?'

All forms of contraception were forbidden in Italy though, as with everything else, there was usually a way around: a few *farmacie* bootlegged stuff and friends coming to visit were sometimes surprised by the requests they received.

At some point Wendy would come home. We'd hear her moving around — and she must sometimes have been able to hear us. Not that we made a lot of noise. Betty did not encourage exotic by-play, just the no-frills version, though strenuous. 'I don't mind if you can't take your time,' she said that first night. 'Just so long as you're good for a quick comeback.' Kissing her goodnight, I sometimes felt a handshake would have done. Round heels or whatever, she was a really nice girl.

That night, a handshake was all I got. Betty had already singled out a tall blond guy, Pan Am pilot so the lucky winner informed me when we were introduced. I wondered if he could do something about my sign.

So, a wasted evening, except for the arrival, in a drum-roll of heels on the tiled staircase and a bass rumble of greetings all round, of Mungo Dingwall Macbeth, stocky, bearded, Scottish and drunk.

He fixed me with watery blue eyes, clearly wondering whether to pick a fight or try to remember if he had seen me before and where. 'Jerry's,' I said. 'We met a couple of nights ago. I was with Digby Tucker.' It would have been a surprise if he had remembered. My human tripwire stunt on the Via Veneto that time led to quite a night.

In his effort to simulate a New York saloon, Jerry, a minor mobster from Louisiana, had installed an L-shaped bar at the far end of the narrow room with a row of booths down either side. In one of these, a couple of people could sit comfortably each side of a table. Three meant a level of intimacy not always welcome. Some of the stalls were jammed four-a-side, mainly with movie carpetbaggers and their well-worn broads.

Mungo Macbeth had been towing a tiny blonde with a flawless enamel face and huge dark blue eyes. Digby introduced me in a crushed stand-up between the tables. 'Wasn't for this chap,' he muttered in my ear, 'there wouldn't be much of an Italian movie industry. Saves the buggers from themselves.' There was some bar-side jostling and joshing, and the Macbeth couple eased away into a booth.

'Saves *who* from themselves?'

'Big directors,' Digby mumbled into his moustache. 'De Vito, Pasolini, Carlo Ponti. Script goes arse-up, they send for the doctor. Mungo's a script doctor, a movie doctor. Brings 'em back from the dead.'

I would have gone to talk to Doctor Macbeth, except that there was a tug on my sleeve and a woman's face looked up from someplace around my waist, 'You're holding up the traffic,' she said. 'Why not sit here?'

It was going to be a squeeze. On her far side was a bulky guy a little older than me. Swarthy, sprang to mind. As did sulky. Still, I was holding up the flow to and from the bar so I sat. 'I'm Delphine,' she said. 'This is Beenak,' she said. 'Niki.'

Niki reached around her and stuck out a hand. We would be taking the shake across Delphine's extensive bosom. I stretched, he leaned forward to clear the impediment, and a small pistol clunked down in the dregs of his bowl of Texas-style Chili. Delphine wiped it off with a napkin and stuffed it back inside his jacket. 'He's Albanian,' she said. And in case I was still wondering. 'He's a Moslem.' Niki came up with a silly grin.

'Let me get some drinks.' I was thinking, what...?

'How kind of you. Gin and tonic, please.'

'And...?'

'He'll have the same.'

'But...'

'He's a *sinful* Moslem.'

She was English and, hardly to my surprise, an actress. Delphine Delisle. 'And, I'll have you know, a graduate of the J. Arthur Rank Charm School. You've heard of that, surely?'

I think she was grateful for someone to talk to since Niki didn't seem to go in for that kind of thing. But bearing in mind that he was packing a gat, I didn't want to seem too appreciative of her attention. I let her chatter on while I looked over at Mungo and the toy-like blonde who had settled in a couple of booths along. 'The only thing that's stuck in my mind was the old pansy who used to give us body care lessons. Ladies, he would say, *never* submerge the bosom in the bath.'

The guy sitting opposite Mungo was giving me a once-over. Another moustache. Nothing as luxuriant as Digby's, more the neat little number those old-time actors used to go for, Errol Flynn, Clark Gable. This one was grey, as was the small amount of hair atop a high forehead.

The forehead gave a little dip in my direction. I left Delphine and went over. 'You're the chap that tripped up the buggers trying to take Arabella's picture this afternoon, what?' He sounded like Digby talking through a sock.

'On the Veneto. Arabella Frost. She's m'daughter.'

No mistaking that. Adjust for age and gender, wind the genes back a generation and the faces had a distinct likeness. Overlooking the moustache, of course. He levered himself out of the booth, leaving his companion, a glitzy lady of a certain age, to the Macbeths and grabbed my hand. 'John Frost. Call me Johnny. I'd buy you a drink except that I'm with all these people. You must come around and see us. What?'

I wondered if that was actually a question, but he had folded himself back down among his tablemates. When I turned back to mine, Delphine and the drinking Moslem were on their feet. Niki patted his jacket to settle the hardware.

'I see you know Johnny,' she said. 'His daughter's another J. Arthur Rank charmer. We used to be friends before she... moved on.' She looked over to the Macbeths and wiggled her fingers. 'And Lia Macbeth. Just *love* her stuff. Roman Kiss cosmetics. Most divine creams and things. She's Hungarian.'

Thus bra-less?

'Sorry to see you go,' I said. 'Looks like people are settling in for a long night.'

'Love to stay, darling. But we have to go and see His Maj.'

I blinked. 'The king. King Farouk. *Ciao*!'

*

Macbeth's appearance in the Colony looked like a chance to expand on the intriguing snippet I'd heard about his script resuscitations. Prescribing cures for great Italian movies was a ready-made mailer. 'Would you like a drink?' I asked.

'*Babee*,' he said, not bothering to look at me. 'Bell's. No ice. Water.' He kept his eyes fixed on the bottle display behind the bar while he knocked back half the drink. 'Mungo!' A bellow from the darkened fringe of the little space.

'Mungo, my man. How you been?'

'Oh, shit!' said Macbeth, not bothering to look in the direction of the voice. 'Hello, Winny. I thought you'd been put away.'

Out of the shadows sidled a figure dressed like a mid-west farmhand: check shirt, bib-overalls, clunky boots. This was Winchester Starr, an embarrassing piece of American surplus

71

around the Via Veneto and a thorough pain in the butt. He was got up like that lest anyone forget that not only had he played the role of nasty Jud in an Italian production of *Oklahoma!*, he had been the stand-in for Curly, the wholesome lead. The company went bust, leaving the cast stranded, and Winchester had been looking for his next part ever since. Alfredo hated him because if people bought him drinks he would blast out 'Oh What a Beautiful Morning' and the place would be cleared out before he got to the chorus.

'Don't call me that, Mungo. You know I don't like it. It's a girl's name.'

'You're lucky I call you anything I can say in public.'

'Look, if it's about the money it won't be long now. We've got nearly all the investors we need. Might even be able to refund you if you want out.'

He turned to me. 'We're gonna open the greatest restaurant Rome's ever seen. Entire piazza over in *Trastevere*. Whole damn neighbourhood, really. Performing animals, dancing girls, fire-eaters. Wanna invest? Grab a slice while it's hot?'

-7-

One thing Rick said to me showed there was a twitch left in his old newshound nose. 'Good move to come here, kid. Things happen in Italy you don't get anyplace else. After a while, they start to seem normal, and that's when you know you've gone native. But they're not normal for the people on the other end of the wire. That old soda jerk.'

The first such story I spotted didn't even make most of the Rome newspapers. It came up on the ANSA wire, lifted from some local sheet, and it was so vague and wandering that I needed to read it over a few times before I could see it in soda jerk terms: Village Mayor Kidnaps Schoolteacher For Love.

Make that *pretty* schoolteacher. This had happened, according to the brief ANSA take, in a village down in Calabria called Roghudi.

'Put in a call,' I said to Aldo, going over to look at the big map of Italy. Couldn't see it there so I started to get down some dusty gazetteers that might tell me where the place was.

Aldo finished talking to an operator and flung out his arms like an orchestra conductor. 'No phone.'

'Who'd you try?'

'Nobody. There's no phones in this Roghudi place.'

'No phones?'

'No fuckin' line even.'

This was going to take some thinking about. In London, I had been mildly surprised to find that not everyone had a phone at home. The system was still catching up from that black-and-white time. In Hungary, well, there had been phones but the lines were usually dead. Here was a town without even a line? An entire town — well, village — not hooked up to the rest of the world? In Europe? In the middle of the twentieth century?

Charlie came out of his office followed by Fernando the Newspix guy, who often came over for a huddle. He read out the copy I had ripped off ANSA. 'In an effort to get the girl to respond to his approaches the mayor repeatedly shot out the light in her bedroom with his *lupara*. That's a shotgun. Sawn-off. Blasted it through the window. Real hillbilly courtship.'

I was seeing it as love Calabrian style, Emilio an impetuous rustic Romeo. The girl's name was Giulietta already. No age, damn. But she had to be young. And pretty.

'It's here,' said Aldo, nose in a pre-war atlas. 'Thirty-six kilometres out of Reggio Calabria. Up in the Aspromonte Mountains.'

'Deep South,' said Charlie. 'Bandit country.'

Cristof got off the phone. 'Girl's from Bova, on the coast. Reporter in Reggio talked to the family. First we've heard from anyone down there since the last time Mount Etna erupted.'

I punched out a twenty-three, taking in Cristof's notes:

ROME 19:05:57. A HUGE MANHUNT SPREAD ACROSS ITALY'S DEEP SOUTH TODAY AFTER THE MAYOR OF A REMOTE VILLAGE ABDUCTED A PRETTY YOUNG SCHOOLTEACHER AT GUNPOINT.

Giulietta Spadafora had rejected Emilio Pastorelli's advances. In events worthy of an opera plot, her brothers vowed to track her captor down and avenge the family honour in the only acceptable way: death.

'Could do with a live dateline,' said Charlie. 'You should get down there. Could be a great colour piece. Kind of thing Roger wants you to do.'

'We send photographer,' said Fernando. Charlie opened his mouth but decided not to let whatever he had thought of emerge. A photographer wouldn't be on the bureau charge anyway.

'Train at one pm,' said Cristof. '*Avanti!*'

'I'd better get an overnight bag.'

'And then some.' In my haste to get to grips with a live one, I didn't think too much about Charlie's enthusiasm for the story. I had tried several times to get out of town but he never wanted me to go too far from the slot.

'Meaning?'

'You'll be a long way from home.'

*

The photographer was easy to pick out, standing guard on the pile of gear they always lugged around. It was a surprise, however, to see it was Lucinda. It hadn't occurred to me that she might be a photographer rather than... whatever she was, apart from the boss's girlfriend. In the flurry of collecting tickets and finding the train, we didn't talk much until we were settled into the compartment. It was a relief to find she spoke fairly good English.

Back in the States photographers, still mostly male, made a point of dressing like they worked for a bank: suit, white shirt, unassertive tie. They had leather cases the size of a plumber's toolbox slung over their shoulders and chunky quarter-plate Speed Graphics. In Vienna and Budapest, I had seen they did things differently over here. Cameras tended to be smart-looking Rolleiflexes, little 35-mm Leicas or Nikons, minimum of three, slung across a military drab jacket or fly fisherman vest with lots of pockets.

Only when Lucinda — Lucy, soon enough — peeled away the outer layers and pulled off her beret could I size her up.

Standard black hair in what a professional magazine scrutiniser like myself easily recognised as a shingle cut, light make-up around light brown eyes. She seemed also to be lightly tanned but that might be the skin she had been born with. She was a tad short in the leg but there was a promising bulge upfront. The train timetables and the map of Calabria I had looked over suggested that we were going to be together for a few days. My chance to test Rick's theory of Italian female sexuality, that could easily be — as I was beginning to think about much of his output — about three-fifths checkable fact and two-fifths interpretation.

I slung my backpack in the luggage rack and helped her stow her stuff, our arms stretching up in enjoyable proximity. I got a stimulating sniff of whatever she had used in the shower. There was only a split-second in which to savour it, however, before my eyes strayed to the window in which was framed the stupid grin, surrounded by the stupid moustache, of Digby Tucker.

'Hope you don't mind me joining you,' he said, shoving a suitcase into the compartment a few minutes later. 'Happened to pop up to Century for a look at the Outgoing and saw the service message saying you were off to the badlands. Thought it would make me a good little *Daily Express* feature. *Buon giorno*, Lucinda. Pictures available to all, I assume.'

Fucking Special! He actually gave the ludicrous moustache a twirl.

Surprised Fernando let you loose with this young buck.'

'Fernando say Signor Shelby is *gentleman*. Not say anything about *you*.'

It sounded more edgy than playful. Had Digby been waving those whiskers in her face?

The train began trundling out of the station and Digby tried to warm up his welcome with chit-chat. 'Saw Rick up there this morning.'

At Newspix?'

'No, Century.' That was, in fact, worth remarking on, Rick's visits to his putative workplace being so rare. 'Looked as though he's decided to take an interest in the pope's hiccups.'

That story had been stuttering for a while; even the Latin Americans were losing their appetite for daily updates. Pius had a throat condition that produced uncontrollable hiccups, fits of which could last for days. We'd pretty well run out of all the jokes about it. It was not really a laughing matter — for Pius, anyway. He couldn't eat, even drinking was difficult. Poor old guy lost weight, and for a while, the bedside bulletins had been alarming. Everyone in the bureau had set to updating obituary stuff and the files on likely successors.

Everyone except the Rickards. Why would Rick be taking an interest in the pope now? They had never shown any, far as I knew, in the other enduring saga, the Montesi case.

'How are you getting on with Charlie?'

'Fine. Why do you ask?'

'Just that he's the kind of chap gets nervous easily. If, say, he thought someone was after his job.'

'Well, I'm not after his job.'

That was a glaring untruth. Every ambitious Centurion coveted the job of the guy next above; how else were we to get ahead? But trying to push things along was not the way to go.

Even if I got a chance to pull the rug out from under Charlie I was no more likely to take it than I had been to pick up on Traynor's heavy-handed invite to snitch. Or so I believed.

'Doesn't mean he doesn't *think* you are. Know what they say up my way? First duty of a new editor, new chief is to identify his successor — and fire him.'

'Charlie couldn't fire me.' That would be up to the aforementioned Traynor or Richard Hammond.

'Doesn't have to, old boy. Just let you go off in the wrong direction one day.'

*

Reggio Calabria was 700 kilometres from Rome, say 450 miles. About the distance from New York City to Columbus, Ohio. I don't know how long that trip might take on Amtrak but this one took all of thirty hours. Unpredicted stops in sidings, mysterious shunting about, no food except an occasional stale *panini* scrounged on some dusty platform. Digby provided the only relief to tedium: a bottle of scotch produced from the old army knapsack. 'White Horse,' he said proudly. 'Vatican duty-free. Monsignor I know.'

Lucy wouldn't have any, displaying the general Italian caution about anything stronger than Campari, but I took a slug from time to time. Didn't help much. It was a stinking hot late afternoon when we eventually arrived, grimy, starving and ill-tempered. We checked into a hotel opposite the station and took to our various beds.

Hertz and Avis had yet to reach Italy and the desk clerk we tackled in the morning seemed baffled by the concept of renting a car. Digby's Italian was better than mine but still halting. We let Lucy take over and after an intensive two-way interrogation, the clerk wrote down the address of a garage where we were offered a fairly roadworthy Fiat. I had feared they might want the value of the car as a deposit, which would have stretched the CNW resources. 'He say no need,' Lucy told us. 'Everyone

78

know who car belong to. But he ask where we go. We can tell him?'

When she did the guy's eyebrows shot up. 'He say we no take this car to Roghudi.'

'Because?'

'Because there is no road to Roghudi.'

Instead, we went about twenty miles further on to a place called Melito, the very toe of Italy and nowhere near as nice as its name. The view on the way, though, was spectacular: sparkling blue sea with Mount Etna smoking away across the Strait of Messina.

At the police station we were directed to some guys heaving themselves out of beat-up four-wheel drives, yawning and stretching. They were dressed like peasants, but since they were hung about with hardware, it seemed reasonable to assume that they were on the job. *Tessera* in hand I addressed myself to the one who stood and looked on while the others unloaded weaponry and boxes of ammunition.

Maresciallo Salvatore Bonnacorso of the *Polizia Nazionale* hid any flattery he might have felt at attracting international attention under a heavy layer of suspicion. Even so, I could see him warm to the notion that a little newsmaking could be a career boost. The posse had just got back from the closest point to Roghudi that could be reached by road. They had a good idea, Bonnacorso said, of where the mayor and his unfortunate hostage were holed up. He was confident that by tomorrow they could begin negotiations. Negotiations? If they knew where my Romeo and Juliet were why not just go in and rescue the poor girl?

Ah, *signore*, that would be dangerous. If the fugitive and his victim were together Signor Pastorelli might become desperate and harm her. If, on the other hand, he was alone and would

79

not surrender there was a strong likelihood the police would have to kill him. Suppose he had left his unhappy victim bound and gagged somewhere else in the wilderness. She might never be found. It would be preferable, said Bonnacorso, if he and his men handled matters the way they thought best. 'This is our country.'

The word he used was *paese*. Country, village, implicitly the way of life down here.

Ideally, the story called for several building blocks. Giulietta rescued and providing a vivid account of her ordeal. Her abductor captured and explaining why he thought such a novel way of making his feelings known might have won her heart. A close-up piece on the mysterious village where the outlandish events had taken place. All with pictures, of course.

Lucy took Bonnacorso off to pose with some guns. Digby and I talked to the squad, who once they saw their *capo* had come round were quite forthcoming. Reinforcements had been pulled in from all over the region, they told us. If anyone between here and Reggio needed a cop they would have to call the *Carabinieri*. That set them smirking. Why?

A barrel-chested heavy, probably the sergeant, put us straight. Down here the *Carabinieri* were — without wishing to cause us offence — *stranieri*. Foreigners, outsiders. *Ignoranti*... Their regulations did not allow them to be stationed in a part of the country they came from so how could they know anything about a place? The *brigadiere* in Bova up the road was from Genoa. At night he and his men holed up in their *caserma* and barred the door.

No, *signori*. If anyone was going to catch the perpetrator of the vile deed it could only be this fine squad of *polizie* from the Aspromonte. We understand this guy. We can read his thoughts. He knows that. He's going to walk into our arms. You want to go up to Roghudi? Don't. It's a shithole. Just wait around here for a few days and you'll see this monster in a cage. Meanwhile, God have mercy on his victim. Her life was already ruined.

The *maresciallo* had been softened up by his photo call. He wrote down the names and addresses of the missing teacher's family; even sketched us a map of the way from Bova to Roghudi. Lucy wanted to know what the *agente* had told us. Why would they say Giulietta's life had already been ruined? I asked her.

'It is the mentality of these peasants. They cannot imagine a woman could be together with a man — even if she didn't want to be — without... you know.'

Good line to work into the story. I wasn't sure about another that I had, rather ignobly, been chasing around my mind. Could the Rickard theory of Italian womanhood apply in reverse? If a guy couldn't get laid the nice way without all that baggage, could he be blamed for going about things the nasty way?

*

Seven o'clock the following morning we were looking out across a vast shallow valley to where the village of Roghudi straggled down a distant ridge like a trickle of orange and red vomit on the toe of a giant sneaker. Sneakers came to mind because Lucy was wearing some and I wasn't. There would be about ten miles to cover, far as I could work out from the map. It would be all uphill along a *torrente*, a dried-up river bed that looked like a stretch of US-Route 66 with every inch of surface broken up by jackhammers. Sneakers would have been useful.

It took us until early afternoon to reach the final stretch, a track grooved by cartwheels at the end of which a gate in a

81

crumbling wall led, presumably, into the village. This close, I could see why the rooftops we had seen from afar glowed bright red. They were carpeted with tomatoes.

'They dry in the sun.' Thanks, Lucy. Never would have guessed.

I certainly wouldn't have guessed at the next revelation. Down towards us, capering zigzag across the dried-up ruts, came a small figure in a skirt. No, a clerical robe, a black cassock with a girdle at the waist, tattered and stiff with stains.

This was unlikely to be a priest. It seemed to be a boy about sixteen who was plainly not all there. His eyes were cocked at different angles. They rolled around, trying to get us in focus. Lucy, behind me, sucked in her breath and I felt her move closer. The poor creature's head was jerking non-stop and his lips, ringed with crust, hung open. He was making gargling, guttural sounds in a sort of sing-song.

'Bloody hell,' said Digby. 'They've sent the village idiot out to welcome us.'

There was not much we could do other than follow the dancing fool in through the *portone*, crude slabs of planking nailed together crosswise.

Once inside, we stood at the head of the main street — the only one as far as I could make out. It followed the spine of the hill upwards. Most of the tumbledown houses seemed to depend on each other to stay upright, though a few on the valley side were separated by stairways that led down a kind of canyon wall. There were glimpses of straggling vegetable plots and garbage heaps at the bottom. Not a person in sight, except for the boy jerking away like a marionette.

The silence was spooky but unconvincing. There were people in those houses, peeking at us through the cracks. With the confidence of a man who had spent years on unwelcoming stoops, Digby took a couple of strides and banged on the nearest door like a bailiff. Nothing. Nothing from the next one either, nor the one opposite. 'I wonder,' he said, 'if there might be a bar.' We turned to see if we could get some help from the boy but he had gone.

Alert as an infantry patrol, we walked in single file up the street. Occasionally Lucy stepped ahead and zoomed in on something that caught her eye, shutter clicks echoing. Digby lifted up a foot and showed the sole flapping away from his shoe. He sat on a stoop while Lucy found some tape in her camera bag. A little further on we reached a shady space by a well. Three gnarled old men sat around a camp stove and a blackened, litre-sized *napolitana* — one of those aluminium things you turn upside down so the coffee can splash out and burn you — drinking from thick chipped cups. If there was a bar, this was it.

'*Buon giorno,*' I said, establishing myself as leader of our expedition. Digby followed up with some cheerful remark but the locals took no notice. On all three faces, narrow and sallow, lined and pitted, expressions morphed and mixed like a slide-show. Surprise. Wonder. Disbelief.

Ignoring us, the dotards began a rattling chatter among themselves. I could not make out a word. Nor, I saw, could Lucy.

She stepped closer to the old guys. Speaking so slowly that even I could understand most of it, she explained that we were foreign journalists. What could they tell us about the dramatic incidents that had taken place here?

The three looked at Lucy, mouths open. Another expression clicked into place: reproach. The silence spun out, then the men's joint gaze swerved behind us. The boy was back and, with him, a man whose coat and trousers matched only in that both were black, tattered and greasy. He had on a shirt with no collar that, nevertheless, suggested he could be a man of the cloth. He said something unintelligible to the coffee drinkers, looked Lucy over just as wonderingly as they had, waved a hand to cut off a stream of gibberish from the boy, and said to me: '*Non parlanno Italiano.*'

These Italians did not speak Italian? Nor, it seemed, did they speak to women, apart from wives and close relatives. Lucy's forward ways had quite offended them. But that we did not find out until later. First, we had to get used to the idea that apart from Padre Piero, as he now introduced himself, no one in Roghudi spoke Italian. They spoke *Greki*. Greek of a sort. I looked at Lucy. She shrugged and got busy with her camera again.

I composed a couple of sentences all by myself to put to the padre, who at least seemed to understand what we were and why we were there. Greece was several hundred miles away, was it not? On the other side of the Aspromonte? To say nothing of the other side of the Ionian Sea? This, Piero agreed was the case. But there had been Greeks here once, he explained. About a thousand years back. Not much had changed in Roghudi since then.

He walked us around to the scene of the crime, Digby stumbling because his sole had come adrift again. The schoolroom from which poor Giulietta was abducted had also been her bedroom and everything-else room. A few bits of clothing hung from wall pegs. It was here, Piero explained, that her impetuous suitor had wrapped her head in his jacket and, according to the neighbours, slung her over his shoulder and taken off. 'She was the third teacher sent by the ministry in the last few years,' he said. The others had been men. None stayed more a few weeks. 'She was good at her task. The children were

84

making progress. Even in Italian.'

The overhead socket from which, we were told, the mayor would regularly shoot out the bulb in a display of affection, dangled from a twisted wire. Lucy squinted at it through her viewfinder. 'No electricity now,' said Piero. The generator that had been the only power source belonged to Pastorelli. 'That is why he was made mayor. Now no one knows how to make it run.'

The room looked to me as though it had once been a chapel. The roof was domed, there were alcoves for statues. Paint was peeling but there were faint traces of saintly murals like the phantom slogans of Rome. Piero guessed what I was thinking. 'People stopped coming to worship. This is not a godly place.' I took that to mean Roghudi as much as the sinister schoolroom.

Our guided tour ate into the day. We were not going to get back to Bova before dark, even if we got Digby re-shod. Thus, we could hardly refuse Piero's offer of somewhere to spend the night, even when his house turned out to be home to the gibbering boy and a shadowy female presence who was not introduced, addressed, explained or even acknowledged. 'Sinful priest,' Lucy whispered.

Dinner was one of the more memorable meals of my life. The room was much like Giulietta's, although the size of the bed in one corner suggested that, normally, the entire household would sleep there. Something that looked like a small altar was shoved in another corner, covered with a purple velvet throw. It looked as though whatever rites and services Piero could get anyone interested in were also held there.

We dined by candlelight. The woman and boy had been banished to the underpinnings of the house that stretched down against the side of a ravine but a trapdoor in the floor flipped open and she handed up a large loaf of bread with a wedge already cut out, and a plate of tomatoes puddled in slightly rancid oil. In the dim light her face was sharp and angular, her skin dark. Behind her, the boy peeped over the edge of the trap like a rodent from a hole, the rolling whites of his eyes picked out by the flickering candles.

Digby got out his bottle. The priest's eyes brightened. '*Grappa*?'

'*Grappa*,' said Digby. 'Scotland's best.'

*

The alarming events of the night, we later decided, must have been due to fragments of our overheard conversation reassembled piecemeal by the boy's shaky synapses. Piero was apologetic when it became apparent that the bread and tomatoes were all we were going to get. 'You have seen this is a poor place,' he said. 'The police who came ate everything. They did not understand there was no pasta, only bread. They ate the four chickens that gave us eggs. Now there is only the rooster left.'

He said *pettino*, a word Lucy did not know. She and the priest batted around a few idiomatic alternatives and she finally translated it as 'cock.' Digby smirked.

'I like *pettino*,' said Lucy. 'It sounds sweet. *Pettinos*, *pettino*.'

A croaking echo floated up from the trapdoor. '*Pettino*, *pettino*…'

Then we all went to bed. I had been wondering how this was going to work out but our host and hostess had a plan. The crone came right out of the hole to clear the table. She handed the dishes down to the boy and tugged Lucy by the sleeve towards the trapdoor. 'The women will sleep downstairs,' said Piero. 'It is more correct.'

Lucy was clearly not happy about this but she took some stuff from her kit and stepped down the hatch. Piero opened a door into the side alley and showed us menfolk a sort of metal sink fixed on the outside wall. He offered guidance by pissing in the street and diluting the puddle with a splash of water from a pitcher. I followed his example, then produced a toothbrush from my little toilet kit. That amused him.

Back inside, Piero extinguished all the candles except one, over which he lowered a hollow glass figure of Jesus Christ, craftily designed so that the flame would illuminate a large crimson heart in the middle of his chest. The three of us, still in most of our clothes, stretched out on the bed. I feared the glowing heart might keep me awake but it had been a long day and the scotch sneaked up on me. I went straight to sleep and stayed completely out of it until the screaming started.

*

Even when we were well clear of Roghudi the following morning and could compare impressions it was hard to be sure exactly what had happened. We guys on the bed were startled awake by a medley of shrieks and yelling. Lucy was crawling out of the trapdoor. Even by the light of the Jesus lamp, I could see that the long T-shirt she had on was covered in dark stains. Blood?

That's what it was, all right but, happily, not hers. Nor was all the noise coming from her. We lunged across to haul her up into the room. The noise from below modulated into speech of a sort. Piero left her to us and slithered down the ladder.

'*Dio la stramaladica!*' said Lucy, trembling. I didn't know what that meant but it sounded like a serious curse. 'That creature! I woke up and he was there holding this...this *pettino*

87

over me. Its head was gone and there was blood everywhere. The woman took him away. She is angry.'

The sounds from below suggested everyone down there was angry. The boy was howling, Piero bellowing and the woman wailing like a siren, 'Poor boy,' said Lucy, calming down. 'I think he just wanted to give me a gift.'

We showed her the wash-trough outside so she could clean up, then we went to sit on doorsteps outside to wait for daylight.

'A whiskey priest, as the Irish say.' Digby had his shoe off and was flapping the sole dolefully. 'Sent here as punishment.'

Lucy disagreed. 'Not for whiskey. Woman.'

I liked that better. 'Maybe he fell in love. They ran away to romantic Roghudi'

'No. She always here. I not understand everything she say but she is *una sagage*. Brings out babies.'

'Midwife,' said Digby. The axis of power between the pair of 'em. Spirit and the flesh.'

'Also *strega*.' Witch.

'Wish she'd apply some magic to my bloody shoe.'

Piero came out.

'Even if the shoe is mended it will come apart again. The stones are hard. You must take *l'asino*.'

'The donkey?'

'Oh, yes,' said Lucy, cheering up. 'We must take donkey.'

So there we were, picking our way back down the treacherous *torrente*, Digby astride a poor undersized beast, feet barely clearing the ground. The stones, rather. Behind and above us Roghudi glowed like a fairy castle in the rising sun. We stopped for a picture session. 'Look,' said Lucy. 'People. Come out now strangers gone.' A couple of dozen figures were gathered around the distant gateway. We had never seen more than six inhabitants, even counting in the boy. Lucy was snapping away. 'It will look fantastic. Fairytale town. No one will guess about the tomatoes.'

I had colourful copy to drown in, but the story still needed punching into shape. In Bova, we went straight to see *Maresciallo* Bonnacorso.

'There was quite a lot about Roghudi,' I said, 'that you might have told us.'

-8-

The lead, of course, was the question of whether the beautiful young teacher would be rescued alive from the clutches of her evil captor. Police had found his hideout in the rugged mountains and were trying to persuade him to surrender which, Bonnacorso warned with multiple shrugs, could take days, even weeks.

The sheer improbable theatricality of it all made the story sing: dedicated young schoolmarm, isolated village, outlandish attempt at courtship, operatic abduction. The *Griki* angle would be confusing so I saved it, just referring to 'local dialect'. I left out the boy, of course, but got Padre Piero in: dedicated priest in wilderness.

Aldo punched it straight on to the Teletype. If it had been Charlie I might have worried about by-line banditry, but Aldo wouldn't have dared.

Charlie himself came on when I made a check call half an hour later. 'Great stuff, my boy. Herograms from all over, clients thrilled, Old Apathy sick as shit. UP, too.' He sounded genuinely pleased. I supposed he might have been expecting me to blow the story, if not something worse, but now he could claim credit for having sent me. Century was on the spot, nailed down the dateline. Owned the story — except for the claim Digby would stake. Though there might be a way around that.

'Lucy thinks they've already got them,' I told Charlie. 'Our fugitives. They just don't want to say so yet. The *polizia*, that is.'

She sidled up to me after our audience at the *commisario*, keeping her back to Digby, who was making nice to Bonnacorso a few yards away. Scribbling my notes, I had noticed her drift over to the gang of cops who were shooting the breeze. Her eyelids were lowered like a movie conspirator and she tried to talk without moving her lips. 'Those guys there are talking like they already seen them.'

'Seen who?'

'*I fuggitivi!*'

'Really? Where?'

'Maybe they already here. In *commissario*.'

'Why wouldn't Bonnacorso say so? Bring them out?'

'So he have time to talk to them. Maybe mayor pay to be let go. Maybe they want girl to say she *want* be kidnapped. Then mayor no go to prison. These are *polizie*. Do what they want.'

'Jesus!' said Charlie, digesting this. 'But it could easily be. I told you Italy wasn't like home.'

'If I could get Digby out of the way, maybe I could persuade the *maresciallo* to produce them for us. We'd have it exclusive.'

'Tell Digby I'm sending you across to Sicily to do a mailer on Etna erupting. He'll think it's all over for the moment and come home. When he's gone you can nip back to the mainland and take up where you left off.'

'Etna's erupting?'

'Etna's always erupting.'

*

'We'll go over in the morning, first thing,' I said to the others when all the filing was done and we could go for something to eat.

'Want to come along, Digby?'

'Not me, old boy. I've got a double-page spread for Sunday already wrapped up. I'll pop into a shoe shop soon as they open, then I'm home to Rome.''

I had actually enjoyed having Digby along. But apart from the prospect of scooping his ass, being left one-on-one with Lucy put the Rickard theory back on the agenda.

Going across on the ferry from Reggio to Messina we saw plenty of smoke, but the cabdriver Lucy found to take us around the slopes was already shooting down the story. 'He say must smell like metal,' Lucy told me. 'Like hot iron.'

To my surprise the slopes of Etna looked a good deal more green and fertile than the flatlands below. We hiked past a couple of small villages and an impressive vineyard to reach some bored volcanologists in a hut up near the crater. The previous day there had been what one of them, speaking English for my benefit, called 'flare-out'. The local paper parlayed it up into a scare and some hungry stringer blew that up into an imminent eruption.

I had been worried that we might get back over to Reggio too late for Lucy and me to get to know each other properly. As it happened, we were stranded in Sicily. The ferry terminal at Messina was locked, barred and guarded.

'The ship is broken. Another one will not come until tomorrow.'

'What time tomorrow?'

Lucy shrugged. She picked up her heavy bag and looked beyond me to a dim blue neon sign a few hundred metres away that said Jolly Hotel.

I eventually found several reasons to challenge this description but the immediate one was that it had no rooms to offer. '*Mi dispiace*,' said the slick-haired receptionist. 'Every hotel in the vicinity is full. Because of broken ferry.'

Out came my *Stampa Estera tessera*. Lucy had an only slightly less impressive *Polizia di Roma* version. A manager appeared. File cards were shuffled. Fingers walked down a register. A vacant room was found. Lucy at my side shifted nervously. '*Two* rooms. A room each.'

Heads shook, the one dark and shiny, the other just shiny. One room was it, and even then a valued guest who had reserved it might have to be turned away. Which of us was to take it?

I looked at Lucy, unmotivated for the moment by lust. We had been up since early morning. Our clothes were filthy. There was volcanic ash in our hair. She shrugged, not looking at me.

'We'll share it,' I said and reached out. The key stayed covered by the clerk's plump hand. The manager pushed over the passport I had also produced and Lucy's identity card. He leaned over and spoke to her in a low voice.

'He says we cannot have this room because we not married.'

I had heard about stuff like this. It was actually illegal for unwed couples to share a room. Foreigners whose names might not match even though they were married could get a consular certificate to take around with them.

I wasn't going to get into an argument with the smug little prick. I handed the key to Lucy and picked up my backpack. 'There must be someplace else, a *pensione* maybe. I'll call you in a while.'

'Wait.' We moved across to the elevator. The manager had disappeared. The shiny-haired clerk was checking in new arrivals but I knew he had us in his peripheral vision. If we both got in the elevator he would probably hit the fire alarm. Lucy went back to the desk, waited until he was free and leaned over to speak to him.

As she trotted back he smiled past her at me. 'It's OK,' said

Lucy, shoving me into the elevator and stabbing a button. *'Va bene cosí.'*

'What's the *cosí*?'

'I told him you were *uno frocio.'*

Not a word I'd heard before but I got it.

Circumstances seemed strongly in my favour. Opening the door of our room Lucy burst into giggles at the sight of the large double bed. *'Uno matrimoniale!'*

I took care not to display presumption. I would take first shot at the bathroom, I said, then get out of the way. I hadn't known how little in the way of amenities came with an Italian hotel room. No soap, and the sort of towels you found in a kitchen back home. I made do in the shower with a tube of shaving goop I had in my kit. Then I went down to the bar, leaving the room to her.

At dinner, Lucy drank a couple of glasses of wine and told me about being a *fidanzata*.

Youthful relationships in Italy had evidently moved on from Rick's sour analysis. Literally, it meant to be engaged, as in *fiancée*. But not so much engaged to be married as merely promising not to stray. There was a way to go before she and Fernando made a *promessa di matrimonio*, filling out forms to register their intentions formally. Until then they were really just going steady.

Well, back home I'd occasionally been able to persuade a girl to forget about her steady for a while. When Lucy let me pour us a third glass I thought it was a done deal.

Until we walked back into the room. While I had been downstairs acting the gentleman, Lucy had re-landscaped the bed.

A long bolster that had been underneath the pillows now lay down the centreline of the *matrimoniale*, dividing it into his and hers. 'Which side would you like?' she asked.

I tried to be sporting. 'You really didn't need to do all that. I'm not going to make you do something you don't want to.'

'You not make me do anything.'

I moved in for a comradely kiss but she twirled out of reach and pointed me to the bathroom. When I came back she was sheathed in one of those long T-shirts. I could see she still had her brassiere on underneath and, I would bet, skin-tight panties. I got a glimpse of her legs. They hadn't gotten any longer but the sight of the smooth honeyed flesh jolted me like a bellringer.

Pride, to say nothing of basic biological compulsion, would not let me give up without a struggle. Not a physical one, of course, but I could argue. Which I did for half the night, some of the time with my arm slung across the bolster, groping for a handhold. Never found one, though. Lucy was rolled up in her sheet like a leg in plaster.

My hard sell, I must admit, was repetitious. I found her irresistible. The Roghudi experience we had shared deserved a memorable celebration. No one in Rome would ever know. I assured her of the efficacy of the Trojan condoms I had pilfered from Betty's PX stock. '*Preservativo*? You show me?'

Breakthrough! I started up.

'No, not now. In morning. Now must sleep. You too, Shelby. Go sleep.'

If only I could, but the thought of what lay beneath those windings kept me awake until grey morning light showed up the water stains on the ceiling. She knew I was simmering away there and, still wrapped in her sheet, she leaned over the bolster, felt around for my stiffened presence and rather clumsily jerked me off.

It only took a few strokes and made a mess of my side of the bed but I guess it was better than nothing.

So much for Italian womanhood, I thought, finally drifting off. Back home, a high school senior balancing virginity against dating prospects would have done a better job. Still, she was *in rodaggio*.

*

We didn't have to do a number on Bonnacorso. He was waiting for us at the mainland terminal. *Buon arrivato*. We were the first journalists to be told that his men were even now bringing in Signor Pastorelli and his captive from the hideout to which they had been tracked down. Well, perhaps not quite the first. 'Your colleague with the *baffi grandi* is already at the *commisario*. He told me you would probably arrive on the first ferry.'

It was all Digby could do to stop from curling his stupid *baffi*. 'No eruption after all?'

Saying don't talk dirty would only make things worse. 'Thought you were heading home,' I said.

'That was the plan, but then I popped into the *Gazette del Sole* office just to check, and they told me the police had sent for an examining magistrate. So I presumed there must be someone to examine. Anyway, you know what old reporters say — never be first to leave the story.'

If Bonnacorso had been keeping the pair on ice somewhere while he worked things out, the show he put on to delivering them gave the story new legs. They were driven up to the *commisario* in a dust-covered police van, escort vehicles, tommy-gun muzzles sprouting out the windows. Flanked by the *maresciallo* and his heavies jostling to fit in Lucy's viewfinder, Pastorelli made gratifyingly villainous pictures, even if he didn't look as though he'd spent a week holed up in a cave. Giulietta was also less bedraggled than we might have hoped for and seemed to be sticking to a script. It had been an unpleasant ordeal, but she had not been harmed, certainly not *violata*. The mayor had behaved like a gentleman.

'What else could she say?' asked Bonnacorso, afterwards, palms and eyeballs ceilingward. 'Anything different and her family would not take her back. They might not, even now.'

'Even if they do,' said Lucy, her expression baleful. 'No one will believe she could be alone with him and not... Now she can be nun or *puta*. Nothing else.'

It might have made an even better story if Lucy was right, and something had gone on between the couple and the cops but there was no way of finding out. I had seen enough of Italy by now to know there never would be.

The long, long train trip north was only bearable because I found a corner of one railcar with a fold-down table where I could use my Olivetti. 'I'm sorry I had to call you *uno frocio*,' Lucy said when Digby had gone to the waterless john to work on his moustache. She leant over and dropped a light clean kiss on my nose. 'But you must not worry. Italy is full of pretty girls. You find one or one find you.'

Magari.

Maybe.

-9-

Pretty wasn't the only consideration. Nor was sex, yearn for it though I might. I needed some enlightened companionship as well. I had not expected it to come in the absurd shape of Caddie Rickard.

Caddie's reasons for appointing herself my Roman rabbi are as hard to work out as the real motivation for many things she'd done in her extraordinary life. Not rabbi as in synagogue but as in New York cop slang adopted by newsrooms. Guide, mentor, back-watcher.

Rick picked up on it. 'She likes it that you showed some respect. Kept calling her Mrs Rickard until she told you to quit. Too many people think they can call her Caddie soon as they stick out their hand. Like she was a tame gorilla or something.'

I thought it might also have been that we were both Columbia alumnae. Americans care about such things. I didn't find that out for a while — well after I, too, had started to call her Caddie — and it came as a bit of a surprise. Not only that she'd been to the same university but that she'd got into the School of Journalism. 'Class of thirty-five. Only three women. But once I started looking for a job I kept quiet about it. Hardnosed eyeshades didn't like the idea of J-School graduates.' I felt much the same way, but back then it must have been a hell of an achievement for a girl from a small-town paper in Iowa or someplace.

Thinking about it later, as I did intermittently for years, I decided that she moved in on me simply because of the affliction most reporters suffer from: the compelling need to *unload*. Get the story out. She had this mental notebook-load of experiences she'd accumulated down the years and no one she felt like telling it to. I asked her early on why she didn't just write it all up and she showed me two fistfuls of knuckles like clamshells. 'Can't run a typewriter anymore. Arthritis.'

Whatever motivated her she was mighty helpful. When I got back from Roghudi she swept me around to that shoe shop in Via della Propaganda to replace the wrecked wingtips with some natty black loafers. 'This young man gets a discount,' she told the salesman. 'He's an important member of the *Stampa Estera*.'

Only a slight exaggeration, I felt. My Roghudi file had shaken up a few of the time-servers over there. Century news stories wiped out AP and UP, both of which made the mistake of settling for straight-up stuff from local stringers. The rotogravure spreads I put together with Lucy's pictures played in weekend supplements all over. I got a professor of ethnography to analyse the weird linguistic isolation of the locals and a researcher from FAO to explain how there could be Italians too poor to eat pasta. The only person around Century who didn't keep on complimenting me was Charlie. All he wanted to know was whether I'd made out with Lucy.

*

I found myself looking at Caddie's unmistakable rear end while strolling along the Via Margutta. She turned into one of the arched doorways just along from Parigini's Seventh Heaven and there were a couple of sharp reports that even to my untrained ear sounded like gunfire. The smart thing would have been to turn on my heel and get out of there but curiosity kills more reporters than cats. Caddie was inside the arch, yelling something through a doorway. I could see dozens of half-finished chairs and tables piled up in a kind of workshop.

'Mrs Rickard! What's going on? Are you all right?'

'Oh, did you get a scare?'

I probably looked as though I had. 'I thought those were gunshots.'

'They were. But it's just Fabrizio the Faker here blasting wormholes in his new antiques.' Back in the shadows, I could see a hunched old guy in a carpenter's apron hugging a stubby shotgun. 'Old creep's got a batch of new chairs need a bit of age on 'em. That's how he does it. I've told him he'll get into trouble.'

'For faking?'

'No. For shooting off his damn *lupara*. This is supposed to be the quietest street in Rome.' She steered me through into a courtyard, leaving the trigger-happy antiquarian muttering to himself.

'What he's supposed to do, he wants to know. Bore the fuckin' holes by hand? Wanna cup of coffee?'

She — and presumably Rick — must live in this intriguing place, and I soon saw why anyone would want to. On one side of a gravelled square stood a cream-coloured building with huge windows rising through a couple of floors. In the roof were glass skylights and, on the lower level, terraces with awnings. In back of the enclosed courtyard a cliff-face covered with ivy reached up to the road leading from Piazza di Spagna to the Pincio. I could hear voices, birds. Caddie was right about the quiet.

Some celestial hand had turned down the volume and the Roman cacophony was no more than a murmur in the background.

'Studios,' she said. 'Sculptors, painters. Or used to be. Now it's more likely to be actors. That *Roman Holiday* movie? This is where the lovers were supposed to be shacked up.'

'The Audrey Hepburn and Gregory Peck characters? They weren't actually lovers, were they?'

'Weren't they? I never saw it. But they shot some scenes right here.'

The Rickard apartment — their name was on a chain bell-pull — was one of those that had a terrace out front. I would like to have seen more of it, got a better look at the framed photographs hung along the passageway that Caddie hustled me through. There was a shot of her in one of those old Dawn Patrol leather flying helmets, climbing into an antique plane.

'What a great place,' I said.

'Damp. Given me rheumatism.'

A fat maid brought out coffee. American coffee; I'd forgotten how feeble it was.

'That's Prudenza'.

I said *buongiorno* to Prudenza who dumped down a plateload of little macaroons and wobbled back inside. 'Is she one of those that Ezra Pound frightened?'

'You remember that? Matter of fact, she's that cook's daughter. Prickly, embittered, card-waving Commie who thinks everyone richer than her ought to be put up against a wall. Except us, of course. We pay, she eats.'

'I've been thinking about that stuff you started to tell me when we first met. The Fascist days and being here when the war started.'

I was still catching up on what had gone on in Italy over the past twenty-five years or so — the span of my own lifetime. I knew that Italy had gone into World War Two on one side — Nazi Germany's — and come out of it on the other. Ours.

I knew that Benito Mussolini created the Fascist party in the early 1920s and that Franco in Spain, the other guy in Portugal, and — above all — Adolf Hitler, had modelled their own thuggish political movements on it. I knew that in the 1930s Mussolini embarked on colonising Abyssinia — another name for Ethiopia — and that he had sent troops to help Franco overthrow the legitimate government in Spain. But I was short on detail.

Caddie was giving me that armour-piercing stare, probably wishing she'd left me in the street. But in that sunny quiet I sensed something happening, those mighty legs beneath the table bracing themselves like she was getting ready for a bout of arm wrestling.

'Okay,' she said. 'Whaddya want to know?'

I didn't think boyish charm would get me far but I might as well give it a shot. I worked up an engaging grin. 'Just tell me everything.'

She laughed; a deep rattle that scared off some pigeons. 'Well, if you buy me lunch I'll tell you *some* of it.' I got the impression that Caddie wasn't up for much more walking that day so we went to the nearest place to eat.

Taverna Margutta
Prosciutto melone
Vitello al limone
Gorgonzola
Frutta fresca

-This place is a dump. Worse, a dump with pretensions. Margutta's supposed to be an artists' quarter but there aren't enough artists in Rome to keep a decent trattoria in business. Or poets. Or writers. Never were. Rome missed out on that great bohemian period that made Paris and Berlin so hot in the

1920s and thirties. Down here everything was suffocated by the damn Fascists. As in Spain.

-Rick was with the rebels over there?

-Franco's army. Mostly Moroccan. Arabs. Bloodthirsty.

-And you were with the good guys. The Republicans? Hemingway and people like that?

-Yeah, Ernie was there right enough. Always trying to get himself slightly wounded so he had a bandage to show off.

-That's where you learnt that Spanish dancing? The flamenco stuff, right?

-Wrong. It's not flamenco. It's *sevillanos*. Just a few little steps, really.

-And both of you were filing for Century?

-Sure. First job together. Though we weren't together much, obviously.

-But you were married?

-Yeah, only just. I bet Rick's said something to you about only getting married to have the same name in our passports. How it wasn't supposed to make a difference to our easy-going Bohemian ways. Still be free to boff whoever we liked, and tell each other all about it?

-The goldfish bowl.

-He told you about that? The asshole. Telling each other if we... slept with someone else. I went along with the idea because Rick was so sold on it and, to be honest, I never really thought we'd stay married all that long. Anyway, I liked sex and after I worked out I'd probably never get pregnant I thought what the hell.

-So where did it all begin?

-China. Shanghai. Got my first real job on the local English paper. Rick was already with Century. I liked it there. We might have stayed except...

-Except for the Spanish war?

-Except Rick bit that woman's nipple off.

(When someone you're interviewing tries to shock you the idea is to stay bland and hope they'll come up with something even stronger to try to throw you. I didn't think it would work with a fellow journalist but it was worth a shot.)

-Which one?

-You really want to know?

-Enough to buy you another lunch.

-Somewhere decent next time.

(Another little trick is the quick switch.)

-Why has Rick started coming up to the bureau?

(That got blocked with barely the twitch of an eyebrow.)

-You need to get a new suit, go with those shoes…

*

My thumb picked up the raised lettering on the card in my *Stampa* mailbox. Embossed. The real thing.

Group Captain John Findley-Frost

And in the bottom right-hand corner.

Royal Air Force (retd.)

There was more on the back.

Palazzo Bergamonte,

Corso Umberto

And a scribble. '*Drinks Thursday 1900?*'

*

Digby was downstairs trying to ingest a *cappuccino* without fouling his moustache.

'What's the story with Arabella Frost's father? What the hell is a Group Captain?'

'Same as colonel. He gets a lot of attention here, time to time. Glossies went crazy for him at the time of Arabella's wedding. Princess holds pair of aces in her hand, sort of thing.'

I must have looked dumb.

'Flying aces. World War Two. Prince Riccardo was just as big a number in the Italian air force as Johnny was in the RAF.' He said *raff*.

Another historical link I was weak on: the couple of years before America got into the war when Hitler left the Italians to fight the British for control of the Middle East, North Africa, and — ultimately — the Suez Canal. Bad decision. Had to send in Rommel and the Afrika Corps to save Mussolini's ass.

'They were shooting at each other, Brits and Eyeties? Like dogfights?'

'Johnny and Ricardo each chalked up much the same number of kills. Around thirty, as I recall.'

'I guess Johnny gave the bride away.'

'He and Riccardo both turned out in uniform. Covered in medals they got for trying to blast each other out of the desert sky.'

*

The Palazzo Bergamonte didn't look like much from the outside, just another vast pompous facade in need of a scrub down. But when I walked around it — or tried to — I saw it would barely fit in a football field.

I was getting used to the time it took for someone to answer a doorbell in Rome. Understandable, considering the ground that might have to be covered. In this case half an acre of marble floor and a staircase only slightly less grand than the Spanish Steps. The white-jacketed flunky who eventually heaved the door open pointed up to where Johnny was waiting on a landing.

'So glad you could come, old boy.' We toiled up a couple more floors, marble giving way to worn stone, until we reached a room the size of a tennis court right under the roof. It looked

105

like the set of one of my *telefono bianco* movies when the Klieg lights had been turned off: dingy, worn and probably damp. There were faded chocolate-boxy murals of boudoir scenes

'Welcome to my bachelor pad, what?' Johnny said *what* a lot. At first, I thought he expected an answer but it was a verbal tic. Like saying *like*. 'Truth is, I'm not really supposed to be here still. I'm hoping I've just been forgotten about.'

He started to clink bottles and glasses. 'Gin and tonic, what?' He showed me the seal on the bottle. 'Riccardo's best.' The seal said Vatican duty-free.

There was a cluster of framed photographs on top of the drinks cupboard. Arabella. Johnny with Arabella. Arabella with small boy. Small boy with handsome guy. 'Yes. That's young James. And Riccardo.' There was also a shot of Prince Riccardo, much younger, in flying kit.

It probably wasn't good form to ask an English gentleman about his wartime exploits, but what the hell. 'Did you guys actually shoot it out back in the war?'

Polite snort.

'Suppose I should say that if we had then the bugger wouldn't be here now. Truth is, neither of us really knows. We were certainly in the same bit of sky at the same time and I imagine he could as easily have accounted for me as me him. Most Eyeties were hopeless at any kind of organised war-making, but every so often one came along you needed to watch out for.'

'Like Ricky.' That crisp fresh scent wafted in and there beside me was the delectable Arabella. 'Good-looking sod, isn't he? Ricky, I mean. Johnny, too, of course.'

I must have been looking at her stupidly, wondering where she had come from.

'Door in the wall over there. Blends into the murals. Stairs lead up from a laundry closet on the floor below. The old prince, Riccardo's father, used to smuggle his lady friends up here. Johnny doesn't dare bring his conquests home.'

They really did look remarkably alike — very remarkably, given that one was a beautiful young actress in her mid-twenties, dark hair in glossy waves, and the other a veteran serial killer in his balding sixties. It was those crystalline eyes. But while hers were mischievous, even inviting, his were flat and unnervingly steady. I thought of a story I'd read someplace about diamonds being hidden by freezing them into ice cubes.

Like him, she had the way of not waiting for a response to anything she said. 'We're very glad you could come. We wanted to thank you for saving me from those dreadful *predators*.'

I could hardly pretend that I'd downed those *scatelli* deliberately up on the Veneto. But even if that mistaken impression was what got me there the old occupational imperative required that I ask her something, at least, about the matrimonial drama. Worst that could happen would be that this stunning woman would fade back into the mural, and Johnny would chuck me down the stairs. 'Should I be surprised to find you're still living here? In the *palazzo*?'

'*Living* here? I'm a prisoner. Prisoner of the *palazzo*. The family retainers watch my every move'.

'But, you and the prince are legally separated, no?'

'Means nothing. Under the temporary agreement we have, I am required to behave as virtuously as though the marriage was still functioning.'

She seemed quite light-hearted about it. 'We're not being divorced, you know. And, after all, it's the marital home. One of them, anyway.'

I did know they were not being divorced, this being Italy. I also knew, having researched the matter intensively by asking

107

Aldo, that the prelude to the custody case now wheezing its way through the justice system had been acrimonious. There had been picture spreads of a public scuffle over who got to steer the little boy's pushchair away from the courthouse.

So I asked a few anodyne questions, the answers to which might come in handy sometime. The boy was with his father at the noble family seaside resort on the Gulf of Genoa. They would stay there until she finished her part in the sword-and-sandals blockbuster she was filming, *Queen of Chaldea*.

'Does that mean getting out to Cinecittá at dawn?'

'Thankfully, no. It's not like Hollywood where you have to be in make-up at six am.'

We talked about Los Angeles for a while and the starlet years there that had made princess material of her.

One minute I had Johnny in sight, flying high cover over the bottles and glasses on the other side of the room. Next, he had wiggled his wings and side-slipped in between us.

'That tussle the other evening set me thinking,' he said. 'About the chap who used to advise us on publicity back in LA.'

She picked right up.

'Said the best way to keep things under control was to get *your* version out first.'

Couldn't argue with that. Well-honed method of news management in Hollywood, Washington and other places where people had plenty to hide. But they weren't dealing with the phantom fact-makers of Europe or, above all, the rabid *scattini*.

'Get it on the AP.'

'Or CNW.'

Which, someone like their Hollywood flack would know how to do. Strangely, that was one species that didn't seem to have joined the great movie migration. Maybe they weren't needed because the *sigari* were as tight as freemasons. They wanted a spread for a star, they just rang up a magazine publisher, or vice-versa. Stars often kept it in the family. Gina Lollabrigida got Milko to speak for her. Sophia Loren's mother could get a story on Radio Vaticano if she thought it would do her girl good.

'Actually, old boy', said Johnny. 'I wondered if there might be some way we could all help each other.'

'About the way this mess over James is being seen,' said Arabella. 'The story that's being built up.'

'We know that something like Century NewsWire...'

'Isn't like those ghastly newspapers. Especially the British ones. Or the dreadful magazines here. In France, too. *Paris Match*. Even in Germany.'

'It's just factual, isn't it? Your...'

'Wire service. News agency.'

'Just the facts, ma'am.' Johnny did the tagline from that old stateside TV series *Dragnet* in an American accent. Made him sound stupid as well as sinister.

'Exactly.'

'Then the jackals would be less likely to come howling.'

I could feel negotiations creaking open. 'Well, it's true that wire service stories about your custody proceedings — which is what you're concerned about, I assume — would probably just stick to what was said in the court proceedings. Or whatever, er, Princess Bergamonte said in answer to a question.'

'Arabella, please.' I pumped up a winning smile.

Johnny gave me back that gunsight stare. 'You'd only use things that she actually *said*? CNW, that is.'

'Especially if I said it to you *exclusively*,' said Arabella.

They were timing their shots like doubles players. 'You wouldn't scrape around for other *things*.'

'Well, we'd stick to the facts, obviously. Not throw in too much colour. Thing about the wire is that we're always up against the clock. Very important to be first.'

'But that's what we mean. We could give you the story first. If there was a story.'

'If?'

'If you didn't need to go into *too* much detail. Turn over rocks. Chase us around the streets. Bother our friends.'

That wouldn't have been the CNW way in any case, though I couldn't speak for what some of the stringers might get up to. Seemed like I was merely being asked to do what we'd do anyway, so I didn't speak for myself, either. Just gave my glass a little lift in their direction. Cheers.

I'd noticed before that the rich and famous had a trick of ending your time together with painless ease. One minute you'd be standing there, drink in hand and feeling pleased with the interest they were taking in you. The next it was, 'So good of you to come' and you were on the doorstep, hand still warm from the parting clasp and thinking of what you should have said back in there.

Down on Corso Umberto, I was not sure what I had agreed to, if anything. Even of what might have been proposed. If anything. Far as I could make out, I had merely been asked to give Arabella considerate treatment in exchange for an inside track on the story. Who wouldn't say yes to that? She was always going to get the best of the coverage whatever the outcome. Young prince belongs to Italian father, court rules. Actress mother in tears. I'll never leave Italy until I have my little boy back. Lawyers say case not over yet.

Still, the general chit-chat had filled out my picture of Johnny.

'Is it right that you were in the Spanish civil war?'

'Certainly was, old boy. Good fun while it lasted, what?'

I waited. Knew he'd say more.

'Few of us got off a ship in Marseilles, on leave from India after a bit of wog-bashing.'

He saw there was a vocabulary hitch. 'Naughty tribesmen. Afghanistan. North West Frontier. We used to fly Hawker Harts. Rickety old things with two wings. Open cockpits. Chap in the back just chucked the bombs over the side. Gas bottles, really.'

'Gas?'

'Yes. Boffins in the Air Ministry wanted to see if it would work.'

'And…?'

'Just blew away, most of it. The wogs would merely gallop off. We'd go after them with the Lewis guns. Damn old Harts were so slow we usually couldn't catch up with the buggers. Good fun, though. Good polo out there, too.'

'And Spain?'

'When we got off in Marseille we thought we'd go and see if old Franco needed a hand.'

'You flew missions over there?'

'As a freelance, you might say. Good fun, though, while it lasted. What?'

The best bit, though, had been what the luminous Arabella said to me while Johnny was fiddling with the last drink.

'If you're out at the studios in the next couple of days, I'm on *Palcoscenico Dodici*.'

Stage Twelve.

-10-

With irrepressible curiosity as a given, the single quality that distinguishes reporters from normal human beings is the ability to recognise what makes a story a news story. Whether this or that combination of personality, place and event is sufficiently odd, relevant or evocative to interest an audience. Descriptive skills can be learnt. That fundamental response is instinctive. You either know or you don't.

Rita the Meeter didn't. Either that or she'd gone, as Rick said, native. Covered the beat so long she couldn't tell when something was out of the ordinary and therefore worth reporting. 'Can't,' she said one morning in the *Stampa* when I'd asked her if she was going out to Ciampino. 'Got a dubbing call.'

It was back when she was still having to explain things to me. 'Pays better than Century.'

'What does?'

'Dubbing. You know, voiceovers.' She saw I needed more.

'It's a crowd scene. They'll want a lot of us to shout and holler.'

A little German correspondent came up to the bar looking expectant. 'I'm giving Fritz here a lift.'

'You coming too?' Fritz asked. Of course, I was.

A few more *Stampa* faces greeted us on the line being checked in to a building way out on Via Flaminia: shitpickers mainly. A rangy guy at the door wrote down our names.

'American?'

He evidently was, and on the run from the Pinklist, I guessed.
'Gary,' said Rita.

'Nice to meet you. First time?'

'Guess so.' I didn't quite grasp exactly what I might be doing for the first time. I looked at his pal, who hadn't said anything; tall, sick-looking.

'He's finished.'

'I'm sorry to hear that.'

'*Finnish*,' said Rita. 'He said he was Finnish. From Finland.' And as we moved on, 'He's also a religious nut. Gets out ranting every Sunday up in the Villa Borghese.'

'As well as a...

'*Pedo*? Doesn't seem to worry either of them.'

We were packed into a kind of movie theatre without seats, so many of us that Gary had to shoulder his way through to the front.

'We going to be voice of people,' said Fritz.

'What people?'

'Any people.'

'Attention please, my friends,' yelled Gary over the multilingual gabble. '*Attenzione!* This is the scene outside the Duna in St Petersburg when Comrade Lenin proclaims the Bolshevik Revolution. There would have been people from all over the world there, so when *Grida!* comes up on the screen just yell out welcome greetings in your own language. Or any language you like. Here's Scene One.'

The screen lit up and we looked at a costumed mob waving their fists and shouting soundlessly. 'Why are we doing this now?' I asked Fritz. 'I mean why didn't they record what the crowd was yelling when the film was shot?'

'Always this way in Italy. Put noise in later. Better later than neverer.'

113

It was a lot of fun once I got into the swing of things. Scenes would come up on the screen with cues typed along the bottom. Gary took us through it like a choirmaster, waving his arms and yelling along. '*Avanti popolo*! Down with the Czar! *Vive la revolution!*' On the way out the Finn handed each of us twenty thousand lire.

'*Vages off sinn*', said Fritz, getting his cliché straight that time.

'Sin?,' said Gary, hoisting an eyebrow. 'Want to leave me your number?'

*

Next time I ran into Mungo I told him about this entertaining experience. 'Thing is,' he said, with a sneery lift of the eyebrows. 'There are no sound stages.'

'At Cinecittá?'

'Nor anywhere else in Italy. Never built any. God knows why. Couldn't hope to keep everyone on the set from yakking, I imagine. They *shoot* with mikes. Get the dialogue on the soundtrack — together with every other noise for a mile around. Vespas. Planes landing at Ciampino. Even the cameras: sound like cement mixers they're so old. Then they chuck the track away and make a new one.'

'Actor's voices, too?'

'The lot. Even stars. Drives foreign actors crazy.'

'Having to do it all over again?'

'If it's for an English version, yes. Doesn't bother Italians, though.'

'Oh?'

'They've all got their *uccellini* to dub for them.'

'Little birds?'

'A voice stand-in. The voice in the shadows.'

'So that's not Anna Magnani talking on the screen?'

114

'Magnani's voice could crack windows, but no one's ever heard it in a movie theatre. She's lip-synched by her personal birdie. Same with Silvana Mangano. Fans have never heard her, either. Real voice is a silly little simper. Elsa Martinelli. Lovely girl, sounds like a fairground barker. Claudia Cardinale. Brought up in Tunisia, French accent. Guys, too. Raf Vallone. Rosanno Brazzi. Never hear their real voices on screen. Lollobrigida's an exception. Insists on dubbing herself, and she's big enough to get away with it.'

'And everyone knows this?' Including Rita, of course, who had never thought it might make a good story.

'In the industry, of course. The *uccellini* are in the contracts.'

'I'd like to meet a couple of them. Find out what it might be like to be a voice of the stars. Wonder if they might be ready to talk.'

'Only if they never wanted to work again. Or if you want a set to fall on you next time you're out at Cinecittá.'

*

Rick had indeed taken to showing up in the bureau, sniffing around like a hungry bear. I found him pulling folders out of his file cabinet. He waved a sheet of paper at me. A creased sales note dated sometime in 1939.

Professore Riccardo Galeazzo-Lisi
Via del Corso 129

'Knew it was the same guy. Now he's the pope's personal doctor. Supposed to have cured him of those hiccups.'

'With the help of a team of specialists from Zurich.'

'He's a goddam ophthalmologist. An eye doctor. Look — this is the bill for a pair of glasses the old crook made for me back before the war. Worst I ever had. Couldn't read a thing with 'em. But if he's that close to *Il Papa* now I'd better go see him. Maybe he'll remember me.'

115

'Speaking of remembering, do you know anything about Group Captain John Findley-Frost? Father of Arabella Frost. You know, the actress? He was in the British air force.'

'That prick! He nearly bombed Caddie's ass off.'

'Oh? Where?'

'Him and a few limey chums turned up in Cordoba when I was there. Franco teamed them up with the Huns and Italians to drop bombs on Madrid. Where Caddie was at the time.'

*

GIGI FAZZI

Lasagna casa mia.
Capretto al forno.
Fragione del campo

-I want to hear about Rick putting the nip in nipple.

-Never seen the sense to pasta. Like having bread and butter for your dinner. Can't stand pizza either.

-It's un-American not to like pizza.

-Is it right they call it pizza pie back home?

-Only in darkest Wisconsin. The nipple, Caddie?

-That suit goes well with the new shoes.

A banal topic like clothes can divert an interviewee from worrying they might say too much. I would just have gone into any menswear shop that looked promising, but Digby took me along to his tailor.

-They're silk, but kind of… papery, don't you think?

-*Bella figura.*

-*Grazie!* So, Caddie, the nipple? How'd you get away with that?

-Went to see the poor woman. Gave her all the money I could scrape up. Old John decided he'd better get Rick back

116

somewhere they could keep an eye on him. He was running the service, editor–in–chief. He wasn't old then, just John. Then Mussolini invaded Ethiopia. Century wanted Rick to cover it but he'd only go if they sent me, too. They'd never had a woman correspondent.

-Century?

-No, the goddamn Chinese, who do you think? Listen, Shelby, we're gonna move. I'm getting rheumatism and Rick's snoring like a fucking rhinoceros. Found an apartment out along Flaminia. Three bedrooms and a terrace. Nice elevator. You want to move into Margutta?

- Could I really?

-Sure. But promise me something. Rick's trying to organise a farewell round of the *case chiuse*. You don't wanna go.'

That was not strictly true. A couple of times all that kept me from checking out what was on offer was fear of embarrassment at not knowing the routine.

-Not that I'm against *bordels* in principle. We used to go to them a lot in Paris, out on a date. The Sphinx, OneTwoTwo. You could get a bottle of champagne, shoot the breeze with the girls. Ones here weren't anything like that. In the bargain basement they didn't even offer a bed. The girl stood up in a kind of shower stall, put one foot up on a step. Rick liked that, said it saved having to take his pants off. I had to take his word for it. They won't let women in. Women clients, I mean. It was the left one, if it matters to you.'

-What was?'

-The nipple. Now we gotta work on your shirts.'

-11-

I drove out to Cinecittá with Rita. My car, not hers. Setting
myself up with a Fiat 500 pretty well topped off my *bella figura*.
I'd take it to the bureau and leave it with Giuseppe, a war
veteran with a limp who managed a shoal of cars three deep in
a setback off Via delle Mercede. For a few coins he'd heave
them around according to their owners' schedules. If I stayed
late, he'd drop the key in the *Stampa* bar.

An Alfa Giulietta would have made for a better *figura*, I
suppose, although even the little *topolino* would have been out
of reach if I had not discovered the key to Italy's domestic
economy. No messing around with bank loans or hire-
purchase. You merely signed a wad of forms dated through the
next twelve months. These were *cambiali* — in effect IOUs — for
a total that added some interest to the original amount. They
could be traded around between interested parties but on the
due date one would land up at your bank to be settled from
your account.

I was happy to have the Fiat salesman deal with that. Getting
cash — even your own cash — out of an Italian bank was a
performance. The same guy greeted me by name every time I
went to cash a cheque, but he still wanted to see my passport.
Another, who also knew me by sight, would look in a file to see
if that was really my signature. Yet another poked around to
see there was enough in the account. Finally, someone would
open a cash drawer and, closely supervised by his colleagues,
count out reddish-brown ten thousand lire bills, each worth

about twenty-five bucks. They were bigger even than those London fivers, and with a wodge of them folded down in my pocket, I felt I could take on the town.

Rita was wary when I set up an interview with Arabella for her. 'Why don't you want to do it yourself?'

She was already suspicious because after she'd first taken me out to Cinecittá and shown me around, I'd pulled in Lucy and put together a take-out on the place which got a pretty good play. It was something she could have done anytime because Cinecittá was pretty extraordinary.

It was about the size of Central Park but with bigger water features and fewer street cleaners. There were piles of mysterious junk everywhere: crumbling old sets, a railroad siding, a huge lake, one end of it jammed with cutouts of Roman galleys, pirate ships and ocean liners. There were herds of cows and horses, all kinds of farmyard animals. There were people, lots of them, holed up in little shanty towns. *Gli affollamenti*, the studio cop we had to take around with us explained. Crowd extras, in tribes like gypsies. A gang boss would negotiate a wholesale rate for their services.

'They shouldn't be living here,' said the cop. 'We have to put guards on the animals. They barbecued the little goats from *Samson and Delilah*. But if we put them out they just set up their *baracche* against the front wall. Hollywood people don't like.'

I parked Rita in the *cantina* and went looking for Arabella.

'*Avanti!*' The door of the *camerino* was open but I knocked anyway. She turned around, flanked by a couple of women in white coats, holding her hands up like a begging pooch, wiggling three-inch-long fingernails. 'Glue still drying. Mustn't touch anything.' The attendants sidled out, closing the door.

'She'll just write something... gushing? No questions about the court case? Or about James?'

119

'Anodyne is Rita's middle name. But when the hard stuff comes along — court hearings, lawyers' demands, I'll do it.'.'

She was dressed in a loose toga-like robe, its bodice cut to hold up her breasts. Open sandals showed long elegant toes that could have been carved from marble. She still had her hands raised like a hold-up victim. Those irresistible eyes had somehow pulled me closer. She was powered up, radiating allure. 'There's nothing under this,' she said, conversationally. She wiggled the claws again. 'And I couldn't even fight you off.'

One of the make-up mavens was back in the room. In the shutter-click of a glance, Arabella switched personas. One instant she was flirting magnetically, lips in an inviting pout, diamond-chip eyes beckoning. The instant that she sensed — not even saw — someone else in the offing every contour of her body and face sharpened up: cool, impersonal, matter-of-fact. If the make-up minions were reporting to Riccardo she wasn't going to help.

'Very well,' she said, snapping into brisk-and-businesslike. 'If she's here at four I'll give her a lift back to town. I've got to be in the Via Margutta by five. Having my portrait painted by a man called Vestiglio. I don't think he's very good.'

'That's where I live.'

'Really? How very extraordinary.'

'I've just moved there. Number 51. I'm told it's the apartment in which Gregory Peck entertained Audrey Hepburn.'

If he had then I hope they didn't catch cold. Caddie had been right; damp seeped from the walls where the building backed on to the Pincio. Anything in a closet got mouldy. But there was honeysuckle among the ivy shrouding the little cliff-face and the scent would drift in the window, mingled with whiffs of cat pee. At night there were fireflies. A flock of pigeons hung out

120

in the courtyard and I woke to their gurgling calls. Some mornings a woman in the building opposite would open her shutters at the same time I did mine and we'd exchange a friendly nod. At first she always wore a robe, but once she got used to seeing me she didn't always bother. Very neighbourly.

'That same apartment?' Arabella had been looking me over as we talked, something of her father's marksman scrutiny, but with a smile behind it. 'Perhaps I could drop in for tea?'

The pages of this script seemed to be turning fast. 'Today?'

'Let's not rush things. Next Thursday. Five o'clock?'

*

When Rick saw my mailer package on Cinecittá he said, 'Pity you didn't get the whorehouse in.' He was up in the bureau again, pawing through his papers. I'd forgotten to pressure Caddie about what he was at. He turned up his lewd grin. 'Out in Cinecittá. The brothel. Some of the extras put in time there. Make-up girls, too. Hairdressers. Not all of them beauties, alas. But for a few lire more they'll do it in costume.'

'Where is it?'

'Moves around, depending if there's a set that's got beds. Last time I went out there it was in *Queen of Babylon*. Want me to find where it's at right now?'

'Later maybe. It's just private enterprise on the part of the extras?'

'No. It's run by some of Farouk's bodyguards. Those Albanians.'

*

Couple of days later Caddie took me in a cab to the far side of the Coliseum. She hauled on a bell pull beside an entrance in one of those endless brick walls After we baked in the sun for a

121

while, a knotty face in a wimple appeared at a little barred hatch and squeaked, '*Senora Richetto!*'

The studded *portone* creaked open and the old nun all but fell to her knees. Caddie tramped past her, me trailing, into a room littered with bolts of cloth and paper patterns. Another nun in a white robe and black head-dress was cutting out something with shears the size of hedge cutters. She put them down and sailed across, creaking and billowing like a sailboat rounding a buoy. 'Caddie!'

'Hi, Jo. I've brought you a customer. Shelby, this is Mother Giovanna Orvieto.'

As new experiences go, having a mother superior put her arms around me and bring her virginal lips within kissing range takes some beating. Of course, she had me roped in with a measuring tape at the time, every move monitored by a sterner looking accomplice to jot down my details.

I was never sure if Mother Jo's lips were all that virginal. She'd had a life in the fashion industry before heeding the call, or whatever it is that leads a lady to the cloister. She was a few years older than Caddie but nowhere near as tall and less than half the weight. Her skin, what could be seen of it, was rosy and flawless. Caddie knew her from back when, but all either of them would ever tell me about her past was that she came from a family of silk merchants up near Florence. Caddie went off somewhere during the measuring process and reappeared as Mother Jo and I were getting down to business.

'Single cuff but two buttons.' Jo spoke English slowly, as though remembering it from long past. '*Gauntlet* cuffs, they are called. Collar medium depth. No pocket.'

I'd always had shirts with a breast pocket but Jo said no. 'Too thick under jacket. You look fat.'

Made-to-measure shirt workshop in front parlour of grim-looking convent was the kind of thing mailers were made of. 'When I come back would you mind if I brought a photographer?'

> 10:04:58 VENICE. ALL THREE SUSPECTS IN THE DEATH OF WILMA MONTESI WERE ACQUITTED TODAY AFTER A PROSECUTOR BRANDED HIS OWN STAR WITNESS, MARIA CAGLIO, 'UNTRUSTWORTHY'.

*

'Pronto.'

Don't you want to know *chi parla?*'

'Hello, Delphine. How're things?'

'Depends what things you mean, darling.' After Jerry's, she'd called me a few times, trying to get us to write something about her, but she never pushed too hard and she was always entertaining.

'You were out at Cinecittá,' she said, voice suggesting a reproachful pout. 'And you didn't drop in.'

'Didn't know where to find you.'

'Well, next time you're calling on the topliners, spare a thought for those languishing downstream.'

'You're in *Queen of Chaldea*, too?'

'I'm the *madame* of the dancing girls, my dear. Lots of moves but only about a dozen lines. Third time I've played the part in one *sandalino* or another. Don't seem to be working my way up the scale. Unlike some.'

I was not worried she might guess I had any connection with Arabella beyond the occupational, but I thought I'd take charge of the conversation. 'I heard something out at Cinecittá about a little Albanian operation. Might your Albanian know anything about it?'

'Ho-ho-ho. You mean the little *bordello*? Well, that's what Albanians do, isn't it?'

'Is it?'

'You could ask him about it yourself. Though frankly, I wouldn't advise it.'

'Don't think I need to. Not a Century kind of story.'

'So what is? I give a great interview, you know. Why-don't-you-come-up-and-see- me- sometime?' Mae West impression. 'We could go on to is-that-a-gun-in-your-pocket-or-are-you-just-glad- to-see me?'

'You've already got one of those going.'

'Always ready to peek in another pocket, darling. How would you like to see the boy king eat thirty-six lamb chops at a sitting?'

'Your Farouk? Some boy.'

'Well he was when he took the throne. A mere sixteen.'

'Now he's a mere eighteen. Stones.' I knew about stones from London, the quaint measure of weight the English used to make themselves sound thin.

'And then some, darling. He's coming up to 350 pounds on the hoof, not counting the latest chin. Seriously, would you like to watch him actually scoffing it up? It's quite a sight, I'm told. He doesn't often do it in public but he's become fond of this particular place.'

King Farouk was newsworthy, partly because of his instant recognisability. He hadn't really done much since being booted off the throne of Egypt by the guys who nationalised the Suez Canal, but it often seemed that he was about to. He had divorced the fairly ordinary young queen who came with him to exile in Rome but there was no replacement in view. Nor did he seem to be involved in the comeback plots that might be expected of a dethroned monarch. Mainly, he just sat around,

124

an unmistakable figure with a silly moustache that I sometimes glimpsed, up at Doney's, dark glasses even at midnight, squatting among his bodyguards. They were mostly Albanian, Cristof explained, because of some ancestral link.

And he ate. Everyone had a story about his outrageous feeding habits. He could get through five hundred oysters a week. Some said six hundred. He had begun one meal with a chicken, followed it with a duck, followed that with a whole turkey. He ordered a three-tier wedding cake from the best *pasticceria* in town, setting off rumours he was to remarry. But it was all for him, and he scoffed it at a sitting.

'You might be able to get a picture if you're discreet.'

That was what mattered. Those tales of gluttony were anecdotal; Farouk rarely went to restaurants and the world was yet to see a picture of him stuffing himself.

'Or if Niki doesn't shoot me.'

'He never would. He's a pussycat really. Just don't let on that I told you where to go.'

*

That turned out to be a restaurant on the Via Appia Antica where Lucy and I strolled in like carefree tourists and took a table in the garden. We had partnered on a few jobs by now and she never failed to deliver. The package we put together on Mother Jo — Convent With a Cutting Edge — even ran in the Soviet Union, although I doubt Century Syndication ever got paid.

It was strictly business between us now, but I always tried to find out a bit more about her. A lot of Italians were cautious about revealing too much about themselves but Lucy always seemed ready to chat about her life. She was as Roman as a damp napkin, born in Trastevere, wrong side of the Roman tracks; more accurately the wrong side of the Tiber. Most of the men in her family were *sampietrini*, the workforce of stonemasons and metalworkers, plumbers, painters and wick-trimmers, that kept St Peter's Basilica in shape, 'You got to be born one, like a tribe. Like *tifosi di futbol.'* Football fans, rooted in the territory. The menfolk were also, I was intrigued to hear, communists. This took some getting used to. Back home, MacCarthyist hysteria was fading but the House Un-American Activities Committee was still hounding 'comsymps'. In Italy, a democracy that was America's ally in the North Atlantic Treaty Organisation, the Communist Party held about a third of the seats in parliament and was a power in local government all around the country.

Only a few other tables were set up, the people at them presumably recovering from a morning of poking around the tombs and ruined villas along the Appia. It had to be the right place: the *padrone* looked to be suffering stage fright and there was a lot of waiter traffic in and out of a corner of the garden screened-off by bamboo panels.

'Did you know that this was the original Roman road? Went all the way down to Reggio Calabria.' Lucy threw a little shudder.

It was the first time I'd seen her in a dress. This one did plenty for her at the neckline but her legs were still a little short. Though only by comparison with, say, Cyd Charisse.

'Yes, I did know, but how I can shoot pictures through that?' She frowned towards the bamboo screen.

Outside, cars were pulling up, doors slamming. A phalanx of waiters got themselves in line, bowing and chanting, *'Buon giorno, maestâ!'*

Everyone in the garden watched, fascinated, as the *padrone* led the arrivals along the edge of the garden and settled them in behind the bamboo. A fresh stream of waiters flowed across toting mineral water in ice-buckets, piles of napkins, trays of hors d'oeuvres. Our own lunch arrived, although we barely noticed because next out of the kitchen came the royal *pezzo di resistenza*. It was lugged past us, a vast silver salver piled with neatly trimmed lamb cutlets, a frilly paper sock on every pared-back bone. I didn't have time to count but there had to be at least the three dozen Delphine had promised.

'Okay', said Lucy. 'Now I be tourist.' She took a little point-and-shoot Canon out of the oversized handbag by her feet and breezed over to the enclosure. She got within two paces, clicking off shots as she went, before Niki and a guy who could have been his twin came out and blocked her.

'They just tell me no,' she said back at the table. 'Quite polite. But I see where king is sitting.'

We got on with our meal for a few minutes then she looked around at the restaurant building behind us, a crumbling two-storey one-time farmhouse.

'*Mi scusi,*' she said, picking up her bag. 'I need some moments.' I kept on eating, wondering if she had been spooked by the Albanians. I wondered for about fifteen minutes while the fish she had ordered dried out on her plate and our waiter radiated reproach. Only when I heard the Farouk party rumbling to its feet did she reappear. She picked the Canon off the table and clicked off a few from a respectful distance.

Engines started up outside. The waiters lined up and launched into a farewell chorus. The two Albanians came back across the lawn.

I wondered if Niki had recognised me from Jerry's. He didn't say anything. but when his buddy pulled a chair around and sat down he hung back a step and dropped me a wink. The Canon was sitting on the table and the first guy put a large hand on it. 'Please excuse me *signorina*,' he said to Lucy. 'His Majesty does not wish to be photographed. He hopes you will accept the price he offers for this little machine.' He fished out a small wad and put it on the table.

No one does indignation better than Italians, and Lucy unleashed a virtuoso tirade. We were innocent tourists, she snarled. This was a public place. She had been enthralled to find herself in the presence of the king. He was someone she had always admired. Now she was humiliated and embarrassed. So was her friend, an American who would receive a very bad impression of Italy. And *you* — she pushed out her bosom patriotically — you are not even Italian!

I figured anything I tried to say would come out as mere ineffectual spluttering so I kept quiet.

The lead Albanian had not expected resistance. Perhaps the *signorina* and her friend would feel better, he said, if in addition to his majesty's generosity over the camera we would consider ourselves his guests for lunch. He picked up the *conto* I had called for and wiggled his fingers. It seemed to be Niki's turn to pay.

He leaned forward to reach into his jacket, and his little gun slid out and landed in the remains of Lucy's fish.

Italians do pretty good flouncing, too, so that was the style in which we made our exit. In the car, Lucy counted her takings. 'Hundred thousand. Twice price of new Canon.' She thought for a moment, lower lip out.

'I give Frederico half. Is enough.'

'But no pictures.'

'Nothing from Canon, maybe. But here...' She opened her handbag and showed me a Leica with a six-inch telephoto lens. 'You owe me ten thousand.'

'For?'

'For cook to let me in his room. Upstairs. Not clean but I see over bamboo. I got him, I think, fat pig.'

She got him, all right. Back at Newspix we looked at the pictures, warm and damp from the printer. King Cutlet. The one in his right hand had a king-sized bite out of it. There was a little pile of bones on a plate to one side and in front of him the big platter with plenty more morsels lined up. He'd kept the dark glasses on but it couldn't be anyone else: the silly moustache, the napkin under all those chins.

'Terrific!' I said, making sure the darkroom hands saw that my peck on Lucy's forehead was no more than brotherly.

'He didn't even eat salad.'

I got Rita to write up an interview with Delphine. 'I've always remembered the advice I got at the J. Arthur Rank Charm School. Never immerse the bosom in the bath.'

*

LA CAPRICCIO

Insalata tricolore

Coda di ruspoli con polenta

Zabaglione

-I heard you went singing with the *uccellini*.

(I'd stopped wondering how Caddie got to know stuff when she never seemed to talk to anyone.)

-It was very interesting.

-The Duck set up that industry. All foreign movies had to be dubbed into Italian in case people might want to learn other languages. Pick up ideas. This is the only fish in the whole Mediterranean that's worth eating.

-Seems a bit trivial. Not even allowing subtitles, I mean.

-Nothing was trivial if it helped the Fascists keep control. They told people how to talk, how to dress, how to act.

-All those mob scenes? All those marches?

129

-Rick loved those Young Fascist girls stomping along with their tits pushed out. All out of step. *Giovinezza! Giovinezza*!

(She croaked out the first bar then put a hand over her mouth mock-furtive.)

-I've seen pictures of kids in those outfits. But mainly boys.

-*Figli della Lupa*, sons of the wolf, junior fascists trying to look like The Duck. He only made corporal in the army so he tried to smarm the poor conscripts by creating this *corporale d'honore* costume. You must have seen the pictures. Silly little cap, black shirt of course, baggy trousers stuck in his boots.

-All inspired by the war in Abyssinia. Which you covered.

-Went from Paris to Marseille, took a little steamer to Djibouti, then a train to somewhere. First time I'd met any Italians, apart from gangsters back home, or waiters.

-And Spain came after that?

-They sent us there because by then we could speak Italian. Far as Century was concerned Italian was pretty much the same as Spanish.

(The kind of Italian the Rickards spoke wasn't even like Italian. They enunciated it like they were reading from a children's book, in exactly the same shunted-together Midwest drone that they spoke English. I could understand most of what they said. Italians usually couldn't.)

-Then when the war in Spain was over you came back here?

-Right. Century was desperate to get the Rome bureau re-opened. The Duck was closer than ever to Hitler after Spain, and there were going to be some big moves in Europe.

-The bureau had been closed?

-For filing a story about the Duck the Fascists didn't like. Bureau chief chucked out of the country and the wire cut off. John came over to Paris and said that if Rick could get Rome back online he'd make him bureau chief.

130

-And Rick reckoned he could?

-Rick reckoned I could.

-Speaking of Rick, why has he been hanging out over at Newspix? As Lucy had mentioned, just chatting.

-He reckons he can talk that Galeazzo-Lisi character into giving us an exclusive about the pope's last moments.

-Jesus! That'd be something.

(And it would. Manna — the appropriate word coming effortlessly to mind — to the devout, world over.)

-Think he can bring it off?

-Doesn't matter what I think. Rick says it'll be his last big exclusive. He's even getting the quack to take deathbed pictures for us. That Fernando, whatever his name is, your girlfriend's boyfriend, is hyped up about it.

-Lucy? She's not my girlfriend.

-You've been doing jobs together.

-And that's all.

-If you say so. Just watch your step.

*

Even from the stairs, I could tell something was up. The bureau stank of sweat and *toscano*. Everyone with a chair up at the desk, Charlie in the slot. He had a Band-Aid above one eyebrow. Walked-into-door would have been the explanation he offered the others, who would nonetheless assume he meant his wife Nora, a blotchy English girl who preferred not to talk to me. When we had first met I asked if she enjoyed living in Rome and she all but spat. 'I hate it! It's crumbling, rotten, dirty. So are the people.'

The Band-Aid was clean, unlike the one he'd been wearing when I took delivery of him a few hours earlier.

The phone had rung in Via Margutta about five am. Call to action, I'd thought, stumbling downstairs. The layout of the apartment made answering unexpected calls hazardous. A short hallway led into a huge space filled with light from a skylight forty feet up. In the centre, like some heathen idol, sat a five-foot-high terracotta stove with a metal flue rising to the roof. Ensuring eye contact between people sitting on either side required delicate arrangement of the few bits of furniture. In back, there was a rudimentary kitchen. The rickety staircase led down from a kind of minstrels' gallery running around three sides. The bathroom was at one end and at the other a bedroom looked out over the courtyard. The vast bed had been custom made and was too big for the Rickards' new place. 'Separate rooms now,' Caddie had said. 'I'd forgotten what sleep was like.'

I expected the call would be about the pope, whose health was back on the news schedule, but Charlie's voice croaked: 'Need a favour, my friend.'

'Where are you?'

'Ospedale Monte Aldo. I think it's the drunk tank.'

Happily, I knew where the hospital was. Streets were clear at that time and the *topolino* got me there in minutes. It took a lot longer to find Charlie but eventually a heavy-eyed *Polizia Ospedale* directed me to the inebriates ward. Charlie was one of several bodies stretched out on narrow iron beds and he was damn glad to see me. 'Must have tripped, or something. Don't know why they brought me here.'

'What happened to your head?'

He felt the plaster over his eye. 'Don't actually remember. Guess I was mugged.'

'Who patched you up?'

'Don't remember that, either. Mind running me home, old chap? Don't seem to have any cash on me. Lucky I had a couple of *gettone*.'

We let it go at that: another insight into Rome by night. The bars closed at two am, except for the joint near *Messagero*. Aimless drunks on the street — usually foreigners — risked being slung in the back of a police car, lightly robbed, and delivered to Monte Aldo to sleep it off.

The *poliziotto* was snoozing in the corridor. I asked him if there were any possessions and he produced Charlie's *tessera* and a bunch of keys. *Soldi*? A shrug.

'Never mind,' said Charlie. 'Let's get out of here.' He lived out in EUR, a pretentious marble show town the Duck built in the late 1930s for a Fascist world fair that was shoved aside by the war.

'I don't suppose you want to come in.' I was even less keen to meet up with Nora than he was. After that sour outburst she laid on me I had tried to warm her up with a compliment. She had a fine nose, I said. Meant it, too, I liked assertive noses and hers was the best thing about her looks, a straight narrow blade rather than one of those self-effacing stubs. She let out a squeak and shot off to the other side of the room.

'Know you meant well,' Charlie said the following day. 'Just that she hates her nose. Always trying to get me to buy her another one.'

*

Now Charlie said: 'Old boy's been taken up to Gandolfo.' The Apostolic Residence of Castel Gandolfo, fifteen miles south of Rome in the Alban hills, was the pope's summer residence. 'Vatican insists he's just getting away from the heat but we're hearing that the hiccup doctors are on the way back. And New York says the American cardinals have been put on stand-by.'

When Pius did die the eighty or so cardinals around the world, the princes of the Church, would converge on Rome to get him buried and elect his successor. It would be the biggest story the bureau had handled.

'Trouble is,' said Charlie. 'New York's bound to send the big byliners who'll do their damndest to outshine us locals. Brad Hooper's sure to come.'

Hooper was an amiable Century lifer who built a national reputation as a sports writer, grew out of that and went mainstream as Century's news fireman. He had coasted into a few big prizes, less because of his rawboned prose, which no one could deny was crowd-pleasing, than to having great set-piece assignments laid before him. The Coronation of Queen Elizabeth. Eisenhower defeating Adlai Stevenson, Churchill's return to power, the French defeat in Indochina. The funeral of a pope and the choice of his successor was cut out for him as neatly as one of Mother Jo's shirts.

'Nothing we can do about it,' said Charlie. 'Best we can try is to feed the heavies enough soft stories to keep 'em happy while we guys hit the street and try to grab the action. We'll rope in the Ricketts, too, won't we, old buddy?'

Rick had lumbered in and was riffling through the Outgoing. He looked up at Cristof who shrugged. 'That's it. We've got two *tipolini* inside the *castello*. Trouble is, how they gonna get out to use a phone?'

If the Vatican bureaucrats wanted to keep the pope's downhill progress to themselves he was in the right place. Vatican City leaked like a Via Margutta skylight but the Castel, in the centre of the village of Gandolfo, was lockdown heaven. Like Via del Propaganda and a number of other desirable properties around Rome, it was part of the Holy See, sovereign territory of the church. Not even the *Carabinieri* could enter uninvited.

Up until now, it had been assumed that Pius's last moments would be played out in the Vatican, controlled in typical Sala *Stampa* fashion. The process would begin with an arcanely worded story in *Osservatore Romano* that only seers like Miss Frisk could decipher. Radio Vatican would drop hints the end was nigh. Everyone interested would set up camp in the Sala and the Jesuits who ran it would put out bulletins whenever the spirit moved them. It would be impossible for anyone to get a beat. Even if we set up an inside track to someone in the papal apartments there was no chance of getting a tip confirmed. The pope would be reportably dead only when a posse of cardinals shuffled into the Sala and said that he was. What might happen, though, if he popped off in a less fortified patch of holy real estate like Gandolfo was something new to consider.

'We'd better have an overnight shift,' said Charlie, looking at me. That seemed fair. The other guys had been there all day. I said I'd come back about eleven. 'Question on style. Castel Gandolfo one word or two?' We made it two.

Downstairs, the *Stampa* was seething, shitpickers lined up to read the ANSA wire. The Germans had annexed one end of the bar, the Angloids another. Every time someone came downstairs from the phones, faces lifted up seeking revelation.

I was gripped by the urge for a hamburger and fries, something that struck occasionally to remind me of my roots. I headed for the California but even from fifty metres off I could hear the full-throated warble wafting up out of the Colony. People were already spilling out, among them Betty's friend Wendy. 'You don't want to go down there,' she said. 'Winchester's got the spirit. Anyway, no Betty tonight.'

'I've got to work later. Only came up for some soul food. Want to join me?'

I was just being friendly, not wanting to seem as though I was coming on to her, but she said, 'Sure.'

We sat up at the counter on red-top swivel stools and ordered beers while we checked out the menu. Bit like a teen date. 'She'll be sorry to have missed you. But she didn't feel like coming out. Little drama last night, shook her up a bit.'

'Drama?'

'She slapped a guy with the Jack Daniel's bottle. Blood all over the joint. I had to gallop to the rescue with the Band-Aid. Pretty funny, really. Him trying to cover his you-knows, me trying to play nurse.'

'Why'd she hit him?' Didn't sound like easy-going Betty.

'Seems that proceedings were, should I say, well advanced when she realised the guy was English.'

'Is that all?'

'It was enough. Don't you know she only does Americans? The girl's a patriot.'

There was a disturbance in the atmosphere. Having put one audience to flight Winchester had lumbered upstairs looking for another. Spotting us, he decided some lines from an *Oklahoma!* ingénue number would suit the occasion.

> *I'm just a fool when lights are low.*
> *I cain't be prissy and quaint.*

Wendy didn't bother to turn around. 'Beat it, Winnie.' But on he went in a ludicrous girly voice.

> *I ain't the type that can faint.*
> *How can I be what I ain't?*

I guess he had the entire book off by heart. All the parts.

> *I cain't say no!*

Wendy swivelled around and took a swipe at him but he

jumped back pretty nimbly for a guy full of booze.

I did what I supposed was expected of me: slid off the stool and got between them. 'Come on, Winnie. Don't be a damn nuisance.'

'Nuisance!' he screeched. 'I'm no nuisance. I'm a goddam hero. A *restaurant* hero. A world-class restaurant here. It's gonna happen, man. Zi Peppe. You watch for it. My great Roman restaurant is gonna happen. Zi Peppe is on the way.'

'That's real good, Winnie. Now leave us eat in peace.'

'Don't call me Winnie! That's a girl's name. And you guys'll never eat in my place. Never!'

I went back to the bureau via the *Stampa*. From the mezzanine at that hour the place looked empty but Rick strolled in from the little terrace fiddling with his flies. 'You coulda stayed home,' he said, looking up and spotting me. 'Miss Frisk decided it wasn't a deathbed scene after all.'

I could see now that there was someone back in the darkened terrace. Rita, I guessed. 'Ever get anything back from the quack ophthalmologist?'

'We've talked a couple of times. I think we're beginning to see eye-to-eye.'

That was obviously meant for a laugh, so I squeezed one out. Upstairs, Cristof was waiting to go home. 'What does *Zi Peppe* mean?'

'In *romanesco*? The pisspot.'

I looked at the incoming ANSA wire and pulled over a typewriter.

> 04.11.57 SHELBY STONE. ROME. THE UNCLE OF DEAD 'BEACH GIRL' WILMA MONTESI TOLD A VENICE COURT TODAY HE WAS RESPONSIBLE FOR THE PREGNANCY OF HIS FIANCÉE'S SISTER.

*

If Miss Frisk had called it, she was right. By mid-morning the following day the Vatican pulled itself together and repeated that His Holiness was up at Castel Gandolfo purely because of the unseasonably warm weather. For once we took them at their word. No hiccup specialists seemed to be flying in after all. Far-flung cardinals showed no sign of leaving home. But the bureau had been given some bad moments. If Pius *had* popped off only a miracle would have got us the first flash.

For the moment though there was a more important matter on my mind. It was Thursday.

-12-

'How lovely!' A plume of smoke drifted in the shuttered afternoon light. 'I needed that.'

'The cigarette or…'

'Fishing for compliments?'

She had arrived at ten minutes past time, the merest scrape of the rusty bell chain. I was only feet away from the door. She came in, dumped her handbag and looked around. 'I could recommend a decorator.' But I could tell she liked the place. And being there. She moved close, taking gentle sniffs. I did the same, inhaling something unexpected.

'Turpentine. My painter's studio. It's right next door. There's a little door in the wall. I told him I'm coming back there in an hour. Wouldn't do to let the chauffeur see me come out of a different door from than the one I went in.'

'I'm flattered you're here at all.'

'You'll be more flattered in a minute.' She had her hands behind her fiddling with something. She backed off and stepped out of her dress. It was a marvellous sight, ivory skin, skimpy bra and pants. She kicked off her shoes and dropped a couple of inches. 'Here?'

'Upstairs.' I showed her the bathroom and pointed to where I'd be. That was when I should have asked if this was meant as some kind of pay-off, but of course I didn't. If I was getting into something, I didn't want to know what.

She was warm, knowing and wry, the kind of light-hearted sex I'd had with VeeVee. I guessed it must be an English style.

139

American women seemed to take things more seriously. Even with Betty it occasionally felt like a workout. Disconcerting though that she went for her objective in complete silence, the moment arriving in a ripple of shudders all down her torso, even along her legs, but without so much as an appreciative moan.

'English boarding school,' she explained. 'One joyful whimper in the night and half the dormitory would chuck pillows and yell *We know you're wanking!'*

'Handy trick.'

'Also stops you bleating out the wrong name at the right moment.'

Not wanting to flash a reaction to that, I rolled away to reach for the Luckies.

'Actually, I was beginning to think I might never do it again.'

'Lovely thing like you? Not very likely.'

'You've no idea. I really am the prisoner of the *palazzo*. Any hint of naughtiness, i.e. normality, and my obsessively possessive husband will be off to the courts. The law says that Riccardo is still able to stop me from seeing other men, from going to live in another country, even taking movie parts he doesn't approve of. Anything that makes me look morally deficient — being shown making love *on screen* — and there'll be trouble. He's been known to storm on to a set and drag me out of bed. Even out of bed with Tony Perkins, who's as camp as the Mona Lisa.'

'You have to be English to say obsessively possessive without spluttering.'

'I never splutter. God knows, it's not as though he imagined I was a virgin when we got married.'

'So when were you? A virgin, I mean.'

'Why do men always think things like that matter? Not since

my Indian days, if you must know.'

'Indian...?

'Didn't you know I was born in India?'

'When Johnny was gassing wogs?'

'Perhaps that's why I'm... warm-blooded. Girls start early out there.'

'How early?'

'Fourteen.'

'Was that legal?'

'Don't know. But it was nice.'

'Who was it? An Indian princeling?'

'Violin teacher. Clever fingers. We only did it a couple of times before my mother found out and put a stop to it.'

'Speaking of one thing leading to another, I guess I was a little hasty. Should I have...?'

'Oh, you mean.... No, that's all taken care of. By the good Dr Graeffenberg. I've had a sweet little thing made of gold popped inside me — 24-carat, of course. Riccardo could never understand why we didn't have another baby.' Her belly had just the faintest silvery snail trails of stretch marks.

'I've never heard of that.'

'The Graeffenberg ring? When I'm too old to need it any more I'll have it taken out and made into a necklace. It will remind me of all the nice times I had with it.'

'Like this?'

'You *are* fishing for compliments?' She reached for her watch. 'You've got twenty minutes to show you deserve one.'

Even so, there was time afterwards to finish our conversation.

'So pretty much the only man you can be seen with is Johnny?'

'Correct.'

'He gets off the leash, though. The other night in Jerry's he had a lady in tow. Didn't introduce me. They were with Mungo Macbeth and wife.'

'Lia. She owns Roman Kiss. Cosmetics. They should make her a saint for what she's done for womankind. That was Mitzy Faragó with Johnny. She calls him Johnny Walker.'

'Because he likes a drink?'

'Because he walks out ladies who need a walker.'

'An escort?'

'A gentleman companion to ward off stray dogs and predatory Italians.'

'What about your mother? Where does she fit in?'

'Nowhere. She's dead.'

'Oh, sorry. How?'

'I think Johnny killed her.'

'What?'

'He thought she was having an *affaire* with his aide-de-camp. She probably was. The *memsahibs* got up to a lot of mischief out there. His name was Gus, as I recall.'

'But how?'

'We were all flying somewhere. Polo match, tiger hunt, something like that. Mama was going with daddy — as I still called him then. In one of those old planes, you know, with your head sticking out. I never really liked that. Anyway, Jimmy and mama were going in his plane and me in another one that Gus was flying. Mama got annoyed because the bags got mixed up. You couldn't take much along, just some soft things shoved in a hole. So at the last minute there was a switch. I was put in Johnny's plane; Mama went with Gus.'

'And?'

'Their plane crashed. Just disappeared. They weren't found for ages.'

I guess something like that would have been easy enough to

arrange in those old string-and-wire flying days. Couple of pounds of sugar in the gas tank. Loosen a couple of nuts.

'How does he feel about someone playing around with his daughter?'

'It's OK, Shelby. He knows I'm a big girl now. But I have to say he can be... impetuous. Man of action and all that.'

'Go back to the walker bit. Would that have been Faragó as in Mitzi?' Mitzi Faragó was a minor movie star and a major marrier. Husbands she had discarded included a New York real estate magnate, a laird who owned most of the Scottish Highlands and half the slums of Glasgow, a Texan cattle king and the dictator of a relatively small Latin American country.

'Her daughter. There's another one, as you probably know, Janka. They're both lovely, too. You must meet them. They're Hungarian, like Lia. Jesus! What was that?' She snapped upright, breasts swinging enticingly.

'Just our local furniture forger at work. We've made him promise to loose off only one barrel at a time. Tell me, do you know if they wear bras?'

'Bras? Brassieres? They must. Blanka would be mobbed if she went out without one. Why do you ask?' She sniffed at the pillow. 'Next time I think I'll bring my own sheets. We princesses are picky, you know.'

'I've only got one set. The ones in shops are too small for this bed. Will you still be a princess if you're divorced?'

'I'm not getting divorced. You know that. Anyway, I wouldn't care. I just want to take my James and get out of this bloody country.'

But there *was* going to be a next time.

*

143

Cristof worked the telephone like someone petting a small animal, cuddling it against his cheek, whispering around the *toscano*. Even as close as two feet it was hard to tell what language he was in.

He hung up. 'RAI are talking to the Vatican about putting the whole show on television if the pope dies.' Although all of us in the bureau had to take on whatever stories popped up, there was a general notion that Cristof was strong on government stuff and Aldo on sport. Cristof had a cousin at *Radiotelevisione Italiana*, which had started the TV service three years earlier. Aldo had an uncle with a connection to *Ippodromo Cappanelle*, the racecourse out beyond Cinecittá, and sent in tips that Charlie sometimes followed up. One of these was being evaluated in a conversation that unreeled in counterpoint to the one about RAI. 'Tell him,' Charlie said to Aldo. 'The last nag he gave us is still running.'

'They'll have a camera right there in St Peter's.'

All the wire services were trying to work out what television might mean to news. Up until now it hadn't been much. Live coverage of the Senate hearings showed something of what television could do by more or less finishing off Joe McCarthy. But that was a couple of years back and it was yet to work up real newsgathering power. What you mainly got was just a guy in a suit reading out stuff rewritten from the wires.

'It's just advice. He doesn't fix the races.'

'One camera won't show much. That place is huge.'

'He's supposed to know the guys who *do* the fixing.'

'They've only got two cameras south of Milan.'

'Anyway, what's the horse for Saturday?'

'Wonder how much they'll ask for the rights,' said Rick.

He'd shambled in, wheezing from the stairs. 'Broad down in the *Stampa* looking for you,' he said, spotting me. 'Asked Gino if you were around. Nice looking. Semi-blonde. You getting lucky?'

'It's called Don Giovanni. Like the opera.'

*

Marsha might have looked nice to Rick. After all, she was female. I was shocked by the sight of her: hair drab, eyes swimming, zit by the side of her mouth. 'You look great,' I said.

'I didn't want to phone up to the bureau. Didn't know who might answer. Strange woman asking for you.'

We hadn't met for a while and I'd been missing her. I had come to accept that she wasn't going to bed with me and I didn't miss New York one bit, but it was always good to be with someone on the homeside wavelength. There was a knowing, flirtatious edge to our conversations and I always got in a crack about her twice-a-day habit. I, at any rate, liked to think sex might not be entirely out of the question. Meanwhile, she was a good friend and I cared about her a lot. 'How've you been? How's Ted? How's Lorenzo?'

'In response to questions two and three, fine and fine. Ted's fine because he's got a new job. Lorenzo too, at least if you can call it fine to be posted to darkest Sardinia.'

We'd talked about the *Carabinieri* routine of posting people far from home: Sardinia sounded worse than Calabria. 'So he's been accepted?'

'Sure has. And in a mere year and a bit, I should be a *Carabinieri* bride. Ted's very nobly letting me divorce *him*.'

'Well, congratulations.'

That was obviously what I had to say. The thought of having her slip out of reach behind that forbidding curtain of matrimony made me feel like I'd had my pocket picked or my by-line pilfered.

145

'Not so fast. You might not be surprised to hear that, this being Italy, matters are not straightforward. The Corpo won't let Lorenzo get married until he's twenty-six, which isn't until May 1959. Next year. We're not even *fidanzato*, yet. That's going to have to wait until I've been vetted by the wives. Wives of his fellow officers, that is. To say nothing of his family, who are less than thrilled by the whole idea. They had the daughter of some old friends lined up for him. But none of that's the real problem.'

'You're...?'

'Pregnant? No. Or not so far as I know. Always a bit unnerving that *dentro* or *fuori* routine.'

'So...?'

'Shelby, how'd you like to be my friend in court?'

'Depends what the charge is.'

'Marrying a non-Catholic. I was baptised Catholic but it was like one of those vaccinations that never took. Ted was, I dunno, nothing, really. We got married downtown in the registry office like everyone else in New York, right?'

'And now you'll be divorced.'

'But it doesn't count. Italy — the Church — won't accept that nice neat stateside divorce. I'm going to have to get my marriage to Ted annulled. Like it never happened. Wipe the slate clean. The family sent me along to their friendly *monsignore* to get it all explained.'

'But you only get annulments for, you know, non-consummation, no? Didn't you and Ted ever...?'

'Of course, we did. Before he... discovered himself. But that's not the point. I'm Catholic, right? And, as it happens, I've got the baptism certificate to prove it. Ted was not. So that's something to begin with. The Church is not hot on *mixed* marriages, as it calls them. In this case mixed-*up*. But the big thing going for me — as the family *monsignore* explained — is that Ted was, well....'

'That way.'

'And I didn't know it when we got married. Maybe nor did he, but that's not the point. If the Church accepts that by letting me believe we were going to have a normal marriage my husband-to-be *deceived* me — there could an annulment.'

'And you'll be able to marry your bold *Carabinieri*....' The more she told me the gloomier I felt.

'As though the marriage to Ted never happened. At least if they accept my story. And if I can produce a convincing witness.'

'I see.'

'So you will? Oh, Shelby, thank you!'

*

FELICE A TESTACCIO
Puntarelle salsa d'alici
Coniglio cacciatra
Frutta di stagione

-Bit off the beaten track. My track, anyway. But they have things you don't often get in Rome. Like this rabbit.

-What is this... salad?

-*Puntarelle*? We call it chicory. Maybe endive. Gotta be fresh. That's anchovy sauce.

-I'd never have guessed. Is that one of the seven hills?

-Dunno where that number came from. Rome's built on plenty more than seven. This one here though is man-made. Ancient Roman-made. From broken up amphoras. *Amphorae*, I should say. You know, those big jars they used to keep oil in, and wine?

-You're kidding. It's about ten storeys high.

147

-Guess they got through a lot of wine.

-Some things don't change. Let me freshen your glass, then we'll go on admiring the Eternal City bottle bank.

(If an interview stretches over more than one session you can try leading a person back to things they think they have already told you about. Second time round, they forget to tread wary.)

-Why did Rick think *you* would be able to get the bureau re-opened back in 1937? I mean you, not him.

-Because Rick thinks with his balls, that's why? The Duck had just made Gianni Ciano his press and propaganda minister.

-And Gianni was?

-Gianni Ciano, Count Ciano. Mussolini's son-in-law. Married to his daughter Edda. He was in the air force. Out in Addis Ababa we used to have bottle parties in hotel rooms, then he'd fly out the next morning and drop some poison gas on the Ethiopians.

Wog-bashing Italian style. Seemed to have been a lot of it going on back in the 1930s.

-Mostly, it was me knew him.

-The goldfish bowl?

-Trouble with the goldfish idea was that Rick wanted *everyone* — not just me — to know who he'd fucked. That got to be pretty boring, even embarrassing, because, as you've probably worked out by now, he doesn't really go for regular women. Worst of all, he'd get drunk and tell everyone what I told him. Like, we know the story's true because Caddie fucked Gianni and he told her.

Which wasn't what had actually happened at that time, though it wasn't for Gianni trying.

-So, what you needed to get the bureau up and running again was permission from the press and propaganda minister, who was now none other than your old buddy Gianni.

-Rick set to working up a speech about CNW's integrity, impartiality and world-wide reach but I remembered the way Gianni had always been trying to get a look up my skirt and said I'd go alone. Twenty-five minutes to get through the flunkies at the Palazzo Chigi, two minutes sprawled in a big leather armchair and *ecco*! CNW was back in business.

(And so the news is made.)

-Well, what would you have done, Shelby? A guy with your future in his hands slings you in a chair, pulls down your pants? Says you give me what I want, I'll give you what you need. What, Shelby?

-If the minister was a guy, you mean?

(That brought out one of her eruptive guffaws. I joined in.)

-I guess Gianni thought he could have been a bit more polite about it. So he told me exactly when Italy was going to invade Greece. Helluva scoop.

-Sure must have been.

-So now you know why the Ricketts are still in business, even if we don't do a lot nowadays. Old John promised that as long as he ran Century the Ricketts would have a job. I suppose now you want to know if I fucked the Duck?

-13-

I had no compunction about lying to the Catholic church. After all, it had been lying to everyone for a couple of thousand years. What were they going to do? Bring back the Inquisition?

It was disappointing to find that the address Marsha came up with was not in the sacred heart of Vatican City but a nondescript office building along the Tevere from Castel Sant'Angelo, another bit of Holy See real estate. We had decided arriving separately would look less collusive and she was already there, alone at a kind of bar table in the middle of the room.

I had also imagined red-robed cardinals and a jury of hooded monks. Instead, I found a fat Irishman about sixty with a scarlet trim to the cassock stretched across his bulging belly, a purple sash cinching him like an Easter egg. 'My name is Monsignor Doolan,' he said, hauling out a pack of *Nazionales* from the depths of his robe and firing one up. 'I am an Apostolic Pronotary from the Holy Commission on Matrimony. You address me as *Reverendissimo Signore*.'

A *sigarone* of the church, even if he did look like he needed to be run through a carwash. The upper part of his cassock bore a cloud pattern of faded food stains, the lower was sprinkled with *Nazionale* fallout. The statement I had sworn out before a *notario* was in front of him.

The only other presence was a cleric of some kind, evidently the court clerk, who looked as though he could be one of Cristof's relatives, cadaverous and conspiratorial. He had opened the door to me and now launched the proceedings with a gabbled prayer in Latin. The two clerics crossed themselves. So did Marsha, with a straight face, too.

'This matter has been assigned to me,' said Monsignor Doolan. 'For the obvious reason that, like the petitioner and yourself, I speak English.' He didn't bother to look at Marsha, just jerked his head towards her while glaring at me. 'My report to the commission will be submitted in Italian, of course.'

'Of course,' I said. '*Reverendissimo Signor.*'

I had been given an idea of what to expect by the *avvocato* specialising in canon law who had written up Marsha's petition: a good business to be in, judging by the crowd in his waiting room.

The Cristof look-alike began to read out a document in Italian. Doolan shut him up with a wave.

'Don't need to hear all that. I'll decide later what's got to be written down. The purpose of this hearing, as I'm sure you've been advised, is to allow the Holy Commission to see if the facts to which the petitioner... and you as her witness have testified to, are consistent with the account of the marriage that will be taken from the... other party by my counterpart in New York.'

I was a little surprised when Marsha told me Ted was helping out with our little conspiracy. I suppose he really didn't have much choice, given the pressure she could have applied if she had been the wrong sort of wronged wife.

She was in my line of sight beyond the *Reverendissimo*, who was shuffling papers, cranking himself up into inquisitorial mode.

Her hair was swept back into a virtuous bun and the planes of her face highlighted by soft light from a window high on the wall. The zit had cleared up, her skin looked scrubbed and fresh. I felt a distinct flick of arousal, inappropriate in the circumstances but nothing new.

In the time we had spent together while she had been plotting her moves, scripting our responses and keeping the canon lawyers up to the mark I had become disconcertingly captivated by Marsha. This was a formidable lady, powered by a steely sense of purpose and determination, who might well be wasted on Lorenzo. I had begun to wonder how things might have gone if I had shown up in Rome a few weeks earlier. Before she had met her young cop. That reflection didn't get dwelt on too long. In the news story of my life, marriage was well down the second take. I preferred the version in which she seemed to glow like the glass Jesus of Roghudi, only erotic.

'You are not of the Holy Faith, Mr Shelby?'

'No, *Reverendissimo Signore.*'

'Your deposition says you were baptised in the Congregational Church, a rite I am not familiar with.' Me neither. My parents, although straight-up, swing-voting Americans in most other respects, were blithely irreligious. They told me they knew they had to do *something* after I had been born and simply chose the nearest church. That was in what they called their Early Bohemian Period, before they faced up to a life of small-town schoolteachering and lawyering.

'Nevertheless,' the pro-notary went on. 'You recognise the sanctity of the Holy Writ and will not object to swearing an oath to tell the truth?' Father Cristof-like produced a book with a greasy-looking cover and we got that over with. The whole procedure was a joke, of course, even without thinking about its total irrelevance. Any kid who had seen a Perry Mason movie would know that Marsha ought not be allowed to hear my evidence before giving her own. But the ham-fisted grilling lurched on: how long had I known the parties concerned, did I believe them to be of good character, was I aware that the marriage they had embarked on was what the church would consider a *productive union*?

This, I had been prepped by the *avoccado*, was the critical issue. By letting Marsha believe she was signing up to a 'normal' union, then failing to provide the input necessary to ensure it Ted had deceived her. 'I'm not sure I understand, *Reverendissimo Signore*.'

'Children. Did they intend to have children?'

'Mrs Ford often told me of her wish to have a large family. She believed Mr Ford would make an excellent father.'

Implicitly, had she known he meant to prevent her from conceiving by withholding his contribution she would never have agreed to marry him.

'And did she tell you that the husband had begun refusing to have sexual relations with her?'

'She told me on several occasions that Mr Ford refused to help her become pregnant. I assumed that meant he was insisting on contraception.' A greater sin, of course, in the eyes of the church than merely declining to co-operate.

It had obviously occurred to the *Reverendissimo Signore* that there were indications here of an overly familiar relationship.

'And have you, Mr Shelby, and the petitioner here indulged in sexual relations?'

The best response seemed to be an expression of mild indignation and the sorry truth. 'Certainly not.'

That brought on a *Nazionale* break and a bout of paper fiddling.

I didn't see that my flat denial left much scope for follow-ups, but the salacious old crook was out to enjoy himself.

'And the husband, Mr Ford? Have you ever had sexual relations with *him*?'

153

Marsha had been careful to keep Ted's switch of sexual direction out of her claim. This time I allowed myself a show of mild resentment at being asked such a thing. 'Most certainly not!'

That seemed to be it as far as I was concerned. I could go if I wanted to, said the *Reverendissimo,* or I could stay.

I wasn't going to leave Marsha to his drooling attention so I swapped places with her and watched as she politely stonewalled him.

I thought the Apostolic Pro-notary might expect some sort of compliment on his performance, so when Marsha was through and getting herself together I went up to the bench and offered him a Lucky that he probably wouldn't have been able to taste after what he'd been burning. But he was soon expelling its product appreciatively. 'You're one of those news fellers, aren't you, son? Tell me, do you ever get any good tips for out at Cappannelle?'

Smoke, booze, second-hand sex and backing losers. The guy might never have left Dublin. 'Don't know about *good* ones, *Reverendissimo Signore.*'

'But you do hear things? I bet you fellers do.'

I tried to remember the arcane descant of those unrelated conversations in the bureau when half of us were talking about Radiodiffuzione and the others about Aldo's horse for Saturday? Something operatic. *Don...Don...* 'Only one I heard lately was Don Pasquale.'

'Don Pasquale? I'll have look in the paper. See if he's got some form.'

I had to get back, so Marsha and I grabbed a quick coffee nearby.

'I think I need a cigarette,' she said. So did I. But as I felt in my pocket I got a flash of the Lucky pack slipping into the greasy black folds of the cassock. Pilfering old fraud. 'Sorry.'

'That's OK. Anyway, that was pretty damn noble of you, Shel.'

'Let's hope it works out.'

'It better. But just in case it doesn't... Remember what you asked me? Before?'

'Oh, shit.'

'It wouldn't be so bad if it was just a *bit* short of the wedding date. Do you know anyone?'

'Not in Rome. Probably wouldn't be a great idea anyway, here.' When I'd first arrived I'd asked Charlie about medical insurance, health care stuff. Best insurance policy in Italy, he said, was a plane ticket to London.

'Pretty soon there's going to be a pill to prevent this, you know. One you take before, I mean. They're trying it out in Puerto Rico. There was a mailer about it.'

'I wish they'd tried it out on me. Oh, Shelby, why is it so damn hard being a woman?'

*

It only took an hour or so to get through to Adam and Eve Mews from the *Stampa*. Jeremy picked up. 'Nice to hear from you, old man', he said, as though we'd seen each other last week. 'VeeVee's not in, I'm afraid.'

'I really wanted to speak to Sally.'

'Hello, stranger. Are you coming back to see us?'

'Afraid not.'

I wasn't sure if Sally believed that the matter did not involve me personally, but she was understanding and business-like.

'Call me day after tomorrow to see if I've fixed it up. Can I take it there won't be a problem with the money? Hold on, Jeremy wants a word.'

155

'Hello again, old chap. Do I gather that someone's going to be coming over this way? Mind if I ask a favour? Could you send the Jaguar's logbook along with her?' The ownership document he would need to sell the car.

'If I can find it, I'll dig it out.'

Hell I would.

-14-

I saw what Arabella meant about Blanka Faragó being arrested if she went out without a bra. In a city fixated on tits, her undulations would draw a bigger crowd than a five-car pile-up. It wasn't very different even when she *was* in her cups — her size DD cups that is — especially when playing the violin. Tilting up her bowing elbow hoisted one breast half-way out of the bodice of her dress. There was the flash of a coppery aureole before she bore down on the strings and it popped back where it belonged.

'Gypsy music, *dahlink*,' said her proud mother alongside me, blonde head jerking to the strident *czardas*. '*Vairy* Hungarian.' Mitzi was sizing me up, sharp dark eyes fringed with lashes like electrical wires. 'You like how my Blanka play?'

We were in a *trattoria* near the *Fontana di Trevi*, one of the more extravagant bits of baroque street art around town. It was a Hungarian joint, the Faragós obviously favoured customers. The musicians, a guy on cimbalom, another with a drum like a big tambourine, were happily bopping along with Blanka. She must have borrowed the fiddle from the leader, who was now plucking another stringed something. Waiters hustled around, popping open bottles of sugary Hungarian bubbles.

This was a rare outing with Arabella, although it was supposed to seem — especially to anyone making notes on behalf of Prince Riccardo — that she was being escorted by her father and that I was with Blanka's sister Janka, who was on my other side. The Macbeths were across the table. As the evening went on I should be able to ease over there and into the seat next to Arabella presently occupied by Murdo.

'Janka could be a beard for us,' Arabella had said, a Thursday back. 'A decoy. You know, in the movies you think the chap with the beard has to be the villain but it's actually the clean-shaven one. Like when Ava Gardner lets those photographers take pictures of her with her hairdresser, she's setting him up as the beard. She's actually sleeping with... well, whoever's *not* got the beard.'

'I'd have to pretend I was... doing it with Janka.'

'People would think you must be rich.'

'Would you care to explain to her?'

*

She really did bring her own sheet the second time, just the one, producing it from a Via Condotti shopping bag. She flicked mine onto the floor and smoothed the clean one over the bed. It was only just large enough.

I had never got to spend time with an actress before and I soon saw that while newsfolk were slightly off-kilter, these professional impersonators had them beat hollow, this one anyway. Arabella's urge to *show* far outpaced any urge to *tell* that I had ever felt. I'd seen it when we first met at Cinecittà and she wanted to keep herself in character for the make-up women. When she had flicked that switch into acting — *actressing*, really, since she wasn't playing anyone other than herself — expressions, movements, voice all seemed to be operated by a different being.

Something else also took a while to tune into, too. She was as solipsistic as a cat but disarmingly open about her moves and motives. 'I said that because I wanted him to think...' The acting never stopped. The actressing, anyway.

Now, monitoring Mitzi's metallic chatter, I wondered if I dared bring up the fascinating morsel Arabella had produced last Thursday when this outing was being planned.

'Apart from their being enormous fun, I need to keep in with Mitzi. She's every bit as helpful with a girl's best friends as Lia is with a girl's best features.'

I must have looked dumb.

'You know...

> *A kiss on the hand may be quite continental*
> *But diamonds are a girl's best friend.'*

Hard to imagine anyone looking less like Marilyn Monroe, thank God, than this sleek English brunette with nothing on, but the breathy delivery was a tribute to whoever taught her acting.

'I still don't get it.'

'The family jewels, my dear. If I need to move them around, Mitzi's the one to go to. Faragó Express.'

She explained. Marriage and divorce on the international scale practised by the Faragós meant that they spent a lot of time travelling. 'Eleven husbands between them at last count but don't ask me who's in the lead.'

Whenever there were lawyers to be consulted, the spoils of divorce shared out, new candidates up for auditions, Mitzi and her girls moved as one. As they did when going about the other family business, a line of costume jewellery. 'Mitzi's Marvels. Even she calls them junk *dahlink*, but a lot of people like them. See? These earrings.'

'They look great. Specially when they're all you've got on.'

'I was too overwhelmed by lust to take them off. Anyway, rocketing around the world with their boxfuls of samples, the girls can always find room for a few pieces of the real thing. Just as a favour for friends. My last trip to America all my big pieces

159

went Faragó Express both ways. Saved an awful lot of bother.'

'Big pieces?'

'The Bergamonte jewels. Riccardo's family. Heirlooms. Worth millions. That's the point. You're spared all that tiresome tax and duty stuff.'

'You've still got the family jewels?'

'Well, I'm still family.'

I got it. There had been a raft of stories about Hollywood stars getting stuck with big customs pay-outs for items they were bringing back from Europe, fur coats on a wifely back, diamond engagement rings on a glamorous fiancée. Sure they might be personal items, gifts, but duty had to be paid just the same. In Europe, it worked the other way. People were caught at ports trying to smuggle out stuff that might have been classed as national treasure. Or that would imply they must be richer than their tax return suggested. Or that they obviously intended to sell abroad without declaring the proceeds.

'You can imagine what it's like when those three launch their act on some tiresome little customs man. "My samples *dahlinks* — pure junk! Nothing but lovely junk. Look, here's the factory invoice."—And the terrible twins waving their personal attributes around, dangling Mitzi's Marvels over those massive *lumps*, their clients' real stuff mixed up with the junk.'

'They're not twins are they?'

'Don't be so literal. Point is, they get away with it. They get to New York or wherever, the contessa's tiara or the movie star's diamond necklace goes into a safebox. They tell her where to pick up the key.'

'And collect their fee?'

'They'll have got that already.'

'But what if they just walked off with the stuff?'

'Darling! They're not *dishonest*.'

160

*

Janka, who hadn't really entered into the spirit of her part, went over to the band and rustled up another fiddle. Freed, I achieved my objective of getting alongside Arabella but Mungo stayed put on her far side. She'd been telling him about her visits to the invaluable Signor Vestiglio, her portrait painter. Far as I was concerned, he was the real beard.

'There do seem to be a lot of interesting people living in Via Margutta,' she said, face straight, eyes glinting with mischief. 'There's that big chap like an armchair in a suit that I've seen out at Cinecittá. Sometimes with Giulietta Masina.'

'That's Fellini,' said Mungo. 'They're married. Can't remember his first name. Pain in the arse. They asked me to look over the *La Strada* footage when he was directing. But that was all they had. Footage.'

'No script?'

'Few scribbles. I'd have had to start too far back to make much difference.'

The band had got the spirit, hammers dancing across the cimbalom keys, drum thumping to the dissonant violins. Blanka and Janka tossed their hair about, elbows jerking, eyes flicking over to pick up on each other's fingering. Even the waiters began to stomp their feet.

Huddled beneath the barrage I said to Lia, 'I suppose you know Mitzi from Hungary?'

'No, from the camps.' The displaced persons camps that thousands of refugees had been herded into at the end of the war. No welcome in Vienna that time around. Newsreel pictures swam into mind of grey winter, Soviet soldiers, large-eyed children, women in babushkas. 'She helped my mother.'

Lia's mother was someone else I wanted to hear about. It seemed she was actually the one who had launched the

161

cosmetics business, whipping up formulas in her apartment kitchen. 'That's true. She was scientist, chemist. Beauty products were Hungarian specialty, you know. Before war.'

'Before you were born.'

That was good for a tinkly laugh. 'Not quite, *dahlink*. Anyway, Mitzi was there to help. She had worked in laboratory in Budapest, doing what I don't know. But she knew all the formulas. Skin creams, make up. Even nail polish. But mama had to find the ingredients and do all the blending.'

'I don't get what you mean by she *knew* the formulas.' Formulae, actually, but who says that?

'Mitzi just remembered them. Remembered everything. She calls it photographic memory. She can even remember all the men that she and the girls have married.'

'I was wondering how old she might be.'

'She's older than my mother.'

'How old's your mother.'

'She won't tell me. But if the date in her passport is correct I was born when she was nine.'

The bubbles were doing their work all round. Johnny came over and took Lia off to dance. Mitzi beckoned me back to her side. 'You don't like my daughter?'

'She's great. What a pity she's married.'

'Not *vairy* married. We go to Las Vegas, next trip back, get new divorce. Have those other naughty girls been telling you about my little hobby?'

She told me more than she really should have, considering she knew what I did for a living. But I guess she also knew that being with Arabella meant I was in their sealed circle. It wasn't a particularly comfortable thought, even if I didn't know what I might be able to do with anything Mitzi was telling me. It wasn't a wire service story.

Although it sure would be one if they ever got caught.

'My God,' I said. 'I hope you don't ever get the stuff mixed up. You know, deliver the countess's bracelet to the actor's wife. Or his girlfriend.'

She giggled. 'Never happen, *dahlink*. Photographic memory. *Shit!*'

Blanka's breastworks had come adrift. Mitzi shouted something in Hungarian to a waiter. The man stepped up behind the fiddling sisters, reached over Blanka's shoulder, took her nipple delicately between forefinger and thumb and guided the floppy package back into its container. Applause rippled around the room. He took a bow.

In the scrimmage of farewells at the door, I tried to nibble Arabella's ear and nearly broke a tooth on her ear-ring. 'Careful. These ones are real.'

Inside the restaurant the lights had been turned down. I could see Blanka pinning the waiter to a wall with her chest. Outside, Janka wandered shoeless across to the fountain and stuck her feet in the water. In the street leading into the piazza, a car flashed its lights. The Bergamonte driver.

'Mitzi liked you, by the way. She told me in the loo.'

'Is that important?'

'Could be. Better than if she didn't.'

'Thursday?'

'Wouldn't miss for worlds.'

-15-

Someone told me that the Piazza del Popolo worked like a giant sundial, hours marked by the shadow of the huge Egyptian obelisk at its centre. I could never grasp the idea, but I liked it down there anyway and I sometimes went down to the big cafe opposite the main *Caserna di Carabinieri* for breakfast on the terrace and a look through the newspapers. There were always uniforms there, waiters bleating *buon giorno colonello, capitano*. Getting up to leave I found Rick sitting a few tables behind me, huddled with a guy wearing a homburg hat and those old-style *pince-nez* eyeglasses. I'd never seen them outside a *telefono bianco*.

I turned towards them but Rick spotted me and wagged his head so I swerved out on to the sidewalk. The other guy's attention had been diverted, though; he twisted round to give me a once-over. Hitlerish moustache. Doughy face that would have looked silly even without the dumb glasses. Guess who.

I caught up with Rick in the *Stampa*. He shuffled his feet like a tired old *carrozza* nag. 'Just a contact I knew years ago. One of those guys that might come in handy some day.' I was a little sorry for him. Much of the awe I'd once felt had ebbed away. If he got lucky with Galeazzo-Lisi it might come back.

*

'Problem,' said Charlie. 'His Holiness is not at home. Least not the home where he's supposed to be.' He had been listening on the spare earpiece of the tipolini phone. Cristof was still whispering into the handset. 'Seems he stayed up at Gandolfo. Serve us right for believing the *Sala*-bloody-*Stampa*.' Was *tmesis* an occupational requirement? Might it be catching? 'They told us nearly a week ago that he was back in the Vatican.'

'Does it matter?'

'Might,' said Cristof, hanging up. 'If there's a reason for them to lie.'

'Not that they need a reason. But what if the old bugger is too sick to be moved?' Charlie was rattled. The worldwide surge of attention caused by the earlier health alert meant that New York expected us to get out the first word that the old boy had popped his satin slippers.

'If our *tipolini* in the Vatican didn't even know he wasn't there how can we rely on them for word of his final exit?'

'They did know. They say we didn't ask them.'

'We shouldn't have to ask them. We can't even get them on the phone most of the time.'

'We did ask the *Sala*.'

'And they deliberately misled us, the pious fucking frauds.' Did that count as *tmesis* or merely an emphatic adjective? Charlie swung round on me. 'You'd better get up to Gandolfo.'

'And do what?'

'Be sure you've got plenty *gettoni*.'

*

Not only Century felt that this time there might be more to the papal indisposition than hiccups. A few dubious characters were loitering in the little piazza across from the *castello*, one with a silly moustache. 'Hello, old boy. Thought I'd find you here.'

'Likewise, Digby. And everyone else.' I nodded to a couple of familiar faces from the *Stampa*. Old Apathy and UP were there.

ANSA, too. 'She's over there,' said Digby but I'd already spotted Lucy, decorous for the occasion in a longish skirt.

She twirled. 'Maybe they ask me in.'

'You should have told us you were coming. I could have given you a ride.'

'Came with them.' She waved at a couple of *scattini* I knew by sight. 'Fernando say no hope of getting anything but I come anyway — *scattina!*'

Every so often a limo would roll to the *portone* in the orange-pink facade and the photographers eddied around it like blown leaves. Flashlight salvos illuminated the startled face of a Vatican *sigarone* or some guy delivering a package. If there were doctors in attendance they must already be inside.

Fernando was probably right. The chance of anyone, let alone a photographer, being allowed into the *castello* was nil, and if the pope did go back to Rome it would be in a curtained limousine. Or an ambulance. Or a hearse.

Despite bulletins of stultifying blandness from the *Sala Stampa* it became accepted that the pope was on the way out. 'They're coming,' said Charlie next day. 'The scarlet horde.' The princes of the church were packing their bags again.

So were the princes of news. 'Who are we getting?'

'Brad Hooper for one.'

'As anticipated. And for two?'

'Sylvia Silver.'

'The Bitch of Broadway? The Josephine McCarthy of the Celebrity Bedroom? Sabre-tooth Tiger of the Scandal Mags?'

Sylvia Silver wrote a thrice-weekly column syndicated to Century clients all around the world. Heavy on showbiz and Republican politics, it often packed a well-informed sting amid the saggy prose. She also socked it to straying notables with pieces in outlandish ragmags like *Confidential* and *Whisper*. In

166

addition, she was on the panel of a television show called *Second Time Around* where they tried to game divorcees into remarrying a partner that they had just shed.

'Never met her. Have you?'

'Couple of times. She's come over here, sticking it to celebrity adulterers. First Ingrid Bergman and Roberto Rosellini, then Liz Taylor and that Eddie Fisher. Pretty rich, if what they say about her and Old John is true.' Which was, presumably, the usual stuff about sexual patronage.

'Esther over at the *Daily American* feeds her stuff. Also, I think she and Rick had a torrid moment a few years back.'

'Oh yeah, Rick. Lucy says he's taken to hanging around Newspix.'

'That where the old sod's got to, is it?' If Charlie did know about the Galeazzo-Lisi plot he wasn't letting on.

Cristof claimed to have worked something out with a *tipolino* inside the Castello. He sketched out the facade with its little clock-tower. 'This is where His Holiness must be. But even if he's not, doesn't matter. The important window for us is *this*.' He drew an arrow on the rightmost one on the second floor. 'Every day at *mezzogiorno e mezza* — half-past noon, right? — one of the shutters will open and close quickly. Just once. That means the old chap is still OK. Still alive, that is. Understand?'

It was as well to know that Pius was still alive. If the suspense was to be prolonged a rumour that he had popped off could easily spark a headline somewhere that we would have to either match or refute.

'Then the same thing in the evening at half-past six. But if one time it doesn't happen, don't worry. Our guy might simply not have been able to get away.'

'From what?'

'Emptying the pope's bedpan. More important is if *both* shutters open-close, open-close quickly. Like that.' He showed me with his hands. 'He's dead. The pope, that is. Will you go up today?'

Cristof himself wouldn't get a turn. Charlie kept him in Rome because some of the *tipolini* would not speak to anyone else. 'Stay until eleven. They all go to bed then.'

'What about tomorrow, Thursday?'

'Aldo.'

*

If I hadn't been able to make Thursday with Arabella there was no way to let her know. Calls to the *palazzo* would have been reported to Riccardo. Trying to leave a message at Cinecittá would have been as useful as nailing it to a tree in the Villa Borghese. But she was only a few minutes later than usual, peeling off her top as she went up the stairs ahead of me, heading for the bathroom. I sat and watched her sprinkle herself with the leaky hand-shower. 'Signor Vestiglio had that Fellini chap with him when I got there today. He really is spooky. Fellini, I mean. Looked me over as though he was sizing me up for a Dracula movie. He inspected the painting — which is almost finished. Then just sloped off with barely an *arriverderci*.'

'Lets his art speak for him.' I passed her one of the two bath towels I owned. Seemed a pity to cover up all that ivory splendour. But it wasn't for long.

Afterwards, smoke wafting up from our Luckies, she said, 'Riccardo's on his way back to Rome. James, too. He'll have some fancy dress stuff to do if the pope pops off.'

A little chill came over parts that had just been feeling warm and content. 'Which means?'

'This might not be so easy. Thursdays.'

'It's not the only day of the week.'

There was more to come. 'I need to be... friendly with Riccardo for a while. Get him to be reasonable about James.'

'Isn't that what you're working on already?'

'Yes, but there's a complication. I've started to talk about something in Hollywood, and if it were to happen I'd want James to come with me. The agreement that's waiting to be approved by the court says that he can't be taken out of Italy without Riccardo's permission. If I couldn't take him with me, I wouldn't be able to go anywhere.'

'Such as Hollywood?.'

'I didn't really set the place on fire first time around. Johnny rather got in the way, I think. Too protective.'

'Rightly so. You were young and innocent.'

'Well, young*er*. I'd like to give it another shot.'

She'd been getting herself back together during the conversation. She sat in her more-or-less token underwear, head back, little eye-dropper poised. Blink-blink.

'Magicali. Lia's miracle drops. Makes eyes shine like headlights. Makes me feel good, too. Just like you.'

That brought the warmth back. 'What's the movie? How long would you need to go for?'

'One of those Agatha Christies. I'm to be an unfaithful aristocratic wife. And don't you dare say type-casting. But it might never happen. Plenty of false starts in this business.'

'Meanwhile, next Thursday?'

'As you say, it's not the only day. Never fear, my pet. Love will find a way.'

'Is that Shakespeare?' More like something to be embroidered on a cushion. But it was a bellringer for me. That weighty word, up for the first time.

The vigil at the *castello* settled into routine, reinforcements trickling in from all over. Within a few days, the two bars in town made enough for their owners to retire on and the one decent *trattoria* doubled its prices. Papal gendarmes, dark uniforms musty in the fall sunshine, strung a barrier along the curb and a clerical flunky reminded the motley crew milling around that it represented a frontier of the Holy See. The clock stopped chiming and its face no longer lit up at sunset.

Other news outfits had their own early warning systems. Guys would sit up on the fountain in the middle of the piazza, nonchalantly studying the *palazzo* facade. Every so often a shutter — not ours — would open or close. Vases of flowers appeared on window ledges or weren't there next time I looked. In the October early dark, lights flicked on and off, setting the watchers muttering. Something that to one correspondent might mean *he's gone* told another, *he's going to make it through the night and you can go home.*

Our bedpan guy seemed pretty dependable. When he couldn't make his daytime move he usually caught up in the evening. If the first signal came through, I would stroll around the lake on the edge of town to a little hotel where they served lunch by the water. After a few visits, they let me use their phone, even took messages. If the evening bedpan bulletin gave the OK I would head back to Rome.

*

Lucy kept on popping up to Gandolfo for a few hours at a time. It was warmer than usual for October and far more pleasant up in the hills than in the sweaty streets of the city. A few days in, we went to have dinner by the lake before starting back to town. We wandered back to the piazza for a last check around when

170

a vibe fluttered through the huddled hordes. There was a surge over to the barrier, dozens of reporters wide-eyed for a sign. Photographers bathed the scene in futile flashes.

The front of the palazzo sprang to life like one of those medieval town clocks striking the angelus: shutters crashed open or slammed shut. Curtains were pulled across some windows from the right, others from the left. Figures popped up, waved handkerchiefs and disappeared. Lights flicked on and off. Gibbering plaintively, the watchers strained to catch the signal meant for them.

The room over the *portone* stayed buttoned down, edged with a dim glow from within. So did our window, the second floor right. 'What do you make of it?' I asked Lucy who was fiddling with a Leica.

'*Porca miseria!*' Her flash hadn't worked. It was one of those electronic packs that had now completely replaced flashbulbs but were just as undependable. Most of the reporters, pockets jangling with *gettone*, took off for the bars to phone through whatever message they thought they had received. I was already turning away when the shutters on *our* window swung open, first one then the other. I heard the slam and rattle of the catch as they closed again, barely aware that Lucy's flash had popped. I bolted for the hotel.

'Jesus!' said Charlie. 'Can we go with it?'

'Depends how much confidence Cristof has in his bedpan guy. I think he did his stuff, but there was a lot of shutter activity a bit earlier, too. Anything from the Sala?'

'Nope.'

'I'm going to file it anyway. You decide whether it goes out. Ready?'

> FLASH. POPE PIUS TWELVE DIED APPROXIMATELY 0200 ROME TIME TODAY.

*

The sun was coming up when we drove back down to the city. A flunky had come out about four o'clock and told the bleary-eyed assembly that death had occurred at 0352. No one argued, but no one believed him either. We thought it must have been that earlier time.

There would be nine days of mourning before the burial in St Peter's, the flunky said. The body would be taken to Rome in a few hours' time and once prepared would lie in state in the Basilica. God bless you all.

I took a shower, went in to the office and looked up the file. I said to Charlie, 'You sat on my flash for a while.' I looked some more. 'Apathy got a beat. By three fucking minutes.'

'We didn't dare put it out until we got confirmation.'

'From?'

'Miss Frisk.'

And so the news is made.

-16-

At two pm the following day I was fighting my way out of Roman Catholicism's spiritual birthplace, the Papal Archbasilica of San Giovanni in Laterano on the eastern outskirts of the city. In a pope's notional role as Bishop of Rome, this was the church where he hung up his rosary beads, and where Pius's last journey back to St Peter's hit the road.

The procession led off without the formality of forming up, well outdistanced by a squad of *Carabinieri* motorbikes. Uniforms of all kinds lined the route, wrestling back mourners whenever they made a run for the hearse that trundled along at walking pace, Pius robed and mitred on show through the glass side panels. Before and behind, a contingent of embarrassed- looking guys in musty red uniforms and tarnished brass helmets shambled along: the *Guardia Nobile*, one of them, presumably, Prince Riccardo. Then came a clutch of cardinals and bishops, some in wheelchairs, and troupe after pious troupe of monks and friars: Franciscans in brown robes, Dominicans and Benedictines in black and white, the slap of their sandals like heavy rain. Nuns in flocks like migrating penguins surged along the sidewalk, clacking their beads to clear the way.

It was a no-by-line gang bang for us leg-men. Aldo and Cristof were also moving along with the procession. Whenever it stalled we would duck into a bar to phone over a few resentful pars to Charlie, headphones on at the Teletype knitting our accounts together for the soda jerk. Even if out in

Ohio he would more likely be Methodist or Mormon than Catholic.

It took until mid-afternoon to get as far as Via Labicana, where dreary apartment blocks threw some welcome shade. Three or four bands in the straggling procession each played its own dirge at its own tempo then fell back on old favourites, like The Triumphal March from *Aida*. Down Via Cavour we trotted, the ruined gasworks silhouette of the Coliseum on our left, past the sunbaked Forum into Piazza Venezia and the ludicrous *macchina di scrivere* bulk of the Vittorio Emanuele monument.

Given my feelings about this kind of thing, it would have been a pushover to parody this lush extravaganza of grief. Much the same kind of mob would have swarmed out to cheer the Blackshirts only a few years back. But the emotion surging through the crowds like floodwater was the real thing. Young men dripping tears on the lapels of their smart suits. Old women chanting prayers aloud. Wide-eyed schoolkids crossing themselves in unison.

Down the Corso Vittorio Emanuele we straggled, across the Tiber and up the Via della Conciliazione. St Peter's Square, which is actually the shape of an old fashioned keyhole, was jammed from one towering Bernini colonnade across to the other. The cortege pressed on through, over to the left of the Basilica, where Swiss guards in their silly costume channelled it through the Petriano Entrance into Vatican City.

I caught up with Aldo and Cristof looking over a large RAI truck full of television gear. Lucy and a couple of her buddies from Newspix were there too, watching some guys manhandling a television camera only slightly smaller than my Fiat.

'These will be the only pictures, Aldo said. 'They're not going to let newsreel inside. Movie cameras too noisy. These guys are

174

gonna be here all night, get their stuff in before the *sampietrini* set up the display.' The display being Pius, who would lie in state in the nave of the Basilica for a week of carefully managed homage.

The crowd started to thin. I made a modest executive decision and sent the others off to phone Charlie and ask if they could quit for the day. 'Tell him I'll hang on here for a while in case there's something.'

'I stay, too,' said Lucy. 'No, maybe we go have coffee. Come back later.' We walked a few hundred metres down Conciliazione and found a bar in a side street. A post office opposite was trying to close in the face of a rabid crowd of pilgrims demanding stamps for their holy postcards.

'How's Fernando?'

'We no speak.'

'Oh? Why?'

'No matter.'

We found other things to chat about, and as the light began to fade she said, 'Go back now. Better in dark.'

The temperature stayed high even after sunset. Over to our right was the bland backside of the Palazzo Sixtus V named, as my hasty research had established, for the pope who pronounced the excommunication of Queen Elizabeth I. Couldn't have worried her much. She wasn't Catholic by then. He also made contraception a mortal sin and wanted adultery punished by death.

The *palazzo* housed the papal apartments that were marked out by the unassertive balcony on the upper floor at which Pius made carefully staged appearances at Easter and Christmas. The entire building was dark. We strolled around for a while, Lucy banging off an occasional shot, me interviewing a pilgrim here and there in the hope of finding a story that might fix my

175

by-line starvation,

'*Ecco-la!*' she grabbed my arm. A light had come on in the apartments. '*Papa* bedroom!' yelped Lucy. There was a Leica around her neck but she rummaged in her bag for another one.

'Colour,' she said, checking its film counter. She snapped in a stubby wide-angle lens, sat down on the cobbles, an elbow braced on each knee. I heard her whispering off the seconds of a long exposure. It would be an eloquent shot, the single light shining out in the broad, austere Renaissance facade. Beyond, dying shreds of sunset hung in the sky.

We took a cab back to Newspix and I switched on the Teletype there. First a servicer:

> FOLLOWING TO GO WITH NEWSPIX SHOTS CAPTIONED
> "POPE BEDROOM"

Then:

> 10:10:58. BULLETIN NEW LEAD POPE. SHELBY STONE.
> VATICAN CITY.
> THE LATE POPE PIUS XII LAY AT REST IN HIS APARTMENT
> OVERLOOKING ST PETER'S BASILICA TONIGHT, HOURS
> AFTER HIS DEATH IN NEARBY CASTEL GANDOLFO.

With Castel Gandolfo as one word it would have been twenty-three. The picture and idea of the old boy back in his own bed meant most papers would change the intros on their bull stories. Maybe even stick up my by-line.

*

The *Stampa* was seething. Even the shitpickers had visiting firemen to entertain, interpret for and feed material to. Pius's death and succession were shaping up as a gaudy ecclesiastical extravaganza of purple mourning, white smoke and intrigue that would run for weeks. The newsstands I passed on the way over were splattered with headlines. *End Of An Era. Christian World Mourns. Crowned Heads Bow in Grief. Momentous Funeral*

Suspense Over Successor. Airlines around the world were selling out of first-class seats to Rome, celebrity reporters squeezed alongside cardinals, bishops and politicians. Out at Ciampino, Rita counted them in and fired off bulletins to Lima, San Paolo, Mexico, Melbourne, Tokyo, Seattle: Your local boy landed safely.

The night before, she had come into the bar with a couple of New York *Daily News* photographers toting huge police-beat quarter-plate Speed Graphics, a breath of East 42nd Street in their broad lapel suits and big shoes. As well as the main assignment they were expected to get a shot of everyone from the New York diocese entitled to wear a dog collar or a wimple.

Rick was drinking with Brad Hooper, whom I'd only glimpsed back at head office, never spoken to. He was shorter than Rick but even broader. They turned around, swinging apart like a *portone*, to frame a small blonde with big hair who had been obscured by their bulk. She pushed a spread of crimson fingers at me, a vulture claw, talons dipped in blood. 'Hi! Sylvia Silver.' Who else?

The talons dragged me off behind a pillar, Rick and Brad shambling along behind. We passed a table-full of Germans crouched over maps like they were getting ready to send in the *panzers*. 'You're the guy that's going to save me, right? Okay, so Brad and I missed the big parade. But thanks to Rick here we're gonna get what everyone's after. The pope's last minutes. Deathbed pictures. It'll be the sensation of the century. Well worth the forty grand.'

The what? A guilty flicker ran across all three faces. I kept mine straight.

'I'm gonna write the pope package. Not just my column. All the copy to go with these pictures. *Life* magazine is holding six pages, even though we're not giving it to them exclusive.

Syndication is feeling out glossies everywhere, London, Paris, Madrid, Buenos Aires. But I'm gonna need input. You were up there. Those harrowing last hours at Castel Gondola. We'll reprise that great procession into town.' She said rep*reeze*. 'I need you to tell me stuff you couldn't get into the news story. You know, your own feelings being in the streets, the crowd.'

'Castel *Gandolfo*. But yes, sure.' Who was I to stand in the way of a woman who had Old John's ear? Or whatever.

'I'll get down to work on the big one soon as Rick collects the stuff from you-know-who. We need to get it across well before the actual funeral. Sunday, right?'

'Seven days to go.'

'That'll be Brad's big moment. Crowned heads. Princes of the Church. Towering world figures. Secretary of State Dulles. It'll be the jerk-off piece of all time.'

Brad saw me looking at the typewriter he'd carried over. The case was the same size and shape of my own Olivetti but made of some *merda*-coloured material. 'Louis Vuitton,' he said. 'Wife's anniversary present.'

His role acknowledged, he left me to Sylvia and steered Rick back to the bar. Brad had merely shown faint amusement at Sylvia's assumption of command but Rick looked distinctly uneasy. When he reassumed the drinking position his feet started that nervous cab-horse shuffle.

'Meanwhile, there's some other stuff I wanna get to work on.' Sylvia had a list in her notebook. 'I looked out that mailer you did on the holy shirtmaker. It even made it on to the shopping page of *Vogue*. Does she make for ladies, too?'

'I don't know. But I'm sure she'd love to see you. Mother Jo.'

'You'll take me along? What a darling! Then there's the Roman Kiss lady, Lia... .'

'Lia Macbeth.'

'You know her, too? You're a real find, sonny.'

Was I trying to impress this sharp-clawed harpy in the hope of, a little career boost? If I fed her enough stories she would not want to call me sonny? Did I want to show the Frosts I could actually land them some promotion without compromising myself? Did I think that doing so might rid me of any obligation to them? Without actually considering any of these questions, I said: 'There's another story you might like to take a look at. Italian nobleman and movie-star princess battle over son being taken to Hollywood.'

'Sounds great. Let's go!'

*

The tickets for the great event that the *Sala Stampa* sent around weren't impressive: thin cardboard stamped with the papal arms and space for a name. 'For Christ's sake, don't lose them,' Charlie said, handing them around. 'You'll also need your *tessera*.'

*

Some of the days before Pius was entombed in the crypt of St Peter's would be reserved for VIP mourners, but for the moment the Basilica was open to anyone ready to stand in line for a few hours. I'd already taken a quick look-in. The corpse, in a new set of magnificent robes and mitre, was on a stand a little above the shoulder level of the pilgrims shuffling past.

A Swiss Guard stood at each corner of the bier and a few Vatican gendarmes hung around, waving off anyone who produced a camera. The only pictures allowed were being shot by the *Daily News* guys on their sacred mission. Every second day or so the *News* was running half a feature something like Our Guys and Gals at Pius Rite. Priest after prelate after cowled nun stepped into a little square chalked on the floor, faced the

179

Speed Graphics and *flash*! When they got back home, five bucks would get them a glossy print for the vestry wall, holy stiff over their shoulder.

The photographers came into the bar at lunchtime. 'Glad to be out of that,' said one, Marty. 'Guess they haven't caught up with deodorant over here.'

-17-

'Quite a gal your Sylvia,' said Johnny. 'What?' We were in the Roman Kiss salon on the Café de Paris side of the Veneto, an elegant shopfront picked out in Lia's colours, chocolate and strawberry. Her buddies often gathered for champagne and gossip when she shut up shop. This time it was also goodbye Farragó girls hello Sylvia Silver.

'They're leaving sooner than they planned.' Arabella had shaken my hand decorously. 'With all that holy coming and going out at Ciampino, Mitzi reckons she could march through wearing the crown jewels.'

'Might be able to take her around a little,' Johnny went on, taking aim at Sylvia, who was lying back in a make-up chair having Magicali dropped in her eyes. 'Should have a bit of time on my hands once the girls have gone.'

'Christ's sake,' said Mungo, tuning in. 'Don't tell that bitch anything. They've had to stop work on Helen of Troy out at Cinecittá. Liz Taylor and Burton won't leave the house while she's in town.'

I felt a little more charitable. Sylvia had been thrilled by Mother Jo. 'That place makes a great piece. You know what it used to be? A refuge for Fallen Women. Cute term, no? That hatch-type thing by the door? The fallen ones stuck their babies in there for the nuns to take care of. Isn't that sweet?'

When she put together a handy piece about my glamorous young princess's lonely battle for justice in heartless foreign courts, Arabella worried she might come down too hard on

Riccardo. But when I told Sylvia it was really the fault of the Italian legal system she let him off light.'

'What's the penalty for murder? That's what I'll be up for if Rick doesn't bring along those fuckin' pictures pretty soon. Where is the bastard?'

That was the first whiff of worry. But back at the bureau messages were soon dropping from New York and London with the same question. Rick wasn't answering the phone. Caddie neither. 'And where *is* that Caddie? Doesn't she want to see her old buddy?'

It went on to be a night to remember at the Hungarian restaurant. For those who could remember anything. Fiddles screeching, skirts whirling, waiters doing that silly sit-down-fold-arms-and-kick dance. Sylvia tried it and fell on her ass. Johnny picked her up.

Arabella started out in actressing mode, barely conceding that I was there. When she went off to the co-educational john I slipped in and pawed at her. 'Not here!' I pushed at another door, a closet full of mops and brooms. We kissed for a while, hands wandering. 'No! We can't.' We could. Lust brought up an image of Rick's whorehouse cubicle.

There was a bucket on the floor and I flipped it over. 'Put a foot up on that.' She shook off her shoe and obliged.

We weren't long about it; both in hair-trigger mode. 'So,' she said, shaking down her dress, 'my first knee-trembler. Heard about it in school. Interesting, though not to be made a habit of. But I've missed you, too.'

She went to the john. I went back to the table and took the chair next to Sylvia. She ran her iceberg eyes over me and flicked her napkin across my lap.

'Better zip up, honey, or I'll be asking if you're good for an encore.'

182

Gino behind the bar was waving his phone at me. Listening to Charlie up in the bureau, I raised my gaze to the mezzanine and there was Rick, looking down like Nero sneering over the embers. I took the stairs, grabbed his arm and steered him out that way. 'Your chum is holding a press conference over at the *Circolo Stampa*. You better come along.'

The *Circolo* was to Italian journalists what the *Stampa* was to us: a haven and a corral. It was also a good deal smarter, elegant even. Galeazzo-Lisi stood beneath a chandelier, a pile of handouts in front of him. The room was packed; he looked it over slowly through those silly pince-nez. I expected his glance to linger on Rick but it passed across us, indifferent as a lighthouse beam.

Much of what he said I had to reconstruct later in consultation with Aldo, but I grasped enough of it at the time to be as astonished as everyone else there. It might appear, said Galeazzo-Lisi in effect, that in recent years his time and talents had been entirely spent keeping the Holy Father in good health. But he had also been preparing for this sad moment. Those present were no doubt acquainted with the traditional practice of embalming bodies to avert putrefaction. Internal organs were removed and the corpse injected with chemicals.

However he, Galeazzo-Lisi, had long ago decided that such crude and intrusive treatment would be inappropriate for such an illustrious personage as the late Holy Father. Thus he, Galeazzo-Lisi, had devoted years of study into one of the central mysteries of Christian belief: how Jesus had been able to spend three days in the tomb and reappear none the worse.

That was not, Galeazzo-Lisi continued, the miracle that the uninformed assumed it must be. Visits to the Holy Land had convinced him that the seemingly miraculous preservation of

Christ's body had been due to the effect of particular herbs and plants with which people of the time prepared the dead for burial.

He, Galeazzo-Lisi, had therefore arranged that rather than suffer the indignity of being eviscerated Pius would be garnished with just such a combination of foliage, which had been flown in fresh from Palestine the morning after the tragic event. Thus, the natural process of decay would be delayed until the rites and rituals which had begun in St Peter's were concluded.

Before anyone could come up with a question, he headed for the door trailed by a couple of Vatican heavies who had been sitting behind him. Rick had been working up a penetrating stare to try to capture his guy's attention but Galeazzo-Lisi bowled by without a glance. 'Guess he's been pretty busy,' said Rick, shuffling his feet like a skater.

The Italian papers hadn't known what to make of Galeazzo-Lisi's extraordinary pronouncement. Most ran the story straight-faced, as did the wire services, including Century. Readers could either cross themselves or burst out laughing.

After I'd filed as lucid an account of the event as I could figure out I said to Charlie, 'Did I hear Sylvia say something about forty grand?'

'I guess you did. And it's dollars, not lire. Only just found out about it myself. Seems Rick fixed it up with Old John.'

There was a plan of St Peter's on the desk. 'For once the *Sala Stampa* are being helpful. *Telefonica Vaticano*, too. They're putting a row of phones in the Wenceslas Chapel, here.' He pointed. 'We've been given one. Or rather, we're paying a thousand bucks for one.'

'Did you know that ITT gave the pope a solid gold telephone as a sweetener for the deal to update the Vatican system? When

184

he rang someone up they had to take the call on their knees.'

'Bet you could work that into a mailer.'

Phones in church might sound odd to anyone who'd never taken a good look around St Peter's, but the Basilica was the size of a small town. There was even a bar behind one of the chapels; I'd had a drink there one morning among a clutch of Benedictine monks from Ireland. 'So we'll be able to file by phone? Direct to...?'

'London. All prepaid. Hooper, me and you will dictate our stuff by turn. Each of us put over a take at a time. He'll do the big picture, the bull piece. I'll do the ceremonies step-by-step. You do sidebars, concentrating on the audience. Forty-three governments represented at last count, lots of mid-range royalty, fifty-odd cardinals. And, of course, Secretary Dulles. Aldo and Cristof will be inside, too, mopping up leftovers. They'll get the phones when we're not using them.'

'Who'll be minding the shop here? What if there's a plane crash or something?'

'Rita. I'm giving her a bonus for making the stairs.'

Aldo held the *tipolino* phone out to me. 'It's Doolan,' said the caller. 'Monsignor Doolan. I heard this was the number to ring.'

What in hell did he want? The Holy Commission had been three months back. Last time I'd seen Marsha. 'First, I want to thank you for that tip. You remember. Don Pasquale. The racehorse. Came in at eight to one.' 'Well, congratulations.' I didn't want to utter his name or title for the others to hear.

'What can I do for you this time?'

'Can you get me some odds on the Archbishop of Genoa?'

The what?'

'Cardinal Siri. He's bound to be the favourite for next Holy Father.'

I took a phone number from him. 'About that other matter,'

he said, meaning Marsha. 'It's out of my hands, now but I've no reason to think all won't be well. As long as the usual procedures are followed, if you get my drift.'

I supposed I did but mainly wanted him off the phone. Aldo was looking curious as I hung up; I'd never had a *tipolino* call. 'Satisfied customer. Had a win on your horse. Don Pasquale. He got eight to one.'

'It wasn't Don Pasquale. It was Don Giovanni.'

*

IL GIGGETTO
Carciofi alla giudia
coda alla vaccinaria
fiche con marscapone

-I don't want to see her, OK?

-Just she keeps asking for you. Every time I see her it's Where's Caddie? Doesn't she know I'm in town?

-Everyone in town knows she's in town.

-Are you keeping out of her way because they're all asking about Rick?

-That's not it. Though I'm not sure how deep a hole he might have dug himself into. I'll come and see them when things get straightened out. Hooper, anyway. But I'd just as soon not see Sylvia. That's something, I dunno, personal.

-These are delicious. Whole artichokes, just deep-fried?

-You eat all of them. Leaves too. Thing is, Sylvia's the only woman I ever thought Rick might leave me for.

(Say nothing. Silence is a vacuum into which words that might otherwise go unspoken will often rush.)

-You know I told you how we used to go to the big bordels back in Paris? Well, Sylvia was there, too. She'd come along,

186

sometimes with her husband. First husband, redneck oilman from Oklahoma, Randolph Winkler. The Silver bit came later. Her maiden name, if the term had ever applied in her case, was Grant. Said she was descended from the general.

-Speaking of Oklahoma, all the visitors want to go to this place Winchester's opened, Zi Peppe. Esther wrote about it in the RDA and Women's Wear picked the piece up.

-She used to get pieces in the big mags, *McCalls, Colliers*. Fashion shit, mainly. Gossip.

-Esther?

-Sylvia, you asshole. Helped along by Randy's cash. She got a huge payout when they split.

-But before that, you'd all go cruising the bordels together?

-We figured it was better to keep the guys in sight. We didn't mind if they succumbed to the occasional blowjob, long as they let us watch. Saved us the trouble. That Winchester's playing round in dangerous waters. One step out of the marital line and that new *mafiosa* wife will get papa to dump him in the Tiber with his balls in his mouth.

-Speaking of balls...

-Yeah, well, once in a while Sylvia or I might get horny and take the guys off with one of the girls for a threesome. That was the house rule, at least one of their girls per couple. You couldn't just get a room.

-Rick with Sylvia?

-Sometimes. And I'd go with Randy. Plus one of the girls, of course. I didn't mind that. The whore was like a kind of chaperone, emotionally speaking. Anyway, I always thought Sylvia was more interested in the girl.

-And you?'

-Depended on the girl. Anyway, as I said, I didn't mind until one day, out of nowhere, Rick said, I fucked Sylvia today.

-He told all in the spirit of the goldfish bowl?

-Fuck the goldfish bowl. That was only for hookers and the like. Not friends. Now he was telling me they went to a maison de rendezvous, some cheap joint near the Opera. Just the two of them. Anyway, I made them cool it. Every time I've seen her since she managed to remind me about it. What does she look like?

-Signs of wear.

-I like the sound of that.

-Amazing that we're still getting figs. But I guess it's hot for October.

-You couldn't get them with prosciutto here, like most places. This is a Jewish joint.

-So I gathered from what the artichokes are called. I guess it's no comfort to them but it wasn't as bad for Jews here as in Germany, was it?

-Bad enough, though. The Fascists stole their houses, property, money. The Duck hated them. Just didn't have the guts to go through with what Hitler wanted.

-Ah, yes. The Duck.

-You still want to know, don't you?

-Not as much as I want to know what Rick is up to. And where.

-He'll show up.

Magari.

*

Brad called me at home. I didn't really want to see him on my own, Sylvia neither, because if Charlie heard he might suspect me of infidelity. They were sitting outside Doney's, taking in the evening *passagiata*. Sylvia arched an eyebrow. 'I got a cable from *Life* at the hotel. They're holding page deadlines for those

188

pictures.' She siphoned up her *americano*. 'We are trying to resist the conclusion that Rick has gone off the air somehow.'

'The air into which forty thousand bucks has evaporated.' Brad was drinking a *babee con molto ghiaccio*. 'I've been going through that stuff you and the other guys slung together on that big procession. Reads good. Even a couple of days later. Evocative.'

'Redolent,' said Sylvia, probably not knowing she was referring to smell. Which cued me to bring up the other Galeazzo-Lisi problem. There had been new reports from the *Daily News* guys.

'They've put him in a plastic bag.'

'Moving all the barriers back, keep people away from the smell.'

'I think a finger fell off.'

'Pope rots! Stinks out St Peter's.' Brad guffawed. No way we could put that out. Even if it's true.'

'*Especially* if it's true,' said Sylvia. 'People be puking all over Brooklyn. The Latins would go ape. Think what the communists would make of it. Is that Queen Soraya down there? The one with the big ass?'

I looked. 'Ava Gardner.'

'Jesus,' said Brad, squinting down the glittering slope hemmed with cafe tables, sidewalk crowded with the svelte and the stocky, beauties and bullshitters, dreamers and dopesters, chancers and thieves. 'What a fuckin' beat.' He swung on me with a third-degree glare. 'Do you reckon Rick's gone rogue?'

Down the hill a bit Delphine was sitting with Niki. 'It's his birthday,' she said. 'Look what I bought him.' She made the Albanian stand up, held his jacket open by the lapels so I could

189

see the gun, neatly nestled in an armpit holster. 'Gucci,' she said proudly. 'Made to measure. No more dropping in the soup.'

*

Thursday, the Jesuits in the *Sala Stampa* were at their blandest. The second day of public viewing in St Peter's was cancelled. Now Friday rather than Saturday would be reserved for illustrious mourners, royals and heads of state. On Saturday the Basilica would be closed for the Holy Father to be taken down from the catafalque and re-robed for the last of the last rites on Saturday. 'They're gonna stuff him,' said Aldo.

Charlie took the fly-ins across to check out the scene. Even with press passes they had to wait in line for an hour. 'It's true,' said Brad. 'He's turned green. Smelled like a dead dog in the woods.'

Sylvia was quite pale. 'We couldn't get closer than forty feet. Not that we wanted to. Nearly made me retch.'

'The guards were changing every ten minutes. You could see they had stuff shoved up their noses. Damn glad we didn't wait until tomorrow.'

I spent most of the day failing to get either Rickard on the phone. I went out along Via Flaminia to ring their doorbell though I knew there would be no answer.

'Wonder who's going to explain things to Old John,' said Brad.

Friday was a stinker for reasons well upwind of St Pete's. Glossy magazines dropped from all over. *Picture Post, Paris Match, ¡Hola! Bunte, Illustraten.*

In all of them, the main spread and cover were virtually the same, and none the less riveting for being in black and white. Pius in hospital-type bed, nun in white habit looking down at him. Pius laid out, guys in cassocks one side, men with stethoscopes on the other. Close-up of Pius with eyes closed, in a cute little fur-trimmed jacket with matching cap. All shot with Rick's point-and-shoot in those missing hours between the shutter frenzy up at Castel Gandolfo and the *Sala Stampa* announcement.

There were deep captions and a long story. Whatever the language the same by-line stuck out.

Professore Riccardo Galeazzo-Lisi, personal physician to Pope Pius XII

Scooped. Duped. Pooped.

'I'm going home,' I told Charlie. 'Maybe Rick'll call me there.' But when the phone rang it was Johnny.

'Sorry to trouble you, old chap. Bit of a worry over some pictures we're hearing about.'

It took a moment to grasp that he was talking about some *other* pictures. 'Publicity stuff shot out at Cinecittá, I gather. Not what they seem, at all. But they might cause a bit of trouble with you-know-who.'

'Your gal Rita seems to be involved. Would you mind having a word in her ear?'

'I'm trying to keep this line clear, Johnny. Can it wait?'

A second or two passed before he said, 'Of course, old chap. Phone you tomorrow, what?'

*

I had almost forgotten about Johnny's call until I went back to the office later and found Rita there, alone apart from Rinaldo. In two years I'd never seen her above the ground floor. 'Charlie thought I'd better start finding my way around,' she said. 'If I'm going to hold down the slot on Sunday.' She had a pile of pictures in front of her. 'Catching up with my captions. So much time out at Ciampino I'm way behind.'

'Are there any of Arabella Frost?'

191

'Just the one, but it's a beauty.' She riffled through the pack. 'I got through to her in Cinecittá, but she hung up in my ear.'

'What did you say?'

'Just asked her if she was enjoying hot moments with Steve Sempregado.' The co-star, a French-Canadian wrestler who had flopped into acting. Rita held out an eight-by-ten glossy.

I wouldn't have felt anything beyond mild erotic interest if it had been another woman in the picture. As it was, I had difficulty keeping my voice normal as I flicked it over. The name on the back meant nothing. 'Nice shot. Who took it?'

'Dunno. One of the *scattini*. Came over in yesterday's batch from Newspix. Looks like the real thing, though I don't suppose it could be.'

I wanted to stop looking at the picture but I was trying to check out every detail. Arabella was lying back on a sort of divan. Her legs were spread, Sempregado standing between them. She was wearing that white toga which had parted to show the leg nearest the camera exposed right up to her crotch. From the three-quarter back view he seemed to be in full costume but the lower part of it was a silly little skirt that hardly contained the cheeks of his ass. What worried me was what might be happening around the front.

'You want a copy, just ask 'em.'

'I'll hang on to this one. The mailer batch won't miss it.'

'Sure. Lots of papers wouldn't use it anyway. Too crotchy.'

Locked in the downstairs john, I went over the picture as intently as Caddie scrutinising a menu. Did that curve in Steve Sempregado's little skirt mean it was turned up at the front? Was there a panty line at the apex of Arabella's gaping robe? What was that whitish blur in the corner of the frame? On the floor? I'd never slipped Arabella's panties off. She'd always done it herself with a couple of deft flicks.

Never knew a woman who could get naked so fast.

I phoned the Palazzo Bergamonte from the bar, and after the quarter-hour wait while the flunkey went up and Johnny came down, I said, 'What the hell is that picture?'

'Is there only one, then? We were worried there might be more.'

'The one's bad enough.'

'Open to misunderstanding, what?'

'It's not the best kind of image-making, that's for sure.'

Then Arabella came on. 'It's all a fuss about nothing! Just those bloody little photographers scuttling about everywhere like rats. We were *acting* for heaven's sake!' *Acting*? Actressing?

'What does it show? Can you actually see my...?'

If Johnny hadn't been around she might have said 'cunt'. I'd never heard another woman use that word — a *pragmatic* as semanticists would call it: having different meanings according to context. But she did, quite often. The impact it made on me seemed to give her a kick.

'No, but it's a pretty good crotch shot.'

Johnny came back on. 'So, old boy, what can we do?'

*

We, in the person of me, went around to Newspix. Lucy was there alone. 'Where is everyone?'

'All gone early. Big day tomorrow..'

'Fernando?'

'*Svanito. Scomparso.*' Vanished? Disappeared?

'What do you mean?'

'Yesterday everyone work making prints for *professore qualchecosa*. You know, the pope man.' She made a pince-nez with fingers and thumbs. 'Many prints. Ship out everywhere.

193

This afternoon, Fernando tell me he leave, not come back. Go to Milano, maybe Paris, open picture agency all his own.'

I went through the last few day's negatives, ranked in transparent plastic sheaths. There was a strip of three shots, none showing any more — or less — of Arabella than the print. I stuck them in my pocket. Lucy didn't even ask why I wanted them. Fernando had left her plenty else to think about, I guess. It was still early so we locked the place up and went for a drink in the Piazza del Popolo.

'I no care about Fernando. All over with us anyway, you know.' I didn't know. No reason why I should. But she wanted to talk about it and I was ready to listen on the grounds that it kept me from having to think about Arabella.

'What went wrong?'

'You know Mother Giovanna? What she does?'

'Holy Shirt? Of course. We went there together, you and me.' Mother Jo preferred to call her expanding operation Convent Comicie but I liked my name better.

'Not shirts. Real work. Work with women?'

'Maybe I don't. What kind of work?'

'She make that place *un... ospizio.*'

A hospice. 'For whom?'

'Women from *case chiuse* who got nowhere to go.' A home for fallen women? Well, good for Jo. 'Maybe sick.' Indeed, some of the *case chiuse* ladies might not be in the best of shape.

'What's that got to do with Fernando?'

'He want Giovanna give him shirts for free because we make publicity. Greedy pig. I tell him she need money for her work. He just laugh. I say *va t'a cazzo.'* Go fuck yourself.

Neither of us needed to be anywhere else. We strolled around the piazza into the Corso. The entrance to Via Margutta was up ahead. Lucy said, 'You still got that *preventativo*?'

194

'Not the same one.' Though it probably was.

*

The October days were as hot as July but the evenings were cool and the apartment dank. I lit the tall terracotta stove and soon the air vibrated with warmth. We stayed down there on the sofa. She was shy about undressing, quaintly keeping her bra until last. Unhooked, it released breasts round and perky as pomegranates.

Whatever Fernando had done wrong he must have done plenty right in some areas. To pursue that crude *rodaggio* metaphor, she was thoroughly run-in and well-tuned, moving parts in fine order. We slipped smoothly through the gears, braking cautiously, accelerating confidently, coasting gently to a standstill. A little while later we took the same road back.

We both knew it wasn't going to happen again but I was glad that it had and hoped that she was too.

A guy never really knows.

She didn't want to stay so I took her down to the Fiat 500 in the courtyard and gave her the key. She would leave the car with Giuseppe the parking *maestro* outside the *Stampa* in the morning. Before going upstairs I slipped the strip of negatives into the firebox along with the expired condoms. Only in the morning did I miss my numbered St Peter's card.

-18-

It was after eight o'clock and I needed to be in the Basilica by nine. A brisk canter across the Piazza di Spagna got me to Via della Mercede in minutes. I scanned Giuseppe's parked fleet but the *topolino* wasn't there. Rita was already up in the bureau, lifting items off the incoming feed for Rinaldo to put on the Italy service. Was there a spare funeral pass? Of course not. Downstairs, the Stampa was empty. Everyone with a St Pete's ticket would be on their way there, anyone without one wouldn't want to advertise it. Gino was fiddling around behind the bar. '*Buongiorno, signor* Shelby.' He was as surprised to see me at that early hour as I was to be there. I wondered if Lucy might have left the car key with him. No such luck.

Waving my *tessera* out the window at cops, I jockeyed a cab halfway up the Via delle Conciliazione. Then I had to get out and shoulder through the keening crowd like a running fullback up to a cattle run of barriers funnelling eminent mourners into the Basilica.

None of my belligerent credential display and pleading to the Swiss Guards and Papal Gendarmes was any use. It was a fuck-up of the first magnitude. The rest of the Century team were inside and on the story. Brad, Charlie, Aldo and Cristof would soon be describing this momentous event to the world via that bank of telephones and I was AWOL, barred from my duty by a bunch of spear carriers in fancy dress.

I couldn't imagine Lucy had thought through the effect when she pilfered that scrap of cardboard, but my entire fucking career was slipping away underfoot.

I skirted the crowd and turned into the street with the post office. It seemed untouched by the sombre atmosphere leaking down from the square. The line of postcard senders stretched out on to the sidewalk but no one was waiting at the *Telegramma* window. Glumly, I addressed a form to Johnny at the Palazzo Bergamonte and wrote PIX DOWNSHOT RELAX.

In the bar across the road people were gulping down their mid-morning *espresso* shots. None looked like pilgrims. Religious tourists never spent money on anything but postcards and pre-blessed rosaries. No one knew what they ate or where. A *scopone* game was starting up in a corner and there was some action around the Totocalcio terminal, the soccer-based lottery I had never been able to understand.

I tried to size things up. I would be fired of course. The chances of any other wire service hiring me here — indeed anywhere — were slim. So I would have to quit Rome. Give up my beloved apartment in Margutta. The *topolino* too — if I ever saw it again. How many *cambiali* were left to go?

So, back to the States, look for a job. I'd probably find something. Maybe even on one of the New York sheets.

Which brought me, unavoidably, to Arabella. Leaving Rome would mean the end of all that. Of all what? Were we having an affair? Did we have some kind of deal? Would she be sorry to see me go? Should that picture with Steve matter to me? If it *hadn't* been acting it should have mattered like hell. Or was the shameful truth that it didn't matter who else she put out for so long as I stayed on the list?

An electronic chord blasted out. I thought it was the Totocalcio set-up but it was a television receiver up on a shelf.

A foggy picture the size of a tabloid page showed the inside of the Basilica. Black-and-white images swam around a bit then

197

came into focus. There it all was, the vast space under the cupola packed with the world's great and good. At the floodlit centre the illustrious corpse lay stretched out on a catafalque that raised it above the surrounding heads, toes pointed heavenwards.

On either side candles tall as lamp-posts picked out the glitter of his magnificent vestments and the spearhead of his mitre. Moving closer to the little screen, I could see the guests had been herded back about fifty feet from the centre-piece, packed into a tight circle. Some held handkerchiefs. Not to their eyes. To their noses. I wondered where Galeazzi-Lisi was. In Paris with Fernando, probably.

This broadcast was going all over Italy, although since few people had receivers at home most would be watching in bars like this or parish halls. It was also being relayed to France, Germany and Austria, although not to Britain or beyond. The United States, Latin America and the rest of the world would rely on newspapers and radio for their coverage that in turn depended on the news wires — Old Apathy, UP, Reuters and, above all, Century-fucking-NewsWire. *Tmesis* had settled in.

Everywhere out there newsdesks were waiting for the first takes. Where it was late in the day morning papers would be drawing up spreads and crafting headlines. Where it was early. the brash evenings would get first bite, pouring in news-agency feeds unedited. Everywhere, radio jerks would rip 'n' read, working up appetites with choice chunks of wire service copy. When the official pictures from inside the Basilica eventually dropped they would hit the front page and centre-spread of damn near every newspaper on the globe.

On the screen, a figure dressed almost as grandly as the corpse stepped up and started sprinkling something. He had to reach up high to get it on Pius. Holy water? Disinfectant?

There would be a fine crop of jokes around the *Stampa* tonight about the decay of the papacy. I was going to miss that weird place, its cosy clubbiness and camaraderie. I thought of the cheery greeting from Gino earlier as I hurtled through looking for my car key and as the scene came back to mind something in it didn't belong.

I re-ran my recollection as the television camera swivelled away from the main attraction to the high altar, sweeping around the less privileged packed tight against the walls by waist-high wooden barriers. My mental lens zoomed in on the bench behind the affable Gino to a close-up on a plate of *focaccio pugliese* and a bowl of eggs.

I dropped a *gettone* and called the bureau. 'Rita. I know you've got Rick there someplace. Downstairs having breakfast, isn't he?' She didn't say anything. I could hear Rinaldo gabbling away in the background. 'Rita?'

'Well, yeah, Shelby. All right. He's here. There. So what?' So what indeed. 'Anyway, you're in St Peter's? Got to the phones, right?'

'No. Not right at all.' That puzzled her. Then most things did.

'Well, you'd best get busy. New York and London are going crazy. They say nothing's being filed from inside. Far as we can make out, talking to ANSA, they had to move all the furniture around to keep everyone out of smelling distance of the pope and no one can reach the telephones. But you've been able to get to one, right?'

'Say all that again, Rita. Nothing's coming out of the Basilica?'

'Only Radio Vatican. Not really descriptive. Just reading out the programme. ANSA says they had to move so much furniture around....'

The phone was in a passageway beside the bar. I looked down at its grey metal box. There was a number, thank Christ.

'Call me back in ten minutes. Meanwhile... .'

'Oh, shit! Here's New York come up on the wire. It says, wait…. "*ex… ex… expedite St Peter copy urgentest*". What do I tell them, Shelby?'

'Call me back like I said. Ten minutes.' I read out the payphone number again. 'Meanwhile, go downstairs and get Rick. Get the bastard up there with you.

Hoping no one else in the bar would tie up the phone with a lengthy call, I went down the street to a postcard shops and bought *Osservatore*, its front page edged in black as it had been all week. I also took all the *gettone* they had, just to be sure.

Somewhere in the dimmer reaches of Roman Catholic doctrine, I once read, there was a theory that mortal sin could be committed even in circumstances that could not have been envisioned at the time. For example, if someone killed a creature from outer space that was later decreed to have had a soul, it would have been murder and thus a retrospective mortal offence. I was about to commit something of that kind in reporting terms. File a first-hand account of events I had seen only as electronic images, a concept way beyond the ken of the Reporting Angel.

I got back to the phone in time to pick up on the first ring. 'Shelby? Rick.'

I told him what I planned to do. 'And you're going to punch it out for me, right? Straight on to the wire. Make sure it's clean and tidy.' There was a brief silence while he thought it through then he guffawed. 'Let's go for it.'

I could hear him moving Rita out of the way. There were some clicks and I guessed he had gone into the wire room and plugged in a headset. 'You're *taking* copy, Rick,' I told him. 'You're not a fucking re-write so move it on straight. Also, you touch my fucking by-line, I'll break your head open.'

I had a good view of the television screen, so long as no one stood in front of it, a firm grip on the phone and *Osservatore* folded back to the Order of Service that listed who among the eminent functionaries was designated to do what.

19.10.58.BULLETIN. SHELBY STONE, VATICAN CITY. ENFOLDED IN MAGNIFICENCE AND SPLENDOUR WORTHY OF A MICHELANGELO PAINTING, POPE PIUS THE TWELFTH WAS TODAY LAID TO REST IN ST PETER'S BASILICA.

That got Who, What and the other Ws out of the way. Then on, I winged it like a jet plane. I goddam soared! A vocabulary that blew wire service strictures sky-high. Grandiose, opulent, resplendent. The sombre but colourful last rites. The measureless spaces of the great church ringing with Mozart's Requiem Mass. The angelic resonance of the Sistine Choir. The incense. Cardinals in crimson — I had to assume — in contrast to the drab suits and dresses of the rest. With *Osservatore* for programme notes I could track most of the plot and principals of the mighty production. From my earlier wanderings around when everything in Rome was new to me I had a stock of figments and factoids about the Vatican and St Peter's that I worked into the copy with demented relish. Every so often Rick would stop me to query something or other. Sometimes I'd get him to check a name. When I threatened to bubble over he brought me down. 'Remember the soda jerk, buddy.'

What I was mainly remembering was that stuff from Howard Russell about describing only what had occurred under his own eyes. Rather than before a television camera.

I put across three new leads as the proceedings unreeled, and I was quite sorry when it all came to an end — well ahead of schedule. In not much more than an hour, those entitled to the privilege were trotting past the display, flicking up a token sprinkle of holy water at the corpse and hi-tailing it for the exits.

Before the camera cut back to some *monsignore* in a studio telling the viewers what they had just seen, it caught a team of *sampietrini* popping out of a trap in the floor to get the remains out of sight — and smell.

'Thanks, old buddy,' I said to Rick. 'Tell Rita to keep her mouth shut and I'll buy you one this evening in Piazza del Popolo.' Then I bolted for the Basilica, slightly handicapped by a pocketful of *gettoni*.

Cardinal Spellman, *capo dei tutti capi* of the New York team, was one of the first into the open air and I cornered him for a few words. He looked distinctly red around the eyes, and I doubted it was from weeping. 'It's all very unfortunate,' he said. Then realising he might be quoted, 'I mean the death of the Holy Father.' He asked what outfit I was from and, when I told him, said, 'You'll be positive in your account, I'm sure.'

Brad came up, toting his Vuitton typewriter. Charlie was hard behind, flushed of face and panicky. 'Did you get to the goddam phones? We were fucking trapped. I could see everything but we couldn't move for fucking bishops. Had to stand there and breathe in that stink.'

He hadn't taken in who was on the other side of my notebook.

'Please give my best regards to Old John,' said His Eminence, letting an acolyte tow him away.

Charlie barely noticed. 'For Christ's sake, have you filed?'

I thought of trying to bluff my way through the whole fuck-up but there were too many footprints. I wasn't going to admit to being parted from my ticket, though, so I said I'd got in just before the doors were closed. I'd seen that everyone might be forced to stay where they were and decided it would be best not to get shut in.

'So how did you see what was going on?'

It was sort of amusing to watch their faces. Brad was the one to see the upside. 'Well fuck my woolly slippers,' he said. 'You just sat in front of the *television*?'

'Stood, actually. It seemed to show most of what was happening.'

'You probably saw more than we did. And you missed out on the stink. That's brilliant, my man. Saved the day.' Which was exceedingly generous of him, considering that he'd had the big story snatched from under his suffering nose.

Charlie could hardly disagree, much as he seemed to want to. 'You put over *three* leads?'

'And a few sidebars.' I could see Cristof and Aldo out in the portico, working the crowd for quotes. 'Where's Sylvia?'

'Fainted. Some nuns hauled her away. Let's get back to the bureau.'

And so the news is made.

*

In Piazza del Popolo, Rick was at the table he had been with Galeazzo-Lisi. I ordered *babees*. 'You saved my ass.'

'Pity you won't be able to save mine.'

'What happened?'

'*Italy* is what happened. There's not a straight-shooter in this whole fucking country. That quack eye-doc took the money, went straight down and made a deal with Fernando whatever his name is. One of ours!'

'Was. He's split. Gone off to start up his own agency.'

'They must have made a million bucks.'

I waved to the waiter for more scotch. Rick was not in sipping mode. 'He didn't even give me back the goddam camera.'

The *topolino* was parked outside Newspix. The place reeked of developer and drying prints. The darkroom guys were cleaning up. The glossies laid out on the benches were all from the same angle, somewhere to the left of the catafalque, just where the cardinals and others so privileged got to stop and shake their little shower of holy water.

There were about twenty shots, all she would have been able to get on the roll of XP120 film in the camera she had stuck down her shirt, lens peeking between the buttons. She'd picked her marks well, Spellman and a line-up of other top faces doing their stuff.

'Good job,' I said. '*Bravo.*'

She held out the car key. 'I knew you would get in some way.'

I gave her a hug. Without friends who would there be to two-time?

She called out when I was halfway down the stairs, 'You see *Messagero* today? Roghudi story?' Back in the bureau I looked it up. The mayor and the schoolteacher had been married in prison. Pastorelli had been given a lightweight twelve-month sentence that the judge said would be suspended if Giulietta forgave him.

*

RISTORANTE PICCOLO MONDO.
Cappellini in brodo
Coda di Rospo al forno
Zuppa inglese

-It seemed the only thing to do. In the circumstances.

-It probably was. In the circumstances. But I don't like the feel of it. I'm an old-time correspondent, Shelby. Or was. Need to see and hear stuff for myself.

-Fact remains, Century got damn near a half-hour beat on everyone else. What's this fish called in English?

-Monkfish. Back home people steer clear of it because it looks so ugly.

-It's delicious.

-It's also a godsend to crooked restaurants. Those fancy lobster dishes, mornay, thermidor, what you likely get is chunks of cheap monkfish. In sauce it tastes about the same. Like second-hand reporting.

-Please, Caddie.

-There'll be a post-mortem, you know.

-They're on their way. Roger Traynor from London, Richard Hammond from New York. Though they're really coming for Rick.

-And me, I guess. Guilt by association.

-Well, before they bring out the blindfold and put you up against the wall you better tell me about the Duck.

-You're not going to let that go, are you?

-I'm a tenacious reporter. Specially at first hand.

-Of course I fucked the Duck. Wasn't much choice. If he knew I'd put out for his son-in-law would have been an insult to turn him down. We could have had the plug pulled on the bureau again and CWP chucked out of the country.

-This is 1940, right? Italy's not in the war yet?

-Not yet, though the Germans have almost got France beaten and the British are scared shitless. I'm in the Palazzo Venezia on my regular rounds when one of the creepy Blackshirts comes up with a leer on his face and tells me Il Duce is offering the American press an interview and he particularly wants me to represent Century. I guessed I was getting the once-over.

-You didn't have to go.

-I suppose I could have made myself look like a dog and hope he'd give me a miss. But I was curious. Couple of days later about a dozen of us got led into the Sala del Mappamondo, the room with that balcony looking out on the Piazza Venezia. The Duck was at his desk right up the far end. You had to walk the entire length of this marble floor tiled with the map of the world.

-Showtime.

-Anyway, the Duck stepped down and shook hands with everyone. He had to squint up. All the Americans were taller than him and I was tallest of all. Also, like I said, I was the only female and I could see from his look that I was in for it. The question was when.

-And when was when?

-Few days later. Letter to say Il Duce would be pleased to grant me an exclusive interview. The flunky met me at the door with a smirk. It was all over in a couple of minutes, me sprawled all over his big desk counting the bits of the chandelier. All those fascisti were like that — ram-bam, *grazie tanto.*

-Well, least they said *grazie.*

-Afterwards, the Duck shuffled around a bit with his baggy pants still tucked in his boots and dragging on the floor. Showed me a little door, led to a sink and a rickety bidet in an iron stand. Didn't look any too clean, so I just used my handkerchief. Came out, he'd disappeared. I had to face going down the big staircase on my lonesome, all those flunkeys smirking.

-Then you went home and told Rick all about it?

-No. I went back to the bureau and filed my exclusive interview with Il Duce. Then I told Rick. He always wanted to know what their cocks were like. The Duck's was just like the rest of him, I said. Short, fat and brutal.

-Was that the only time?

-I'm happy to say. Wasn't the last time I was in the Sala del Mappamondo, though.

-19-

The inquisitors assembled in a nondescript *birreria* halfway down Via Babuino where, Charlie said, no one would guess what was going on. He chattered non-stop through the cab ride down from the Excelsior, where Richard Hammond and Roger Traynor had also booked in, testing for a level of confidence. 'How's Old John, Hamm?'

Hamm?

I hadn't heard directly from... Hamm since he sent me off from New York three years ago, or from Roger since I left London. They were both bleary-eyed from travel and uncomfortable in suits too heavy for still-warm late October.

'Haven't seen him for a while. He's tied up with his new baby.'

'The Newstower,' said Roger.

I was about to ask the obvious question but the driver swerved round a *carozza*-load of tourists, hit the brakes and they all piled out, leaving me to get the fare.

I was exonerated as soon as the proceedings opened. 'Thing that matters,' said Hammond, 'is we got a thirty-minute beat over Apathy, which is almost unheard of, and that the clients lapped the story up. Stories, I should say, because Shelby here kept filing away all through the... whatever it was.'

'And never once mentioned the stink,' I said, shaky bid for a laugh.

'More than fifty minutes on the phone,' Hammond said. Definite note of approval. 'And the stories were sound. I've read all of 'em through and I don't mind saying they're as good a wire service product as ever I saw.'

Charlie shifted uneasily. 'Even if it was, well, kinda, second-hand?'

Hammond wasn't interested in an ethical debate. 'Listen', he said. 'We're going to have to come to terms with what TV is doing to news. There's this video*tape* now, on reels just like a big tape-recorder, only with pictures. They'll be able to plug in and feed stuff straight on air. What does it matter if Shelby here saw it on a television screen? He could have seen it through a fuckin' telescope.'

Roger lifted his stein of draft Peroni towards me. 'Good for you, kid.' Now he knew what Hammond thought he was on safe ground. He wanted it seen that his boy had pulled it off.

I also knew where things stood with Charlie. If I had been pushed to the edge he wouldn't have reached out to stop me going over.

Being off the hook should have felt better but I actually shared Charlie's misgivings. And Caddie's, although I hadn't been ready to let her know. A reporter looking at pictures was not the same as being there. That huge TV camera was as blinkered as the old nags clopping down Babuino. It didn't go round corners. Didn't see who was making nice or nasty with whom *behind* it. The camera wasn't going to chase someone outside, shake them down for the killer quote.

'Even so, guys, we're not going to advertise what happened.' Hammond was still thinking things through. 'Apart from anything else, if Apathy and the rest get to know too much they might not feel so bad about Century wiping them out. Let's just keep it in-house, along with the stuff about Rick. Now, where is that bastard? Charlie? Shelby?

He swivelled from one of us to the other. I've got to have a serious talk with him. Forty thousand bucks-worth serious.'

I submitted a plea in mitigation. I told them of Rick's heroic copy-taking without which my story would never have got on the wire. Then I reprised everything I knew about the Galeazzo-Lisi disaster. 'And remember, Hamm.' I watched for a sign that I was pushing my luck with the Hamm. 'Even our own guy at Newspix double-crossed us.'

'Yeah, Newspix,' said Hamm. 'I saw those pictures from St Peter's. There was a good one of Sylvia being hauled away, out like a light. I'm keeping that for gags.'

I told him about Lucy; said she'd worked her way into the Basilica somehow. 'A chick? Really?'

'You need to meet her.'

'Send her along to Rich. Newspix is Europe, not stateside.' He finished off his beer, missing Rich's simper. 'Why are we drinking this cat's piss? We're in Rome, fellas. Let's get a new pope elected and meanwhile — get on the town!'

The iron law of inter-bureau hospitality decreed that visiting firemen had to be appropriately entertained. A bureau chief might not build a reputation on the lunches or dinners he drummed up, but one could surely be demolished. The bar-room annals of CWS were replete with horror stories of ill-judged amusements. Hamm looked from Charlie to me and back. 'Guy on the plane told me about this great new joint by the river everyone's going to. *Zeepeepee*?'

*

I was overdue for a turn in the slot. It was conceded that covering the Conclave of Cardinals that convened after the funeral, and the new pope it would produce, was all Brad's. Waiting For The White Smoke would make up any ground my St Peter's scoop had whipped from under him. He installed

210

himself in the *Sala Stampa*, the *tipolini* number glued on his phone there. Renaldo punched out a quick-start tape and hung it from a clip over the Teletype:

FLASH—BY BRAD HOOPER, CENTURY NEWSWIRE SPECIAL CORRESPONDENT, VATICAN CITY. TONIGHT THE WORLD HAS A NEW POPE.

Soon as Brad gave the word, whoever was closest would feed the perforated strip into the guide on the front of the machine, ring them bells and hit send. Word would clatter around the globe seconds ahead — we hoped — of the competition. For such a momentous announcement, time and date could go on the bulletin that Brad would go on to dictate.

I got on with the housekeeping:

26:10:58 SHELBY STONE. ROME. THE ITALIAN COLLEGE OF PHYSICIANS TODAY EXPELLED PROFESSOR RICCARDO GALEAZZO-LISI, SAYING HIS POST-MORTEM TREATMENT OF THE LATE POPE PIUS XII 'BREACHED PROFESSIONAL RESPONSIBILITY'.

Hyphenates count as one word.

The fifty-six cardinals in the Conclave used the first day to flatter pals or patrons by putting their names in the early ballots. The token voting papers were burned in a little stove producing, with some chemical assistance, black smoke from a vent on the chapel roof. The first sign of serious activity came at the lunch break on Day Two. No deal.

The days were still warm and sunny but ending earlier; it was nearly dusk when the chimney spoke again. A strange cracked tinkle spread around the bureau. Charlie was in the slot, I was batting away at a mailer. The others were winding up their own chores. '*Porca miseria*', said Cristof. 'It's ANSA.'

First bellringer that machine had ever produced.

URGENTISSIMO. FUMA BIANCA AL VATICANO

211

Someone turned up Radio Vaticano, which had been muttering reverentially all day. Out spilled excited squeals. '*Abbiamo papa!Fumata bianca! Abbiamo papa!*'

The *tipolini* phone buzzed. Charlie picked up and we could hear Brad across the room, 'Fire off that tape! Someone take copy.'

Aldo stepped over to the wireroom. I grabbed the spare earpiece, ready for Brad's bulletin. Cristof turned up the radio: nothing but scuffling sounds.

Charlie was flushing red. He flapped a hand to stop Aldo. 'You sure, Brad?'

'Came up on Vatican Radio. It's official.'

'The smoke? You saw the smoke?'

The ANSA machine was chattering. '*Fumata bianca,*' said Cristof.

The seconds were ticking off. Apathy and UP would be hearing and seeing the same stuff. They too would likely have a flash tape ready to run. 'I say send it,' Brad yelped. There was shouting in the background. 'Now it's on ANSA. Flash it for Christ's sake.'

I could see Aldo in the wireroom door, blinking at Charlie's raised hand. Cristof and I focused on it, too, he still bent over the radio, me with the earpiece pressed to my head, trying to make sense of the multilingual gibbering coming from the *Sala Stampa.* Charlie scowled around, face faded to pink and patchy like a slice of *mortadella.* 'It's too thin.'

Shaky ground here. Brad didn't answer to Charlie. If anything it was the other way round: the bureau was at the service of Century's top by-line, whose world beat was slipping away by seconds. But I knew what Charlie was thinking: Roy Howard. Proclaiming a new pope before there was one might not be on the scale of ending a world war prematurely, but it would bring the faithful all around the world to their knees.

And lose Century plenty clients once they found the effort had been wasted.

Brad came back on, his tone edged with anxiety. 'Did the flash go? Fucking kill it! That smoke's as black as Sylvia Silver's heart. Seems it looked white for a couple of minutes because some idiot turned a television light on it. Now I'll do a piece on the false alarm. You gonna take my copy?'

'This second-hand stuff seems to be catching on,' Charlie said, ostentatiously not looking my way. Whatever else he might be he was a Centurion all the way through.

Cristof put down the other phone. 'They took that Radio Vaticano guy away in a straitjacket.'

Sylvia was miffed that the *Sala Stampa* didn't respond to her request for first interview with the new pope. 'Anyway, darling, can't hang around on the off-chance. I'm due in Estoril to see the Prince of Naples. That's in Portugal. He ought to be king of Italy, you know.'

'Except he's not allowed into the country.'

'It's things like that make Europe so interesting, isn't it?

*

Pronto! Chi parla?'

'Don't give me that, Shelby. You've been in this place too long.'

'Hi, Marsha. Where are you?'

'Mamma Lucia's. Well, our bar, actually, down the hill. Come over and I'll buy you a drink.'

'Guess you're not married yet. I would have got an invitation, right?'

'Next month. I'm in town with my honeymoon shopping list.

'She looked fine. Better than that, lovely. Clear skin, good haircut. Better dress and shoes than I'd seen her wear before.

Italy was showing. 'In town from…?'

'Sardinia. You remember those old movies about the French Foreign Legion? It's like that. Only mountains instead of desert. And Italian. Well, sort of.'

'Sounds interesting.'

'I suppose it is, in a way. I'm having to live in a *pensione*. When we're married I'll move into the *caserna* with the other *Carabinieri* couples. One big happy family.'

'You're really going to do that?'

'Too late now. Lorenzo's parents have shelled out for that damn annulment — which I didn't know about until they'd done it.'

'How much?'

'Million lire. The going rate, their bishop told them. What have you been doing, Shel?'

One answer could have been that for the last ten minutes I had been wondering if I could persuade you to put out for one carefree, throwaway farewell fuck before you faded into matrimony.

Instead, I came up with a bulletin-style roundup of recent events, suitably fudging my St Pete's performance but headlining the Galeazzo-Lisi saga.

'Forty thousand down the drain!'

'To say nothing of the slap in the face for Newspix. They'd presold the deathbed shots all over. Rick's had a grilling from Richard Hammond and Traynor. Don't know if they've come to any conclusions, but the drop-ins are all due to drop out Wednesday, and Hamm wants a big dinner tomorrow night. Wanna come?'

'Sure. I'll be leaving the morning after. Our last date, Shelby.'

If there was a whiff of promise there it was overlaid by a sharp aftertaste of bad timing.

In my pocket was the one-word telegram I had collected that afternoon: *Thursday*.

*

'They're all hot for this place Winchester Starr's opened,' I told Caddie when I got around to her. 'It'll broaden your horizons.' Most of us rarely ventured across the Tiber except to call in at the Vatican, Trastevere had a couple of half-way decent restaurants in picturesquely crumbling piazzas, but the surroundings were pretty grim, a maze of smelly ill-lit streets with piles of garbage for landmarks.

'Anyway, you need to come and so does Rick. Show 'em what you're made of.'

Although Charlie was the nominal host — he cleared out the petty cash to fix the bill — I got stuck with organising things because I knew Winchester and could see we got treated right. I had my doubts about that but there was no time to heed them. The idea of a reservation would have baffled most Rome restaurants. Getting a table was never a problem, even if there was sometimes a bit of hanging out on the pavement, passing a *carafa* around.

From what I'd heard this was a huge place; there would surely be room for a few more. Even, in this case, a dozen.

I hadn't tried to achieve a gender balance, far less fix anyone up with a date, but when Hamm heard I'd invited Marsha, whose ex-husband, it seemed, was still at 42nd Street, he said, 'Don't ask any company for me. I'm bringing my own.' He winked. 'Used to be on the road myself, remember. Know how to shake out a territory.'

We met up at the *Stampa*. The place was still bubbling, visiting firemen from all over hanging around while the new pope was *in rodaggio*, minor enclaves in session around the room: Miss Frisk's, the Spaniards, Kurt Leder hosting a bunch of DPA clients, Digby Tucker and a gang of Fleet Street thugs.

Our guests straggled in, Lucy in a dress that stuck to her curves, Brad and Sylvia together, Nora Flynn, alone and sour about it, no less so when Charlie came down to join us. Traynor's eyes lit up when Marsha made her entrance, as did mine. She looked like a million bucks at the top rate of exchange.

Brad came over to the bar with me to get drinks. 'What's with that sourpuss wife of Charlie's?' He was a good old boy for a home office big-timer, and I'd come to admire the easy-going way he went about things. I told him of my embarrassing blunder with her. 'Just don't mention her nose.'

Hamm came in. He started to introduce me to his companion who grinned and stuck out her hand, 'We've already met, haven't we, Shelby?'

'Hi, Betty.' Guess he *did* know how to shake out a territory.

Sylvia let out a squeal. Rick was lumbering across the room, looking his usual slept-in self, trailing Caddie in a vast, brightly coloured floor-length gown that made her look like a runaway Indian tee-pee.

'How wonderful to see you,' Sylvia yelped. 'We were beginning to wonder if you were in jail or something.'

That might have been all joke or just part, but no snappy exchange ensued because down the stairs came Rita, her heels clacking on the marble like warning shots. 'Rick! Are you all right...?'

The next minute she was on the floor. Caddie decked her with a roundhouse right that would have broken her jaw if she hadn't turned her head away to scorch the rest of us with an accusing glare. Caddie hadn't minded her providing services for Rick but she wasn't letting her get possessive.

I turned to getting everyone out of there and into taxis on the rank in San Silvestro. There were plenty of helpful hands to get Rita back on her feet. Actually, she looked OK, if a bit shook-up. She managed to work up a killing glare for Caddie's back, even while trying to make out if her jaw still worked. Rick was shaking his head in admiration. 'Still got that knockout swing!'

We needed three cabs, an Italian speaker in each to make sure we got where we were going. One of the drivers yelled out the name of the piazza to another and Lucy gave me a startled look. 'You didn't tell me Trastevere.'

Roman cabs made a noise like someone rolling a bucket of bolts around but even so, we could pick up the noise from *Zi Peppe* half a kilometre off, something between a mob of Cinecittá extras baying for overtime and three operas being sung at once.

The sight was even more astounding. We had to leave the taxis a hundred metres away and march in line, me leading, along a narrow alley that debouched into a floodlit tumult of colour and action.

'*Dio la stramaladica!*' Lucy muttered. The restaurant filled the entire piazza. Beneath a network of coloured lanterns, people sat at long tables, gobbling and gabbling, waving for wine, bellowing over the din. Waiters wriggled between them, tray-loads of plates over their heads, dodging teams of acrobats, musicians, jugglers, can-can dancers, pan-pipe players. A couple of guys on ponies were handing down trays of *espresso*. Girls and small boys hauled away trolleys packed with dirty dishes.

'Like a Breughel painting,' said Marsha. 'Everything but a dancing bear.'

'Nope. There he is.' And there he was, a poor mangy little bear being led around on a chain.

Our way was blocked by a guy dressed like a Walt Disney pirate. If he was the maître d' there was a worrying lack of deference about him. We needed, I said politely, a table for twelve. We were, I said more firmly, a party of important foreign journalists, in Rome to report the accession of the new pope.

'Impossible.'

I slid across a folded *dieciemille*. 'Maybe one hour. Maybe more.'

'Is that Winchester?' Betty had worked her way up alongside me. The others had spread out, taking in the astonishing scene. I looked, and sure enough, on a platform built up at one end of the piazza sat Winchester and, I assumed, the gangster bride. He was got up like a circus ringmaster, riding breeches and boots, cutaway coat and a stars and stripes vest.

'Back in a moment,' I said. I pushed past the pirate and struck out in that direction, dodging a somersaulting dwarf, a couple of fire-eaters and an old-fashioned cigarette girl with tray and bottomless cleavage. A few steps along a hand reached out. 'Fancy meeting you here.'

Delphine and the pistol-packing Albanian.

'Why not? We seem to meet everyplace else.' I looked around the table they were at. People along it were shovelling in *spaghetti alla carbonara*.

She shrugged. 'Don't know who these others are. These were the only seats.'

Winchester spotted me. I could feel him zeroing in as I shoved and dodged through the Breughalarama. I took the couple of steps up to where he sat, switched on my best shit-eating grin and stuck out a hand. 'Hi, old buddy,' I said, or something similarly fatuous. 'Helluva place you've got going. I'm with a bunch of visiting firemen, important news people from New

York. Thought you'd be able to fit us in.'

I turned and offered the bride an ingratiating little head bow. She was about my age, good-looking in a shadowy way, dressed like Cleopatra. No asp. No smile either.

Winchester looked at me like I was something scraped off the bear's hindquarters. He let a beat or two go by then said, 'Get the fuck outa here, you stuck-up bag of shit. You didn't wanna let me sing, I don't hafta let you eat here. Ever.'

Since that seemed a fairly conclusive response, I made my way back towards the entrance, fingers in pocket counting off the big ones I had left.

Delphine and the sinful Moslem were extricating each other from the bench they'd been sharing with the *carbonara* eaters. 'Gotta go collect His Maj.'

Niki had got one leg out but the other was trapped under the table. They'd obviously been giving the prophet's poison a bit of a trouncing. I tried to lend a hand but he lurched forward and his pistol slid out, clattering on to the cobbles in front of me. Gucci probably didn't have a lot of experience in holster design. 'Silly!',said Delphine. 'I showed you how to click in the little stud.'

I picked up the gun and handed it to him. He took it then gave it back to me to hold while he fiddled with the shoulder harness. Then I shoved it back to him. It was like trading moves with the performing bear. Eventually, he slipped the piece under his arm and gave me a hug. 'Great picture,' said Delphine as she sidled by. 'Steve and the princess, I mean.'

Still working that out, I looked around to see that the pirate had been taking an interest in that little game of pass the popgun. Whatever he thought Niki and I might have been doing, the display of light artillery seemed to have changed my status. 'I have a table for you, *signori. Un angolo discreto.*'

A corner discreet enough, I was relieved to find, to keep me out of Winchester's line of sight. Lucy gave me a sharp look as we were led over: how? At gunpoint, I'd tell her later. I settled her in alongside Brad to counterbalance Nora Flynn on his other hand. For now, the evening was airborne and I could hand over the controls to Charlie.

I brooded a bit over the idea that Delphine must have seen that picture of Arabella and Steve, but not for long. There was a lot of fun to be had once we paid a Sicilian *pizzicato* band and a pair of shepherds with bagpipes to leave us be. The main wine supply arrived in a trolley towed by a dwarf who needed both hands to get a *litro* up on the table. I sent him off for a bottle of the stuff Lucy liked, a sticky *rosato* called Caruso. Think Mateus *rosé* with double sugar.

He also delivered a couple of *babees* that Charlie ordered on the side. The waiters were dressed as bandits, the point of which became clear when the bill arrived. But before that we ate *frutta di mare*, bowls of various pasta, a large fish of some kind, a pair of suckling pigs, *patate fritte* and an *insalata mista* served in a baby's bath.

Some seat-swapping went on, though I stayed put, as did Charlie who was obviously keeping a safe distance from Betty. He was keeping up the *babees*, too; they came along two at a time. Nora just sulked over hers, so after a while he'd drink that, too.

To begin with, Sylvia was between Caddie and Rick, but when an enormous *mamma* plunked down a spirit stove on that end of the table and started to whisk up *zabaglione* in a copper kettle she came over and sat by me. 'I'm gonna fly out day after tomorrow. After I'm finished up in Estoril, I'll go to Lisbon and get the *Andrea Doria* on to New York. It's the Italian Line. *Molto* chic.' I could see she was working up to tell me something hot.

Reporters are like that. They get a story, it's hard to bottle it in. 'Listen, Shelby, keep this to yourself, right?'

'Sure.'

'I've got you to thank for it, after all.'

'Right.'

'I'm going to have to check it out when I get back home, but it's a big one. Keep my column going for a week.'

Wait. Lean in a little.

'Lia's sold Roman Kiss to Glamglo Inc. It's a big deal, five million bucks, easy. And they're going to keep her on as the elegant face out front. Boy, will *Women's Wear* be sick when I break it.' I supposed they would. I could see that could be a big-time beauty and business story. Pity it wasn't coming from the bureau, but you can't win 'em all.

'So I owe you for introducing me to Lia. And Johnny, too. Johnny Walker.'

She giggled. 'We had a couple of nice... walks. He's coming to Portugal with me to see the prince.'

She hadn't finished. 'Hope that pretty princess of his appreciates all you've done for her. Never hurts to play the flack a little, well as the hack.'

A real one-two, right where it hurt.

Hack. n. Person hired to do routine, often dull, writing; literary drudge.

That was bad enough. Centurions were known to josh about themselves being hacks, but no one else could.

But *flack*! Flack probably wasn't in the dictionary. The jerk in Hollywood who advised them — rightly, alas — to get their own story out first was a flack. The guy in wide lapels who tried to get in the way when you went to interview some actor. Or who stepped up and tried to explain why someone like Joe McCarthy hadn't meant what he'd just said.

But I screwed up a light-hearted grin. 'Guess not. Anyway, congratulations on the Lia scoop.'

'Yeah. Just too bad those Magicali drops won't be the same. They'd never get away with mama's secret ingredient over in the States.'

'There's a secret ingredient?'

She wasn't listening. 'Know why *I* didn't make pass at you?'

Wait. Say nothing.

'If I had and you didn't take me up on it I'd have had to wreck your career.'

The seats on either side of Caddie were empty. She was sitting still as the Sphinx. Rick had gone off to pee, or maybe escape from a guy in a moth-eaten tailcoat who had hauled up at the end of the table and was priming himself to burst into song. 'Leave him be,' said Caddie when I snuck over to her, crouching to stay out of Winchester's sight. 'I like those Neapolitan tenors. He'll do *O Sole Mio* with that funny little gargle they throw in.

'So how's it going, Caddie?'

'Did that bitch grab your cock?'

'Not that I noticed.'

She cranked out an evil chuckle.' She did it to Rick, I swear. She was sitting here between us, swapping old-time stories. I looked over and she had her hand under the table. Under his fuckin' napkin.'

Rick came back, red and sweating from an encounter with the fire-eaters. There was some more seat-swapping and Lucy slipped in on my other side. 'Never thought I'd be at this place. I heard about it but.... '

'You live over here. You could come any time.'

'Never! This not our *petacca*.' Our...spot. Place. '*Son fori dar vassetto.*' That was dialect, but I got it. She was on hostile turf.

222

New Yorkers understood such things. 'My people *sampietrini*, honest. Here everyone bad people, thief or...maybe worse. Even police. They hear my name.... '

She drew a finger across her throat.

'You're kidding, right?'

'Not right. When we go out of here stay together, please?'

'Sure. Don't worry.' I wasn't convinced she could come to harm but who was I to argue with a local? 'Did you talk to Roger about Newspix?'

'*Si*. Maybe he give me job.' She looked around suspiciously at the seething piazza. 'Also, wrong football team.'

Charlie started to lay down big ones on a *conto* as long as my forearm. It had arrived at the table in a little barrel strung round the neck of a St Bernard dog. 'That's so cute,' screeched Sylvia. 'Anyone got a bone we can give him for a tip?'

Charlie's face was aflush from the *babees* he'd been knocking back but, feeling good about everything, I thought why the hell not? He'd steered the bureau through some tricky waters these last couple of weeks, managing a major story with one hand and this clutch of demanding home office heavies with the other. He didn't like the way I'd dealt with the St Peter's problem but he'd accepted that others did. The Galeazzo-Lisi disaster was not his fault. Tomorrow, the visitors would all be gone, apart from Brad, and the dust would settle. All in all, Charlie deserved a drink or two.

Everyone else was gabbling and I could lean across to Betty, keeping my voice right down. 'How did you know Charlie wasn't American?'

Her eyebrows went up and she made a mock shut-up signal with her lips, but she was amused. I looked around for Nora. She was sitting up straight, resentment emanating like a death ray, patting at her eyes with a handkerchief. Brad had been on the other side of her from Charlie, but he had slid along to talk to Marsha. I picked up a modulation of the surrounding din. A far-off throaty howl.

'OhhhhHHHHHHH what a beautiful morning....'

Everyone had a fight to get out of those damn benches but eventually we were all more or less upright, ready for the big farewell scene. Lucy seemed really unnerved, so I stuck with her while she went around offering her hand to the guys and giving the women a peck on the cheek. The only one who didn't seem to welcome it was Nora. 'What's wrong with Mrs. F?' I muttered to Brad.

'Oh, shit! Her glass was getting low and I said, can I give you some....that pink stuff you got for Lucy. She's cute, by the way.' I blinked at him, get on with it. 'I was meaning to say *rosé*, but right then that story you told me popped up in my mind.' He gave a little shrug. 'What came out was: can I give you some more *nosé*.'

I'd assumed we would group up for cabs much as we had arrived, but if the Flynns were going to sulk off to EUR right away then Roger could see Lucy home. Hammond broke away from the ripple of kisses going around. 'Great night, Shelby.'

I was reaching for the hand he stuck out at me when Sylvia let out an ungodly screech. 'She bit me! That bitch bit me.'

Caddie, in her great tent of a dress, was teetering off towards the street and the line of taxi lights, Rick trying to catch up with her.

'I was just reaching up to give her a goodbye kiss and she chomped her damn jaw on my cheek. Omigod! Am I bleeding? Are there toothmarks?'

Marsha and Betty hauled her round into the light. We guys stood rolling eyes at each other. I looked around for the Flynns. Gone.

'No blood,' said Marsha.

'Maybe I should go to the hospital. Will I need a rabies shot?'

'There *are* toothmarks,' said Betty.

'I'll be scarred for life.'

'Probably not for life.' Marsha was taking a closer look. 'Skin's not broken.'

Sylvia was muttering, scrabbling in her bag for a mirror. 'I'll sue that crazy old whore. Fuckin' *vampire*.'

'My place,' said Betty. 'It's right near their hotel. I've got a PX aid kit.' I had to fight down a giggle.

'I'll come along,' said Hamm, stepping up like a gent.

'How can I go to see the Prince of Naples with bite marks all over my face?'

Betty clearly expected Marsha to help her out with Sylvia, so the tender scene back in the Inghilterra I had scripted came down to a quick public kiss. 'Take care,' I said, feebly. 'Call when you're next in town. After the honeymoon.'

The other guys, seasoned shitstorm-evaders, saw no reason to follow their leader's example. 'I'd better go check out the wire,' said Brad. Whoever had been holding down the slot would have left, but we'd given him a key to the bureau. He winked at me. '*A domani*. G'night, ladies. It's been vivid.'

'I'll go with Brad,' said Roger. 'Take the cab on to the Excelsior. See you in the morning, Sylvia.'

I took Lucy home. It was only a ten-minute ride to a piazza just like the one we'd left but nothing in it other than a crumbling fountain and some dilapidated cats. 'Did you really think it was dangerous back there? What are the locals going to do, cut your throat?'

'Not throat. Maybe, you know.... ' Guess I did. She opened her bag to show me the little point-and-shoot Canon. 'I got picture of bite.'

225

'*Pronto, chi parla?*' The sniffle at the other end could only belong to Nora. It was a bit after five am. 'He got out of the taxi somewhere along the Corso. I've been waiting up for hours. Where could he be?'

It took me a while to remember where I'd left the *topolino*. The sun coming up over the Pincio picked it out for me down at the end of Margutta. I drove across town through empty daybreak streets. The *poliziotto ospedale* greeted me like an old friend.

-20-

Rick and Rita were eating breakfast in the *Stampa*. He was eating anyway, that salty *focaccio*. 'I went up to the bureau. No Charlie.'

'He's not coming in.'

'Found this.' Rick showed me a servicer from the backroom in New York.

> RICKARD BOOKED NEWYORKWARD ANDREADORIA
> ITALIAN LINE EXNAPLES 29:10:58. TICKETABLE AMEX
> ROME. COLONEL SAYS UNMISS.

'Looks like our visitors filed their report. Hamm, anyway.'

'That's tomorrow. Can you make it?'

'Guess I gotta.' He headed back upstairs.

I hadn't seen much of Rita since Caddie decked her that night. She didn't seem any the worse for it. She showed me another carbon Rick had brought down:

> 26.10.58. ROME. CONTROVERSIAL DIRECTOR FEDERICO
> FELLINI TODAY DENIED THAT HIS NEW FILM 'VIA VENETO
> NIGHTS' WAS BASED ON REAL-LIFE EVENTS SURROUNDING
> THE WILMA MONTESI SCANDAL.

'Title is about the only part of a movie he's got.' Mungo Macbeth had told me, snorting into his scotch in Jerry's. 'Last I heard they'd shot ten hours of film and no one had written a word of script.'

He seemed a little distracted, which was understandable if

227

Sylvia had been right about Lia's big deal.

'Maybe you'd like to be in it?' said Rita. 'The big movie. They want some real-life foreigners for a scene set back in Occupation time. Other guys here are going to help out.' I was about to brush her off and go on up for my stint in the slot but she went on. 'It's gonna be set in the Palazzo Bergamonte. Seems Fellini's a chum of that Principe Riccardo. You know, Arabella Frost's husband.'

*

'Fucking American Express doesn't know anything about a ticket. No reservation for me. Nothing. I wasted an hour there. I'm gonna need my passport.' Rick unlocked his file cabinet. 'Also, Caddie's gone apeshit. Says she oughta go see Old John instead of me.'

'What about the Italian Line ? Where's the office?'

'Up on the Veneto.'

'Call us from up there.'

He did, another hour later. 'No ticket here either, but they'll give me a berth. Gotta pay for it, though, and they won't take a cheque. I'm going back down to the bank.'

Aldo and Cristof had come in and I told them what was going on. 'Should be OK,' Aldo said, looking at the clock. 'Plenty trains to Napoli.' The phone light flashed and he picked it up. Rick again.

'They won't give me the dough without my passport. And I left that back up at the Italian Line.'

'Jesus! The bank knows who you are.'

'They know *me* but you know *them*. No passport, no fucking money. Can the bureau cover it?'

228

I left the phone open so he could hear me ask Cristof. 'No way. The visitors cleaned us out. Won't get our reimbursement for a week. You want me to call Caddie?'

'Sure. She's got to have a few hundred bucks squirrelled away someplace. I'm going back up the Veneto.'

I dialled the Via Flaminia apartment. 'Not a fucking red cent, Shelby.'

'Hey, Caddie, it's just a loan. There's been a balls-up at American Express. Don't you think Century's good for it?'

'Rick knows why he shouldn't go on that ship. He comes here to get his clothes I'll put the locks on.'

'What the hell's the matter with you, Caddie?'

'That *Andrea Doria*'s the ship Sylvia's gonna go home on from Lisbon.'

It was 3:30, half an hour before the bank closed. Aldo had been picking up calls from Rick. 'He's back up at the Veneto. Café de Paris. Italian Line shuts at seven.'

In between the calls I'd seen Aldo and Cristof batting looks. Now Cristof came out of the office and put down a pile of 10,000 lire bills. 'Three hundred thousand. But we need you to give us a note for it. Sort of a *cambiali*.'

About five hundred bucks. Enough for Tourist Class, probably. Steerage. 'Who's we?'

'Aldo and me. We got ten to one. 'On Roncalli. *Il Papa*.' Or, as the guy now installed was to be known, Pope John XXIII.

'You bet on Roncalli for pope? How come?'

'Aldo's cousin — one of them — is *capo cameriere* at Crema di Mare.' A big seafood place near Ostia Antica. Caddy and I had it on our lunch list.

'Well, all the French cardinals went down there on the Saturday. Night before the funeral.'

'When they should have been deep in prayer for old Pius's departed soul.'

'Sure. But they're French. They paid for the place to put the shutters up. Had it to themselves. Brought along their own French wine. Franco waited on them himself.'

'And heard them talking?'

'Words that kept coming around were *le vieux*.'

'So we asked ourselves who *le vieux* might be.'

'Roncalli wasn't the oldest but he was the oldest who wasn't, you know, ga-ga.'

'So he was probably *le vieux*. He was years in Paris as papal nuncio there. The French had his number.'

'So we thought it was worth a bet.'

Especially at ten to one. I couldn't argue. They hadn't short-changed Century. Nothing in that story would have been strong enough to have gone on the wire. 'I'll write you a receipt for head office. Aldo, grab a cab and get Rick along to the Italian Line. Tell him not to go home. Caddie might lock him in. On the way, duck into *Rinascente,* get him some underwear and a couple of shirts. And wish him *buon viaggio*.'

I looked at the servicer just in.

> 29.10.58 SUBVERSIVE POET EZRA POUND UNINTERVIEWED HERE ON RELEASE. ARRIVING NAPLES LEONARDODAVINCI 22.11.58. INTERCEPT ETSTORIFY COLOURFULLEST.

I had been counting on a mock double-take from Arabella when she saw me stroll into the Palazzo Bergamonte but she didn't show a flicker. 'How nice to see you again', she said.

Then, turning to the guy beside her. 'This is Mr Stone. He's American.'

'Shelby,' I said, giving her prince a firm American handshake. I should have expected Riccardo Bergamonte would have the same sharpshooter's mid-distance gaze as Johnny. His eyes were blue, though. With dark blonde hair, it made for a look you sometimes saw in Italians from the north. He was in tails — what they called a *frak* — and white tie. Arabella wore a sleek evening gown.

'Mr Stone is a reporter, she said to Riccardo. Fair warning.

'Are you writing about this?'

'Not tonight, I'm going to be in the movie.' I could see a few Stampa faces, Digby's among them. Miss Frisk was there, wearing an evening variation of her daytime turnout. No parasol but gloves up to her elbows and a glittering geometric hat. Little Fritz was dressed as a German soldier: rough grey tunic, big boots. Beside him on the floor was one of those coal-bucket helmets.

'How amusing! So are we.'

'But can you...?'

'Be in two movies at the same time? This isn't a real part, just a little cameo to go with the *palazzo*. Look, my co-star is here, too.' Sure enough, there was the hateful Steve Sempregado in a Roman toga and sandals, chatting to a guy in full-scale SS uniform, all black and silver: swastika, cap with death's head badge. Jackboots even.

One beery night at the bar I had asked Fritz and his boss Kurt Leder when they had first come to Rome; implicitly, how? Fritz smirked a bit and said he had been in a tank during the German retreat, seen how things were going and deserted. Shacked up with an Italian girl and only gone back home a couple of years after the end of the war. Kurt listened behind a shadowy smile, and when I turned to him, said his story was not nearly so adventurous. 'Never saw the place, before I came here for DPA. I was spared the army for a weak heart.' He tapped his chest

'Spent the war in Berlin. *Öffentlichernformationsdienst'* Public information service.'

'When I told Fernando he could use the place he insisted that we must come with it.' Riccardo was giving me a good once-over which, unlike most Italian guys, he could do without looking up. His English had one of those crotch-tingling accents. Not my crotch, obviously.

'I believe all this is just for *una sequenza sola*, so I hope it's a flattering one.'

All this looked even more of a mess than the usual movie set-up. The vast *entrata nobile* I'd glimpsed on my earlier visit was a snakepit of tangled cables out of which Klieg lights on black metal stalks towered like giant cobras. A set of rails laid on the white marble floor let a huge camera crane roll forward and back. The camera itself was pointed at a broad staircase that rose to a mezzanine. More marble, mostly pink. At the top, a small boy leaned over the balustrade. 'My son,' said Riccardo. 'James.' He waved and the child waved gravely back. *My* son. Not our son.

'If I'd known people were going to dress up I'd have put on tails, too.' Digby seemed quite miffed. 'I've got my own, you know.'

'*Deegby!*' A blonde in pared-down evening gown rammed her tits in between us, gave him a sloppy kiss and whirled away, heading for a cardinal. Cardinal Johnny, I realized when he tipped his little hat to me.

'Who was *that*?'

'Anita Ekberg. Fellini's big Swedish discovery. Wrote a piece about her last week.' People started to yell for silence. They didn't get it but it brought *il maestro* shambling out to explain to the prince and princess what he wanted them to do, which was, apparently, walk up the stairs. Seemed simple, but before

232

they set off there was to be a pan shot of the whole scene. Trays of champagne glasses full of bubbly mineral water were passed around, the big lights crackled on, the camera rose and dipped, Fellini sitting beside it on one of those metal tractor seats.

Then the lights were rearranged and a minion went to call the princely couple away from the conversation they'd got into with Steve and his uniformed friend. Riccardo, eyes trained on the top of the staircase, arm crooked for Arabella's hand to rest on, took a casual half-step backwards and ground his heel on Steve's bare toes. Steve yelped and hopped around whimpering. Hardly anyone noticed except the guy in the SS outfit who burst into giggles, slapping a riding crop against his boot. He pulled off the death's head cap. 'Bugger me,' said Digby. 'That's Kurt.'

I wondered if Herr Leder had decided to come along in some old clothes he hadn't been able to bring himself to part with. Public information service my ass.

The less figurative ass, that of my beloved, was making its way up the staircase shielded from the gaze of the mob by, I was ready to bet, no more than a single layer of fabric. Fellini yelled something and Riccardo shook her hand off his arm and slid his own around to enfold one perfect buttock. I didn't want to entertain one of those logical inferences Professor Peirce had been so fond of, so I allowed the pang of rage I felt to be assuaged by a fleeting impression that my keen reporter's eye had harvested-. The heel I had seen stomp down on Steve's toes had been of the Cuban variety. It made me feel slightly better to know that Prince fucking Riccardo needed stacked heels, and probably lifts in his shoes, to bring him up to eye-level with the rest of us. Including Arabella.

233

-21-

No way was I going to get an exclusive with Ezra Pound. All the wire services turned out on the dockside to meet the *Leonardo da Vinci*. The Apathy guy must have come down to Naples on the train before mine. Reuter and United Press International sent stringers and a couple of local photographers.

In New York we would have got an early start on the story, going out to the ship in the pilot cutter. I'd enjoyed the few such jobs I'd done, climbing onboard into the chaos of arrival, passageways choked with baggage, stewards hustling last-minute tips. Here, we had to wait for the *Leonardo* to tie up alongside and disembark half her passengers. In late afternoon she would pull out again to take the rest of them, including the Pounds, to Genoa.

Only when consulting the embassy about his legal status had I discovered that Ezra was accompanied by Mrs Pound, the former Dorothy Shakespear. Ever since, I had been trying to work out how, if I needed to mention her, I could prevent someone from adding 'e' to her name.

They had been married for forty-four years and she visited him nearly every day of the thirteen years he spent in that hospital, St Elizabeth's. What's more, he had been released into her care: she was his legal guardian.

Caddy produced a malign cackle when I told her that. 'First thought when I heard they were letting him out was that he would be able to get away from Dorothy and back to Olga.'

'Olga?'

'Olga Rudge. Third corner of the triangle. Their *ménage a trois*. Ezra was a tireless pussy hound and Olga was lady friend number one. She was English. She's still around, far as I know. He kept Dorothy at their place in Rapallo and Olga at hers up in Venice. He'd shuttle between the two. But when they got stuck in Italy they lived at Olga's all through the war, three enemy aliens packed in a little house on some back canal. She played the violin.'

'Dorothy?'

'No, Olga. You're really going to see the old nutcase, are you?'

'Wouldn't want to miss it.'

'Well, if you get stuck for questions, ask him if it's true the American embassy wouldn't let him on the train.'

'What train?'

'The one I told you about. After they brought us down from Siena they sent us and all the other Americans across to Portugal, which was neutral territory.'

'Pound wanted to go home too? I thought he wanted to stay.'

'Well, that's what he *did*. Who knows if it's what he *wanted*? Something happened just as the train was leaving for Lisbon, I don't really know what. A couple of people said they thought they'd seen Ezra there, arguing with embassy people. But they weren't sure. So ask him?'

No one had mentioned that the Pounds were accompanied by a Mr Oliver Pangler of the State Department. He awaited us up on the sundeck, undiplomatically turned out in linen slacks, a Hawaiian shirt, grey crew-cut matched by a moustache like a dab of froth from a hasty *cappuccino*. 'Good morning, gentlemen. My, but isn't this a sight to inspire?'

He pirouetted on a rope-soled espadrille to make sure we took in the glories of the Bay of Naples: Capri, Ischia, Vesuvius and, for balance, the slums beyond the tumbledown waterfront of which from that height we had a peerless view. 'In case you wonder what I am doing here, you must remember that Mr Pound is still a guest of the United States government and will so remain until the appropriate Italian authority accepts him when we reach Genoa.'

'You mean the Italians are going to take him into custody?'

'No, no, no. We merely need to confirm the assurances we have asked for to permit Mr Pound to take up residence in this lovely country.'

'*Doctor* Pound,' said a little old lady sidling up and holding out a cool hand.

'All right, Dorothy. *Doctor* Pound.' Pangler smirked at us over her head. 'He's picked up a few honorary doctorates and he likes the sound of it.'

Mrs Pound stepped neatly aside to let us focus on a shrunken wiry figure. Wild rust-spattered grey hair and a spade beard made him look like a dehydrated version of one of those Elizabethan voyagers, Walter Raleigh, or Francis Drake. Just needed the ruff.

Pound was close enough for me to see his eyes were green. If those winged tufts of hair on either side of his long skull had once been red, as the traces left suggested, the effect must have been luminous. As it was, he looked crazy.

'Dr Pound,' said Apathy. 'I'd like to get a couple of things straight. You're age seventy-two, right?'

Pound didn't seem to think that was worth a response so Dorothy provided one, 'That's correct.'

'Born in Idaho, right?'

No answer to that, either.

'And just to keep the chronology straight, when exactly were you released from that mental hospital?'

'Never was,' said Pound.

'Excuse me?'

'When I left the hospital I was still in America. All America is an insane asylum.'

Apathy preferred not to get into that, but Pound was flexing up. 'America is governed by ignorant people. Congressmen and Senators know nothing about the great events of history.'

One of the stringers stirred. Great, greater, greatest. Reporters respond to superlatives. 'Who would you say is the greatest American poet of the age?'

'Ezra Pound.'

That was good for a polite laugh, which seemed to encourage his pal.

'Dr Pound, how do you think Italy might have changed since you were last here?'

'Last time I was here my view was what little I could see through the bars of my cage.'

Notoriously, the American army unit to which he turned himself in back in 1945 had locked him in an outdoor cell improvised out of the steel mesh used to lay airstrips. 'GIs would come and feed Old Ez like an animal in the zoo.'

There had been a war to get on with, the army later explained. Pound's bewildered custodians had been worried that hostile partisans might snatch him for ransom. They kept him caged up for most of a winter, during which he slept on the cold hard ground and wrote much of the Pisan Cantos, the epic and blissfully obscure series of poems that revived his reputation.

Now that I could see how Pound was likely to handle things I thought it was time to get serious.

'Do you think your return will remind Italians of some unpleasant aspects of their past?'

'I don't think it will even remind them of *me*. Most Italians will never have heard of Ezra Pound, let alone remember that I supported their great movement.'

'*Il Duce avete sempre ragioni?*'

He liked that. I wasn't sure if anyone else there would recognise a Fascist slogan from under the paintwork.

'Sure he was right. At least at the time.' The other reporters kept firing off questions but Pound was bent on mischief. He took a step back and swung up his right arm in the infamous salute. '*Viva Il Duce!*'

There was a card-sharp riffle of camera shutters. 'Ezra!' Dorothy pushed his arm down. It swung up again like a pump handle. She grabbed it and hauled him around.

'Oh dear.' Pangler was by my side. 'I think he's been meaning to do that all along. Just waiting for a cue.' Indeed, Pound looked like an unrepentant naughty child.

There was little more to be had in the way of news. That picture was the story. Any words filed would be boiled down to caption and headline. In papers whose readers might have heard of him it would be *Back in Italy, Ezra Pound gives Mussolini salute.* In the others, *Mad poet...*

The photographers headed off. The stringers tossed a coin for the shore telephone. Apathy was watching me, so I said, 'There'll be a line in the passenger terminal.' I let him lead the way but at the head of the gangway, I dodged aside and let him be first to quit the story. I still had questions to ask and didn't want the answers shared.

The guy in the purser's office looked like he might be a serious obstacle, but a back-a-de-front-teeth Brooklyn accent reassured me. 'You're aways from home,' I said.

'Comforts the Americans and makes the Italians think I know all the best addresses in New York.' He stuck his hand out. 'Filipo Bonfiglio. Flip.'

I told him I wanted to bum a lift to Genoa. 'Sure,' he said, handing back my *tessera*. 'Anything for the Press. We'd be breaking the law to charge a fare between Italian ports, so you'll just have to have it on the company. Tomorrow morning, go ashore with the shipping reporters that come on in Genoa and no one will know you were ever on board.'

I went across the passenger terminal and dropped a few *gettoni*. 'I'll be back by tomorrow night.'

'Even sooner if you want,' said Aldo. 'You can fly from Genoa now, you know.' Italy's first internal air routes had just started up, Rome to Milan or Genoa.

'Just might.' I had never flown in a plane.

Back up on the sundeck. Pound and Dorothy were stretched out in deckchairs, looking through newspapers. I told them I was coming along for the last part of the trip. 'Maybe we can have dinner together?'

Pound gave me a green-eyed glare. 'Which one of those mendacious two-faced outfits you from?' The answer didn't seem to mean much, but after an attenuated moment he said, 'And how's Old John?'

'I guess he's OK,' I said. 'Though we're not in regular touch. You know him?'

'Used to. Way back when. We had things in common. Both hated adjectives.'

*

Between then and dinner time I lay on a comfortable bunk and thought of Arabella. On the Thursday after the *palazzo* filming she got to Margutta before me. I'd shown her the spare key for Prudenza, hidden under some broken tiles in a flower trough. It was the size of a socket wrench; I hung mine from a clip on my belt.

239

She was standing at the head of the stairs wearing my bathrobe. As I started up she let it fall open. A few steps from the top I stopped and knelt down, my face within nuzzling distance of her neatly trimmed wedge. The faint scent was like a shot in the arm. No, not the arm. She shifted a foot, parting her long thighs. Her hand on my head pressed me closer. Christ, I'd missed her.

'I hope you're not being *too* nice to Riccardo,' I said to her in due course.

I listened to the laugh she came back with as intently as one of those guys in a submarine movie trying to hear his way through a minefield, but didn't pick up a giveaway note.

'I'm not being *that* nice. In any case, he's having it off, as they say, with that Ekberger.'

'Riccardo is? Really?'

'That's what my old charm school chum Delphine Delisle tells me. She was always a sneak, that one, but not a liar.'

'Riccardo trod on Steve's foot. Deliberately. I saw him. Must have hurt like hell.'

'It's that bloody photograph.'

'Riccardo's seen it?'

'Heard about it. Probably from whatever little toad took the damn thing.'

'Or from Delphine.'

'I never thought of that. Anyway, it's jolly good if Steve's a suspect.'

'Why? '

'If Riccardo thinks I might be being naughty with Steve then *Steve* will be our beard.'

'He's even got one.'

*

240

Soon after the *Leonardo* pulled out of the bay I came across Pound sitting alone in an enclosed deck space. He waved a glass at me. 'Wanna drop a mountain dew?' He was doing hillbilly. Later he would try out more drawls, brogues and twangs, none very convincing. He was putting up warnings against taking anything he said seriously; even truthfully.

'You-all livin' in Rome? That *Stampa Estera* set-up?' I acknowledged that was the case.

'Heard the Rickettses got settled back there again. Elwyn and Candace. You ever come across 'em?'

'Sure. They're still around.'

'We used to be friends, back in the old days. Close friends. I'm going to get some more of this bourbon whiskey. It's half the price here on board as back in DC.'

I wasn't going to let on how well I knew the Ricketts but I thought an account of the Galeazzo-Lisi events might loosen him up for what I really wanted to ask about. And indeed he listened to my condensed version, clowning suspended, a malicious snigger rewarding the punchline about Rick not even getting his camera back. I was working up a double-whammy to fire off once the fresh round of bourbon arrived.

'What I hope you might tell me,' I said, 'is whether you really wanted to stay on in Italy after America got into the war. Or that you had no choice because the embassy people wouldn't let you on the train?'

'On *that* train? With all that human flotsam and jetsam bleating for the homeland, they'd been so scornful about when they were living it up in sunny Italy? There's another one, you know, besides flotsam and jetsam. Another sort of marine debris.'

Misfire. The greatest American poet had fallen back on the first line of interviewee defence: ignore the question. And

241

swung neatly into an evasive move: introduce an off-the-wall topic.

I ignored the answer. 'Just something Caddie Rickard told me.' No harm letting him think I knew more than I did.

'That Caddie, he said. 'Had the finest ass it was ever my privilege to prod.'

'I've heard she was a looker.'

He switched off the mimicry. *'The long flank, the firm breast....'*

'Is that something you wrote about her?'

'It's called *ligan.*'

'What is?'

'Flotsam is stuff that floats off a sinking ship. Jetsam refers to things that have been chucked overboard. Ligan is something left on the sea bed until the owner comes back to get it. A lost anchor, say. That was me in Italy. Ligan.'

It was chill even behind the glass, but neither of us wanted to move inside to the warmth, and lose sight of the coast of Tuscany a few miles off, aglow in the setting sun.

A big ship going through the water produces a lot of noise, exhaust stack blast and the slap of its wash. It was a moment before I realised Pound was reciting something.

> *What thou lovest well remains.*

I recognised that line from the Cantos.

> *The rest is dross.*

He cranked up the volume.

> *What thou lovs't well shall not be reft from thee.*

I remembered 'reft'. Pound specialised in putting language under strain. Over on the far shore lights were starting to come on in the hills.

> *What thou lovst best is thy true heritage.*

He turned a little and looked up at me, a mischievous gnome pushing a dubious explanation of something.

242

This is not vanity.
Here, error is all in the not done.

I was mesmerised. He might simply have felt that seeing Italy again called for some kind of a reaction and those were just a few lines from the hundreds of poems he had written, not yet blanked out by dotage. More likely he was reflecting on his return to a land where he had been well treated by the natives and atrociously by invaders from his own tribe.

In the *not* done. Something he had not *done* had been an error. Implicitly, not getting on to that train, but he wasn't going to say so.

I didn't care.

Sitting there alongside Ezra Pound, mentor of T S Eliot and James Joyce, friend of John Galsworthy, Joseph Conrad, H G Wells, a living monument to literature; hearing a voice like an old phonograph record intone the lines distilled from his hours penned up in that floodlit cage, was one of the mighty moments of my life.

Easily a match for my first glimpse of those Russian tanks in Hungary and the first sight of Arabella naked.

*

I found Pangler alone at a table for six, working on a martini the size of a fire bucket. 'Might as well order,' he said. 'As best I can establish, the great poet has decided to extend his early evening nap indefinitely. You might be able to catch up with them in the morning. I'm sure there'll be paperwork for Dorothy to attend to.'

He looked around the half-empty salon. 'Guess the tourist trash got off in Naples. We're left with the natives.' It was true. The ambient sounds were Italian, though subdued. The real last night of the voyage had been the one before Naples; this was anticlimax evening, ordinary right down to the menu. 'Have they found you somewhere to sleep?'

Somewhere better than I'd expected, in the two-berth outside cabin *con bagno* my new friend Flip Bonfiglio had come up with.

'What number?' I looked at the key tag and told him something a couple of digits different. I was already picking up on Mr Pangler's interests. 'Join me in another of these?' He hefted the martini glass.

'What's the paperwork Mrs Pound has to do?'

'Oh, residence permits, that kind of thing. She's his legal guardian, remember. Far as the United States is concerned, he — Pound — is mentally incompetent. Insane. Of course, I don't know what the Italians might think.'

'What if they decide he's OK?'

'That's their business. Frankly... .'

'Shelby.'

'Thank you. I'm Oliver. Frankly, Shelby, I'll be glad to see the last of them.'

'Haven't enjoyed the company of America's greatest poet?'

He snorted. 'America's greatest phoney. That's not poetry he writes, it's claptrap. Garbage. There are real American poets, Robert Frost, Whitman.'

Of course, it would be Walt Whitman.

I could have won a bet on what he then came out with.

> *Passing stranger!*
> *you do not know how longingly I look upon you.*

I just fed him back an enigmatic smile and remembered Caddie asking what I was prepared to do for a story. I sure wasn't going to do it for this story. 'I was trying to get Ezra to tell me more about why he decided to stay in Italy, back in 1941.'

'And did he?'

'Some. I'd heard he actually tried to get on that train the embassy fixed to take the stray Americans over to Lisbon.'

'What did he say?' A glow of martini cunning warmed Pangler's eyes. I looked straight into them and lied.

'He said he wanted to go but they wouldn't let him on.'

'Far as I know, he's never said that before.'

'That's why I thought it was interesting. Do you know if it's true?'

Pangler was weighing the odds. Was there something he could offer that might help win my favours? Would telling me get him into trouble? Should he or should he not? I stayed in say-nothing mode. Silence is a vacuum.

'There was a memorandum I caught a glimpse of once. Classified, of course. Don't remember who wrote it. Someone who was there at the time.'

Wait. Wait.

'Said Pound showed up just as the train was due to leave. Two women with him. Dorothy and...someone else.' Dorothy and Olga Rudge.

'Thing was, only Americans were allowed on the train. The other woman was American but Dorothy was English. Sure, she was married to Pound but they'd never lived in the United States and she'd never become naturalised. Still had a British passport. So Pound and the other woman could go on the train, but Dorothy couldn't. So none of them did. His decision, I guess.'

'But if all three *had* been allowed on Pound would not have spent those years in Italy? No Fascist broadcasts? No cage? No mental hospital?'

'I guess not. But that was the way that particular cookie crumbled. What say we have a nightcap in my stateroom?'

And no Pisan Cantos.

'I've got some notes to write up.'

Later on, I stretched out on my bunk and listened to Pangler banging on a door down the passageway. 'It wasn't true. What I told you wasn't *true*. You try to print that anywhere I'll deny I ever said it. Ever spoke to you, you...*prick*!'

Maybe Joe McCarthy had been right. The State Department was a nest of perverts and subversives. Well, not necessarily subversives.

Pangler had nothing to worry about, of course. There was no way I could back up his story. Though it probably was the way things had gone, as Pound had let me know in his own weird way.

*

The ship was already alongside in Genoa when I opened my eyes. I had expected to be woken earlier by the bumps and grumbles of people getting off but it was oddly quiet. My porthole looked out on a tumbled city older, more serious-looking than Naples; a strange squared-off lighthouse sprouting over the port, built-on hills rising behind. On the pier below stood clusters of baggage. Buses and cars were lined up, but no one seemed to be tending to the passengers straggling down the gangway. I dived in the shower with the toothbrush and paste I'd bought from the ship's pharmacy, slung on yesterday's clothes to go with this morning's bristles, and soft-footed down the passageway in case Pangler was lurking behind one of the doors.

Flip Bonfiglio was in the gangway lobby, also dressed from the day before and darkly unshaven.

'It's the *Andrea Doria*,' he said.

'Rammed by some Swedish ship off Nantucket Light. She's sinking. Maybe sunk already. Lotta people drowned.'

'She's gone.' Aldo sounded as though he might burst into tears. 'Like the fuckin' *Titanic*! Dozens dead. Maybe hundreds.'

'What about the other ship?' All that day, in and out of the Italian Line head office in Genoa there had rarely been a mention of the *Stockholm*, the liner that had, so it seemed, ploughed into the *Andrea Doria* in a fogbank. In a way it was understandable, The *Doria* was the pride of the fleet, newest, fastest, most luxurious of the Line's half-dozen transatlantic liners. As Bonfiglio said when he told me what little he knew, 'These are sister ships. Crews swap round. Everyone on board them is family.'

There was also the unhappy fact that the *Doria* had been holed on her starboard side. In line with the rule of the road at sea, that could put her at fault. But, in Genoa, if the *Andrea Doria* was the *Titanic* the *Stockholm* was just the iceberg.

Fault-finding, however, was yet to come. The collision happened about eleven at night. *Doria* stayed afloat until ten in the morning but with a bad list that — as with the *Titanic* — meant she could launch only half her lifeboats.

I burned up the phone line to Rome with what I had been able to wring out of the Italian Line, the bureau scraped together what it could from various authorities, but no way could we compete with the stuff coming out of New York: who was safe and who not.

Several rescue ships had taken *Doria* passengers on board and a few injured been picked up by Coastguard helicopters.

It might take days for a full count.

In East 42nd Street bulletin bells would be going off like fire alarms, reporters and photographers all over the piers along the Hudson and over in Jersey, coaxing stories out of the bedraggled survivors. Shipwreck was the greatest of news dramas, trumping skyscraper inferno, earthquake, train wreck. And Century held a couple of aces that would sweep up the game when they hit the table. Queen and knave, more accurately. 'Rick will be storifying soonest,' I said to Charlie, keeping it light. 'To say nothing of Sylvia. Our gal in the lifeboat. *Shipwrecked in my nightdress.*'

'New York didn't know she was on board until we told them. Are you sure she caught the ship?'

'Who can be sure of anything where she's concerned?'

For a second or two, there was only the standard coppery hum on the line. 'Now we're seeing pictures, it looks like that big gash in the *Doria*'s side is right by the first-class cabins. You got the passenger list yet?'

'Cabin plan but no names. They're to be released in Rome by the *Marina Militare.*'

'The navy? What the fuck for?' Then he answered his own question. 'Government want to be sure there was no one on board who shouldn't have been. Fucking creeps. Anyway, you'd better rebase *subito*. Is it right you can fly down?'

'What about DOWNHOLD? Alitalia might not do a Stampa discount.'

'Fuck DOWNHOLD. Fly anyway.'

Bonfiglio was on the dockside getting a hard time from a flustered-looking elderly woman. 'Just tell them it's Olga. That's all you need to say. Olga.'

The airport was just a sort of pier sticking out into the bay. The plane was only a bit longer than a Rome bus, but not as wide. A guy dressed like Bonfiglio got me strapped in next to a priest keeping a good grip on his rosary beads. The engines started up with the sound of a hundred Vespas, there was a jolt that pushed the seat into my shoulder blades. I felt a worrying dip as we came off the end of the runway, but the plane stayed dry and high. Two hours and a bit later I walked into the terminal at Ciampino looking around for Rita. Safer than sea travel.

There was no Silver on the list of names the navy finally released. Not surprising. That was a by-line, not a name. Rick's was there: Tourist Class six-berth cabin down by the screws.

Caddie answered her phone. 'They fished that old asshole out of the drink yet?'

'Should hear something any minute. Meanwhile, what did you tell me Sylvia's real name was? Was her *last* married name Grant?'

'Far as I know. But no need to worry. Be like trying to drown a spider. She'd walk on water in her little spiky heels. Goddamn, she'll be unbearable. The shipwreck queen. Listen, Shelby, soon as something comes in about Rick, you call me *subito*, right?'

Grant was the name against Stateroom 53. We tried to match the cabin plan with aerial shots of the *Doria* starting to go under. It did indeed look as though number 53 might have been right where *Stockholm*'s bow sliced in. 'Thing is,' said Charlie. 'Even assuming she's *that* Grant, we don't know if she actually got on the ship. This list is bookings, not boardings.'

I went downstairs to use a *Stampa* phone. 'Evening, Johnny. Sorry to disturb you.'

'Not at all, old boy. We're just going out the door. Dinner with Macbeth and his lady. That's what we call Lia, y'know. Lady Macbeth.'

249

'It's about Sylvia.'

'Of course. Hope she's all right. Terrible news, what? Expect it's been keeping you busy.'

'Somewhat. So, Johnny, you know for sure that Sylvia was on the *Andrea Doria*?' I could all but hear him wondering if an answer might incriminate him.

Indeed. Put her on board in Lisbon meself. Then flew back here. We had a jolly nice time in Estoril. Splendid fellow that prince. Not like some we could mention, eh?'

Indeed. Speaking of which, do I hear your beauteous daughter in the background?' Christ, I sounded like him. That stupid stiff-upper-lip style was catching.

'Hello, Shelby. Nice to hear from you.'

'Tomorrow?'

'I'll give your love to the Macbeths, shall I?'

> ROME PROHAMMOND SILVER PASSPORT NAME BELIEVED
> GRANT. CONFIRM BOARDED LISBON CABIN 53.
> APPRECIATE EARLIEST RICKARDWISE.

As of that morning, only about thirty *Doria* passengers were left unaccounted for. Where the fuck was the old fraud?

*

'And it's not even Thursday.'

'Riccardo's gone to Genoa. The family's got a big investment in the Italian Line.'

'A sinking fund?'

'I'm glad you can joke about it.'

'Don't need to, now you're here to cheer me up.'

When we got around to the cigarette stage, I rattled off some catch-up stories. I was only slightly surprised that she had never heard of Pound. That drama school had given her an impressive grip on the mainstream English playwrights,

250

Shakespeare especially; she could reel off speeches and snatches from most of the big female parts. Lots of poetry, too, but my new friend seemed to be outside her orbit. She was intrigued, though, by the idea of the *ménage a trois*. 'Did he write any poems about either of them?'

'Not far as I know. There was one that made me think of you, though. *The long flank, the firm breast... .*'

I had looked it up soon as I could get to the English bookshop in the Corso — *Canto CXIII*:

> *The long flank, the firm breast*
> *and to know beauty and death and despair*
> *And to think that what has been shall be,*
> *flowing, ever unstill.*

*

There was no milestone moment to mark the general acceptance that Rick had gone. We just started speaking of him in the past tense. All the rescue ships had reached port, all survivors put ashore. All the bodies recovered had been identified. Eventually, the few names left might be matched to some sodden remains washed up on the New England coast, but for now I started to focus on Caddie.

'I'm OK, Shelby. Guess it had to happen sometime.' No, she didn't want to come out. No, she didn't want me to visit. 'Just let me know soon as you hear something.'

I talked to Esther, with whom Caddie maintained a fractious friendship. 'Listen, Shelby. There's nothing either of us can do. I went round yesterday and she couldn't wait to get me out of the place. Just wanted to be left alone. That was the all-time love-hate deal, y'know, her and Rick. Wait and see which bit lives on.'

I had the occasional drink with Esther in Jerry's and elsewhere. She was silly and syrupy but basically a good sort.

Needed that *Daily American* job to stay afloat after her last divorce from some Air Force guy left her with a couple of kids and not much alimony. Feeding stuff to bigger beasts like Sylvia was a handy side-line for her.

'Hope Sylvia put your payments through already,' I said, keeping things on a suitably detached plane. No one was happy to see Sylvia dead, but she hadn't been one of us here. Family.

'I billed direct to accounts before she left, slugged it REQUESTED CONTRIBUTION PAYMENT DUE USED OR NOT. I hear Caddie gave her a Dracula kiss at your big wrap-up supper. Sorry I missed that.' We elided into the hang-up phase then she remembered something. 'Shelby, what's with all that stuff Caddie's getting from the other passengers?'

'*Andrea Doria* passengers?'

'She had a whole pile of cables there from some guys on the ship. Guys who got saved, obviously. And she's got one of those plans that show where the cabins are.'

'Guess she's just trying to get the picture. Last moments, sort of.'

'Either you get out of there and meet me at the Capriccio,' I told Caddie. 'Or I'm going to come camp on your doorstep.'

*

Hamm called from New York. Charlie picked up and jerked his head at the second earphone. 'You know how much Sylvia meant to Old John. He's planning to give her a big send-off.' We hadn't known, but that was OK. 'He'll be writing the obit himself. Is young Shelby around?'

Charlie's eyebrows went up, but we swapped the phone parts over so I could talk. 'Hi, Hamm.'

'Shelby. Sad times.'

'Sure are, Hamm.'

'Not all bad news, though.'

Why did that make me edgy? 'Glad to hear that, Hamm.'

'Good news for you, anyway.' Tick-tock, tick-tock. Suspenseful pause. 'You've been nominated for a Pulitzer.' Charlie's eyes, a foot of phone cable away from mine, flared like an electric fire.

'You're kidding!'

'No kidding about it, son. Old John himself put your name up. International Reporting category. It's for — and this is *his* citation — distinguished and sensitive reporting of the funeral of Pope Pius XII that enabled readers and listeners all around the world to share in the majesty of the occasion. Unquote. And it's been endorsed by Cardinal Spellman no less.'

I sagged down without looking to see there was a chair. Aldo and Cristof were staring, convinced I had been given seriously bad news. Which was how it felt. 'But doesn't he know...?'

'Button up, Shelby. Why argue with good fortune? Anyway, no need to get *too* excited. Nomination doesn't mean you actually win a prize. Many called but few chosen.'

I was still trying to dredge up something to say that wouldn't make me sound like I didn't want to sound when Rich's tone became even more avuncular. 'Mind, if you *did* get lucky, it might mean you'd be back over here in time for *our* big deal.'

I was clearly expected to ask. 'What big deal's that, Hamm?'

'Betty and me. Betty from Rome, my boy. You practically introduced us! We're getting married.'

*

Am I the first reporter to want *not* to win a Pulitzer?' Marsha showed up at the bureau without calling, bringing Aldo and Cristof crashing to their feet. We went down to the *Stampa* bar.

'Guess you didn't get married, then.'

253

Wry but slightly cheeky grin. If she'd looked delicious as a bride-to-be she looked positively radiant now.

'No dashing young officer of *Carabinieri*? No Sardinia?'

'Especially no Sardinia. I would never have been able to hack it.'

'Lorenzo?'

'I think he's glad, really. He's acting hurt and *tradito*, but I don't think he really wanted to go through with it. The women sure didn't. His mother, his sisters but mostly the *Carabinieri* wives.'

'Sounds interesting.'

'I suppose it was, in a way. The guys, the other officers, weren't so bad. Usual *bacio la mano* shit, and they liked to show off their English. It was the women who did nice cop, nasty cop. They were OK with me for a while, when they thought I was just disposable foreign tootsy. But once they saw Lorenzo was serious, the *fidanzamento* and all that, things got rough. Those congressional committees back home could take interrogation lessons from that pack of haughty broads. "You take job teaching English! Impossible! Undignified. Officer's wife is officer's life." Or something like that. Then it was children. At my age, I shouldn't leave it too late. Jesus, Shelby, I'm twenty-six! I think some of them even got to my gynaecologist.'

She was toughing it out in wry New York style but I could see she was saddened.

'Eventually, a couple of Lorenzo's pals put it to me more or less straight. The *Corpo di Carabinieri* was an exclusive club, they said. Like a college fraternity but with clout. Guardians of the nation, the good guys in a bad world. Which they tried to shut out as much as possible. Most of them — and the wives — were born into the tribe. Foreign wife, especially an American with, you might say, liberal views was bound to have problems fitting in. Which would make her a career liability for her righteous Italian husband.'

'And Lorenzo's family?'

'I paid the parents back for that damn annulment. Cleared me out, but Ted's sent me a ticket home.'

'Noble of him.' Which was not at all what I felt. 'Not via American Express, I hope.'

'Just picked it up from Pan Am. Out tonight. New York in a mere twenty-four hours or so.

He's a noble guy. But I think he's got a reason.'

'I heard he got a new job.'

'Which may be the reason. So what have you been doing, Shel?'

Not wanting to get too deeply into the Pulitzer pros and cons, I told her about Ezra Pound. 'He taught me a new word. *Ligan*. Though it can be *lagan*, I discovered.'

'Sounds like that yoga word for the gentlemanly part.'

'That's *lingam*.'

'And I'm *yoni*. Hi.' She hauled up a big grin, but even with my pants astir I saw through it.

She was not happy. Nor was I that she should more or less simultaneously declare independence and hi-tail it back to the States and out of reach. I sort of admired her for keeping me at arm's length while she was with Lorenzo, though I was pretty sure that I would have been able to tempt her back to Via Margutta that night at *Zi Peppe* for a carefree once-before-you-wed if Caddie hadn't pulled her Dracula stunt.

Not much point in going back to that now, it seemed. I phoned Rita to smooth the way through the airport. Then we retrieved the *topolino* and jammed her bag in back.

It had started to rain and, fighting the suicidal evening traffic, we got nearly to Cinecittá, before I could come up with something that didn't have the ring of disappointment. 'You going to try for a job in New York? Back into the book biz?'

'Actually, I thought I'd like to do something like you do.'

I didn't want to say that she needed to have started a few years back. The best I could come up with was: 'And end up like Caddie Ricketts?'

Silence suggested that I could have done better. I concentrated on blocking bloodthirsty overtakers.

But she reached back to my Ezra Pound report. 'So jetsam is stuff that's been chucked overboard?'

'And flotsam is like driftwood, just flotted off. But *ligan* — lagan, whichever — has been deliberately left underwater, but marked so that someone can find it again.'

'Like sunken treasure? Jesus, Shelby, watch out. You're driving like an Italian.'

*

The Pulitzer nomination was not the only issue of conscience I was grappling with. Up until now, Arabella had left project management to Johnny. But on that last visit to Margutta, pleasure had been followed by the business I had all but forgotten about. 'Remember I told you that Riccardo was getting off with that Ekberger? Well, he's taken her up to Bergamonte with him.'

'So?'

'Well, I suppose I should be happy about it in a way. It means I get James all to myself. But it does seem a little... off, don't you think?'

'You mean in front of the servants and all that?'

'The all that, mainly. Look at what I'm not allowed to do — like walk out with you, or whoever I want to — while he can do whatever he bloody well likes. With that blonde... .'

I lent her a hand with the next word. 'Actress?'

That's what was getting at her. Riccardo had not gone off with someone else's wife, or a girl behind the counter at *Rinascente*. Anita Ekberg was an *actress*. I had seen Arabella sizing up other actresses, those crystal eyes searing into them like a welder's torch; probing, unzipping, reading their moves. Dizzy Delphine did it too when she encountered another of their competitive species, but my lissom Arabella, damp from the trickling hand-shower, snapping her bra and pants back on, was the hands-down champ.

'What if,' she said... 'there were some pictures of them together? Riccardo and... Ekberger. Nothing horrid. Just enough to show that he's not the sort of snow-white father he wants the judges to see him as. Could we do that?'

We...?

Everyone in the bureau had promised to keep their mouths shut about the Pulitzer but when I walked into the *Stampa* bar that evening Gino said, '*Buona sera, commendatore.*'

*

LA CAPRICCIO.
Seppi all Romano
Cacciucco
Ensalata mista
Torta caprese

-You look like you could use a decent meal.

-Thanks, Shelby. That's a fine way to make a widow feel good.

I was being kind. Caddie looked awful. Actually, she looked awful at the best of times. Now she looked ghastly: drained, grey. She had on dark glasses but they wouldn't stay put. Slipped down her nose showing make-up around the eyes that seemed to have been put on without a mirror. When I took her hand the skin felt loose as a glove. There was a faint unwashed smell that I hoped was in my imagination.

-You can't be sure yet that you're a widow. What's actually in these things?

-You mean Rick's gonna turn up clinging to an iceberg, or something? It's been the best part of a week. Anyway, I know. And I know *how*. Bits of meat, peas. Rice mainly.

-And deep-fried. They're great. What do you mean, how?

-I mean because of where he was. I tracked down every one of the guys who were in that steerage class cabin. He was supposed to be in. Spoke to some of 'em, too. Lacrosse team from upstate New York they were, coming back from somewhere. They never saw Rick after the first coupla nights out of Naples. After Lisbon, which is where salivating Silver got on. Never slept in his berth another night. Didn't even leave a bag there.

-Didn't even *have* a bag, as I remember.

-Whatever. Those guys used his bunk for a store-shelf. He was up sprawling around in first class with that slut.

-You can't know that's what happened.

-Hey, Shelby, I'm a reporter, remember. The truth is that if Rick had stayed where he was supposed to he'd be here now. That fuckin' Sylvia was the only one he'd swim outside the goldfish bowl for. I'm pretty pleased she drowned, too. Just the same, if anyone was going to go into the sunset with him it shoulda been me.

-You want to be dead, too?.

Which might even have been the way she felt. But there she was, picking her way around a bowl of fish stew, sopping up the Frascati.

-You were up in Genoa? *Cacciucco* there's better than this.

258

-It's powerful stuff. We should have something sweet after it. What's the *caprise* in the *torta*?

-It's *caprese*. From Capri. Supposedly. No flour. Just almonds and chocolate. This place puts a shot of Strega in it.

-Anyway, it's good to see you.

-Likewise. But we won't be doing it again for a while.

*

Mungo was outside Doney's with some Cinecittá strays. He stood up and steered me away from the table. 'All people want to talk about is this stupid Fellini movie. *Morando*, he's calling it now, whatever that means. Let's go and have one, shall we?'

We went down to Jerry's. 'Congratulations due, I hear. Digby told me.' And, a couple of *babees* later: 'Terrible about that Sylvia. You know she was going to break the news about Lia's big deal?'

'Which has yet to break?'

I hadn't seen any stories, but they could have flowed past me on the wire or been in the business pages back home.

'Far as I know Lia hasn't told anyone else. Ask her yourself if you like.'

So the following day I did. It was always a surprise to see how tiny Lia was; that china doll thing. Except that you knew that if someone dropped her she wouldn't break. She sounded as Hungarian as the Faragó gang but with fewer *dahlinks*. All business, ready to push the story out. Must work Lady Macbeth into the copy.

The New York end of the takeover deal wanted to get some headlines before releasing all the details. She called them up right there and we worked out a schedule. I could only pick up the overflow from the phone against her delicate ear, but Magicali crackled through a couple of times.

Struggling through a thicket of figures in the stuff she gave me, I saw that though no bellringer it was an important business and fashion story. When I was ready to go back and write it up I fired off the time-honoured exit question, the one that sometimes hits a mark you didn't know was there. 'Everyone goes crazy for Magicali. What's the secret ingredient?'

I was standing close enough to see her pupils flash out that split-second dilation that means a hit. '*Eef* I tell you that, *eet* no more secret.'

Playback was instant and gratifying.

LIAOFROME MERGER STORY FRONTING WSJ, NYT, NETWORK RADIO. UPFOLLOW DEVELOPMENTS. HAMMOND.

When Prudenza saw the copy of *Gente* I took home, Riccardo and Ekberger on the cover, she said, 'That's *lo svogliato* who came to the door once, asking who lived here.' *Svogliato*, someone you like to dislike, came up often in our dealings. To Prudenza, anyone not clearly of the working classes was ideologically toxic. Including, probably, me. 'If I'd known he was a prince I would not have been so polite.'

'What *did* you tell him?'

'Just that whatever he was selling we didn't want any.'

'I mean about who lived here?'

'I said I didn't know and if I did I wouldn't tell him. If he was a friend of yours he would know where you lived. If he wasn't a friend you wouldn't want him to know.'

'*Bravo*, Prudenza.'

-23-

Rome absorbed. Enfolded people, softened them with sunshine, wine, mellow yellow walls and easy ways; immunised them to the passing of time and events beyond. Half the *Stamperini* had merely dropped in on the way to somewhere else and never got round to moving on.

I had been there for nearly three years and might have been in danger of going the same way but for the bureau schedule. Even so, the days slipped by all too pleasantly, seasons marked off by weighty considerations like whether to eat dinner indoors or out. I strolled over to the office the same way most mornings, checking out the cheapjack tourists on the Spanish Steps like a gardener brooding over weeds. Coming home in the afternoon heat I would stick to the shady back streets.

My mother and father visited, a breath of crisp Connecticut rectitude. She wore sensible shoes that went with the guidebook borrowed from their local library. He brought along the stiff-brimmed straw hat girded with his prep school colours that he wore every summer. Boaters, the English called them.

They had come over on the SS *United States*, spent a while in London and flown down. Rita got me airside at Ciampino to greet them, which they found impressive. We took a taxi into the city but the following day I introduced them to the *topolino*. I thought they were going to burst out laughing, but mother squeezed in back for a couple of trips. At lunch, they checked out the cutlery.

'No spoons?' my mother said. 'For the spaghetti? The Italian

261

place we go to back home sets out spoons and forks to eat spaghetti.'

'Maybe they've never been to Italy.'

I had booked them into the Inghilterra, an old-fashioned hotel set back a little from the Piazza di Spagna. The bar was cosy; heavy furniture, club chairs that made me think of Mamma Lucia's place. I told them about the *Roman Holiday* association with Via Margutta.

'Very authentic, dear,' said mother after their first look over Number 51. 'Is that damp rising or falling?'

They'd seen the movie and wanted to check out all the locations, especially the Bocca della Verità. They held their hands in the marble mouth while they recited a couple of amusing lies and faked relief that they came out intact. (Months back, when I told Caddy I'd been to take a look at it, she said, 'Always meant to get Rick to stick his cock in there.')

I had worried they might pressure me to ask Century for a job closer to home but I wasn't their priority. My kid sister and her husband, an adjunct professor at Brown, would soon be producing their first child; parental concern was concentrated on that, and whether he was going to get tenure next year. I didn't need any reminding of Marsha, but if I had my parents' straight-up American ways would have done it for sure. Listening to them talk about this kind of stuff, my mind drifted into a sort of home movie starring us as a happy couple, which was stupid, considering we'd never got around to exchanging more than a hug and a peck.

Around sunset, my father's need of a serious drink would surface. So we sat out on the Veneto most evenings, downing a couple of *americanos* before dinner. They liked that, though mother complained she could never get used to eating dinner later than seven. She was ready to concede that the girls parading past were pretty enough, 'But there's always the Catholic thing, isn't there? Was that Gary Cooper?'

'Charlton Heston. He's here for *Ben Hur.*'

I knew more than I wanted to about *Ben Hur*, the mammoth production that had taken over Cinecittá. Arabella had been up for the ingénue part but it went to an Israeli actress, Haya Harareet about whom no one on the Veneto knew zilch. 'More a squeal than a name,' said Arabella, and never uttered it again.

Life, or what passed for it in news schedule terms, trundled on. Rome was warming-up to host the Olympic Games in 1960, a year off; stadiums being built, new hotels, new airport out towards the coast to be called Leonardo da Vinci. The site was swampy and regularly fogbound, but the price was right for the crooks in office who made the deal.

Fellini kept on shooting his movie, setting up locations in unexpected places around the city. He came down to the *Stampa* and invited everyone to meet the actors. The *stamperini* turned in a spirited performance of bawling out questions, most of which Ekberg and a bewildered-looking actor called Mastrello someone, ignored.

The intrepid reporters didn't seem to notice that the camera was on them rather than the players.

I gave the event a miss but Lucy came by a couple of days later with some prints. 'Need names for people.' She passed the shots around.

'What's he doing there?' asked Aldo, stabbing with a fat finger. We all looked at the stranger amid the shitpickers. Riccardo.

'Keeping an eye on his treasure,' said Rita.

She was too dumb to get suspicious about the stories about Arabella and son that I had nudged her into doing, like the one that made the *Gente* cover.

'Everyone call her Ani*tona*,' said Lucy. Big Anita. 'She no like.' I could understand why, even if it were true, at least about some parts of her. 'You know what he call us? In the movie?'

'Who?'

'Fellini. He put all *scattini* from Via Veneto in film, too. He call them *paparazzi*.'

'I thought you said you weren't one. Una *scattina*.'

'Not *paparazza*, either. What mean *paparazzi*?'

Aldo and Cristof went into a shrugging fit.

'Make sure mine's *al dente*,' said Esther.

Esther was there because, working around the DOWNHOLDS, I had signed her up to cover fashion, about which we were getting more and more client requests. She got her teeth into the Roman Kiss development. 'It's a really big deal, Shel. They're setting Lia up with a plane, crew all togged out in her colours, flying her all round the States pushing the products.'

She kept me updated on Caddie. 'Doesn't want to see me either, until she's ready. Nothing personal. Just wants to get used to being the Widow Rickard.'

Even so, I worried. Driving along Flaminia, I stopped and went up to the apartment. Faint guitar music drifted out. My finger hovered over the buzzer. Could I hear a shuffle on the floor tiles? Soft handclaps? The record ran out. I heard the needle scraping. It started again. I envisioned the darkened room, a vast shape, swaying, shuffling, tapping.

*

'Did you know that he calls Ekberg Ani*tona?*' I had to explain. Italian suffixes took some decoding. 'He came along to the *Stampa* the other day to watch her do her stuff.'

'Just like he used to do with me. He'll start showing up on set

264

next.' Arabella giggled. 'Well, she must be a bit of a handful. *Double* handful. Shit!'

She snapped upright on the bed, setting her own more manageable handfuls jiggling. There was a second blast from the wormhole *lupara*.

'Fabrizio's got a double-barrel order in. Four dozen brand-new antique gold-leaf ballroom chairs for some hotel in Miami.'

'He should blow a whistle when he's going to shoot that thing off.'

Temporary command of the bureau meant I could shift my diary around for opportunistic encounters. We had been shaken by Riccardo's mysterious appearance at my door and she stayed away from Via Margutta for a while. But he never said anything to her and, frustrated by the few public set-ups we could manage, normal relations resumed. 'Far as I can tell,' she said. 'He doesn't even know you exist The only time he's seen you was at that silly Fellini event at the *palazzo*.'

'Once in my life, I'm happy to stay obscure.'

'He was probably looking for Steve.'

Even though I was far from happy with the arrangement, Steve put in some useful beard duty during that dry period, taking her places I was also invited: a dinner to mark the Roman Kiss deal, a terrace cocktail party thrown by a couple of Hollywood agents trying to worm into the Cinecittà flesh market. The easy-going double act they pulled off could have meant anything anyone wanted it to. I kept her in the corner of my eye while listening to Mungo's misgivings about Lia's breakthrough. 'She says I'll be able to do things in Hollywood if I go to America with her. Why would I go to Hollywood when Hollywood's pouring in here like a re-run of the bloody Allied invasion?'

Arabella did a fine job of treating me like just another guest, at least until other women there got Steve in their sights and moved in between them. That let me get within dirty muttering distance of her, but there was no chance of another knee-trembler. In the crush of people getting into their coats, I slid a sly hand around her silky Simonetta-wrapped ass and she pushed into it just long enough to let me know there was nothing underneath but her.

Eventually, she called me at the office — neat impersonation of someone from the British embassy — and we were back on track. There were no more sittings with Signor Vestiglio, so encounters had to be squeezed in between hairdressers, dressmakers, and other plausible outings. Afterwards, she would phone for the chauffeur to pick her up at the top of the shopping streets.

'What happened with the portrait, anyway?'

'Riccardo's got it somewhere. It's horrible. He doesn't want to pay for it.'

She'd been there an hour, which was usually her limit. I expected her to head for the bathroom any minute, but there was something on her mind. 'Have you ever been to Cannes?'

'Cannes, France? Where they have the film festival?'

'*Chaldea* been accepted for it.'

'You're kidding!'

'I'm as surprised as you. It's a stinker. But that bloody *Ben Hur* seems to have given *sandalini* a boost There's no chance of it — or me — winning anything, but it's a big deal just to be invited. Steve, too.' She had those glittering eyes on me, mischief surging up in them like champagne bubbles. 'It's in mid-May. Want to come?'

'Of course.' Where the beard went, there went I. Charlie was due back in early May so I could take some vacation.

'It will give me a chance to see Gabby.' Her stateside agent, a faceless guide to her universe. 'The wheeling and dealing there is more important than the movies.'

'You serious about taking another crack at Hollywood?'

'Need you ask?'

But if I did go up to Cannes with her, I later wondered, what would be the set-up? The territory belonged to our Paris bureau and fly-in showbiz writers from New York. The Festival was notorious for management and manipulation. Everyone would be told where to stay, what invites to accept, who to walk out with.

Walking out was Johnny's department. 'You and I can stay with Mitzi, old boy,' he said when I checked with him. 'She's taking somebody's villa there. Always does. Arabella will be in one of those awful hotels most of the time but that needn't worry the rest of us.'

I was still not sure if he knew how close I was to his daughter or what he might think about it. Let alone about how *she* might really think about it. I didn't know that myself. 'We're trying to get Riccardo to let James come along but he's being tricky as ever. Personally, I think he's got his eye on the new nanny.'

'Didn't know there was one.'

'Wendy. Been with us a month, now. English, of course. Pretty girl. Ghastly name.'

*

Cristof shoved a *Paese Sera* story under my nose.

CRIMINE SPAVENTOSO DOPO MATRIMONIO IN GALERA.

I had learnt to start reading Italian newspaper stories at the half-way mark. Before that, they were all flowery flexing of style and no traction. But I went back and read this one through from the top. 'Check it out,' I said. 'Put a couple of short takes on the wire, just for the record.'

> 25:01:59. A YOUNG ITALIAN SCHOOLTEACHER WHO
> MARRIED HER KIDNAPPER IN PRISON WAS YESTERDAY
> CHARGED WITH HIS MURDER.
> GIULIETTA SPADAFORA WAS ALLEGED TO HAVE STABBED
> HER HUSBAND EMILIO PASTORELLI TO DEATH ON THE
> FIRST NIGHT OF THEIR HONEYMOON THAT HAD TO AWAIT
> HIS RELEASE ON PAROLE.
> POLICE IN REGGIO CALABRIA DESCRIBED THE INJURIES SHE
> REPORTEDLY INFLICTED AS 'UNSPEAKABLE'.

'Means she chopped it off,' said Aldo.

-24-

We flew, up to Nice in a jet airliner. Another first. Great machines but an important wellspring of Rome datelines would dry up when they took over the long-haul routes. They used less fuel, which meant fewer last-out-first-in landings at Ciampino. This one was a Caravelle, proudly introduced by Air France only a few weeks earlier. 'Quite safe, old boy,' said Johnny next to me, as we blasted off at a frightening angle. 'Engines are British.'

And Nice was French. All I'd seen of France before then was the wintry view from the train to Rome three years earlier. The little airport at Nice was a perfect *entrée* to the French Riviera: warmth in the early evening air, sea murmuring on the other side of the runway, rustling palm trees, cheerfully indifferent customs agents and a cab driver who flatly refused to take us the twenty-five kilometres or so to Cannes for less than fifty bucks.

It ended up closer to a hundred because there wasn't enough room for Arabella's bags and we had to put them in a second cab with Steve. 'Keep them with you, please, darling,' she said when we dropped him off at the Carlton Hotel. 'I'll come back and check in, soon as we find this other place.' I didn't care for that *darling*, but I guessed there'd be plenty of it flying around in the days ahead.

'We need never have left home.' Every head turned towards Arabella when we went out on the terrace of the Carlton that evening. Everyone looked cast to type. Americans with the wrong clothes, Italians with the right ones, Frenchmen with beards, Frenchwomen with black tarantula lashes. The English just looked English. 'I think,' she said, offering the cinematic rabble a lofty smile, 'I would like a dry martini.'

She liked a second one, too. After that, we strolled along the Croisette, the strip fronting the beach, exchanging volleys of *darling* with Veneto regulars and ended up in a pizzeria called Vesuvio. 'Gabby said this was one of the places to go.'

'I never eat pizza in Italy.'

'You're not in Italy. Besides, it isn't about pizza. We were lucky to get in.' I had seen, beyond the guy at the door who gave us a sharp once-over before leading us to a table, that this was no ordinary pizza crowd; more Carlton arrivals sizing each other up.

She was on full alert, taut as a wire, eyes glinting, every move a gesture. Every so often that spotlight gaze would snap past me to check out the audience. Half a pizza and a couple of glasses of red wine, both better than we were used to in Rome, eventually unwound her. She patted the corner of one eye with her napkin.

'Is that a tear?'

'Bloody Riccardo.'

'James?'

Far from letting the boy come along with her, Riccardo had taken him up to the ancestral estate for some early seaside time. It was in Liguria, just across the top of the Mediterranean from here, the groin of Italy.

'And Riccardo definitely won't let him leave the country?'

'He just laughed. Said if I didn't understand the legal position I should get some better lawyers.'

'Shit.'

'Quite. I couldn't go on with the conversation. Couldn't even talk to James when Riccardo put him on. I started to snivel, had to pass the phone over to Johnny. Don't look now but when you have a chance to turn your head tell me if that's Harry Wangler at the table by the bar. With the badly dyed blonde.'

I didn't know about the dye job, but when I swung around to look for a waiter I saw she was right. Harry Wangler, the Miniature Monster of Maximum Studios, was hard to miss despite being only about five feet tall. Even sitting, the blonde across from him had a top-down view of the yellowing thatch plastered against his little skull.

The table lamp threw a pink glow on the extraordinary moustache I had noted in glimpses of him on the Veneto. It was not a luxurious growth like Digby's or the semi-professional style Johnny wore, but the thinnest line of hog bristles imaginable, sticking out like a toothbrush; he must use a magnifier to trim it. 'Bristles or not,' said Arabella, when I suggested that. 'He's the most powerful producer in Hollywood this year.'

I wasn't sure how the evening was going to end but back at the Carlton she said, 'Stay.'

'I haven't got a clean shirt.'

'I haven't got a clean thought.' We had never spent a night together.

*

The villa was at the eastern end of the bay, beyond the casino. Mitzi had greeted us there and displayed, among other comforts, a couple of neat little Renaults with fringed canvas tops we could use to run back up the Croisette and, as Johnny discovered, a speedboat tied up at a pier. Rolling back the cover left him awestruck. 'Bloody Riva Tritone!' He slid into the

271

driver's seat, looking over a bank of instruments. 'Mitzy, have we got the keys to this thing?'

'We got keys to everything. Just ask *gardien*.'

He crawled out on to the varnished deck and pulled open a couple of long hatches. 'Twin six-cylinders. Bloody fast boat, what?'

I looked down, read *ChrisCraft*. 'American engines.'

He grinned, remembering what he'd said about the Caravelle. 'Thirty knots, easily. Let's take her for a spin.'

I was put up in a sort of attic reached by a staircase bolted to the outside of the building like a New York fire escape, only wooden. Never did work out how many people were sleeping in the villa, let alone where, when or with whom. Janka and Blanka were around some of the time. Mitzy, too, though she was usually saying hello or goodbye to some sleek receiver of smuggled sparklers. Breakfast at Tiffany's every day. Lunch and afternoon tea, too. 'Make me feel so good, *dahlink*, give them back their treasures.'

'Long as the right lady gets the right treasure.'

'Photographic memory, *dahlink*. Photographic memory.'

Regular sleepovers at the Carlton might have attracted snoopery, so for the first couple of days I would slink up to Arabella's room in late afternoon when she and Gabby had finished their go-sees with producers and directors.

Most of the time I liked Gabby, who was small, squat and well-named.

What I didn't like was her clear assumption that I was as dedicated as she to pushing her client's prospects. 'Johnny told me all about you,' she said when we were introduced. She hauled me down by a lapel to whisper.

'We're going to fix this beautiful broad to knock Liz Taylor off her perch.'

272

We?

I had been trying not to brood over the late Sylvia Silver's advice about leavening hackery with flackery. But as much to amuse myself as anything, I did make a sort of game out of rehearsing Arabella for the interviews the disorganised *Chaldea* publicity people set up.

'If it's a man, lean forward, show some cleavage. If it's a woman, don't.'

'What a genius!'

'More seriously, politely decline to discuss Riccardo or James. Just say the legal situation is delicate and that you must put the child's welfare first. Think you can tear up?'

'Weep? At will, darling. At will.'

'Don't say anything critical about Italy or the legal system. You love the place. Plan to spend the rest of your life there to be close to James.'

'I can also lie readily.'

Then I'd watch my beautiful broad dress for the evening: a screening or a party with Steve. There were several days to go before *Chaldea* was shown in the main theatre where the judges and critics did their stuff. That evening, and the final one at which the awards would be announced, were when she got to put on her best outfits and flounce around on the red carpet.

With the ever-obliging Steve. The problem was what to do the rest of the time.

The set-up for accredited press was down behind the Palais des Festivals, so I made sure to stay clear of there. That left the Croisette, the beach teeming with shameless beauties shedding their tops, the restaurants and sidewalk cafés, the sumptuous shops in the Rue d'Antibes; the prospect of running into Brigitte Bardot.

I guessed I could deal with such hardships for a few days, then we'd all go back to Rome.

A couple of mornings I stayed by the villa pool, pretending to ignore indecent exposure on the part of the Faragós. Johnny formed a close attachment to the Riva and we'd stick Janka and Blanka in the back seat for a lunchtime cruise up to the main harbour. He'd let the boat idle around the sterns of some ocean-going cruisers so the people on them could size up our passengers, then ram the throttles forward and we'd thunder off, our wake surging under the big yachts, 'Shake up the bloody marys, what?' He gave the girls his Spitfire glint. They loved it.

Usually, I ate dinner with Johnny and whichever Faragós were around. Later, we would meet up with Arabella and Gabby at the Carlton, too much confusion on the terrace for a snooper to see who might be with whom. There was a lot of table-hopping — outright *leaping* in the case of the Hungarians. Mitzi had something going with most of the Hollywood names, including the Miniature Monster. 'My good friend, Shelby,' she said to Wangler, during one gabble of introductions. Close up, the moustache looked like it was made from those metal pads you cleaned pans with. I'd warned her not to mention Century. Without a tag for him to grip on to, Wangler just dropped my hand and waited for me to get out of the way of the Hungarian tit show.

Before I got too deracinated, though, I needed to check in with the bureau — the Century imperative, vacation or not. There was a phone at the villa but every time I looked one of the Hungarians was using it. I took down the number and that afternoon at the Carlton asked Arabella if I could charge a call to her room.

274

She shrugged. I had learnt to read the signs about what was going on out there. Or, more usually, not. 'Bad day?'

'Frustrating. Gabby's actually come up with something. Or something that might be something.'

'Cinecittá?'

'No! The real thing. Hollywood but this time with a *name.*'

'Name of what?'

'Actor, silly. Or should I say *star*?' She wanted me to ask but she was going to tell me anyway.

'Cary Grant!'

OK, I was impressed. 'What's the...movie?' Should I have said *property*?

'Doesn't matter. I wouldn't be able to do it anyway. Go to America. Anyway, I've got to get dressed.' She headed for the bathroom. 'Make your call.'

*

'Wondering when we were going to hear from you.' Charlie was back to his old needling ways. We'd only spent about half an hour together in Rome when he came in to reclaim his territory, but he'd looked healthy and pink rather than red and harassed. I told him I was going up to see some old friends in the south of France. 'Hamm wants to talk to you. Can you call New York where you are?'

'What's it about?'

'Well, I guess it's got something to do with this. Italcable message yesterday. Slugged personal but we've all read it. Want to know what it says?'

He read it down the line, putting in all the STOPs with leaden teasing. I envisioned the smudgy strips of tape pasted on the cable form.

23:05:59 PROSTONE EXHAMMOND STOP PERSONAL STOP. CONGRATULATIONS YOUR PULITZER STOP. ALL HERE DELIGHTED STOP.

'All here delighted, too, dear boy,' said Charlie. Maybe not all.

Hamm sounded like he was, though. 'We thought the sooner you got across here the better. What about, say, a couple of weeks from now?'

A couple of days from then I was over at the Cunard Line office in Nice negotiating a trip from Southampton, England, to New York. 'Best not stretch our luck and put you on one of those Italian boats,' Roger Traynor had said when he called from London. 'Besides, we'd like to give you a send-off here.' He also let drop the intoxicating words 'First Class'.

Neither the *Andrea Doria* events nor my maiden voyage over in the utilitarian lower reaches of the USS *United States* had diluted one of my lifelong secret dreams: an Atlantic crossing in the grand manner — black-tie dinners, bowing stewards, glamorous fellow voyagers. If anything, the brief taste of luxury afloat that went with the Ezra Pound experience sharpened it. Not on the Italian Line, though. The two great British liners, the *Queen Mary* and the *Queen Elizabeth*, were the only way to go. I signed up for an Outward Passage, as the Cunard guy called it, on the *Queen Mary* two weeks from then and told him to send the bill to Century London.

I had come over from Cannes on the train, crisp, sparkling Mediterranean one side, grey-blue crumpled hills on the other, cute little stations in between. I started to wonder how much the years in Italy might have conditioned me. For all the mellow beauty of Rome, away from the city centre it was ramshackle, shabby and disordered. Here, at least in my brief uncritical assessment, everything looked well-kept and prosperous.

276

Things seemed to get done properly with only about half the effort and confusion. The trains ran on time.

The big item in Nice was the Promenade des Anglais, a sweeping seafront curve of fanciful hotel facades and sinuous palm trees, about three times as long as the Croisette. I strolled half its length and back, wandered away into shady streets behind for a poke around the temples of commerce, had a civilised lunch and looked through my alluring little Cunard pack: colourful baggage labels, a booklet of instructions and another titled What to Do in New York. I hadn't thought much about New York lately, except in regard to Century, but whenever I did the same image flicked up, sure as the logo on a television screen. Marsha. American Marsha over there in the arms — well, maybe not, but in the intimate vicinity — of her recycled and, presumably, still unappreciative husband. What a waste.

*

I hadn't been sure if anyone back in Cannes would be interested in something as far from the movie world as a prize for reporting. Gabby understood though, and drummed up some applause. She gave me a big hug and kiss, as did the Hungarians. The one I got from Arabella was best, of course, more so when she repeated it later when we were naked.

She seemed to choose such moments for hot news items. 'Cary Grant wants me. We talked on the phone this morning. He's seen the rushes of Chaldea.'

'And he still wants you? That was a joke.'

'The question is: will Wangler? It's a Maximum production.'

'You've talked to *him*?'

'Not yet. But he's told Gabby to fix it.'

'So why aren't you happier?'

'You know why.'

*

When I found her at the Carlton that evening she was emitting distress signals I could pick up across the length of the terrace.

'What's up?'

We were in a quiet corner of the sprawl of chairs our party generated. The Hungarians had taken over its far end and behind the wall of noise they created, we could pitch our voices on a private wavelength.

'Riccardo has told James his mummy wants to go off to America and leave him. I told the poor little chap that wasn't true but I'm not sure he believed me. Sooner we get back to Rome the better.'

'So, no Cary Grant?'

Gabby came squirming through the chairs. 'Has she told you?'

'About Cary Grant?'

'About Harry Wangler. About my sensational deal. About the contract I've just spent three hours working on that the Maximum lawyers are looking at right now. That she's going to sign in the morning. I told you we'd make this gal a star!' Arabella pinned me with a glare: shut up.

Steve turned up to take her to the evening's party. It was on some monster yacht. He had on a blazer and white pants.

She slipped me the room key. 'Back about eleven. Talk then.'

*

'Of course I'm going.'

'I guess you always were.'

'Only after we got the OK from Wangler.'

'What about James?'

'James is my business, Shelby.'

The small silence that ensued was due to renewed wonderment at her lightning flickovers from persona to persona. Lover to actress. Mother to actress. Anything to actress — then back again.

A little affectionate action seemed to lighten the mood. 'If we could only straighten things out, I'd come with you on the *Queen Mary*. What are you looking at?'

'Just checking everything's in the right place.'

It was, of course, but I always took pleasure in looking it over. The pink-brown nipples only slightly pulled out of shape by baby lips; the same colour scheme around her nifty little asshole, of which I got an occasional glimpse as we tossed and tumbled. Now, leaning on an elbow, admiring the neat folds and furrows of Arabella's downy delta, a faint line of abrasions caught my eye. Back in my days of opportunistic frat house sex, a frequent complaint was 'carpet burn' — grazed buttocks, knees and elbows. Was this a case of moustache burn?

'Well, now that you've found the right place... .'

I had no intention of mentioning that unhappy sighting. I didn't even want to think about it. But of course I could think of nothing else. I had this vision of *the Miniature Monster* and his spiky upper lip nibbling away at my beloved like a terrier.

The following day I said to Gabby, 'Guess no one gets cast in a *Maximum* picture unless *Harry Wangler* gives the OK.' I might just have been making conversation if, unable to shut myself up, I hadn't added, 'Actresses, I mean.'

We were on the terrace of the Carlton once again-, and once again screened off by the soundwall of Hungarian shrieks, squeals and chatter. Her look turned beady. 'You trying to say something, Shel?' I was, of course, but I didn't. 'Then let me ask you something. You got any idea of the competition for a part

279

like that?'

I took that as a rhetorical question.

'In all of Hollywood maybe twenty, thirty girls might put up for it. Some who've broken through already, some just hit town. Some more beautiful than the rest, some more cute. And, really, any of 'em could probably do the work just as well as the rest But first, they gotta get the work.'

'Which is what you do.'

'No, Shel, I find the work. Who gets it is up to people like Wangler.'

'But if Cary Grant...? '

'If Cary Grant thinks Arabella will stir up some kind of chemistry that will make him, the leading man, look good? Sure that's a big help. But the guy who decides is Wangler.'

'Who strikes me as being the ultimate Hollywood jerk.'

'It's no good getting uppity about the little prick. In the real world, he couldn't get laid in a whorehouse. He and all those other old guys at the top of the studios. Which is why they run their whole weird world like a whorehouse. Except they don't even care about the sex. What I've heard, Wangler doesn't even do sex as most people know it.'

I hadn't actually mentioned sex. And I wasn't comfortable that she had.

'It's ownership. Competition. Showing off to their buddies. Some guys collect Van Goghs, automobiles, vintage wine, old books. These guys collect people. Beautiful people. It's not that Wangler wants his girls to DO things. He wants them to BE things.' It was obvious to her that I didn't like any of this.

'It's hard, Shelby. Hard for a girl. But that's the way it is out there. Some of them, if they need to, pay their dues and reckon it's worth it. They get the part and if they turn out good box

office they can tell Wangler and the rest to kiss their ass —
except that's exactly the kind of thing he likes to do, so I hear.'

She kept on talking, but it was Caddie's growl that sounded
in my ear. 'Well, what would you have done, Shelby? '

Gabby and she would have got along fine, I should try to get
them together sometime.

'This isn't real life, Shel, it's the movies. So don't let shitbags
get in the way of what's real. Live with it. Go along. Hold her
up.'

*

Thus, I was back in Nice a couple of days later, listening to an
embarrassed Englishman explain why the Cunard Line could
not allow Arabella and me to share a double cabin on a crossing
to New York. 'Moral turpitude,' he said, barely able to get the
phrase out. 'It's in the ticket conditions. If the immigration
authorities over there see people with different names in their
passports and the same cabin number they may refuse to let
them land.'

'They couldn't refuse me. I'm an American citizen.'

'But your... companion has a British passport.' As I had put
down on the lengthy booking form. 'The company would be
obliged to take... Mrs Frost back to England. There would be...
publicity.'

I got it. This was an eddy spun off the storm of righteousness
that had been whistled up by the Mothers of America or
Daughters of the Revolution, or another such coven of
hypocrites, after Ingrid Bergman, saint of the silver screen,
respectably wed, had run off with Roberto Rossellini, an Italian
director. Also married.

Why the forces of marital righteousness had seized on that
particular recoupling remained puzzling. Neither of them was

American, even. The real offence seemed to have been that they were open about their romance and the child it produced. Rossellini, in Mungo's view, one of the few genuinely talented Italian moviemakers, was threatened with lynching if he ever came to America and Bergman was denounced as a degenerate homewrecker. In the United States Senate, for God's sake. Sylvia Silver and her like had pushed out stories that the bedroom Macarthyites were limbering up for Liz Taylor and a couple of other big movie names.

'One solution does suggest itself, sir.' The Cunard man was bracing himself. 'You already have a single cabin booked. Why not take a double in the lady's name? The same passageway? Adjoining, almost.' He riffled through his lists. 'I can jiggle things around a bit, but you'd be getting the last First Class stateroom on that crossing.' Then he threw in a man-of-the-world bit. 'You could always use the single for your baggage.'

*

Back in Cannes, the Festival lights had come on at the far end of the Croisette. Usually around then the Hungarians would be winging around the villa, trying on each other's evening clothes. The sound from the big living room leading off the pool seemed unusually muted, so I wandered over. The Faragós were sitting around, rather stiffly. There was also a young woman I'd never seen before, in some kind of work outfit. Johnny was turning back from the bar, gin and tonic in hand. He looked sun-reddened and tousled; been out on the water. All of them were focused on the centre of the room where a small boy in a playsuit was bouncing a large rubber ball off the expensive furniture. He gave me an indifferent once-over.

Arabella's heels clattered across the pool space like a bolting horse. She burst into the room, ran across and picked up the boy. Swivelled around and zeroed in on her father with a burst of stress *tmesis*. 'Jesus fucking Christ, Johnny! What in bloody hell have you done?'

'Piece of cake, old boy.' Johnny nudged me out on the terrace. 'Knew the little beach they use over there. Knew they went to it most days. Only a couple of hours to get across in the Riva, though I was a bit worried about fuel. I just tied up to the jetty, spotted James on the sand with Wendy, asked if they'd like a turn around the bay, and took off. She was a bit upset, but I told her we'd sort things out with Riccardo. Main thing is we've got young James out of Italy and where he belongs — with his mother. And one in the eye for that pretentious little dago prick, what?'

'Look, Johnny,' I said. 'Even if you could get away with snatching the kid on the grounds that he's your grandson, what about Wendy? Effectively you've kidnapped her.'

'We'll just send her back. Put her on a train. I'll pay the fare.'

'It's not the bloody fare, Johnny.' Arabella had come out poolside, where I had led her father. Inside, the women were rushing about, trying to decide where the new arrivals could sleep. 'She hasn't even got her passport, let alone proper clothes. But never mind about her. What on earth were you thinking of?' Her eyes were flashing with rage. 'You've wrecked everything. Riccardo will go crazy. The Italian court will go crazy, Bloody lawyers, judges, the police. Maximum Pictures will go crazy.'

'Perhaps I should take them both back?'

For a couple of moments, I thought Arabella was going to buy that. But she was sizing things up, riffling through likely scenarios.

'I need to talk to Wangler. To Gabby. They've got their publicity people working up stuff about me. They were going to announce it tomorrow. The Cary Grant movie. With me. This will fuck up everything.'

Johnny, reddening and crestfallen, said: 'Let me have a few words with young Wendy.'

'Don't!' Arabella was directing the scene. 'Leave her to me. What you can do is talk to the Faragós. No one outside must hear a word about this. Not a bloody word. We've got to keep it quiet until I can work something out.'

She and Johnny, in harmony once again, turned to enfold me in conspiracy. 'We can do that, can't we, Shelby?'

A warm fluttering had begun in my solar plexus or, as I believe it is properly called, the celiac plexus. A girl I knew who dabbled in the mysteries of the East told me this core of our being was not a mere bundle of nerves but the energy centre from which we drew confidence, personal power and self-esteem.

In my case it was where those old imperatives lurked that divided hack and flack. Getting it right, getting it first, getting it out.

'Actually, it might be a story that would do you some good.'

'No!'

'This is the kind of thing our little understanding is about, isn't it, old boy?' said Johnny. 'Kind of thing we need to count on you for. Keep it off the record?'

Hell we could. This was hard news. Erectile, even. Apart from what was going on in my gut, my brain had lit up like the Croisette.

Riccardo's reaction? Police complaint? And, as ever, how to file.

'Not quite, Johnny. That's not how it works. We didn't agree to keep anything off the record.'

Had we gone on, I might have conceded that a lot of people

didn't understand the fine lines to be observed if they wanted to keep a reporter from reporting, such as a clear understanding beforehand. Anyway, it applied to stuff people said, not what they did.

'You mean you're going to let us down?' Arabella's look modulated into cold appraisal. She turned around and marched into the house.

'Doesn't look that way to me, Johnny. You can't keep the lid on this. It's a hell of tale. Even if you didn't mean it to be.'

Arabella kept me in sight from the open door. She had James in her arms, one foot dangling. Poor little guy had come away without shoes. I took a step towards her but she turned away into the house.

*

The urge to file was as pressing as a full bladder. I had already decided the casino was the place to go. There would be phones there for big losers to call home. I strode down the hill, feeling for a fistful of francs, but my fingers hit bottom.

A couple of heavies, one in evening dress the other turned out like a French admiral, watched stone-faced as I patted myself down, trying out expressions for their benefit — puzzled, exasperated. Pleading would be wasted. I had my passport, so no problem there, but it cost five thousand francs to get in the casino, a lousy ten bucks, plus whatever it needed to get my bag looked after while I was on the phone.

I knew what had happened. My neat fold of small franc and big lire bills had been sitting alongside the stuff I was ramming into my bag. I was separating the Cunard pack, ticket, labels, checklists, Advice to Passengers, into his and hers when Arabella came up to the room. 'Please, Shelby. Don't ruin everything for me.'

285

She was as beautiful as I'd ever seen her. No make-up, eyes glistening with gathering tears. "Why should it? More likely to do the opposite.'

'You don't know that! They're so moralistic, these Hollywood people. Can't it at least wait until my contract's signed?'

'Don't see how. It'll break somewhere, anyway.' Or would if I could get these goons to let me at a phone.

*

'Well, look who's here! Sammy? Solly?'

'Shelby.' It was the guy from the dubbing session lurching out of where I wanted to go. Gary. I'd seen him up and down the Veneto a few times with the religious Finn *pedo* trailing half a step behind. Like he was now, drunk as only a Finn could get: waxen, sweaty, ready to throw up.

'Bad night, old buddy?' asked Gary, swaying gently. 'Clean you out? Went the other way for us.' He opened his jacket to show a clump of bills in the inside pocket. 'Plenty for a good night on the town. Wanna come along?'

'Sorry….'

'Sure? Might be fun, away from home base and all that. 'Sorry, pal.' I turned away but a heave to the shoulder spun me around. I thought the Finn was trying to hug me, but he was stuffing 10,000 franc bills in my top pocket. *'Vages off sinn,'* he mumbled. *'Vages off sinn.'*

Beyond him, Gary shrugged.

'Go try 'nother spin of the wheel.'

'I'll pay you back,' I yelled as they tottered away.

'Get the headset,' I told Aldo. 'After I give you the bulletin, call me back for the rest. Then get on to Newspix. They've got plenty mother and son shots. See if you can get someone out from Genoa to knock on the father's door.'

23:05:59.BULLETIN.SHELBY STONE. NICE, FRANCE. IN A
DRAMATIC TWIST TO AN ARISTOCRATIC CUSTODY BATTLE,
MOVIE STAR ARABELLA FROST'S FATHER TODAY
SNATCHED HER YOUNG SON FROM AN ITALIAN BEACH.

Then I took a cab up to the railroad station. If there wasn't a train to Nice there were enough francs left for a cheap hotel. I could lie in bed, look at a peeling ceiling and brood on the cost of that exercise in reporter sovereignty.

As I resumed my packing, Arabella had focused on me like Johnny squinting mercilessly down his gunsight, eyes aglow, lips moist and parted, breath like a flowerbed.

'If you don't send the story until we're ready, I'll make you a promise... '

She was sweating slightly. That smelled marvellous, too. 'No matter what else happens, we can go on doing this whenever you like.'

'This?'

'You know. Fucking.'

'Whenever I like?'

'Well, whenever I'm around. Do what I'm asking and you can have me any time you like. Anytime. Anyplace.'

Hell of a promise. And as fine a piece of actressing as she'd yet turned in.

287

-25-

'Just as well you're getting out of town.' Charlie probably had the reputation of the bureau in mind rather than my welfare, although as ever with him, it was hard to tell. But it helped make my homecoming even more uncomfortable.

First, there had been police all over 51 Via Margutta, most of them crowded into Fabrizio's workshop by the entrance. I sidled past into the courtyard and joined a group of fellow-residents. 'What's going on?'

'Fabrizio found this guy storming around the place, yelling. He waved his *lupara* at him and they started pushing each other. The gun went off.'

'Good God. Anyone killed?'

A guy guffawed. 'It was just birdshot. Only enough powder in the cartridge to make those wormholes in furniture. Wouldn't even draw blood.'

'You wouldn't say that if you'd had a dose of it.' It was my neighbour from the window opposite. I hadn't recognised her with clothes on.

'Do we know who it was got shot?'

'That's the best part. It was a prince. Or that's what he was shouting when the ambulance came. Yelling out names.'

'What names?'

'His own, I think. Bergamonte? And something that sounded foreign. *Chames?*'

The bureau pieced together a workmanlike account of the event from police sources, recapping on some of my copy of the day before. As soon as he realised his son had been abducted, the story said, Prince Riccardo rushed down to Rome. He had not, at that stage, known of Group-Captain Findlay-Frost's dramatic coup, or that the boy was in France. He suspected he might have been taken to Via Margutta — 'haunt of the city's bohemian set' — by someone close to his glamorous actress wife. The accident that followed was due to a misunderstanding with a watchman.

From what Aldo and Cristof had been told by the police, Riccardo seemed to have had his suspicions about Number 51 but not, it seemed, about anyone in particular living there.

The story didn't just have legs, it took off in leaps and bounds. The Maximum publicity people grabbed the twister Arabella threw at them and ran with it. She — and James — vanished on the eve of the *Chaldea* screening, leaving Steve to make a carefully calculated stroll along the red carpet on his lonesome. Great picture that made the covers of three Italian glossies and *Paris-Match*, no less: He Walks Alone.

Still, as Charlie said, it looked like a good time for me to get out of Rome for a while.

I escaped from the *Stampa* without too many questions about how I had pulled off our scoop, but walked into an ambush in Jerry's that evening. Digby, who would have given half his *baffi grandi* for such an exclusive, was hungry for the inside stuff. Mungo was slightly disapproving. 'But you were their guest, old chap? Staying in their house.'

'Don't know whose house it was, really. But what difference does that make? Johnny was quite upfront about what he'd done. No secret about it.'

Johnny had also gone missing. None of the coverage mentioned the villa but even the dimmest of showbiz reporters must have found it.

I called the number half a dozen time but it rang out.

'Well, they're in the shit now,' said Digby. 'Or will be if they ever come back here.'

'She won't need to come back. Off to the big time, now.' Mungo had caught up with the movie moves. 'Cast opposite Cary Grant in a major Maximum production, title yet to be announced. Daresay Lia will be after her to endorse the new Kiss line for America.'

'Anyway,' said Digby, sliding a *babee* over to me. 'Who are we to quarrel with a Pulitzer prize winner?' He meant it graciously. 'Here's to the *dolce vita*. Don't let them keep you over there too long.'

Mungo downed his *babee* and looked around for the next.

'That's what that oaf Fellini is going to call his monster movie. *La Dolce Vita*. Not very original, is it?'

*

I dialled Caddie's number. '*Chi, parla*?' Prudenza. A tommy-gun rattle of questions. Was I all right? Had I been involved in the dramatic events at Via Margutta? What had happened there? Was this so-called *principe* the *bighellone* she had seen skulking around there?

'Prudenza, please let me speak to *la signora*.'

Silence. 'Prudenza?'

'*La signora non c'e.*' She seemed surprised I should be asking. I realised it was several weeks since I had left Caddie to her miseries. I called Esther.

'Hi, Shelby. Nice story. Even made our front page.' The *RDA* was notoriously cautious about using any but the most anodyne Italian stories for fear of offending local sensibilities.

'I saw. I'm flattered. Look, what's with Caddie?'

'I wish I knew. Ask that nun with the scissors?' She sounded hurt.

'Mother Jo?'

'Of *Vogue* magazine, *Women's Wear Daily* and other glamorous showcases. Caddie seems to have moved in with her.'

*

Lucy was also pissed. 'You didn't tell me those things happen in Cannes.' We were at Newspix, drinking that pink Caruso. 'You know whose pictures of *la principessa* got used everywhere when this big news happen? Fernando, that's who. With his little *agenzia*. Why you not tell me your big story?'

'Because I didn't know it was happening. Not until I was up there, anyway. Listen, Lucy, what's going on with Sister Jo? Cadence Ricketts?' I didn't think she knew Caddie, or at least not well. But she dropped in regularly to Holy Shirt.

'Why you not ask *them*?' Partly because I didn't know if Caddie would appreciate me checking up on her. Mainly because I thought I might not like the answer. 'Anyway, I been invited to your big send-off celebration.'

I knew this was in the wind. Charlie was organising something with the bureau people and a few *Stamperini*. I thought it wouldn't be polite to enquire, except to say that yes, of course I was free the following evening and, no, there wasn't anyone I'd like to bring along.

'Where are we going? *Zi Peppe*?' Smile fades to frown.

'Joke.'

'You don't know?' She flicked some news cuttings out of a basket. 'Must have been day you left.'

I hadn't looked that far back in the file, and there had been other claims on my attention. The clip was from *Messagero*. Start reading half-way.

> ... *e così il corpo acquerellato del famoso ristoratore, attore, ballerino, cantante Winchester Starr fu trasportato a riva*

> *dall'antico fiume Tevere, accanto al quale aveva fatto la sua*
> *casa e il suo più grande successo come....*

'Drowned! Winchester drowned himself?'

Lucy rolled her eyes.

'Someone did it for him? Who'd want to kill Winchester?' Apart from anyone who'd ever heard him sing.

'Naples wife father, of course. Winchester lost him much money.'

'Lost? That place must have been taking in millions?'

'And those *ladroni* who work there take it all out again. I told you. More *truffatori* in that piazza than in Regina Ceoli.'

'And poor old Winchester got the blame?' Where is the mafia bride?'

'Gone. Maybe gone with your *principessa*.'

'Very funny. Put that stuff back in the *frigo* and I'll buy you a drink that I can drink too.'

*

Gino gave me a big hello when I came into the *Stampa* after a fairly embarrassing tussle with the bank. Booking that little old *Queen Mary* stateroom in Arabella's name had eaten up all but a few of the thousand bucks worth of traveller's cheques I had gone up to France with.

But he was looking past me, and I turned to a smartly suited guy struggling out of one of the sagging chairs. I missed the name he announced when he stuck out a hand but caught the part that mattered. '...*tenente di Carabinieri, Ufficio dei Stranieri.*'

Out on the terrace, he explained politely that he was in charge of the investigation into the recent dramatic, not to say shocking, events concerning the distinguished family Bergamonte. It seemed possible that a serious crime may have been committed and he would be grateful if I, who had produced the first account of the apparent abduction of an Italian citizen — the young prince — would agree to a brief interrogation.

I knew enough about policemen to fall back on basic principles. Reporters got stuff out of *them*, not the other way around. Naturally, I said, I would do everything I could (consistent with my professional obligations) to help his enquiries. Might I offer him a *caffè*? A Lucky?

Our conversation was painfully polite. I told him everything he already knew, or should have if he had read the newspapers. He asked how I had become aware of the alleged kidnapping. I told him that while on assignment in Cannes, I had called on *Il colonello* Frost, who was an acquaintance rather than a friend. Quite by chance, I arrived just as he was returning from Italy with the young prince. No, I lied blandly, I had not seen him or his daughter the princess in Cannes before that time. I returned to Rome rather than stay until the end of the festival in case there was more work to be done in the matter.

Was I saying, he wanted to know, that I had no idea where she or the boy might be now?

As cops usually do eventually, he slipped into heavy mode. I must be aware that keeping information from him could get me into serious trouble. I could see, though, that his heart wasn't in it. Nor was mine, since I really didn't have the slightest idea where she might be holed up.

Nevertheless, I had one for him. I could see that recent events might create difficulties in the civil proceedings over custody of the boy. But I knew that James had been born in London and that Arabella had him registered, as the British allowed a parent to do, in her passport. Could it be a criminal act, I asked, for a mother to take possession of her own child; one who, as I understood it, was a British national?

293

He seemed not to have known that little James was a Brit as well as being Italian. He thought for a moment and said that an Italian court might not consider the nationality of the child relevant. In any case, while the mother might be violating a court edict by keeping the child out of its jurisdiction, the actual kidnap appeared to have been perpetrated by the grandfather. *Il Colonello* Frost must expect to be pursued.

This was helpful stuff for future stories and, since no one had agreed otherwise, all on the record. As he got up to go, he said, 'I believe you are acquainted with an old friend of mine. *Signora* Ford.'

Marsha? I took my first look at the card he had handed me while we had been talking, *Tenente* Feltrini, Lorenzo. Shit! Lorenzo, the former *fidanzato*.

'She told me a lot about you,' he said.

'Nothing good, I hope.' I also hoped he realised that was a feeble joke. 'Have you heard from her lately?'

'Just one letter. She returned to her husband. I forget his name. The one she divorced from. They were getting married again. Do things like that happen often in America?'

*

I hadn't been to Holy Shirt for a few months; had enough of the products to last me a while. But Mother Jo gave me a big hello. In the workroom two nuns were laying out patterns on the table, so we sat in a corner. The sister who had opened the door to me came along with a *napolitana* and poured us coffee. The essentials of the place had not changed since Caddie first took me there but there were signs of expansion: a sort of showcase in the *antecamera*, photographs taken by Fernando, and later Lucy, on the walls; the stutter of sewing machines in the next room.

'We are grateful for the publicity you and poor Senora Silver made, but the extra business gives us some problems. People say we should move but where could we go? We are a community *in seclusion*. Making shirts is not our principal vocation. That is why we will never be able to export, except via an agent — if I could ever find one to trust_ So, people who want Convento shirts must come to Rome.' She gave the nuns at the table a little sign that sent them wafting out of the room. 'You know what this house is, Shelby? Apart from a shirt factory, that is?'

'The women from the *case chiuse*?'

'You have heard about that? It is the sacred mission of this Order, going back to medieval times. To care for women who have suffered, in the main, simply for being women. Maybe you know about the little *oubliette* in the wall outside?'

'Where women used to drop off unwanted babies.'

'Quite so. Caring for those abandoned souls was also part of our mission, as was looking after their mothers and others who, as I said, were suffering the penalty of gender.'

'Caddie doesn't quite fit in there.'

'Perhaps not. But she needed a haven and we are happy to have her here. She does not want to see anyone for the moment. Not even old friend like you.'

'At least get her to call me.' And a few days later she did.

'I'm going to New York next week', I said. 'People are going to ask about you.'

'Tell 'em…' There was that grunting laugh. 'Tell 'em I've got me to a nunnery.'

*

I went back to my real preoccupation of the last few days: wondering about Arabella. Had she realised that I left her the Cunard ticket? Some kind of dumb gesture of… I dunno, hope?

I hadn't been thinking about detail during those parting words at the villa. But it began to dawn on me that while she sure wasn't going to come to the United States *with* me, if she needed to go anyway — particularly with James — the *Queen Mary* would offer a better chance of ducking Riccardo than the cattle run through a couple of airports pursued by half the world's reporters.

Wondering if I should just have tried to get a refund, checking off the things that had to be done if I was going to leave for London in forty-eight hours, I walked half the length of the Forum before remembering the *topolino* and had to go back for it. I wasn't scheduled for the slot but I told the others I'd come in and take a turn.

As I pulled up by the *Stampa* building, Giuseppe the car wrangler signalled me to stay put. Usually he would have three lines of cars up against the recessed kerb, heaving them around with his one good shoulder as owners came and went. Today there was plenty space and I could see why: a big *Carabinieri* saloon was parked, the driver and another uniform sprawled in front. 'Not allowed to block them in,' Giuseppe said. 'Their boss went into *Stampa Estera*. Been there half an hour.'

I'd never seen a cop of any kind in the *Stampa* until Lorenzo showed up the day before. Not to worry, I told Giuseppe and drove around to Margutta.

'Ah, there you are, *signora*,' said Charlie as soon as he heard me on the phone. He got it right away, of course. 'Do you know where Shelby is? There's a gentleman here waiting to see him.'

'Carabinieri? Tenente Feltrini ?'

'I thought you'd be the best person to ask. Do you know if Shelby is on his way here?'

'No chance. I think he's planning to leave town.' I didn't think Feltrini could get anything serious on me but there was every chance he would try a little bullying to see what more I knew. Even lift my passport which, given my schedule, would be a great inconvenience.

'That's a *very* good idea,' said Charlie, arch and theatrical; enjoying himself. 'I'll ask Rita. She'll be in her usual spot.'

Ciampino. I called her there. When she finally grasped what was required she said: 'The British European flight from Athens is due in at 1600. It's got pick-up rights.'

Most of the long-distance flights that dropped in to refuel were not allowed to take on passengers for European destinations. But the London-bound BEA flight could. 'You got your ticket?' Nope, but Century now ran an account with the airline and both Charlie and I could sign.

'Better hurry.'

Rita breezed us right on through the customs and border police barriers into the departure lounge, big smiles to all in sight. 'See you in a month,' I said, giving her a hug. It was like heaving at a mattress.

I left her the key to the *topolino*.

Three hours later I was in London, much as I'd left there three years earlier. Suitcase, typewriter and no money.

-26-

London was so goddam *quiet*. In the way that eating in France had shown me I had been conditioned to the pleasant but limited flavours of Italian cooking, I realised I had also become inured to the clamour of Roman life: honking cars, rasping Vespas, mindless music, every voice cranked up to be heard over it all. The buzz and clatter of the Century newsroom down off Fleet Street came as a relief.

Roger Traynor wanted all the details. Charlie had filled him in on the reason for my early departure and predicted that the problem would have faded by the time I was through in the States, especially if Arabella and the boy stayed out of Italy. Johnny, too, of course.

'So if she decides to surface, with or without the boy, let's hope we'll be the first to know.'

I would be the first to know if she decided to use that *Queen Mary* ticket but I wasn't going to let Roger in on that highly tentative possibility. I hadn't the slightest idea what I might do if she did show up but I didn't want Century making up my mind for me.

He took me to the White Elephant again, to celebrate the Pulitzer, in which he clearly believed he held a stake for having posted me to Rome. This time it was lunch. Even in daylight hookers crowded the sidewalk. 'Legal now, aren't they. Along with homosexuality?'

'Typically British. They've legalised the girls right enough, but it's an offence for them to let you know they're on offer.

298

You're supposed to think they're waiting for a taxi. As for the queers, it's practically become a requirement in some quarters.'

We had to talk of Rick, of course, and when he asked about Caddie I just said she wasn't feeling good and had moved in with some friends for a while. He wasn't that interested. The Rickards belonged to New York. His territory was Europe. But it brought him around to the *Zi Peppe* dinner. 'You must have seen I was right about Charlie having a problem. I'm going to try to do something about it. Anyway, you'll be happy to go back to Rome when the day of glory is behind you? Still as Charlie's deputy?' I assumed I was supposed to pick up the slight emphasis on *deputy*.

'Why not? He runs a good operation.'

'One that's likely to get bigger. The file out of Rome is a damn sight hotter since you went down there. Lots of play, all along the wire.' That was true. I had broken a lot of new ground with those mailers, and the picture spreads with Lucy. I had also polished up the routine coverage, even put some zing into the dreary political stories, mainly by working the dread words *Communist Party* for all they were worth. Italy was relatively untouched by most of the Cold War truisms but God-fearing Americans liked to keep themselves scared.

'I've been thinking of putting in an extra hand down there. Someone like you when you started out. Could lead to a few other changes.' The pings were getting louder. I was wondering how to move the conversation on when he slid off-script. 'Thinking of our party evening reminded me. Ever hear anything from that Marsha?'

'Only that she went home and got married to her husband again. Divorced husband, that is. Ted. Ted Ford.' I wouldn't have told him or anyone else that I had found myself brooding about that. Marsha's adventures in Italy and the way she dealt

299

with them showed she had more going for her than a neat ass and some worldly smarts. Sure, I had seen her as a target of opportunity, even if the opportunity remained elusive because of Lorenzo then, farcically, because of Caddie's snack attack on poor Sylvia.

'Yeah. People thought she might have come back from Italy..' He performed a little cupped-hand *gesto* around his belly. 'But, it seemed not, far as I know. Now they're in Washington.'

'DC? He still with Century?-'

'Bureau Manager.'

Manager explained why I hadn't heard of this before. Switching from journalism to administration was usually a career backslide but in Washington, with some twenty specialist correspondents to be managed and maintained, the back office would be as powerful as the newsdesk.

Way down beyond the hormone layer, I had harboured the dim expectation that she and I would, at some stage, get it — something — together. Now, in some way beyond my understanding, she seemed to have taken herself out of the game and doing Ted a mighty favour he had in no way earned.

'She's working too, I heard. In television. Not on camera — be a while before we see a girl doing the news. Something technical.'

'Well,' I said, having to say some damn thing. 'I guess those old marriage vows mean something after all.'

'Loyalty. Loyalty's the glue that keeps this business together.' And there I thought it was booze. Champagne by the pint and vintage claret still counted as booze.

'What about a glass of port?'

*

I had only two days in London, mostly spent getting management to redirect my salary and come up with some walking-around — not to say crossing-the-Atlantic — money. Outside of places like the White Elephant, much of the old town still seemed to be showing in black-and-white. The Aldwych Hotel, where Century grudgingly put me up for a couple of nights, had a tea dance every afternoon: dim chandeliers, string quartet, gigolos with shiny hair pushing prospects around among the potted palms.

I expected the Boat Train from Waterloo Station to be more of the same, but it was a blaze of rich purple velvet, gleaming mahogany, shimmering brass. Tea in fine china cups and dinky little three-corner sandwiches. A steward delicately detached the top layer of my ticket. He shuffled through the rest of the pack 'No *Not Wanted* items, sir? Bags not wanted on voyage, he meant. My single suitcase was parked in a bay at the end of the car showing off its glossy Cunard stickers. 'You'll be able to go straight on board, then. Bon voyage.'

I was in for five more days of that slightly assertive servility. It emanated from the assistant purser, or whatever he was in the passenger terminal at Southampton, who peeled another sheet from my ticket pack. My fellow passengers were standing guard over heaps of Not Wanted but a flunky in a striped apron cut me out from the herd and led the way along a covered gangplank into the First Class sumptuousness of the *Queen Mary*. We took an elevator down a couple of decks and I followed him along a passageway, sharp right into a narrow corridor to Cabin 56.   Cabin, not stateroom. The stateroom was 58, the door opposite, no more than four feet away. *Advice to Passengers* had told me that US dollars were standard currency on board so I gave him five. Then I checked out my quarters: bathroom, bunk, porthole, wardrobe, dressing table, armchair, call buttons and went up on deck.

When I was a kid my parents had held this great ship up as a symbol of grandeur, elegance and technical accomplishment to equal the Empire State Building and the airship *Hindenburg*, although number three slot went to the Union Pacific railroad after the *Hindenburg*'s sad end.

She seemed to stretch forever, forward and back. Also up and down. In addition to the walkway, I'd come along another half dozen gangplanks led directly into decks lower down. Cabin Class passengers were using an entrance half-way down and, closer to the waterline, Tourist Class lugged their own bags on board.

Gleaming brass signs showed the way to bars and dining rooms, cinemas and swimming pools. At the top of a grand staircase, the Observation Bar was a vast semi-circle surrounded by art deco panelling and tall windows. It offered a fine view of rusty dockland rooftops on one side but on the other were a couple of husky tugboats getting ready to haul us out.

'Martini, sir?' The bartender was English enough but I could tell he knew about Americans. 'A Perfect Martini. Speciality of the house.'

'Of the ship, shouldn't that be?'

'Of course, sir. Ha-ha.' I hadn't heard of a Perfect Martini in three years: 50-50 sweet and dry vermouth along with the gin. What the hell, it matched the decor.

After a while I went back out on deck. The atmosphere had shifted from shoreside bustle and confusion to serious seagoing stuff. There was a thunderous blast from the steam whistle on one of the three tall smokestacks, the deck trembled underfoot and the tugboats took the strain. The last mooring line splashed down in the water, as glaring a symbol as anyone could read. Clean break.

Even without the tips in the Cunard welcome pack, I knew the score. Black tie for dinner but not on the first night out nor the last; I could stay dressed as I was, just wash up a little.

Back in Cabin 56 I had visitors: Martin the cabin steward. 'Just press the button for tea in the morning, drinks, anything else you wish, sir.' Kate the stewardess. 'I'll collect your things for pressing, sir, and for the laundry. Fresh bed linen every day, of course.'

It was a real bed, too, not a bunk, though I noted it had boards on each side that could be slid up and down to stop me rolling out.

I had my shirt off and was splashing around to check the hot water supply when the next caller arrived, guy in a smarter uniform than I'd seen so far, officer's cap under his arm.

The little badge on his jacket read Passenger Relations Manager.

'Awfully sorry, sir, to have to barge in but I'm obliged to check this boring moral turpitude stuff.'

He was shifting from foot to foot like someone who needed to pee. 'You mean you want to see if I've smuggled someone in here? Look under the bed?'

'Not here, sir.' He swung a glance over at Number 58. 'Just need to make sure you're settled in here. Not over there in the stateroom.'

I took a close look at him. The dim light in the passage threw a shadow across his face like the dumb moustache I had first seen back in Adam and Eve Mews.

'Jeremy, isn't it? What the hell are you doing here?'

He sidled into the cabin, looking as though he feared I might grab him by the throat. 'Hadn't realised it was you,' he said. 'Behaving turpitudishly. Never knew your second name.'

I made him sit on the little dressing table stool. Took the

armchair for myself. I would have liked a drink but that would have involved ringing for my man Martin, who might not approve of hobnobbing with the help.

Jeremy kept on apologising, which I assured him was unnecessary. 'How're things in the Mews? How's VeeVee?'

'Great. Just great. She'll be chuffed to know I've seen you.'

I wasn't too sure about that.

'She's on the *QE*.'

'*Queen Elizabeth*?' The newer sister ship and the venerable *Mary* made alternate crossings, one steaming eastwards across the Atlantic as the other went west.

'Trainee assistant purser. So she's rather junior to me. Makes for a laugh.'

'Means you can't be seeing much of each other.'

'Best way to keep a marriage together, some say.'

'You're married? Congratulations.'

'Three years, now. Bit rushed at the time. VeeVee's mother looks after the little boy.'

'You've got a child?' An uneasy stirring in the plexus. 'Any chance of a discreet drink?'

'Each of us gets a day or so with him each trip. And we get a week off, one crossing out of ten. I'll nip along, see if there's something in the steward's pantry.'

I was still counting on my fingers when he got back with a half-full Johnny Walker bottle.

'I'd better not have any. Got a few more welcome-on-board calls to make.'

'More turpitude suspects?'

'Well, the immigration people over there do get nosy.'

'Tell me about it.'

'There's just another couple. Couple of couples, actually, old friends. Always make the crossing this time of year. One lot's

American, other French. They come on board in their right order, adjoining cabins. First night out they swap partners. Stay that way for the rest of the voyage. Since they're marrieds it wouldn't be a problem if one pair weren't foreigners.'

There were thumps and scuffling of baggage being hauled around the passageways, loud American voices calling to each other.

'I'll see them settled in and after that I'll only need to make sure everyone's back in the right cabin night before we dock and that they haven't been cheap with the tips so the servants stay quiet. Apart from them, it's just the usual bunch of card sharps, jewel thieves and con men to keep an eye on.'

'So have you got a dossier on me, or what?'

'Nothing like that, no. Just word passed along from head office that you shouldn't be allowed to share quarters with... Number 58. And that we ought to try and keep the two of you, er, separately occupied, during the crossing. You and... the princess, that is.'

'Well, looks like you won't have to worry about that. I suppose I could even spread myself out over there.'

Jeremy looked even more dumb. He seemed to think I was making a joke beyond his grasp. Losing the moustache had been a mistake. 'Not much time to enjoy it, sir.'

'Christ's sake, don't call me sir. You mean the stateroom over there is going to sit empty the whole damn voyage?'

'Just for another few hours, sir. Sorry. You get in the habit, you know, sir and madam to everyone. Only till we get to Cherbourg.'

I had completely forgotten the ship would put into the French port just across the Channel. A trickle of hope sprang up to dilute the dregs of disappointment that were souring this epochal experience, mingling like the two vermouths in that perfect martini.

There were plenty of places in the first-class dining room, a great cavernous art deco box rising through a couple of decks, one end of it dominated by a mural of the Atlantic with the ship's course picked out. 'Wherever you please, sir,' said the man with the Chief Dining Room Steward badge. 'No seating plan until lunch tomorrow.'

I sat at a large round table, an empty seat on either side and a dreary looking British couple opposite, too far away for any but rudimentary communication. Then I went back to the Observation Bar and watched the lights of the French coast draw near.

Only one narrow gangway was run out. I looked down on it from three decks up. In the bar I passed through there had been talk of a very short stopover; something to do with the tide. There was a pungent salt smell, mingled with a strong whiff of Humphrey Bogart. I could imagine him sidling out of the waterfront shadows in the light drizzle, fedora brim down, trenchcoat collar up, butt stuck to lower lip.

The new passengers trickled across from a sort of warehouse. The first of them looked to be Tourist class, shambling along with their bags. A squad of crewmen in porter's aprons shouldered past them to collect baggage for the high rollers. I could see the Cabin class batch being mustered and into the wall of light spilling from the ship they came, led, I was appalled to see, by Johnny goddam *tmesis*-inducing Findley-Frost.

That was going to take a bit of thinking about but not now. First Class began to straggle out, middle-aged mostly, gesturing at the porters who outpaced them, even with cabin trunks on their shoulders. Umbrellas opened up, marring my view, but I picked her out, perfectly dressed for the occasion in a light coloured Bogart-ish raincoat and beret.

James marched along by her side.

Clangs and rumblings suggested we were getting ready for departure. I had no idea how to get to where the end of the gangplank came into the ship so I took the elevator down and found my little alleyway jammed with bags. Martin and a porter had filleted out the Not Wanted stuff and were about to take it off somewhere.

James stepped forward, made a little bow and put out his hand. It was unlikely he remembered me from the brief glimpse we had of each other at the villa, but he knew what was expected of a gent.

'Hi there,' I said, meaning it for Arabella, too, who I could see inside Stateroom 58. She still had the coat on but not the hat; a few raindrops glistened in her hair. She was pale, slightly disarrayed and unbearably beautiful. 'Hi there,' I said again. With one hand she hauled James inside. With the other, she slammed the door in my face.

*

When it came to segregation Jim Crow had nothing on the Cunard. Once onboard, the passengers in each class were herded up in their own corral, out of sight or sound of the others except for the boat deck which was divided — unevenly — between First and Cabin by a ropework curtain like a huge tennis net.

Up there a gang of weather-beaten guys in caps and reefers ran some kind of deckchair racket. It was the custom, I discovered, for passengers to negotiate with these genial exploiters for a sunny corner where, after an extravagant breakfast, they would be wrapped up in blankets like disaster victims and fed cups of steaming bouillon until it was time for lunch. It seemed a questionable pleasure since once the ship worked up to speed the blast from the stacks, the roar of huge ventilators sucking air down to the boilers, made a noise like a hurricane.

Johnny spotted me the first morning out, mooching around, and we talked through the ropework squares, the deckchair heavies keeping close surveillance.

'So here we are then, old chap. Despite your best efforts.' The wind flattened the hair against his scalp and his skin looked scraped thin. Even though his age was showing the harsh sea light picked up that killer glint in his ice-chip eyes.

'Meaning?'

'You could have wrecked everything, putting out that story.'

'You serious? It was priceless publicity. Might even have clinched the contract.'

He shoved a sheaf of telegrams at me. '*Life* magazine, *Look*, all the glossy magazines, want pictures. Interviews. Perhaps you'd like to repair a bit of the damage. Lend a hand to keep these wild beasts at bay, what?.'

'Doesn't look like damage to me.'

'You couldn't...?'

'Sorry, Johnny. Get yourself a flack.' The word tasted good.

'Well, think about it at least We don't have to decide anything before we get to New York and the Maximum people smuggle us off. No one knows where we are. That's something we do have to thank you for, I suppose. The ticket. Though I had to pay for James.'

'Arabella won't even speak to me.'

'She may feel it's a bit risky. The Cunard people read her the rules.'

'Who needs rules? I'm in my cabin, she's in hers. Which I paid for. How did *you* get a ticket, by the way?'

I knew the crossing had been booked solid.

'Wangler. He had some influence.'

'Not enough to get you over on this side?' I wiggled some fingers through the netting.

'No position to demand favours, old chap. Don't suppose a few days with *hoi polloi* will hurt, what?' His gaze slid past to range across the more generous stretch of sundeck behind me, the hooded companionways leading down to the delights of First Class. 'Though I did spot some familiar names on the top end of the passenger list.'

I could read the calculation in those icy eyes. 'But if you and Arabella are no longer on speakers, you might consider... '

'Swapping berths with you? Nice try, Johnny. See you in New York. What?'

*

Jeremy and his gang had obviously worked out a drill to keep the moral degenerates well clear of each other, but they were wasting their time. Arabella behaved as though she'd never seen me before and didn't want to know me now. The first couple of nights out the ship's officers hosted twee little cocktail gatherings for passengers to meet and mingle but we were never invited to the same one. I rarely saw her during the day, although she always came to *Luncheon*, as the programme had it, where the seating plan kept us as far apart as possible.

Similarly at dinner. The traditional honour of a place at the captain's table had been watered down to accommodate demand. The table was round and seated a dozen, eleven of whom were passengers, rotated at each meal. I was not at all surprised to see that on the night the routine kicked off the seat to the captain's right was occupied by the longed-for flanks of my beloved.

'That's that Italian princess, had to run off with her little boy,' my companion at the table to which I had been banished — the purser's — informed me. 'Papers in London were full of her. Nice Simonetta, she's got on. Saw it in Florence last year but in turquoise. Looks better in yellow.'

She was a princess of Seventh Avenue herself, part of a large delegation from the garment district heading home after looking over the fashion season in Europe. I'd seen her already, cutting a rug in the Starlight Room along with the rest of the *schmatte* crowd, cha-chas and sambas polished to perfection at vacation classes in the Catskills and Miami Beach. Made me feel homeside already.

'We get 'em all on the old *Mary*, honey. Movie stars, crowned heads. No one gawks.'

'You make the crossing often?' I was getting a grip on the vocabulary.

'Every year. For the show, you know, Paris, London, Florence. There's a dinky little synagogue and you can keep kosher if you want. On the *Elizabeth* it's just the chapel. Ecu-*men*-ical. Mannie and me are Reform but we don't eat shellfish or pork products.' Across the table, a guy in a blazer and striped tie wiggled his fingers at us. 'We're in coats and cloaks. He cuts, I seam. Along with the rest of them, that is. We got thirty in the workroom. You're not Jewish?'

'Sorry.'

'Oh, well. Someone's gotta buy retail — that's a joke. I'm Sophie, by the way.'

So Arabella had been made. If this one knew who and what she was so would everyone in these parts by tomorrow. The inevitable was shaping up. Meanwhile, being Not Wanted On Voyage gave me plenty time to explore. The delights of First included spaces dedicated to most of the activities a passenger might wish to perform or commission: pray, play, eat, drink, read, write, exercise, swim, smoke, bank; be barbered, manicured, massaged, coiffed, get children cared for or have your fortune told. Elsewhere in the vast hull were swimming pools and squash courts, garages packed with limousines, kennels — and, for all I knew, a village green and a goddam cricket pitch.

These distractions, however, could not stop me from brooding and, often as not, it was Marsha who stood in the foreground rather than Arabella. I wasn't exactly mad at Marsha for getting remarried, but I was goddam puzzled. Disappointed. Deprived, even.

I had got stuck on the idea that she and I were of the same ilk. Maybe not the same label but products that belonged on the same shelf. We were counterparts in *affinity*. I was quite pleased with that concept until my junkyard brain recalled that the mathematical model of affinity showed that even if lines were parallel they would not necessarily converge. Thanks a bunch, Euclid.

Jeremy cornered me at one cocktail *soirée*. 'About the Jag, old chap. Could be worth quite a bit, you know? Sotheby's has started vintage car sales. Same model — slightly better shape, mind — brought nearly five thousand quid last time. Ours might do as well with a bit of touching up.'

Ours?

'Where is the car?'

'Chap I know runs a garage. Trouble is, we couldn't put it up for sale without the logbook.'

'Told you I wasn't sure where to find it.'

'Same with the garage then, I'm afraid, old chap.'

It had been a mistake to let him stop calling me sir.

*

Even the goddam ship's doctor had a table and he was a sight to stop anyone reporting sick. He had weaved in its direction, tottering downhill on the heft of a wave and came up all standing, looming over his guests, plainly smashed. A couple of stewards who had been scuttling in his wake grabbed an elbow each, the ship rolled the other way and he fell back into the chair that a third steward stuck under his ass. There he sat in his white evening gear, like a mound of crumpled Kleenex.

'Don't worry, honey', said the woman I had wound up alongside in that round of table swapping. 'There's a nice little hospital downstairs with proper doctors and nurses. I guess it's your first time on board.'

Eleanor, thirty-five or so, blondish, brown-eyed and promising fun; a lingerie buyer from Saks Fifth Avenue. 'All things slinky and frilly. You know — stuff that's meant to look good on the floor.'

Nice teeth, too, when she smiled. 'A reporter? Know anyone on *Women's Wear*?'

Then, the ritual New York checklist School? College? Where do you live? Parents and siblings? Married? Never? Not once even? How come?'

'How come you *are*?' She had a wedding ring, although it was lost among the clutter of metalwork weighing down her fingers.

'What I mean is.... '

'Do I like girls?'

'Pretty sure you do. I watched you checking out that princess.'

I checked out Arabella every time I could pick her out amid that well-heeled horde. She would take James along to the Children's Suite, part nursery, part playroom, in the morning and either stay there with him or do some ladylike stuff in the salons. What she did in the afternoons, I couldn't make out. Not what I would have wanted, that was for sure. I cornered her on the big staircase. 'Why the hell won't you talk to me?'

'You know why. We're not supposed to be... turpiduous?'

'You can't say that. It's not a word. But anyway, we can *talk* if we want to.'

'Then I suppose I don't want to.'

*

It was quite easy to miss people in that vast floating warren of passages and playgrounds. I didn't see Eleanor again until the day before we were due to dock. The only experience I'd been denied, I told her when she asked if I'd enjoyed the voyage, was being able to eat in the Veranda Grill, an *a la carte* restaurant high up under the bridge. The maître d' who turned me away seemed surprised I was even trying to get in. Smart passengers booked in there when they bought their tickets. Or the voyage before.

'I can get a table.'

The Veranda existed in a different dimension from the slightly patronising atmosphere of the First Class dining room. The lights were low, we could see stars twinkling through the windows in the curve of the superstructure and make out the mainmast gently ticking across the night sky with the roll of the ship, one side then the other. There were only about thirty tables, all set up for two or four and the help was craven beyond redemption.

A solid block of the tables was occupied by Sophie and friends all, like me, dressed down for the last night. A sly old strolling fiddler billed as *Moshe and his Stradivarius* was sidling about, scraping out *schmaltz*. 'So, you come here often?'

'Most nights, in case any of that crowd want to pitch a deal.'

313

'I meant the ship. The crossing'

'Four years running: London, Paris, Rome, Florence. I'd go to Rome anyway once a year, just to stock up on Roman Kiss.'

'Lia Macbeth?'

'You know her?'

'Among others.' The preliminary interrogation had established that I worked in Rome.

'Like Princess... whatever? They can't get over it, the garment crowd. Finding themselves on the same ship as a royal runaway.'

'Not royal, really.' Close enough though, for a headline.

*

In the *telefono bianco* remoteness of the *Queen Mary* at sea, I had been able to put off doing anything about the incipient exclusive I had to face up to. But with New York no more than a night away, I knew the celebrity freaks on board were bound to point Arabella out to the shipping reporters. Some might have mentioned her already in a homecoming cable.

That afternoon I had followed signs to the Wireless Telegraphy Room. Beyond a little reception space, several guys in smart jackets were tapping away at telegraph keys, just like in an old-fashioned Western Union office. The honcho at the counter had shoulder flashes reading International Maritime Radio Co. He saw me look over at a Teletype behind him and shook his head. 'Only in port, I'm afraid, sir.'

'Cable then.'

'Certainly, sir. Radio, actually. Forms are over there.'

'And you'll send it before we actually get to New York?'

'Ha-ha. But there's always a bit of a pile-up before landfall.'

CENTNEWS NEW YORK. 10:11:60 SHELBY STONE. ABOARD THE QUEEN MARY. ACTRESS ARABELLA FROST WAS ON THE WAY TO NEW YORK TODAY WITH THE CHILD SNATCHED

FROM HER ITALIAN HUSBAND PRINCE RICCARDO DI
BERGAMONTE.

New York would roust out Rome and Hollywood to fill in the rest of the story. But by-line bandits would have a hard time beating that. *My* scoop.

'Thank you, sir. Four dollars a word. One hundred and sixteen dollars. We don't charge for the cable address.'

'Jesus! Is there a press rate?'

'Sorry, sir.'

'Take out *di*.'

'That'll be one hundred and twelve, then.'

He read it again. 'Perhaps, sir, you'd like to make it *On board* instead of *Aboard*? More maritime, like. *Aboard*'s what the train conductor says. You know? All aboard!'

'So back to a hundred and sixteen?'

I handed over the shiny new American Express card the London back room had given me. Maybe the bill would get lost.

I didn't want to go on talking to Eleanor about princesses. 'You'll be able to get Roman Kiss stuff all over the United States soon. I wrote some pieces about it.'

'Won't be the same, though. I hear the magic's gone out of Magicali.'

'Really?'

'The not-so-secret ingredient.' She leaned close to whisper. It was like having a basket of flowers shoved in my face. Nice, though.

'You're kidding!'

'That's the word in the trade.'

A check appeared from nowhere. I reached out but she grabbed it and signed. I thanked her sincerely and she gave me a shy grin, twisting away at her rings.

'Thing is, these trips give me a kind of get-out-of jail card. You

315

know, out here on the ocean, who's looking, right? But time runs out when we get back home. In the morning. There's just this chance, Shelby.'

It was tempting. She was nice-looking and, as Marsha once said, it had been a long drought. Shit, *Marsha*. Even before Roger told me about the marriage rerun, whenever I tried to settle on some new emotional wavelength she kept butting in like an FM station just out of range.

Perhaps that split-second flashback put something in my face that Eleanor's deal-making smarts picked up on. 'There's a girl, isn't there? Wasted my time, I guess. Maybe you should wear a badge.'

She stood up with a jangle of metalwork. Not angry, just a bit rueful. 'Change your mind, I'm in number 36.'

Moshe was pushing his fake Stradivarius under her nose.

I gave him five bucks to go away and sat there finishing my glass of fine French wine. The metallic clanks faded then got louder again and Eleanor was back.

'You're not a Republican, are you?'

-27-

Not all the celebrated monuments of travel are over-rated. All that stuff left over from ancient Rome is wonderful. The Eiffel Tower is a genuine marvel, so is Tower Bridge. I'm ready to concede the grandeur of the Grand Canal and even, sight unseen, the Grand Canyon. But that righteous emblem of my native land, the Statue of Liberty welcoming all who steam up New York harbour, is liable to let you down.

To begin with, the main ship channel runs up the East side of the bay, quite a distance from where Liberty lofts her lamp over the New Jersey shore. Secondly, there's so much industrial haze and skyline clutter across there that she's hard to pick out. If it's raining, as is often the case, forget it. But what mainly prevents arriving passengers getting a good look at this legendary symbol of all America holds dear is that they are likely to be stuck below decks, awaiting the mistrustful attention of the Immigration Service agents who come on board with the pilot.

When this moment arrived we were herded into the main First Class lounge. Distinctions were at last abandoned, the watertight doors that sealed off the Cabin section rolled back, its denizens peeking around to see what they had missed.

Us versus Them became Americans versus Aliens. US citizens were dealt with fairly efficiently, marshalled into alphabetical groups. I could see Eleanor way upfront. I'd never grasped her last name but it was way ahead of Stone.

She spotted me as she collected her passport and turned to walk out. Came up with a wiggly wave. Too bad.

Aliens, including Johnny as well as Arabella and Son, lined up around the Cabin class dining room where the process would take much longer, straining the impatience of the reporters and photographers who had pulled alongside in the wake of the pilot boat. Especially the photographers, old hands with Speed Graphics and a police pass stuck in their hatbands, expert at persuading glamorous female arrivals to perch on the sundeck rail for a leg shot. What they were after this time, of course, was the crucial princess-and-son picture.

The Century team found me in Cabin 56. The photog squeezed out a little whistle when he shuffled the handful of pictures the ship's photographer had snatched for me in the Children's Suite when Arabella was having tea with James. Fine, sharp, black-and-white prints of a mother hug, one vertical, one horizontal, a steal at fifty bucks. I had taken his strip of negatives, too, in case he got other ideas.

'Only story in town for days,' the Century reporter said. 'Bet you got a great interview.' 'You know how to hurt a guy. Five days at sea, she wouldn't say a goddam word to me.' Which was true, far as it went.

*

Still wondering if I should take up Eleanor's kind offer, I had opened the door to my little cabin and found James sitting up in the bed, leafing through a couple of *fumetti* he must have brought on board.

'About time you got here,' he said. 'I'm supposed to be asleep by ten.'

On the other side of the passageway it was Hollywood already. The lights were low. There was champagne. We sipped it from shallow *coupes*, the way the Cunard liked to serve it. Looked deep into each other's eyes. Kissed long and eloquently. Frilly folds slithered downwards. I didn't bother to check if

318

they looked good on the floor. 'Is this... ?' Reconciliation? Resumption?

'Not at all. Offer withdrawn. You didn't keep your part of the bargain.' It didn't seem like the time to say that there hadn't been any bargain, at least not so far as I was concerned. 'Just think of this as...off the record.' I nodded like a dumb jerk and Ezra Pound moved in.

The long flank, the firm breast...

And to think that what has been shall be flowing, ever unstill.

Flowing went on for quite a while, but sometime in the early hours we ran dry. I've heard the postcoital arrangement we'd wrestled our way into called spooning, but there's too homely a ring to that. In the restricted bed space, my knees in back of hers flexed those long flanks downwards, spilling organ warmth from her cooling parts on to my depleted ones.

Across her shoulder I watched the surface of the champagne, flat now, tilt with the gentle roll of the ship. Those *coupes* were said to have been modelled on Marie Antoinette's tits. If that was the case, Napoleon could have done better in that department. I certainly did. Arabella's were not large but they had made a firm comeback from having to deal with the baby James. One filled my hand, the other lay soft against it. Her nipples were always sensitive, the slightest squeeze was good for a gratifying shudder. I squeezed. 'We could have been doing this for the last four nights.'

'No we couldn't.'

'So tell me why.'

'Because I didn't bloody feel like it, that's why.'

'And all because of a story that seems to have helped, at least, to get you the part you were after?'

'I would have got it anyway.'

'Well then, whatever I did doesn't come into it.'

'You talked to Gabby about Harry Wangler.'

'So what?'

'It was none of your business. You had no right to ask her those questions.'

'What questions for Christ's sake?'

'She told me you wanted to know what Wangler wanted.'

'Only in a general way. She gave me an interesting little lecture on how stars are made.'

'I can imagine. She likes to tell it straight from the shoulder.'

'From someplace, anyway. So I guess you knew how it was going to be with Wangler.'

'How do *you* think it was?'

'From what she said, it seemed to me that the deal depended on you letting him gnaw your crotch and whatever?'

'We say *crutch*. And there wasn't any *whatever*. That's what Wangler does, it seems. Whenever he signs someone up.'

'Like Cary Grant?'

She giggled. 'For all I know. But I think it's just actresses. It's his little... ritual. Everyone's had to put up with it just the once, Gabby says.'

'Put up with it? Like a dutiful wife? Lie back and think of England?'

'Of Beverly Hills, actually.' More giggle. 'Look, Shelby, it doesn't *matter*. It's over. Gone. Finished. No need to do it again.'

'You hope.'

'Yes, I do. But listen, Shel. It's *my* crutch. Crotch. What I do with it is *my* business.'

'I still don't know why you wouldn't at least speak to me all this time.'

'Just so everyone could see we weren't *turpituding*. It was just *acting*.'

Actressing.

I carried James over, still asleep, and put him in his bed. Then I took a shower, dressed, packed up my stuff, put the suitcase out for the porters and went up to meet the guys off the Press boat. They'd bought a pile of morning papers, all with my story somewhere on the front page, if not always the wood. By-lined. When I got back Arabella's bags were also out, Martin would be along in a moment for his tips.

The door of Number 58 was open. She was at the dressing table working on her eye make-up. 'The nice stewardess has taken James off to breakfast so I can get myself ready. I'm glad we've started speaking again. It's a pity you always have to *write* things.'

There ensued one of those pauses that form the great punctuation marks of life. 'You're not going to write about *this*, are you? Me and James being here, I mean?'

Not going to... Perhaps because what might come next is always uncertain, most languages don't have a range of future tenses to match those of the past, the broad grammatical reach of the *preterite*.

It would have been good to chat with old Ezra about the preterite and lament that, by contrast, actions that were yet to occur had to be marked out with flabby auxiliary verbs — *will, won't, going to, not going to*. As in I was not *going to* answer Arabella's question.

As it was I didn't need to resort to evasive verbal sophistry because my eye fell on the little bottle in Arabella's hand, and Eleanor's mischievous whisper replayed in my ear.

'Is that Magicali? For Christ's sake, don't try to take it past Customs.'

'Why ever not?'

'Because it's full of cocaine, that's why.'

'Not *full*, darling. There's only the teeniest *tincture*, Lia says.'

'So you knew that was the secret ingredient?' I seemed to be the only person around who *didn't* know.

'Lia's mother says there's nothing like it to give the eyes that certain glow.'

'Get the rest of you glowing, too. But if they found it in your stuff you could go to jail.'

I unscrewed the heavy porthole fastening and flipped the little bottle out.

-28-

My first audience with Old John took place the day after I had checked in, fresh off the *Queen Mary*. Hamm set me up for it with no warning at all. 'He said to send you along soon as you were settled in but that's not what he meant. John doesn't cut any slack. I'll tell him you're on your way right now. He likes to be called colonel, remember.'

The apartment building was on Sutton Place South just up from East 53rd, one of those massive granite-faced fortresses from the 1920s, doorman in dove-grey uniform and silly hat. Inside, a guy at a desk, whose jacket said *Concierge*, phoned up then nodded me over to the bank of elevators standing ready for take-off.

The doors slid open right in a foyer. There were impressive pictures all around and a couple of hefty sculptures. First I thought the little guy in work clothes standing in the centre of half an acre of oriental rug must have come to fix a pipe. But since he said, 'Hi, Shelby,' I decided he must be the oddball media monster who ruled my destiny. 'You know what floor we're on?' He had his head on one side, that birdlike way old folk do when they're sizing you up.

'Thirteen.' It wasn't a $64-question. The elevator indicator had said fourteen, but as in most New York buildings like this, the scary number got skipped. I had seen twelve go by.

'You noticed that, huh? That's good. Reporters gotta notice things.'

No one had told me Old John was so *small*, built like a jockey, the wrists sticking out of his shirt cuffs thin as twigs. As I followed him across the carpet I looked down on his shiny scaly scalp, no bigger than a New Jersey turnip.

Nor that he was quite so old. Because I knew he had that time in common with the Rickards I'd vaguely assumed he was their contemporary, but a quick look at *Who's Who in America* before I left the office showed he had been born in 1865, the end of the Civil War for Christ's sake. In this year of 1960, he was ninety-friggin-five.

The outlook from the huge room he led me into was stunning: to the left the great spans of the Queensboro Bridge and, to the right, open water all the way down to where the Century building peeked out from behind the UN.

'Great view of the river! *Colonel.*'

'It's not a river.'

I gave him the rest of it, something any kid who'd been to school within a hundred miles of the city could have done. 'It's a strait.' Which, of course, the East River was, a channel that linked two larger bodies of water: Long Island Sound and the Bay that I had steamed up the day before.

He cackled. Another bird-like characteristic, but it seemed to conclude the entry exam.

'You here to collect that Pulitzer, right?'

'And I heard I've got you to thank for it... colonel.'

'What they give it to you for, now?'

The correct answer was probably *because you told them to* but maybe he really had forgotten. 'The funeral of Pope Pius.' I wondered if I should add 'in Rome,' but he might have thought I was being smart.

'Shit, yes. Great colour story that was. Lots of play all over. Not me you should be grateful to. Thank Cardinal Spellman. He sent your piece round to every priest in the diocese. So why has Caddie Rickard become a nun?'

Was there a link there I'd missed? With people as well plugged in all over as John, it's hard to tell how much they might know about what. 'I don't think she wants to be a *nun*. Just looking for some peace and quiet.'

'She never looked for any when I knew her. Hell-raiser, that girl. And what a looker!' I still found it hard to envision Caddie looking anything other than she did all the time I'd known her. She could have slipped Old John between her tits and presumably once had.

'She was badly shook up by what happened to Rick. We all were.'

'Best thing for her. Pity it didn't happen years ago, not that I wanted him dead. Everyone always knew though, back when they were hot stuff with that double-dip by-line, that most of their best work was hers.'

John perched himself on the edge of an upholstered chair. If he sat back in it his feet would have been off the floor. I didn't want to stand hovering over him so I folded myself down on to a sort of footstool that brought our faces more or less level. I wondered if I should say something in Rick's defence just to be sporting, but it was as well I didn't.

'I wanted to tell him to his face that he had made a fuck-up over Galileo... what's his name?'

'Galeazzo-Lisi.'

'Yeah, him. Bad enough losing the money but losing the story, too...' The bird eyes were aimed past me, across to the shambles of Queens on the far bank. It probably looked better at night. 'Guess he thought I was going to fire him at last. Which I surely would have, if I'd known he was going to get Sylvia drowned.'

I couldn't let him go on talking to himself, so I said, 'Way those ships came together, colonel, she didn't have much chance in that cabin. Wrong place, wrong time.'

'Took me years to train that slut up to be a public bitch. Even though she was a natural for it. And we had some sizzling fun along the way.' He seemed to have got over the dislike of adjectives Ezra Pound had told me they shared.

'That Caddie was something in the sack, too, let me tell you. That sound disrespectful, talking about a nun?'

'I don't think she wants to be a nun.'

'Ah, yes. You said that, didn't you? You know the age is getting to you when you start to say things twice. Three times. Start to forget things. Memory is the first thing that goes.'

He had me fixed with those birdy eyes. I wondered if he had forgotten what he was going to say. But no. He pointed down at Welfare Island, the two-mile-long strip in midstream previously renowned only for a large looney bin and a few crumbling colonial buildings. 'You heard about this, right?'

By now all Centurions knew about Our Founder's crowning folly. On the southern tip of the island stood the Newswire Newstower. Come the first of next month, Century's half-century anniversary and, coincidentally, Old John's ninety-sixth birthday, a huge mushroom-shaped steel structure over there was to light up, and a news ticker twice the size of the 'zipper' that ran around One Times Square start to roll. The flow of text, snippets from the A-wire, would intermittently switch from right-to-left, putting up languages like Arabic and Hebrew that went in the other direction.

Then there was that sleight-of-foot hustle I'd had before from the imperious. Servant with coat — in this case an oriental houseboy, like in the best old movies — and an eye cocked towards the way out. Brisk jostle of handshakes, farewells, good-of-you-to-come and I was back in the elevator, thinking of stuff I *could* have said.

*

The Pulitzer event took place a week later. The evening before, I went to dinner at the Traynors. 'Betty's been asking when she's going to see you,' Hamm said. 'I think she's planning to fix you up with a date.'

The apartment was in the East 50s, well inland from Old John's place and a fraction of the size. If Betty was worried I might drop a hint about her carefree Colony nights there was no sign of it in her greeting. The other guests made for a pretty straight-up party: a downtown lawyer and a *Herald-Tribune* section editor, each with wife; divorcée travel agent named Donna, who also lived in the building, matched with me.

The women all had wide red mouths, hair piled up, swirly skirts that threatened to sweep plates of snacks off the low tables. In London, young girls had been wearing hemlines hiked up to the crotch. Crutch. Here I'd seen a few hiked well north of the knee but occasionally a skittish gust of wind would deliver a glimpse of that old deterrent the panty-girdle. For all that we were hearing about The Pill, American womanhood had not entirely abandoned the first line of defence.

The talk was wary, too, much the same as when I had left four years ago, a granny-ish feel to it, the autumn tones of the Eisenhower years. In Italy, the Cold War was well over the horizon, but back here it rumbled under the news every day like subway noise along the avenues.

Betty wanted to know if I'd heard from Marsha.

'Not from. About.'

'That she and whatsisname got remarried?'

327

'Ted. And that she was working in television. Washington.' I didn't want to sound too interested in this matter even though I was. Very.

I had forgotten how and how much New Yorkers drank: martinis and highballs before, wine with, scotch on the rocks or sticky killers afterwards: Drambuie and Amoretto.

Which may explain why I said what I did to Betty.

A black maid had been around to help serve dinner but she'd gone, and while everyone else was jammed in the hallway getting ready to leave I helped take some stuff out to the kitchen. Betty was a little glassy-eyed, too. 'Guess you didn't hit it off with your date?'

Donna had given me a pretty thorough once-over and not bothered much after that.

'Maybe I look a tad sleazy to her.'

New York men were still turned out as they had been far back as I could remember. Suits solid and stiff, pants riding high, three-button jackets like folded beetle wings. I'd wondered if I should go that way but I was embarrassed to go shopping, even for a shirt. I didn't know what size I should be. In anything. Everything I wore, down to my hand-sewn Roman shoes, had been made to measure.

It came out before I could bite my tongue. 'Something I'd really like to know?'

Betty looked over to the open door but we could hear the others beginning their goodbyes a safe distance off in the hallway.

'How could you tell that Charlie Flynn wasn't an American that time? I've always wondered.'

She giggled. Bent to scrape off a plate into the garbage pail. Straightened up and patted a closed door alongside. It said Service Entrance. 'Honey, he only wanted to use the back way.'

'Oh? But...'

'American might do that, sure. But they'd try the front first Only polite.'

She gave me a comradely kiss on the cheek. 'You ought to go see Marsha. She might have something to tell you.'

'Like?'

'Go see, Shelby.'

'*Ciao.*'

She put a finger to my lips, 'The clothes are fine, Shelby, but don't be the sort of guy goes around New York saying *ciao.*'

*

The consensus was that a month or so would be long enough for the Prince Riccardo thing to cool down and I could go back to Rome. Charlie promised the bureau would try for a discreet word out of someone official that there wouldn't be trouble waiting for me. I defied DOWNHOLD TRANSAT CALLS to talk to him, using one of the new wonders of communication, the international dial codes. To get Italy, you just hit 0039 then the number over there and *chi parla?* No operator. No wait. No connection a lot of the time, though, if half of Brooklyn was calling *nonna.*

I took a sublet up on East 81 Street from a Broadway hoofer turned hooker who was moving in with a boyfriend. 'The kitchen's pretty small,' I said.

She wore strappy open sandals that showed toes like walnuts. 'Honey, eat out.'

'Why don't you take a little vacation,' Hamm said.

'After that, I'll find you something to do.'

'Thought I'd go take a look at the nation's capital. Haven't been there since I was in school.'

'Say hi to Ted from me. And give Marsha a hug.'

-29-

'She'd love to see you,' said Ted in the back room of the Washington bureau, writing down a number. 'Often talks about that Rome time.' He made it sound like history rather than just a few months back. I wondered what he thought there might be in the way of history with me and Marsha, and if I was looking to revise it.

I also wondered what the hell had happened with them. If he had really gone pink or, having done so, switched back to... what would the straight colour be? Blue? Green? Either way, he didn't have to worry. The Lorenzo episode had seemed to confirm what Marsha told me way back: she took life one guy at a time. What a goddam waste.

Not that I was short of company in Manhattan. Sex was not the challenge it had been only a few years earlier. The panty-girdle might live on for girls who still had to answer to their mothers, but for the older ones — those over twenty-five, say — the Pill changed things with astounding speed. Quite a few I met hardly needed to be asked, although there sometimes seemed to be a certain kind of resignation as they took their clothes off.

Sometimes I had to enliven the occasion with a fantasy of Marsha. It would be good to see her, even fully dressed.

*

OLD EBBIT GRILL
Chesapeake oysters

Hamburgers
French fries
Roquefort dressing

-You really know how to treat a gal, Shelby.

-I'm a stranger in these parts. I just picked someplace near the White House.

-Welcome back to America. Pass the ketchup.

-You look great.

No lie. She was leaner and maybe even a bit mean: the blonde hair darker, cut in a fringe and shaped around her taut jawline. Eyebrows and lashes marked out but unassertive; lips a sort of burnt orange. She looked cool, crisp and fiercely stimulating.

-You just forgot what I look like, it's been so long.

She had kept me in our greeting hug for an extra microsecond.

-I haven't forgotten anything. Don't want to, either.

-So how long are you over for?

I told her about how I had to duck out of Rome.

-Don't really think they'd get out the handcuffs if I flew in, but it seems best not to tempt them.

-Them? You mean Lorenzo! He made *both* of us flee the country. But he's a pussycat, really.

-Did *you* do the right thing?

-Leaving Lorenzo? Oh, sure. I guess I was kinda naive.

-You were kinda in love.

-That, too.

I laid out a carefully edited version of my Cunard adventure and an only slightly immodest one of the Pulitzer event up at Columbia.

-So what if you did look at it on television? The images were just as real as the images that come up in the minds of people when they read what you write. More so, since they're not

331

filtered through your preconceptions. You've got some catching up to do, Shel. TV news might walk all over you guys soon.

-Centurions aren't allowed to have preconceptions. What does a news producer do, exactly?

Truth was, I was no longer offhand about TV news. It was beginning to get audiences like radio, even if most of what was broadcast came off wire service rip 'n read.

-Just about everything most people think the guy on screen does: line up interviews, write the script, look out the film clips, tie his tie right. I'm coming up to New York next week for a job interview.

I did wonder how she'd got this first job. No real background in news, but maybe that didn't matter anymore.

-Do tell.

-This stuff is moving so fast it's hard to keep up. Everyone involved is so young. I know more than most of them just from hanging out with Centurions. Dropping a few such names didn't hurt. Yours was one.

-What did you say about me?

-Lied that you let me pick up some experience over in Rome.

-If not the kind I had hoped for.

-Ha ha. Now NBC's got a project to get news out of the studio. Broadcast direct from where things are happening. No waiting for film to be processed. Shoot on videotape, plug right into phone lines and feed stuff straight on air. There's this thing in the sky now, like a big mirror a thousand miles up. You bounce pictures off it back down to earth.

-Echo. It's a communications satellite.

-You know about that? Echo One. Soon there'll be more like it. The network's built this trailer full of electronic gear. Big mobile home with the NBC logo all over it. Needs a team of producers and it looks like I might get a shot at it.

-What about Ted?

-What about him?

- If you got the job would he come back up, too?

-Why should he?

-Well, he's your husband, for one. You got married again, so I heard.

-Not really. We just told everyone we did. He-'d got this job, and he was terrified of winding up on the Pink List. Washington's a poisonous town for gossip.

It was one of those switch-flick moments after which everything is a different colour.

-So you've been living in sin with your ex?

-He gets to do most of the sinning. I'm too busy.

I was treading water, keeping myself afloat while I got the conversation back on a suitably light-hearted track. Marsha was not a re-married lady? She was a goddam beard.

-And here was I thinking you could do plugs for that show of Sylvia's.

-Poor Sylvia. That was weird, those great big ships crashing up against each other out of nowhere.

-Bit like us, really.

-In Rome, you mean?

-Even now. Each of us knowing the other was out there, but not which way we ought to turn.

-And you feel that way now?

-Remember that word I told you I picked up from Ezra Pound? Flotsam, jetsam and...

-What was it? The other thing?'

-Ligan, lagan. Something left on the sea bottom to be recovered later, like an anchor. Sunken treasure, maybe marked, with a buoy, or on a chart.

-Think that might have an application here, Shelby? Treasure left underwater to be hauled up when the time came?

-Might this be the time?

-Depends if I might be the treasure? Up in New York, Shelby, pick someplace dark and romantic.

-30-

Rome showed up in town from time to time, in the person of Mungo Macbeth converging with Lia as she flew in and out of New York in the Roman Kiss plane. They stayed at the Plaza but Mungo liked to drink at PJ Clark's or Costellos As sometimes happens when people step outside their natural setting, he seemed diminished. A script he'd been working on in Los Angeles had been put, as they liked to say out there, *in turnaround*.

'All anyone wants to do are these so-called Spaghetti Westerns. They don't even make the bloody things in Italy. They go to Spain. For the landscape supposedly, but really because it's easier to *cucinare i libri.*' Cook the books, ho ho.

The Macbeths took in the New York premiere of *Dolce Vita*. The *Times* critic had called it 'an awesome picture... licentious in content but moral and vastly sophisticated.' Mungo called it pretentious bullshit.

Even if I'd got an invite I would have steered clear for fear Arabella would have been there. Old Ezra had it wrong with that line about 'what has been shall be, flowing, ever unstill'. What I had with her flowed like hell in Italy and that last mad night on the *Queen Mary*, but it had dried up and blown away.

Unpacking in my new apartment, the massive key to 51 Margutta dropped out of a bundle of laundry and nearly broke one of my toes. Rather than summoning up a vision of Arabella naked in the cracked old bathtub, the heft of it made me think of Prudenza, hands on hips, railing about our aristocratic intruder. I never saw Arabella again. Except, of course, on the screen along with the millions of moviegoers she brought in for Maximum.

When I did catch up with the movie it seemed a bit dated and sad. Not just that my memories of that time didn't play in dim black and white. None of Fellini's characters seemed to be enjoying life. Still, no small achievement to generate a global cliché. And to re-brand photographers *paparazzi*.

*

'Hey, Shelby. *Roman Kiss* mean something to you?' Guy on the Interstate desk, Henry somebody.

'Sure. Had a few of those in my time.'

'Lady called Lia?' He was reading a Teletype tearsheet. 'Big plane in funny colours?'

'Both of them very glamorous. What's up?'

'Nothing glamorous.'

> BULLETIN. SALT LAKE CITY. ROMAN KISS COSMETICS
> QUEEN LIA MACBETH WAS AMONG THOSE KILLED TODAY
> WHEN HER BOLDLY DECORATED TURBOPROP AIRCRAFT
> PLOUGHED INTO A FLOCK OF SEAGULLS.

'Guess I should give it to International.'

No point in telling this stranger what I felt. 'Sure. Tell 'em to check there are seagulls in Salt Lake.'

'There are, there are. It's the Utah state bird. And Mitzy Faragó? She one of those big-tit tootsies?'

'The mother. Anyone else?'

'All crew by the look of it. Crashed coming in to land. Engines full of feathers.'

'Check that name before it goes on the wire. It's Hungarian. Only one *r* and some kind of accent on the *o*.'

'If it's only the mother we can leave her down-story.'

*

Following morning I took a cab up to the Plaza, the steel plates covering the craters on Third Avenue clunking under the wheels like a backwoods railroad. The story was splashed all over. Front of the *New York Times* and the *Herald-Trib*, though the *Times* kept it downpage. *Women's Wear* made it centre spread as well as the wood. *Facemaker to the stars. Magic mixmaker. Beauties round world mourn.*

Mungo, flown in from Los Angeles on a redeye, was in the Oak Room bar, beard matted and stained, hands shaking. He grabbed at me like a television wrestler. 'Thank God. Someone who's not one of *them*.'

'Of who?' Whom?

'Everyone. Bloody lawyers. People from Glamglo Inc. Fucking reporters.'

It was just after nine and he had a whiskey highball in front of him, the jigger glass alongside evidence of an extra shot. I got some orange juice.

'You're a fucking reporter, too, aren't you?'

'Maybe not right now.'

One gulp took care of half his dark brown breakfast 'She wasn't even supposed to go to Utah. The tour was set to begin in Washington, then Florida, Texas, the West Coast. I was going to hop on over there and we'd come back via Minneapolis and Chicago. Glamglo sprung Salt Lake on her at the last minute, a quick there and back because their outlet had booked the Tabernacle Choir. What the fuck is that?'

'Why was Mitzi along?'

'Wanted to see Salt Lake. Said she'd heard Mormons made good husband material. Can you believe seagulls? In the middle of the bloody country?'

337

'Where are the girls? Mitzi's daughters?'

'Salt Lake. Flew there last night.'

'Is there anything I can do, Mungo? Talk to someone for you?' I knew nothing about Lia's business set-up, but there was bound to be a swamp of sticky detail for him to wade through.

Down went the rest of the highball, and it occurred to me that, distressed as he undoubtedly was, Mungo was also a tad shifty. He said, 'Let's go up.'

At the entrance to the lobby, he paused. 'Those vultures will spot us if we walk over to the lifts.' He turned into the staircase and we climbed up to the mezzanine and took the elevator from there.

The suite was one of the Plaza's finest, a view from the rococo sitting room over Central Park one way, and across to Fifth Avenue the other. The Macbeths leased it for most of the year while Lia was doing her fly-arounds. Mungo lumbered into a little kitchen and started clinking bottles. 'Nothing but bloody fizzy water. Need room service.'

'Had Mitzi been staying here, too?' He was looking cagey again. 'That's the trouble.' He beckoned me into a bedroom: elegant, overstuffed and sterile. On the bed, a Vuitton overnighter lay open. Shaken out across the satin spread were dozens of small keys, some with coloured tags, most without. 'Safe deposit boxes,' said Mungo. 'Mitzi was going to hitch a ride to do her pick-ups and deliveries.'

'Her friends will be disappointed.'

'More than disappointed.' He started to paw over the keys. 'Some of these must belong to people somewhere over here or in Latin America. She would have stashed their goodies in different places around Europe. Others have got to go back to the Europeans whose stuff she's already dropped off around the States. Washington, Dallas, Miami, Los Angeles, wherever.'

338

I was beginning to see why Mungo was twitchy. 'And you don't know which keys belong to who?' Whom.

'No bloody idea.' He looked at me like a drowning man grabbing at a piece of flotsam. 'They're just keys to safe deposit boxes. You know, in banks and, well, safe depositories.'

'And you don't even know *where* the boxes are? That what you're telling me?''

'They could be anywhere. Millions of dollars worth of jewellery locked away in vaults all over the United States. All over the fucking world and only Mitzi knows where. Knew. Let alone who owns whatever's in them..'

Photographic memory, *dahlink*, photographic memory.

'I suppose I ought to go out there, too? Salt Lake.'

'It would look good if you did.'

'But what am I going to do with these?' He stirred the keys around, tearful and blinking.

'First, you need a lawyer. No, first you need to put those keys someplace. Have you got a safe box?'

That got a raw grin out of him. 'I say, old chap,' he said. 'Do you think there might be a script in this?' If there was it could have an unhappy ending. Kind of people who owned what was in those boxes were long on reach and short on scruples. Might even be some Bergamonte heirlooms awaiting pick-up. Somewhere.

Coming out of the elevator I looked down from the mezzanine. The Plaza's great Palm Court was heaving with pelts; a herd of giant hairy caterpillars on the move. It was the day after Memorial Day, first day of fall. The New York ladies had got their minks and sables out of storage. Amid them, Miss Frisk stood out like a museum piece. She waved her umbrella up at me. Parasol.

-31-

One of many things I could never have imagined doing with the austere Nordic goddess of the *Stampa Estera* was taking a cab ride down the East River Drive to the Seamen's Church Institute, a whiff away from the Fulton Street fish market.

Italy and Sweden had asked a US federal court to decide whether the *Stockholm* or the *Andrea Doria* was responsible for the collision and the death of forty or so passengers, including the distinguished foreign correspondent Elwyn Rickard. The Institute had been rented as a venue for a swarm of attorneys and maritime experts to argue things out. 'You must come with me,' said Miss Frisk. 'I send my report from press room there. Also, there is telephone.'

I could understand why *Svenska Dagbladet*, a heavyweight broadsheet with front pages as antediluvian as she was, had sent her over. It might be the *Andrea Doria* enquiry to most of the world, but in Sweden the headlines would be *Stockholm*.

The SCI building was suitably grim: industrial gothic with a sort of little lighthouse on one corner and a big cross on the roof. In the old sailors' chapel that took up most of the first floor, tables were piled with documents: charts, reports, witness statements. Lawyers and experts sat around smoking and chatting, no one paying attention to the witness being grilled up front.

A press section was marked off but people wandered in and out of it as they liked. Miss Frisk sat me down in a pew of the old chapel and went off to the pulpit end where there was a bank of typewriters. The hand-carved benches and uprights made a perfect frame for her ankle-length skirt and wide-brimmed hat. It was about half an hour before she came back and said, 'Let us go around to the corner.'

In Fulton Street, we sat at a scrubbed-down table. The waiter gave her a big *buongiorno*. 'Lady likes our Bloody Mermaid. What about you?'

'Mermaid rather than Mary?'

'Clam juice instead of tomato.'

'I'll just have a regular BM.'

'Ya need to try a mermaid. It's got *fresh* clam juice.'

'Just an old-fashioned Bloody Mary, thanks.'

'You want an Old-Fashioned? I thought you said Bloody Mary.'

'I did, you know: vodka, tomato juice, tabasco, slice of lemon.'

'I'll get ya a mermaid. Ya don' like it, don' drink it.'

The mermaids arrived in glasses that held about a pint, only some of which was ice cubes. Mine tasted like a scoop of the East River with a squeeze of lemon. Miss Frisk downed half of hers in a swig. I had never seen her ingest anything, apart from some kind of herbal tea that Gino would make for her.

'This is a most fortuitous encounter.' She started to peel off a glove, checked the tabletop and kept it on. First I thought she was observing sanitary precautions; then I realised that behind the usual stony cool she was positively edgy.

I couldn't think why that might be, but I said: 'It's certainly unexpected.'

'What I mean is that I am able to talk to you about Senora Rickard.'

'Caddie? Is she all right?'

'I would not say so. Which is why I am concerned.'

'Well, she *is* in mourning.'

341

'I would not say that, either.' The ice rattled in her glass as the rest of the revolting fishy gloop went down. 'It would seem that she does not believe that her husband is truly dead.'

'She told you that?'

'Not directly. But I go to Mother Giovanna for my clothes, you know. Since long before she became so famous. Which was with your help, I believe.'

'Only partly. The biggest boost she got was from poor Sylvia Silver.'

'Poor Miss Silver. I think we should rather say poor Senora Rickard. Because the reason Senora Rickard is so unhappy is that she does not believe Miss Silver is dead, too.' She looked down and gave the ice a shake. 'Dead, either, I should say.'

Wasn't that she wanted help with her English. She was giving me time to brace for the next take. 'Senora Rickard has formed the impression that Mr Rickard and Miss Silver have not drowned after all. That they may have run away together. Although I suppose, in the circumstances, one should say swim away.'

Was that joke? Maybe a Swedish joke.

'I hadn't realised you were close.'

'I would not say we were. We are rather different people. But some time ago she did me a great kindness and if she required some help in her present situation I would like to provide it.'

'Like what kind of help?'

She fished about in her reticule and came up with a page of copy. 'This is the story I have prepared for my paper. An English version, of course'.

She watched me scan it, working down to the third or fourth par.

> Among the recent bodies recovered from the sea was that of the international newspaper columnist Sylvia Silver.

There were a couple more pars about Sylvia's life and accomplishments.

'This was in the evening papers?' It certainly hadn't been in the mornings where it would have been linked to the Salt Lake crash.

'No. Because it is something that... let us say, is yet to happen. But if this little story appeared in *Svenska Dagbladet*, then it would be picked up by the wire services — especially CNW. Senora Rickett will read it in the *Rome Daily American*. She will no longer think...'

'That Rick and Sylvia might have swum off into the sunset together?'

'Exactly.' She was looking at me like some benevolent grandmother bestowing a treat.

'But it is not true.'

'I would not suggest this if I thought it could cause any harm. But as far as I have been able to establish, Miss Silver had no relatives who might wish to claim her body. If she really had been found, that is. Not even any close friends. She must have been a very lonely person.'

I kept looking down at the copy for a while, mainly because I didn't know what to say. For all that she might know the Vatican like the back of her veiny hand, Miss Frisk didn't seem to have much idea of the way news worked in the real world.

'Trouble is, Miss Frisk, there's no way of getting Caddie to read this without everyone everywhere getting to read it, too. Miss Silver might have been friendless, but she's plenty newsworthy. Was, that is.'

There were too many Misses piling up in the conversation. Despite her stern persona, it felt like time for first names, had I known what hers was. We'd been swapping *buongiornos* now for years and I still didn't know what her by-line was

343

'*Women's Wear* sees the story on the wire and they pick up the phone to the US Coastguard or whoever: what did she wear to drown in? And they'd get: Who? *What* body? I don't know where the poor woman was born, but the local paper there would call up CNW for more details. Which we wouldn't have. This simply couldn't be done. Quite apart from the fact that it's not a fact.'

'But if CNW were to put it on the wire, it would become a fact. Or near enough to one. *Non e vero?*'

*

The only good thing about taking the subway uptown was that the clanging, grinding and lurching drove Miss Frisk's dumb idea out of my mind. I had offered her a taxi ride but she wanted to go back to the Institute. That left me free to hop on the Seventh Avenue Express without much thought of where I might get off.

Days earlier, I had been shooting the breeze with a couple of Centurion shipping reporters and I mentioned that I might want to hook up with someone who worked on the big liners. Where did the crews hang out while the ships were in turnaround?

What I told them was true, far as it went. A chance eyefall on the Shipping News in the *Times* had informed me that the *Queen Elizabeth* was due to dock that Wednesday.

Now, without really thinking about it, I got off at West 57th Street and continued on foot towards the sunset.

Coming away from the *Queen Mary* at Pier 90 a few weeks back, I hadn't looked beyond the cab rank under the Hudson River Drive. But just across 12th Avenue a jumble of bars and diners marked the north-west corner of Hell's Kitchen, monuments raised by generations of ship-jumpers: Paris-Brest, Kelly's Irish Pub, Portofino Pizza.

There didn't seem to be a British one, but that would have made it too easy. I stretched out beers in one joint after the other until well after four in the afternoon. The last of them was large and nearly empty. I settled in a corner of the bar from where, in true trench-coat fashion — mine was up on the peg alongside me — I could look around discreetly. Light rain had started up and people coming in were shaking themselves, peeling off jackets, finding hooks.

Guys rolled up to get drinks, spreading themselves out and helping to screen me off. Some had English accents, which was encouraging. Women in twos and threes began to fill up the tables under the half-curtained street-side windows, though most of them seemed to be American, blue-collar and getting on: cleaners probably.

A younger group piled in, four girls and a couple of guys, gabbling away in high English voices and took over a table near the door. A waiter they seemed to know gave them a big hello. One of them with her back to me *could* have been VeeVee.

So what if she was? Whatever I might once have felt for VeeVee, even remembered about her, was heavily layered over by now. No purposeful intention was guiding me; just the sense of disquiet that had welled up now and then since Jeremy told me about that child.

Thing was, my rudimentary understanding of the female reproductive system did not entirely exclude the possibility that there was some arcane, probably messy, reason for her to have put Hans Brinker in place even if she had been pregnant. But if that were so, if I had not been the sucker with the answer to the brown envelope problem, why let me walk away from Adam and Eve Mews? Because if I had stayed the money might actually have had to be spent on the abortion, stupid.

There was a surge around the table I had been trying not to

eyeball too closely. The girl with her back to me turned, and I could see she looked nothing like VeeVee. Nor, while I had not been able to see her full-on, did the one I had been taking peeks at. But now that she stood up and reached for her coat I could see it *was* her. A little heavier in outline, face a little rounder, different hair, but indubitably VeeVee. She gave the bar a scan before turning to the door, her glance sliding over me without a flicker.

I followed her out. Half a block ahead she reached the stop on West 57th just as a bus pulled in, splashing through the potholes. I imagined the sneer I would get from a New York cabbie if I told him, 'Follow that bus!' The best thing, it seemed to me, was to grab the bus behind. I would be able to see VeeVee get out.

That happened at Fifth Avenue. She stuck to the west side of the street and headed downtown, me on her tail, zig-zagging across the sidewalk in case she picked up my reflection in a shop window.

She went into Lord and Taylor and up the escalator to Children's Wear. I hung as far back as possible, mooching around like a hick, fending off sales clerks. When she went off to pay for whatever she was buying I pointed her out to a floorwalker — smart grey suit, carnation in lapel — and handed him the Jaguar logbook that I had recently dug out of my Olivetti case, where it had always been stowed, along with some expired passports and press credentials. 'That lady dropped this.'

Gracious smile and off he went after her; only useful thing he'd done all day, probably. I dived into a down elevator, quite smug about my Miracle on Fifth Avenue. VeeVee and Jeremy might work it out one day. I never would.

346

-32-

-This is more like it, Shelby?

-You wanted dark and romantic.

Around Third Avenue and 42nd Street, common territory to two wire services, three newspaper offices and a broadcast network, there were plenty places in the first category but not the second.

-And now that we're short of time... .

I had told her on the phone, keeping it cool and light, that it might only be days now before I was off back to Italy. The bureau seemed pretty sure I wasn't on an airport wanted list, so I had to give it a shot.

-So you've no sooner hauled me up from the depths than you're tossing me overboard again.

-How was I supposed to know ...?

-That I wasn't a respectable married lady after all?

-I wasn't looking for respectable. But since you're not even married, how about coming with me?

-To Rome? Give up my job? I mean the new one?'

She held up a key. It had one of those gift-shop tags attached. *Captain's Cabin SS Titanic.*

- Meet NBC's new Mobile Broadcast Manager. Captain of the

347

Newsbus.

-They took you on? That's great.

Not what I felt at all, but I needed to keep it upbeat.

- And I didn't have to put out.

She must have seen something flick across my face.

-Joke, Shelby. Those guys think I'm their mother. Anyway, those times are gone. This is the age of Women's Liberation, haven't you been told? This wine is marvellous.'

-Calon Ségur.

I flicked the napkin off the bottle to show her the heart-shaped label.

-Cute. What if Italy won't let you in? If you had to stay here stuck on a desk? No more dashing foreign correspondent.

-Then I might never get to find out if Hungarian girls wear bras.

I'd told her about that back in Rome.

-Quite a few of us don't these days if you haven't noticed.

I'd noticed. Or at least suspected. Political statement?

-Among other things. You're not going to ask me to marry you are you? That heart's got me worried.

-What if I did?

Very prescient. Had she guessed I might have started to think that might not be such a bad idea?

-Come on, Shelby. Only people getting married now are nuns and priests.

That was one of the running stories of those days. The power of the Pill had seeped into strange places, freeing people to do what had hitherto been beyond their dirtiest dreams.

Around once a week some headline name would announce he or she was getting shacked up without benefit of matrimony while priests and nuns were ditching celibacy and flinging themselves into marriage, often with one another.

-When we're through here can we go someplace and make up for lost time?

-You're sure not losing any now, are you?

-Does that mean yes?

We were both a little drunk. She leaned across the table. Something stirring wafted off her. I meant to look deep in her eyes but my glance strayed down to that enticing cleavage. She gave me a dirty grin, did something around her neckline then jerked the front of her blouse right down. What is it with tits and the male libido? The sight of those perky breasts was like punching a *Here Is* key and firing up a Teletype on the other side of the world. Of the table. *Ding!*

Before I could think of something to say she was tucked back together again, the grin downgraded to cheeky.

-Guess we can skip dessert.

I was laying down bills on the table.

-My place?

She shook the key.

-Welcome on board. Think they'll mind if we take that bottle?

*

Marsha's new command, the NBC logo glinting on its aluminium flanks, took up three car lengths in the parking space along East 40th Street reserved for vehicles with the coveted NYP — for Press — licence plates. Inside, it was a television studio on wheels, little control room, big tape decks. Some very big.

'That's videotape. The antenna on the roof can beam the images up to a dish on top of our building. If we can't get line-of-sight, there's another dish on the Empire State building we aim it at, and the guy up there can bounce it over. State of the art.'

349

State of my libido was getting in the way. Beyond the working area were a neat living space, sink and a couple of hotplates. Marsha fiddled under a banquette--type bench and heaved. A Murphy-style bed creaked open, flattening down into a perfectly usable surface for what I'd had in mind even before she flicked me that stirring double vision.

An hour later the place — the space, rather — was a good deal less neat and tidy than when we tumbled into it. I started to collect my clothes from where they had landed, wondering if anyone passing down the street might have heard us and wondered what the hell was going on in here.

My shirt was draped over a phone; new model press-buttons instead of dial. 'Can I call out on this?' Checking in had gone the way of my pants, but the reflex was stirring once more.

'Has to be hooked up to a Bell Telephone terminal and plugged in. There's one every few blocks, most places.' I was watching with some regret as she picked up her own clothes and started to put them on.

'You can send pictures up into space but you need to get down a hole in the sidewalk to make a phone call? What's the number?' I handed her my notebook to write it down. She did, then flipped over a couple of pages.

'You usually peek at other people's notes?'

'If I get the chance.'

'You been dialling 39?'

'Couple of times.'

'Me too.'

'Lorenzo?'

'Just to see how he was holding up.'

'And?'

'He's fine.'

'Is the phone plugged in now?' She jumped out in the street just as she was, and hauled out a cable from a little hatch in the side of the trailer. Since I didn't know quite what she was doing, I just enjoyed watching out the window. It might well have been that bizarre and etching sight: ass in air, shirt blown up to show her briefs, those lovely breasts flat on the sidewalk as she reached down into the Bell Tel depths that shifted my perspective from sex as sex to sex with Marsha as an ongoing project.

Back in, she unhooked the phone. 'Dial tone.'

Roger had the volume way up. 'Where the fuck are you?'

No need-, fortunately, to come up with somewhere plausible because he went straight on to bawl:_' Get your ass up to the colonel's place right away.'

'Colonel who?'

'There's more than one? Colonel John. He's called in twice. I don't want to hear from him a third time.'

'What's this about?'

'*You* ask him. I didn't feel like it. But it's probably to do with your imminent return to work.'

'Work?'

'Rome. You're still on the payroll there, remember.'

'What's happened?'

'I'll tell you later, after you've seen John. I'm going to call, tell him you're on the way. Now *move*.'

*

I got there just at dusk and Old John sat me down by the big window overlooking the river. Strait, whatever. He was clutching a telephone on a long lead

351

'They're ready to flash it on,' said John. 'Just for a few seconds. Only got hooked up to the A-wire today. Anyway, I hear you've been talking to my old friend Frisky.'

That took a beat or two. Miss Frisk? Old friend?

'Well, yes, colonel. She ran an idea past me.'

He didn't say anything. 'It was just something she'd come up with to make Caddie Rickard feel better. Don't know if she'd even checked with her editor, whatever.'

'No need.'

'Oh?'

'She owns it. That *Dagblatet* outfit. The *Svenska* one and a few other titles round Sweden.'

The dumb look on my face made him snicker. 'Used to be a family business. She inherited, but she didn't want to go back up there. She left whoever was running the show get on with it and she hung on in Rome, doing what she'd always done.'

Well, that would sure explain how she might bulldoze that weird story past her editors.

'The company's a good client. Like to keep 'em happy.'

'Guess so. Pity she didn't come up with something we could do.'

'One thing I did think of. That statue in Central Park. The Reporting Angel in bronze. We could make that the Rickett Memorial. Put *his* name on the plinth. Doesn't look a lot like him, but who's to know. Caddie might like that, you reckon?'

He didn't want an answer. Outside, the daylight had all but gone.

'We're not supposed to light up until tomorrow, but whose fuckin' tower is it?' He poked a number on the phone and said. 'Zip 'er up!' Down in the watery gloom between the shores giant letters of light spun out.

h a P P Y B I r T H d A y C O lone L J O h N

'Aw, gee,' he said. 'That's cute. They'll get that typeface ironed out by tomorrow. Now let's see what's on the wire.' He told the phone: 'Just give it a flash.'

The zipper lit up again, barely long enough for me to decipher, among the other cryptic headlines trundling around

> *andreA DOrIA: famoUS ColUMNisT COnFIRm DRO?NeD.*

Then we were in the lobby again. The houseboy took my coat off an ornate stand and shook it out. Beyond him, I could see umbrellas lined up like rifles in a rack, black and masculine save for the one at the end. A parasol.

'You know what I said before, that when you're getting old the first thing that goes is memory?' John had me fixed with those birdy eyes. I stopped myself from saying, 'I remember'. Just nodded.'

Then nothing. I wondered if he had forgotten what he wanted to say. But no. 'Actually, sex is the first thing to go.' There was another lapse. Then the little eyes lit up and he came back on air. 'But, you know, the memory of sex. That doesn't go at all.'

-33-

The embrace that enfolded me left a nosefull of mothballs, garlic, espresso, household cleaner, and Prudenza's armpits. I'd never gotten close enough before to check out the mix.

She trailed me around the apartment as I put my stuff away, rapping out bulletins. The police had confiscated Fabrizio's *lupara*. The landlord had been round three times. If I couldn't pay the rent right away I could give him a *cambiale*. There was a new leak, this time in the corner of the bedroom ceiling. *La nudista* across the courtyard had been beaten up by her husband. She had bought, at her own expense, a new gas cylinder for the water heater. No, not *la nudista*, she, Prudenza. So the young *signor* would be able to shower. If he could get that stupid faucet to allow him any water. It was worse than the one in the kitchen. And if there was any money left over after I settled up with the thief of a landlord, she would appreciate if I could catch up with her very modest salary as well as reimbursing her for the *bombola*.

'And is there any news of Senora Ricketts?'

She blew out her lips like an old *carrozza* nag and whacked off a *segno della croce*. Caddie was still in the convent. Senora *Esta* — Esther — had tried to persuade her to go back to Via Flaminia but she would not listen.

It was a good hour before I could hustle Prudenza out. I had already checked the phone for a dial tone. I didn't need to work out the time of day in New York, I was still operating on it despite having spent the better part of twenty-four hours

354

getting from there to here, first in a bone-shaking SAS Douglas DC7, fuel stop in Gander, Newfoundland, a place I'd barely been aware of hitherto, and another in Stockholm.

*

'Tonight,' Hamm said when I came back down to East 42nd. 'Didn't John tell you?'

'Tell me what? And what's that stuff on the A-wire about Sylvia fucking Silver?' *Tmesis* again. Must be stress-induced.

'Charlie's out of it.'

'What happened?'

'Seems he went missing for a couple of days. Malvolio tracked him down to some drunk tank.' Took me a while to remember that was Aldo's second name.

'Roger's fixed for him to go up to London, take a cure. Him and... .'

'Watshernose.'

'Yeah, her. They've already left. So the bureau's rudderless and Rome's a hot dateline right now. Can't let the place drift.'

'And you want me to leave *tonight*?

'As John didn't tell you. What *did* you guys talk about?'

'That stuff on the wire, for starters. Sylvia's body.'

'There's nothing on the wire about Sylvia Silver.' He was turning over the tear-offs on a clipboard. 'Or her body. What the fuck are you talking about?'

Guess if you own the means of production, you can produce something to make an old friend feel good.

'Anyway, you need to pack a bag. Limo will be at your apartment at nine.'

'What limo?'

'The one from Scandinavian Airlines, asshole.'

*

'I'll update you soon as I get there.'

'On everything?'

'Including, that I assume we're in love.'

'What was that?'

I said it again, but the payphone at Idlewild was hemmed in by farewelling family groups keening like professional mourners. There was also a lot of banging and scraping at her end. 'Crew's coming aboard, Shelby.' *On* board. 'Seems we're off to...' There was background gabble. 'Albany. We're headed to Albany. Interview with the governor. Call soon as you can. I'd like to hear that again. What I think you just said.'

I knew what I had *said* but what I had been thinking about was sex. Thing was, I couldn't work out Marsha's sexual strategy, let alone her sexual *policy*. I'd always thought women must have one or the other. In the case of Betty it had been policy: make the boys feel at home. VeeVee was policy first: the way to a good time. Strategy evolved later — or so I preferred to think — to deal with the brown envelope pile. With Arabella, actressing was all strategy, sex life included. If she enjoyed the role, all the better. Even if she didn't, she'd play the part. A trouper.

Marsha, I guess, had applied the traditional American-girl strategy to get herself married to Ted — even if the effort was wasted. Way things were back then. When she had to play by someone else 's rules, though, things went off the rails. Though she was still talking to Lorenzo, which I didn't particularly care for.

That introductory tumble on the *Newsbus's* fold-down was unforgettable. Shapely smart and deft, she had known exactly what to do for me and for herself. But it had also been a reminder of the wryly reported pleasures she had shared on

356

that Rome massage-table. Nor had I cared for that line she had tossed in about not having had to put out to get her NBC job. She meant it as a joke, but would she have done so if required?

What would you have done, Shelby? said Caddie in my head.

But more importantly, as a backroom planner like Ted would have said, did she have a policy *objective*? Preferably me, whose own strategy had been wrecked. I'd let that word slip out. The genie was out of the bottle, cat out of bag, horse from stable. Like putting a flash on the A-wire, there was no taking it back.

*

SCANDINAVIA AIR SERVICE. NEW YORK-STOCKHOLM.
FIRST CLASS.
DINNER
Gravlax
Sillsallad
Renskav
Räksmörgås
KotbullarKladkaka
Punsch

-I hope it is not too boring to share a table with me yet again.

-On the contrary, Miss Frisk, I could not think of a more delightful travelling companion.

-Even though, I gather, you were made to come away in rather a hurry? The colonel was concerned that it might be onerous for me to travel alone, and since you were going in the same direction… SAS was happy to provide another seat.

-It sure is comfortable up here. Luxurious even.

-The airline is a valued advertiser in my newspapers. We sometimes exchange favours.

-So they *are* your papers?

-It was indiscreet of the colonel to mention that. And it is not

357

quite as grand as it sounds — there are some minor shareholders. Nevertheless, I would be grateful if you did not mention the matter in the *Stampa Estera*.

-Not if you tell me how Old John... I mean the colonel... got that headline up on his tower.

-Surely you should first ask why? To which the answer must be that he wished to please me. Or perhaps simply to make me stop bothering him.

-So he faked it?

-I suppose he asked his technical people to arrange something. But it was not very convincing. In any case, by that time I had come to see the wisdom of your words, Mr Shelby. It would not have been right, my plan.

-And it would probably not have fooled Mrs Ricketts. At least not for long.

-I expect you would like me to explain these dishes to you.

-And a few other things, as well?

-Like why I want so badly to make Senora Ricketts happy? *Räksmörgås* is a little pile of shrimp. On bread.

-An open sandwich? And why the colonel tries so hard to help you?

-And *renskav* is reindeer. The colonel has always been a help to me. Going back to the first time I saw him. *Liberazione*.

-Of Rome?

-In 1944. He rode into the Piazza Venezia like a god in his chariot. Like a centaur!

-And Caddie?

-Whom I already knew, from before the war. She was there the same day: big, strong, dressed like a soldier. We had such an adventure!

-Do tell.

-Perhaps another time. Now I must sleep. No, Mr Shelby.

Both these seats are for me. You will go in the Tourist part. Just through those curtains over there, I believe.

*

I got out my notebook and performed the IDD routine, still novel.

'As I was saying while in that other hemisphere,' I said, smartass.

'Anyway, you made it. No trouble at Ciampino?'

'None at all.' I'd messaged Rita to meet me in case my passport was whipped away or the heavies moved in on me, but told her not to come airside. As it was, neither I nor my passport attracted any attention.

Silence, of course, can't be categorised or qualified. If it could it wouldn't be silence, right? Even so, there was something suspicious in the online echo that took over.

'Lorenzo,' I said, and a crafty giggle trickled down five thousand miles of cable. 'You called Lorenzo, didn't you?'

'I told you we talked sometimes.'

I wasn't sure how I should feel about her leaning on an old lover to help out a new one.

'You could have got Lorenzo to have me turned back.'

'And I near as damn did. I want you, Shelby dear. I want for us to be together. But there's stuff I need to do first. Get myself in solid here. With the network. I've got to make them need me.'

I need you.'

And I need you. Hang in there, Shelby darling. We'll get there in the end.'

'I just want to get on with the beginning.'

There was an ominous undertone to that. Might she actually be saying that she needed NBC? God Almighty! Had she got a whiff of whatever it is that makes the newshound nostril flare?

Take a right at the top of the Spanish Steps into Via Sistina. There are intersections, and the street names change, but keep straight on, shortcut right through the church of Santa Maria Maggiore, and you can get all the way to San Giovanni in Laterano where old Pius began his last ride without even crossing the road. Holy Shirt was out there, and I needed both the exercise and the chance to get back my bearings. Anyway, I had yet to retrieve the *topolino*.

A hug from Mother Jo was a world away from Prudenza's greasy embrace: saintly soapy, crisp and slightly erotic. I'd phoned ahead, and even without checking she told me to come over. 'Caddie was wondering when she was going to see you again. So was I. You know she makes all the publicity for us? Takes calls from everywhere. Makes heavenly press release.'

And there was the old monster herself, trailed into the showroom by the timorous nun who let me in the front door. When someone's been ill people often say they would never have recognised them. There was too much of Caddie for that, but she had sure changed. Pale, thinned down to raw bones. Her hair, usually scrunched into greying curls, was cut close to her head and quite white. She was wearing a stripy robe, nothing religious, more like a hospital nurse. We put our arms around each other and it struck me that, apart from handshakes before she discouraged even those on account of her swollen knuckles, I'd never actually touched her before. When she spoke, though, it was the same gruff honk.

'So, how's the old bastard getting on?'

Mother Jo got the idea that we might need some private time. She swirled her habit. 'Sister Teresa here will bring me if you need anything.'

Convent protocol evidently meant man could not be left with woman. Any woman. Caddie jerked her head at our chaperone. 'Don't worry about Teresa. She hears me cussin', thinks I'm praying. So what about Old John?'

'Didn't you talk to him yourself?'

'Sure. Didn't have much to say, though, aside from the usual stuff about Rick everyone keeps coming up with. Then he couldn't wait to get off the line. Seems I'm still on the payroll, though, which is a relief.'

'He's got a lot going on. Staking out Centurion sites all over the city. To say nothing of the Newstower.' I told her about the tower and the other commemorative stuff. Then we talked for a while about what she was doing for Holy Shirt.

'Christ's sake don't call it that. It's Camicie Convento. Class label.'

Did she plan to go back to Via Flaminia?

'Probably. Some day. I like it here. It's uncomplicated.'

'I think John would like to put Rick up as one of those Centurion memorials, monuments, whatever.'

Her laugh sounded as though it hadn't been used for a while. It gurgled around like a Via Margutta faucet but then burst out in a flood. Sister Theresa jumped as though she'd been goosed.

'A fucking statue! I won't even put up a tombstone, plaque, whatever. I told you how I felt before you went away. I was sad at first, sure. Real sad. We'd come a long way together. Lots of places, lots of stories, lots of good times. But when I realised that he'd gone down with that strumpet Sylvia — and you can take that for what it sounds like — the only one I was sorry for was me. Now I'm not even sorry for myself anymore. I'm a free, happy woman. Old John puts Rick up on a pedestal I'll personally go over there, back up and piss on it. Food here's shit. You wanna stay for lunch?'

361

'Only if we can talk about Miss Frisk.'

*

CANTINA

CONVENTO DEL PRESEPIO

Zuppa fagioli

Pasta al Forno

Ensalata

-You remember I told you that Duck experience wasn't the only time I was in the Mappamondo? Well, the second time was because of her.

-Do tell.

-June '44. Liberation of Rome. Rick and I came in with the US Fifth Army. Different outfits, though. The Germans had mostly pulled out. Guys I was with simply rolled up the Appia Antica and into Piazza Venezia.

-And she was there? You were right. This soup is revolting.

-Along with a few other neutrals who'd sat out the war in the *Stampa*. Or in her case the Vatican. That's when she first saw John.'

-What was he doing there?

-He was our censor. Chief army censor. Then on, all copy out of Rome had to go through him. If you think the soup's lousy, wait 'til the pasta gets here.

-Maybe that's what she meant when she told me he seemed like a centaur. Censor?

-No, no. I get that. John was probably sticking up out of one of those M20 armoured cars. You know, like a tank but with wheels.

-Half man, half combat vehicle. Wheels instead of hooves. And that did it for her?

-Something sure as hell did, because the next thing we knew they were all tucked up together. And she was a woman of maybe forty years old. Dressed like something out of The Little House on the Prairie.

-She fell in his arms right there in the piazza?'

-No, a bit later. That time it was me she wanted to make happy.

-You knew each other from before?

-Sure. From the *Stampa*. Her father was Swedish ambassador to the Holy See. Good contact.

-So, the Mappamondo?

-Oh, yeah. Well, I was giving her — Frisk — all my K-rations and stuff and she saw me looking up at the Palazzo Venezia, you know, the famous balcony? Where the Duck used to bawl out those imperial fantasies. And she said, 'There's no-one in that place now. They've all run away.'

-Mussolini was still alive, right?

-Way up north. Holed up in that stupid little *republicco* the Germans let him set up by Lake Garda. He wasn't shot until months later, right at the end of the war.

-Shot by *partigiani*? Resistance fighters.

-Communists. Then they strung him up like a hog. They didn't want the Allies to get him, case he had too much to say about the deals they'd made with him. I told you the pasta would be worse.

-So you got into the palazzo?

-*Portone* was all closed up but Frisk took me round the back. Via degli Astalli, the street is.

-This is where Clara would come, she said.

-Clara Petacci, the official mistress.

-And friend of Frisk, as I was to discover. They shot her too, the commies. Didn't even give her time to put her panties on. When they hauled her up by the ankles everyone saw she was bare-assed. Took her down and fixed her dress with a safety pin. Then they hauled her up again. OK to murder her, but not to show off her ass in public.

-I remember that photograph. Pretty vivid.

-April 1945. I got up there the day after.

-So back here, *Liberazione*, you knocked politely on the back door of Palazzo Venezia?

-Kicked it in with my GI boots. Not a soul around. Stairs led right into the Mappomundo. Frisk and I sat at the Duck's great big desk that I got spread out on that time. I had some scotch in my duffel. We drank it straight out of the bottle.'

-And got Miss Frisk to tell you all about life under Fascist rule, German occupation? What the Vatican had really got up to?

-Actually, I wanted to DO something. So I stomped out on to that *balcone* up there and yelled down at the people scurrying along, 'Mussolini *stronzo*!' A shit. They looked up at this weirdo in battle fatigues and a GI helmet. Musta thought I was drunk. Which I was.

-That was the first you knew that Miss Frisk was chummy with the Duck's girlfriend?

-Yeah, but so what? *She* wasn't in the war. We used to run into Petacci around Rome ourselves before we were chucked out. I thought she was just another tootsie. But when the Germans took Mussolini up north she insisted on going along. Don't suppose you noticed the little jacket she was wearing?

-When she was hanging upside down? Can't say I did.

-Well, while I was there some of the commie crones were pulling it off her body. Feeling round the seams in case there was some loot sewn in. And there was. Diamond rings, brooches. High-class stuff.

-Jesus.

-So I grabbed what I could. Gold bracelet engraved *Ben and Clara*.

-Ben…?

-What she used to call him, I guess. I heard later that Clara had Pucci sew the goodies in for her.

-Emilio Pucci? The designer?

-And big-time Fascist.

-Great story. Wish I could have read it.

-Never made the wire. John killed it. Said it made the vile Fascist beasts seem too human.

-Anyway, I gave the bracelet to Frisk. Memento of her pal.

-And that would be the favour she wanted to repay you for?

-More likely for keeping my mouth shut about her shacking up with John.

Mother Jo slid up alongside with a starchy rustle. I wondered yet again about her younger days. She wanted Caddie to go take a nap and I had to wind up fast

-'Army moved on, John went with it. Anyway, he was married back home.'

-'How did *she* take that?

-'On the chin. Just moved out of Via Margutta and went back to daddy in the Vatican. All she ever said to me was that it had been an interesting experience but she didn't feel the need to repeat it.'

-'Out of *Margutta*?'

-'That's how we got the apartment. John had commandeered it from some Fascist monument carver and he handed it on to us.'

-'Lock, stock and great big bed?'

-'Maybe that's why Frisk took a shine to *you*.'

*

First few weeks I was back I talked to Marsha so often that I had to declare a personal DOWNHOLD. DDI made it easy to call, but Telefonica Italia had squeezed a hefty deposit out of me and the charge per minute was brutal. I spent a lot of money trying to persuade her to quit NBC and come over to Rome, and as much again listening to her argue, quite affectionately, that it should be me who did the moving.

Bureau life lurched on. There were plenty of soft stories even without the sweaty whiff of the impending Olympics and the regular flow out of Cinecittá and the Vatican. English debutante marries Calabrian fisherman; American heiress buys up village in the Abruzzi as home for religion she co-founds with Kathmandu herbalist; Novella Parigini offers to paint anyone up there ready to get naked.

I didn't go up to the Veneto as much as before and I kept right away from the Colony. Wasn't that I didn't feel horny. Felt horny all the time, but with a narrow focus. I couldn't feel bad about it because if Marsha was truly ready to keep on with what we had finally got going we would work things out somehow.

As the negotiating sessions became less frequent she began drawing ahead on points, and I was getting ready to toss in the towel. A couple of times, I unsheathed the Olivetti, ready to cut my professional throat with a letter to Hamm asking if soon as Charlie got back from the dry cleaner he'd let me move back to New York. Rewrite Row, probably.

As it was, he got in first 'Can we make this private?' he said when I picked up. It was only about seven am in New York.

I had been checking through the Outgoing, thinking about lunch. I switched the phone to the inside office. A call from 42nd Street was a major event. Aldo and Cristof would be straining hard enough to pop an eardrum. There was the usual brief rat-a-tat-tat of pleasantries, then: 'What I told you before is now official.' Capitalisation boomed down the line. 'Hooper at the Hoops. Century News Wire's Gold Medal Sportswriter.'

'Sounds terrific.' Well, I guessed that was what he wanted to hear.

'So I guess you'll be wondering who's going to move into the top fireman slot?'

As would every Centurion worth his pencil shavings. Almost certainly it would be one of the senior bureau chiefs — Paris, Bonn, Moscow, even Charlie. No, probably not Charlie. About whom I hoped Hamm would have something to tell me.

'What we've come around to thinking is that the job might be split. Someone working out of here as Chief American Correspondent, someone over there as Chief European. We've already got the American one lined up — Sage Ashley.'

That was something, giving a job like that to a girl. Well, not exactly a girl. I'd never met Ashley but I knew she was in her forties. She'd been running the Atlanta bureau for a few years, keeping on top of all the race stuff going on in the Deep South. Anyone with an eye for news could see there was going to be plenty more of that, and soon. Ashley would probably do a good job.

Subduing the bitter little spout-up of envy in my personal deep south, I started to say so.

But Roger had a follow-up. 'And you get to do the European side. If you want to, that is.'

In the fraction of a second between those two sentences, the thought flared in my mind, bright as the Newstower zipper. No, you asshole, I want the *American* one. Back there in clutching distance of Marsha.

But I knew better than to ask. What I was being offered was a bestowal, not a proposition. Negotiation was not the Century way. Try it, and I'd end up on Rewrite Row. It was take it or take off. Besides...

'Seems like it's what Old John wants.'

'Nothing to argue about, then.'

'Only the salary.'

'I'll just have what Brad's getting.'

'Hell you will.'

Everyone in the bureau was trying not to look like a human query mark, including Rita, who was sprawled in a chair, puffing from the stairs. I didn't know how much of the conversation they might have overheard, decoded or imagined.

'Charlie,' I said. 'Back at the end of next month.' As Hamm had gone on to tell me.

About the main topic, he said: 'You need to keep all this to yourself for a couple of weeks. Don't want to take any shine off the Brad announcement. Besides, we have to get some ducks in a row. I'll let you know when we're ready to tell the clients about you and Ashley, give it to the trade sheets.'

When I spoke to Marsha I said I'd be out of touch for a bit because some off-base assignments had come up. 'You don't have to wait for a bulletin,' Hamm had gone on. Get started right now if you want. Just pick your hotspot. The Belgian Congo looks promising. Algeria? The French are in deep shit over there.'

What I really needed to say was sliding around my tongue like a bad taste that turned worse when Marsha asked if something was going on with Brad. 'Just that he was in Costellos at lunchtime. Came in alone. I wasn't sure if he'd remember me, but I said hello anyway.'

'And what did *he* say?'

'Wanted to buy me a drink but I had to get back. He seemed a bit, I don't know, *down*.'

'Hangover, probably.'

*

For the next couple of weeks I managed to stay out of phone range, filing by cable, occasionally bumming a few minutes on a handy Teletype. Too hot for a trenchcoat in the places I went, but I came back with some quasi-combat shirts that impressed the shitpickers, if not the Veneto creeps; only foreign battlefield they cared about was Sunset Strip.

I took Lucy along on one trip. Richard had her on some kind of probation before letting her take over at Newspix and she was happy to get out of town.

The story was a spiralling threat from Syria to Israeli settlements just across the frontier between them, place called the Golan Heights. Little kibbutzes were easy targets for the Syrians to drop artillery shells on whenever they felt like it. Apart from the tanks, artillery pieces and few hundred guys in battlegear the landscape was just like Roghudi. I couldn't imagine why anyone would want to live on either side.

We flew into Beirut and rented a jeep to drive southwards through Lebanon. Fieldwork done, we went back to the city to file and spend a night in the St George Hotel, a sooty pink palace on the edge of a fine bay.

If we were ever going to have another shot at each other that would have been the moment, but we stuck to shop talk at dinner and parted decorously at the doors of our adjoining rooms. Weird. A single episode of sex with Lucy — I didn't count the Sicilian backhander — had sealed a friendship, but our hearts had not been in it then or now. By contrast, that single episode with Marsha created a binding deal. At least as far as I was concerned.

A tremendous explosion sometime before dawn brought me out on my St George balcony and Lucy on to hers. We were separated by a little wall that I could stick my head around.

'*Dio la stramaladica!*' She was clutching a T-shirt in front of her. It didn't screen off much, because she was only giving it one hand; the other looped the strap of a Leica over her head. It didn't seem fair to stare, so I turned away to scan the bay while she went back inside. I heard her calling the desk downstairs.

'Not to worry, *concierge* say. Guys go fishing with dynamite. Lazy bastards .'There was nothing to be seen but water, at which we stared for a while, talking around the partition.

'You not found that girl yet?' She didn't know about Marsha. This was the hypothetical girl she'd assured me I would find, after our Sicilian fiasco. 'I think I have, but one of us is in the wrong place.'

'Then someone must go to right place.'

Which, I came to the conclusion in that moment, a pastel dawn spilling down from the low mountains enfolding the bay, and the endlessly newsworthy wars shaping up on the other side of them, was going to have to be *my* place. In the last few days I had begun to slide towards the worst possible solution, even if it meant ending up on Rewrite Row. If I was going to be miserable, at least I would be in the same place as the love of my lifetime, as Marsha undoubtedly was.

I hadn't told her that, though it had surely leaked into the increasingly strained conversations we had whenever we managed to connect. But in that unlikely moment, in that improbable place, I hooked a U-ey. A screeching, moonshiner handbrake, 180-degree back-the-way-you came spin-around. Without even thinking about it, I gave up on the idea of going where she was and went back to thinking of how I might lure her over to where I now planned to dig in. If, however, she had succumbed to the lure of the newsroom, the relentless urge to rake it in, shape it and get it back out there, I didn't think much of my chances. Look at Carrie, for Christ's sake.

Anyway, I needed to do something pretty quick. Having to keep quiet about the moves at Century had given me a chicken-shit excuse for not even telling Marsha about my loaded option, but word would leak out of 42nd Street long before *Newspaper News* got the handout.

Lucy went back to bed leaving me to watch the day spread across the surface of the sea, from the bottom of which — figuratively speaking — my precious item of ligan had been hauled up and, all too likely, would now slip back down again.

*

Normal people feel a chill when the phone rings in the middle of the night. Reporters, though, get a charge. A late-night call had put me on a plane back to Algiers and the French Foreign Legion mutiny that changed the way of the civil war there. Another sent me driving lickety-split up to the south of France, where a burst dam all but wiped out the town of Frejus. This time it was Marsha. My willful, wayward, smartass, faraway Marsha. 'Hi, Shelby. Thought you might like to hear what's going on.'

What was going on at the Via Margutta end was me trying to wrestle the phone into a hold where the wire didn't brush my crotch, encouraging the arousal that the sound of her voice never failed to evoke. I had slithered down the stairs naked and slightly confused after a drink or two in the *Stampa*, eyes half-shut against the light, feeling around for my notebook and knocking over the stool. 'You with me now, Shelby?'

'Sure thing. What's up?'

She'd taken me by surprise. I did the calling, not her. Partly because I wanted to be gentlemanly and pick up the tab. Partly because if she got me in the bureau I couldn't really say what I wanted to. Partly because of the daunting time difference. It was nearly two am; eight in the evening in New York. If I had been over there we might just be going out to dinner. Mainly, though, because I was still trying to figure out what I needed to say to her and how.

As it was, there was an ominous feel to this call. Likely that a leak about my new job had reached her before I pulled my side of the story into shape.

'Aren't you pleased to hear from me?'

'Of course.'

'Why do you think I'm calling?'

'Multiple choice question?'

'You mean multiple choice answers.'

To tell me it's all over? That you're eloping with the news anchor? You're going back to live with Ted? With Lorenzo?

'Then I guess I should say, I hope you're calling to tell me something.'

Like what? You've heard that I've taken on a job that's going to keep us on different sides of the world, maybe forever?

'That you love me?'

'Oh, Shelby, that's old news, I just thought you might like to know that we've signed Brad Hooper.'

'Who has?'

'NBC, of course. All thanks to me.'

'He's going to be on television?'

'To head up our Olympic team. Hooper at the Hoops. We lifted that slogan, too. He'll be great. Won't even have to write any copy. All he'll need to do is read it.'

'You've filched Brad Hooper from Century?'

'There, and I thought you weren't listening.' Weren't talking, either.

'Why didn't you tell me you were taking over his job?'

'Only half of it.'

'Half that matters, seems to me.'

I winced so hard my teeth grated. But she didn't sound angry. In fact, there was a tinge of mischief — archness, even — in her voice. Arch was not a quality she had hitherto displayed.

'Anyway, what we need to talk about now is parking.'

'Parking?'

There was a slight crackle on the line, a stirring I felt rather than heard on the frequent occasions I had replayed the moment she had whipped down her neckline in the Petit Paris.

'In Rome. For the Newsbus. I'm going to be Brad's producer. 'We're shipping the whole rig over to the Olympics. Crew of three, me on the quarterdeck.'

I started to giggle with delight. Had to loop the phone cord clear of a fresh priapic surge.

'Gotta go now, Shell. Isn't this great?'

Sure was. Greater still if I could be sure the Games wouldn't fizzle out in our own personal Closing Ceremony.

'Didn't I tell you it would all work out?'

Magari.

2020

This was the first time I had come up to the old alma mater since collecting my questionable Pulitzer Prize there back in the 1960s. Then there had been lunch in the Low Memorial Library, clink of glasses and the rumble of gossip swirling around the pretentious rotunda. A graduation ceremony, even from Columbia University's grandiose School of Journalism, rated a lesser setting, the Brad Hooper Auditorium. Brad Hooper, for Christ's sake! A goddamn sports writer? OK, he'd become president of ABC News. Maybe I should have gone for television. Or sport. Still, he's dead, poor guy, and I'm here presenting the Elwyn and Cadence Rickard Prize for Excellence in News Reporting.

It was interesting looking over those faces in front of me, ranked up like the rows of keys on an old iron typewriter. In my day they would all have been mid-market white and very few of them girls. OK, women. Here, skin shade spanned the spectrum and women predominated; there were even a couple of hijabs. Also, these were graduate students, which meant quite a few foreigners added to the mix.

The J School marketed its master's degrees hard and profitably, skills proudly packaged in with liberal free press and First Amendment values. Just the thing for Saudi Arabia or Pakistan or Myanmar. Or Google, Facebook and Twitter, the new and future assembly lines of news true or fake.

The dean was at the podium, a woman made famous not by journalism as I still thought of it, but by fronting a television 'reality' show called *What If?* on which semi-celebrities re-enacted and reinterpreted episodes from history: the sinking of the *Maine*, for instance, or the Rogue River Treaties. They would apply — in the phrase that has come to alternately enchant and appal us — 'alternative facts' to decide the outcome.

She was a nice lady, smart and striking in her sixties, and I was flattered she had thought of me for the occasion.

'You're perfect for it,' the dean had said. 'Respected newsman, Pulitzer winner, Even if you're not a J School grad you were close to the Rickards. It's taken a long time to get this award in shape and we want everyone right behind it.'

It had taken that long because the endowment was a legacy from Colonel John Coldfield. On the basis of little other than pure greed, the old villain's will had been challenged by two generations of its beneficiaries, the first one outlived by their lawyers. Old John had wanted to fund a scholarship, but what remained after the court cases would only pay for an annual ornamental trophy and a few glasses of wine for those depraved enough to be still drinking alcohol.

But it was, as the dean insisted, the spirit that counted. 'I heard that Elwyn wasn't actually a very nice man,' she said. 'For myself, I would have preferred to have just Cadence's name. After all, she was the Columbia alumnus, not him. But we weren't going to stir up more trouble.' Now, as she began to speak, the graduates lifted I-phones up to their faces like prayer books and bathed her in flashes.

I knew the students would be wanting to get out of there as badly as I did. They were keen to go party, I was ready to go home. Marsha would have been watching this event on the link the J-School had tapped us into, but she'd be relieved to see me.

We were of an age that when one of us went out alone the other could not be entirely sure they'd be back.

The dean had come down to Two Fifth Avenue to sell me on the invitation. She looked out of our 14th-floor windows, ignoring the rival sprawl of NYU that colonised Washington Square down below, checking over the distant thinned-out skyline of lower Manhattan. 'My God, were you here when the towers...?'

Indeed we were. The Trade Centre had been almost finished when we bought the condo in the early 1980s. The twin towers became the main feature of our cityscape. Always something going on, a nut making a parachute jump, guy taking a mid-air stroll between them on a tightrope. When we grasped what was happening on 9/11, or some of it, I had a visceral compulsion to get on the story. There were still people at Century who knew I used to run the newsroom and they let me stay on the phone for three hours straight. Stuff was pouring in from all over, but my eye-witness stories made the wire. My last by-lines.

Brevity is the essence of news reporting and thus of my warm-up to bestowing the trophy on a young woman called Pandora Perks. It took only a couple of minutes to run through the highs of the Ricketts' career. I'd thought of throwing in the story from Ethiopia about Rick having to stand guard with a gun while Caddie peed in the bushes rather than risk her ass in the Italian army latrine. But in these sensitive times, it would be asking for trouble to say she needed to because she had been the only white woman for miles around. Weren't local females just as entitled to be raped?

Nor did I say anything to warn these graduates of the dispiriting prospects most of them faced despite their exalted grooming: a career chained to those little I-screens or stuck in front of slightly bigger ones, monitoring tweets and shuffling factoids from one feed to another.

I did tell them how rackety and risky foreign reporting had been back in the Rickard era; even in my own heyday. To have gone on to explain that it was also addictive and corrupting might have been asking for trouble. They could not be expected to appreciate what sheer mischievous fun it was. Most of the time, anyway.

Great name for a by-line, I told Pandora Perks afterwards. She was thin to the point of anguish and over-excited. There could have been a tail-wagging beneath the pale blue academic gown. 'You really worked with the Rickards? That's cool.'

'Only on a couple of things, really. They were pretty much at the end of their working days when I knew them.'

'And where was that? Spain? Africa?'

'Rome, actually.'

'Rome. Cooool. That's where we're going for our graduation trip. Me and Vernon.' She pointed with her phone at a small Asian guy on the edge of another group. 'We found this great place on Airbnb.'

'First time there? I'm sure you'll enjoy it. I haven't been in years.' Not since those Rickard days, in fact, although it was a long time since I stopped worrying that I might be being arrested at the airport.

She swiped at her little screen. 'It's a famous old building. It was in that old black-and-white movie, *Roman Holiday*. Audrey Hepburn, she was so cool. And Gregory Peck. *He* was a foreign correspondent. In the movie, that is.'

She held up the phone. 'It's right in the centre. I forget the name of the street...*via*, whatever.'

I took the phone and jiggled my glasses to focus on the images in the electronic brochure. A bright, modern-looking motel-style bedroom. Polished granite walk-in shower. Kitchen with wall ovens. 'Flip over', said Pandora, leaning in with a finger to do it for me. Flip, flip. None of the shots meant anything until up came an orange ochre wall, cobbled street and a wide, arched doorway faced with smooth granite. I handed back the phone.

'That's Via Margutta. You'll love it.'

ENDIT